"The Sword

of

Uncreation"

A Hell and Heaven Novel

By Darren Walker

First Published in 2019 by Blossom Spring Publishing
The Sword of Uncreation Copyright
© 2019 Darren Walker
ISBN 978-1-9996490-9-8
E: admin@blossomspringpublishing.com
W: www.blossomspringpublishing.com

Introduction

"The time for war has not yet come, but it will come, and that soon; and when it does come, my advice is to draw the sword and throw away the scabbard."

Stonewall Jackson - Virginia Military Institute. March 1861

"With the right sword you can keep the scabbard!"

Satan.

Dedications

(Raising a glass to those that didn't make it).

There are many people that I owe the grateful nod of thanks to, their help and support is always appreciated, and I am sure that you know who you are. I will have to name them in my next novel. It's coming, I promise.

However, I must send my love and eternal gratitude to three people that never got to see me become a published author. Gone far too soon and still in my heart.

Firstly, my mother, Margaret, the epitome of patience and caring love. Forever missed but someone who believed in me; even when I wasn't always able to.

Then there is Frank and Brenda Conley, my in-laws, they treated me like a son and made me part of their family. Thank you!

Chapter 1 - A Time Before Time.

Apart from a preponderance of spears tied to their backs and laid along their saddles, plus the unusually large number of swords attached to their belts, to look at them in their dirty and tattered rags they were nothing special. There was nothing to identify the two weary travellers as strong, brave and heroic heavenly angelic knights. No wings or halos and definitely no cherubs, floating overhead, playing tiny harps and singing their praises. The camels, that they rode, were nothing special either. Their lolloping gait was the same as every other camel. Also, the idiotic eyes and gormless, half smiling, expressions could never be accused of being unique. The fact that they were carrying angels didn't make their personal habits any better or respectable either. The loud belching noises, casual spitting and far from self-conscious loud flatulence, was all part of the package that being ships of the desert entailed. But they were comfortable to rise up when kicked out of their resting inertia and, mostly, obeyed orders so the riders had no choice but to take the rough with the smooth. The past few centuries had not been easy for either of the two soldiers so the chance to have a break from the barbarity of war and the discomfort of routine military existence had made this sound, at first, like a relatively easy and comfortable mission. It certainly beat being run through with a sword or having an eye taken out by an arrow; which was, to say the least, in the opinion of most military men a major inconvenience.

Both had seen the real sea on their travels and knew its grace and power. Looking out at the vast and virtually lifeless and barren desert, all around them, they recognised the simile when comparing the wet ocean with the dry and arid wasteland that was stretched out to the horizon. The dunes were like waves caught in time and frozen where they were. As if they could suddenly rise up and swallow any unsuspecting traveller; which in sudden storms they'd been known to do. The shade of an unimaginable spectrum of sea blues swapped for an equally stunning array of gold and yellows as the sun moved across the sky and lit up the ever slowly shifting and undulating sands. The glare first blinding unprotected eyes with its reflection off each tiny grain, then sending long and ghost like shadows across the land. Other than the noises of orderly military breathing, controlled and casual as training dictated, and the various sounds of the camel's bodily functions, the only other sounds were the eerie and other worldly noises of the whistling sand as the wind blew across ridges and played its unique and desolate tune. To the superstitious, and weak minded, the sounds had been interpreted as demons and often driven the unwary listeners to insanity and left them there, running wildly across the dunes, to be lost forever. Skeletons first covered by the slowly changing dunes before eventually being eroded away. Fortunately, the two angels knew what demons really sounded like and they definitely tended not to whistle in such a hauntingly desolate way. Their evil banshee sounds tended to be more like blood curdling screams as they tried to remove heads from shoulders or obtain fresh and warm innards to be used as a light snack. With such loud tactics removing the element of surprise being not much of a problem and allowing even moderately well trained angels the opportunity to defend themselves and keep the pieces of intestine that they had grown attached to. And no angel would ever be stupid enough to point out the flaw in demonic battle strategy to the demons themselves.

2

Mile after long and relentless mile and day after seemingly endless hot day they continued on their journey. Replenishing water whenever they came to a remote oasis and resting before resuming their quest. When the heat of the midday sun was at its most punishing, they rested and slept in the relative cool of the night. Both physically and mentally the monotony of the journey was the most punishing element. The initial magnificence of the scenery long since taken for granted and eventually becoming despised. The routine becoming a dull, seemingly unchanging everyday sight. One towering awe-inspiring sand dune followed by another until the spectacle became first stunningly beautiful, then mundane and finally annoying. The diet of figs, dried goat's meat and water wasn't doing much for their constitutions either. And as for the sand - that was getting into places that the human body was not designed to accept - was making tender places feel like they had been thoroughly rubbed by sandpaper leaving cleft buttocks, and other places, sore and painful.

"Sethbert?"

"I have told you Anderax, shut up!" Sethbert's voice full of weary and pent up frustration.

"But Sethbert we haven't spoken in 15 days." Continued Anderax; unperturbed by the tone of his riding companion's voice.

"So? What exactly have you got to say now that is new and wasn't said 16 days ago, or even 57 days ago?" The tired gaze that Sethbert gave to his colleague would have been enough to silence most people but not the determined and oblivious Anderax.

"But I'm bored!" he continued. His whiney tone making his tired companion cringe at the sound of it.

"So, what? Guess what? So am I. We have been doing the same thing day in, day out, for 228… err no 229 days and I think that even you will agree that there isn't much left for us to talk about. We have shared every possible story from our lives, both on Earth and in Heaven and we have also, on innumerable occasions, discussed what meals we will gorge on once we are safely back home. Now you tell me, what is there that you could possibly have to say to me that will break the tedium and make me glad to be alive and here rather than being happily in Heaven instead?"

Anderax smiled an innocent and optimistic smile. "I know! How about a game of I spy? That should help to while away a few happy hours."

As if by instinct Sethbert's camel stopped its gentle plod and both it and its rider turned their heads to fully look at Anderax. Even though camels can't adopt a look of incredulous contempt this one seemed to be making a pretty close approximation of one; matching that of its passenger. If the beasts head had been closer to the ground the sigh, he released, could have shifted a small amount of sand and created a mini dune. "Anderax, do you remember the last time we played that game? There are three possible letters for you to use covering four words to be actually spied. 'S' for sun and sand, 'C' for camel and 'D' for dune. And before you say it, we agreed that 'C' for camel poo was cheating. So, no matter how bored you are, I have no desire to spend three brainless minutes and play that game."

"There's Carl!" mumbled Anderax.

"What?" Snapped Sethbert, determined that he would not be drawn into yet another vapid and pointless conversation.

"Carl. It's the name of my camel." Anderax gave his animal a friendly pat on its neck. "We have been together for so long walking in the desert. Why have you still got a camel with no name?"

"Will you just SHUT UP?" Despite his gritted teeth he was still able to make himself heard and his anger felt.

There was a long period of tense silence as both resumed their journey; several long miles where the desert was allowed to solemnly whistle to itself undisturbed by any attempts at pointless communication or jejune small talk. Even the camels seemed to get the message and refrained from their loud barking followed by wet expectorations or noises emanating from the other end of their bodies. The uneasy verbal truce, between the two people, maintained due to a complete lack of mental stimulation to create something even remotely worth talking about. Finally, Anderax gave one last try at brokering some form of mutually acceptable topic of conversation. "I'm warm!"

Without turning to look at his travelling companion, eyes fixed on some random sand dune in the distance, Sethbert just muttered unenthusiastically "Don't make me get off of this poxy flea bitten camel, come over there, and kill you!" His hand deliberately, and conspicuously, moved to grip the handle of one of the swords on his belt.

Eventually, after just another three weeks of seemingly aimless meandering across the featureless landscape the weary and, more importantly, silent travellers finally reached the brow of a dune. Much to their relief they were able to see in the distance something that wasn't just more sand, dunes, miniscule oases or shimmering mirages. Every night they dreamed that they must be nearing their destination - just one more day of walking, always heading in the same direction and they would suddenly see it. But each night they would sleep and subsequently be disappointed by yet another day of steady soul eroding travelling. But today was different; they had made it! Small at first and almost imperceptible, the yellow towers, yellow walls, slightly darker yellow windows camouflaged against the yellow background making it look like a yellow optical illusion but, as they got closer, they could see the building properly and make out more details. The whole edifice seemed a structural impossibility; tall and rigid on the undulating and far from solid desert surface. Towers tall and thick with glassless windows designed more to keep the inside of the building cool than for any possible defensive purposes. Too large to provide cover from any invader's archers and anyone that managed to climb the steep walls would have easily been able to scramble through them. Walls equally impressive and imposing, permanence the message conveyed to any passer-by that just might have spent the last few months wandering in the deadly heat and accidentally stumbled across the place. Few knew how long it had been there and even fewer were willing, or able, to tell its many dark secrets. Some things just existed and had to be accepted, question it if you liked but don't expect too many answers. Questions would be heard but ignored. Anyone simply seeking enlightenment there had better just turn their camel around and go back the way they had just come.

On finally arriving at the imposing edifice the two travellers regained their latent warrior instincts. They circled the building so that they could get a full impression of the place they would eventually be entering. The size amazed them, it took them the best part of a day to go all the way around it and the square building could never be accused of being some architect's grand design full of imagination, creativity or artistic flourishes. Each side of it was equally sized with sparse high windows and no signs of life. No balconies, for people to enjoy the views of the bleak desert, no guards and no noises to indicate life. The total silence beginning to make them fear that the whole place was uninhabited, and they had either arrived at the wrong location or made the journey for nothing. The only break from the symmetry of the structure was the giant wooden door in the centre of what they decided was the front of the building. No other door was visible anywhere; their ingrained military instincts seeing a giant flaw in its simple and utilitarian design. If it were to be attacked the defenders would have no method of escape; should the door be breached. However, the biggest defence, of this particular building, was its location. Any army intent on pillaging the place would have to be hardy and determined; with the danger making the possible prizes not worth the effort.

Now that they had something to talk about, other than sand, camels and the heat, both Anderax and Sethbert lost their enforced taciturn moods. As they surveyed their journey's end, they were able to talk and plan their next cautious steps; not that there were many options. They could try and scale the walls, and possibly take any inhabitants by surprise, which considering their complete lack of ropes or climbing apparatus made that idea moot or highly unlikely. Neither of them wanted to spend about two years going back to get some equipment and then return again. So, the only credible, and sensible choice, was to go up to the door and knock on it. After all they were not some all-conquering army intent on pillaging and destruction. Hopefully they were expected and if they weren't then they had made a very long journey for absolutely no reason and they would be facing an equally long and soul-destroying journey back again. A desolate trip that neither of them relished with, or without, possessing whatever they had come for. The game of *I spy* would be just as boring, and lacking in alphabetical options, travelling in the opposite direction.

Dismounting their camels, they walked hesitantly up to the ancient looking door. The imposing height made them feel like dwarves and it also made them both silently wonder where they got the wood for it in the first place. After all deserts were not famous for their rich, green and dense forests and plentiful supply of what looked like oak. Sethbert raised his clenched fist and purposefully struck on the door. Other than the pain he felt on the side of his hand there was nothing; no sound to reward his efforts. Optimistically Anderax tried the same thing and got the same agonising results, a painful hand and silence. Looking at each other they both shrugged in bewilderment, eyes searching the other's face for some clue as to how they should gain entry. Looking up Sethbert began shouting, hands cupped to his mouth in an attempt to amplify the sound "Hello! Is there anybody there?" Anderax joined in but even their combined shouts were met with a haunting silence. Giving up on that futile tactic they both removed short swords, from the three on each of their belts, and began to thud the pommels against the solid wood; the impacts absorbed and, once again, resulting in no discernible noise that might be picked up by anyone at the other side of the giant barrier. Suddenly there was a faint sound of ancient metal hinges being forced to move after countless years of inactivity. To their left a small door opened, built into the main door but so well designed that it was invisible to any casual and uninformed onlooker. Instinctively both angelic soldiers took up a defensive fighting stance, swords raised above their heads, tips pointing at the door ready for any less than friendly welcome. Instead their cautious and aggressive postures, and anxious feelings, were met by the wizened face of an old bearded man as he put his head around the smaller door. His smile was disarming enough to induce the two battle hardened soldiers to return their swords to their leather scabbards.

"Oh, hello there." His voice frail but warm. "I thought I heard something. Sorry about the delay I was just on the toilet. You should have used the knocker." He pointed to a specific place on the main door and paused. Looking down he saw a pile of eroded indistinguishable rusted brown metal laid on the floor. "Aaargh, well, that used to be a door knocker. How did it manage to rust? Never mind, I am here now, and no harm done. Now that you're here you might as well come in." Pausing to look at

9

them with a glance that made them both wonder if he was serious or just joking. "If you want to of course?" With that he disappeared back inside closing the tiny door behind him. The bemusement of the two travellers was brief as the giant door began to open, forcing them to step back. It opened just enough to allow them, then their camels, to get through. Then, once they were inside, it closed again; all movements done with no visible methods of its opening, and closing, evident to the bemused visitors.

Inside they were met by the unexpected sight of a giant grass covered square courtyard with an imposing water fountain in the middle of it. The sculpture, in the centre of the green, was depicting a noble looking human with his hands on the jaws of a giant serpent; dissecting the creature as he pulled the jaws apart. Like all water features, throughout time, the clear liquid was spurting into the air from the figure. In this case there was a torrent shooting up to the heavens from his mouth, like the physical expression of his victory cry, and a second plume was issuing from the mouth of the anatomised reptile. That depiction was more of a macabre representation of blood being released from its body. Beyond the fountain, and square, were wide steps leading up to a columned platform and gold-plated doors leading into what looked like a temple. Many years earlier, after a particular vicious and bloody battle with some Scrark Demons, Anderax had taken refuge in Petra, the city carved into the sheer rock face of what is now part of Jordan, and been left speechless by its magnificence. In his opinion this was even more impressive. Statues of marble, gold and bronze lined the walls and sat in alcoves. They recognised many of the figures as depictions of a few of the demons they had encountered in various throes of death; the stone vanquishers shown as naked men and women with swords and spears despatching the creatures back where they belonged - Hell. Such magnificent art seemed out of place, and completely wasted, in a remote and inhospitable location. Left only to be admired, and perhaps taken for granted, by the residents of the isolated place.

Now that they were closer, they were also able to take a better look at their decrepit host. He was a stark contrast to the heroic statures and physiques of the humans depicted in the artwork. It was impossible to estimate the age of the man but if they had been pushed to give an approximation then they would have gone for a wild guess at *'very, very, very old'*. His beard was grey and nearly reached the floor and the hirsute nature of his facial hair was the complete opposite to the top of his head which was totally bald. He walked with a stoop and it looked like, if you removed his twisted and dirty walking stick, he would have just toppled over. More than likely landing with his forehead on the ground, his body maintaining its bent shape, leaving his bottom stuck in the air. The dirty brown woollen robe he wore gave him the appearance of an Orang-utan that had been rolling in the dust and finally decided to get up and go for a stroll. He turned and, as he looked at them, they saw that the one thing about him that still looked young was his eyes. Bright blue as if the ravages of age had avoided them and taken pity on him leaving him with one last vestige of youth. They seemed to sparkle and be full of a childish mischief that the rest of his body could never deliver. "By the way, my name is Tosoma Skylou. I am the main acolyte, gardener, doorman and event planner for this place." He paused pensively. "Oh, and I also help with the washing up." The last part added more as an aside than a proud boast. "You have travelled far, I will arrange for your camels to be put in the stables and be looked after and you can eat and freshen up before you meet the High Priestess."

"Excuse me" ventured Anderax "but how do you know who we are?"

"Well, you have been sent by God, haven't you?" asked Tosoma casually.

"Yes, of course."

"And you have come to collect The Sword?" continuing with his line of polite but rhetorical enquiry.

"Well that goes without saying. We have travelled countless days and…"

He was cut short by Tosoma putting his hand up to silence him. "Yes, yes, I know that. There is no easy way to get here. Each journey is a true test of courage, strength and patience. We seldom have visitors and it is even rarer for two to arrive at the same time. Usually it takes so long that one person gets on the nerves of the other and ends up having to cut the throat of their unfortunate companion. So tragic but perhaps inevitable if they forget to bring a pack of cards. Imagine having no other mental stimulation and having to resort to playing *I Spy*!"

Anderax and Sethbert looked at each other sheepishly. "Really?" exclaimed Sethbert. "Anyway, surely you want to test us? Ask us some probing questions to ensure that we are who we claim to be. After all we could be demons."

Turning to fully face them Tosoma smiled indulgently at them. "Alright. If you insist. Are you angels sent by God?"

"Yes." Replied Sethbert proudly.

"So, you are not demons in disguise?"

"No, of course not." Sethbert's showing that he was offended by such an implication.

Turning to continue his slow walk he simply muttered "There you go, you've convinced me. Come, you must be tired from being so stupid!"

"But, but, but…" spluttered Sethbert indignantly before realising that further discussions on the subject would be pointless and decided to be quiet. Their presence, and true identity, had been accepted so there was no point in wasting further words. Hardly the most probing of verification processes but it was fit for the purpose intended. After all they weren't demons and trying to persuade the old man to ask them more in-depth and challenging questions would not have changed the outcome.

They followed Tosoma to a hall at the side of the massive courtyard. Despite the scarcity of windows, it was well lit. The, seemingly technological miracle, thanks to large polished shields hung high on the walls and positioned so that any light, that managed to get into the room, was reflected down and spread out so that tables and benches were illuminated. It was empty apart from the trio and Tosoma bid the two tired travellers to sit at the nearest table that was already covered by bowls full of clean water, for washing, and plates full of fresh fruit and a selection of meats. Also laid out on the bench were clean and folded silk robes.

"Please, you are guests here. Feel free to take your time freshening up, filling your stomachs and divest yourselves of such dirty rags. I will collect you later and show you to your rooms. Then, once rested, I will take you to see the High Priestess in the morning." Before they could disagree, and try and arrange for an audience straight away, Tosoma had turned and walked out of the hall, leaving them surprised at his unexpected turn of speed.

"What a strange man." Sethbert casually commented.

"Yes, an interesting fellow, quite possibly madder than a box of angry fire ants though" replied Anderax.

They washed, as best they could. Some of the sand had ingrained itself in far too deep to be removed by the simple application of a bowl full of water. A week's soak in a warm bath and then being smothered in scented unguents by, hopefully, nubile women would have been their preferred method of getting fully clean. But taking into account the limited resources and the total lack of females, nubile or not, they managed to remove the worst of the dirt themselves. There was still sand in a few hard to reach places but neither of them felt like initiating a search for each grain, especially in front of the other. But at least they no longer smelt like sweaty or farting camels. The long forgotten pleasing permanent odour of things not related to dromedaries would have to wait for when they finally returned with their prize. Not wanting to get food on the fine silk clothing they ate naked and only when they had eaten their fill did they finally dress. The fine material gently caressing their skin was a strange, almost forgotten, experience after the endless days of the same coarse clothing that they had been used to. Re-tying their sword belts, around their waists, they sat casually drinking wine and chatting as they waited for their old host to return and show them to their welcome and much needed beds. They didn't have long to wait, while they were focused on watching the door, that they had entered through, he had come in via a door in the far wall and quietly walked up to their table. He coughed gently to get their attention but even that sudden soft noise made them both instinctively turn towards him, hands grasped onto the grips of their swords; ready to draw them if required.

"Please relax gentlemen. I assure you that there is nothing to fear here. You are our honoured guests and no harm shall befall you." Tosoma's voice gentle, calm and reassuring. "Please walk this way." He turned and began to hobble towards the side door, his walking stick shaking uncontrollably as he leant on it.

"If I'd got much more sand between my buttocks, I think I would be walking that way!" ventured Anderax quietly, much to Sethbert's barely contained amusement.

Tosoma turned slightly and smiled at them. "Yes, one of the many perils of visiting us. The sand gets everywhere."

"But..." spluttered Anderax, surprised that his softly spoken words had been overheard.

"My young man, I might be old, walk like a senile and arthritic three legged dog and, quite possibly, occasionally smell like one, but I am not deaf." He gave the two knights a conspiratorial wink to assure them that he had not been offended by their joke; the simple action making his bushy grey eyebrow wave like a hairy fan.

The walk to their rooms was via long, empty, but well lit, corridors. When they finally reached their accommodation Tosoma bid them enter, assuring them once again that he would come and collect them in the morning and take them to see the High Priestess. Both Anderax and Sethbert promptly surrendered to their beds and fell into deep and restful sleep. The next morning, they awoke to the gentle knocking of Tosoma. They both felt stiff and sore, bodies unused to the comfort of soft beds but they dressed quickly and were happy to be finally meeting the High Priestess and be able to fulfil their objective. They knew that there would be an equally long and uncomfortable return journey home but they knew that they had survived it going one way; so, they could find a way to do the same on the way back. Even if it was in complete silence; perhaps they could borrow a pack of cards from Tosoma? As they walked along long and winding passageways, they casually chatted with Tosoma trying to learn a little more about the strange city, that they had managed to eventually reach, but his answers were not very informative. He seemed preoccupied and reluctant to answer too many questions. All they managed to glean from him was that many centuries ago there used to be a wide river that flowed nearby, with the city was built to make the most of the trade from the passing ships and boats. As the river dried up so did the visitors and the whole place became forgotten by the outside world; more of a myth than a fact with the isolation becoming part of its character. Its inhabitants occasionally venturing into the outside world as they visited such distant cities as Tanis, Palmyra and Petra. Not staying for long and never enlightening strangers about the true existence of their home. Tosoma seemed unwilling to elaborate on why they went visiting such places and when he was pressed just said "Ask your God, maybe he doesn't want us making too many swords!" crossly and went quiet for the rest of the journey.

Eventually they reached the vast courtyard and were in natural light. The sunshine making them shield their eyes from the glare. Finally, he gestured towards the steps leading to the entrance to the temple. "That way my young friends, my Lady is expecting you. I will be waiting here for you when you have finished."

They thanked him and began to walk up the steps, past the columns and statues and finally through the entrance into the temple. Again, it was lit by convex shaped shields in the ceiling reflecting down the sunlight streaming through the windows. They were able to take in the magnificence of the vast chamber. The marble floor was decorated with mosaics depicting scenes from legends and tales unknown to the two angels. Along both side walls were painted depictions of numerous men and women in various lovemaking positions. Many of which the two knights suspected might be physically impossible or, if not totally impossible then, at least, liable to leave the participants with serious and lifelong disabilities. But the pleasure of the experience might have been worth the pain.

In front of the paintings were brightly painted sculptures towering up towards the roof. Recreations of men and women dressed in fine robes and all depicted wearing the same gold crown. Both angels quietly speculated, to themselves, that they must be eternal reminders of either past kings, queens, leaders of the priesthood or rulers of the city. They had no way of knowing as the words inscribed at the base of each sculpture was in an ancient language that they were unfamiliar with. As they walked the gentle sound of their soft leather sandals was carried around the hall. The resultant echoes making them sound more like an invading army, that were all wearing slippers, rather than just two visitors. Finally, they reached a plain yellow Phrygian marble altar at the far end of the room. Its simple design and construction seemed out of place when compared to the art that surrounded it. As they stood in front of it, they looked at each other as they expected the other to know what they were supposed to do next. Anderax silently mouthed 'now what?' to Sethbert but all he got in return was a look of uncertainty and a shrug of his shoulders. All they could do was wait and see what happened next.

Fortunately, they didn't have to wait long as they heard the brushing sound of cloth being dragged along the floor and, looking into the corner of the hall, they saw a tall red headed woman in a long flowing white dress walking through a doorway; heading gracefully towards them. In her outstretched hands was a long object wrapped in thick red woollen cloth. On reaching the other side of the altar to the two knights she gently placed it onto the cold marble surface and only then did she allow herself to look up and face Anderax and Sethbert. Her skin was pale and her eyes were dark with makeup. She smiled graciously at them and finally addressed them.

"Welcome travellers, I have been expecting you. I am Monicara, High Priestess of Sadducee. When your God visited me in a vision, and requested my services, I was happy to be of assistance. Even though He is not my god He is fighting against the same demons and devils that we fear and have battled from time to time. If they were to win then the world we know would be destroyed."

"So, your Highness" began Anderax, "do you have that which we seek? Do you have it?"

"The Sword?" her soft voice gently interrupting him. "Oh yes, for several years our finest swordsmiths have been working on it and many have given their lives, and souls, in the process. It has not been easy but we have that which you came for." With that she took hold of the edge of the red cloth on the altar and carefully unfolded it revealing a plain leather scabbard next to a long silver sword. It's shining blade reflecting the light onto the walls. Gold lettering in the unfamiliar language etched into the fuller, several opals in the handle and the pommel inlaid with a single clear red ruby.

"Here it is, in all its terrifying power and glory. The most destructive and dangerous weapon ever created, or will ever be made, by the hand of men – or gods." As she spoke her eyes filled with a mixture of fear and sadness. "Although, perhaps, I wish that we had not been tasked with creating such a terrible thing. Those that possess it will never find peace and those that desire it will never win!"

"Just a sword?" asked Anderax, his voice unable to hide his surprise and bewilderment. "What's so special about a sword?" Revealing, by the bewildered tone and the comment, that God had not been forthcoming with the full details of their mission.

Monicara's eyes suddenly took on an angry and hard appearance. "Just a sword? Just a sword? This *is* The Sword of Uncreation. One cut, or even the tiniest of scratches, will destroy you. Not just kill you and allow your body to rot as your soul merrily makes its way back to Heaven and you wait for your time to come back to Earth and continue the war against Satan. No, that is the end. You die and your soul ceases to exist. Goodbye Earth and goodbye Heaven."

Both soldiers listened in awe at what they were being told. Fear gripping their hearts at the thought of losing Heaven. "And what about if demons are wounded by the sword?" asked Sethbert warily.

"They will suffer the same fate. They will die instantly and their vile spirits will cease to exist as well." She picked up the sword by the grip and pointed it at them both, making them lean backwards as the tip hovered in front of their noses. "Who-so-ever yields this in battle will be virtually assured victory, but be warned, if it should fall into the hands of Satan, or his hordes, then the good fight will end and all will be lost. The power within the blade belongs to whoever holds it and, if they have enough skill, they can then turn any battle to their own advantage and eventually win any war." Returning the sword onto the cloth "Do you understand? Even the slightest scratch and you will be quite literally history and dust but nothing more; a memory for those that used to know you."

Both of them reluctantly dragged their eyes from the sword and stared into Monicara's intense hazel coloured eyes. "Yes, my Lady. We fully understand." Sethbert's voice trembling at the thought of such power being laid before him. "It is a responsibility we accept with honour. We will deliver it to God, err our God, so that He can use it wisely."

"Good. Two people to guard a sword that can destroy whole armies? Hardly seems adequate, but perhaps two can hide from angry demons and avoid any form of confrontation better than a whole army of angels." Monicara was no longer convinced that she had been right in creating such a weapon of peace.

Anderax raised his hand to take her attention away from thoughts of what she had done. "Excuse me my Lady. May I hold the sword?"

Brought back from her private thoughts she smiled and casually pointed at it. "Please be my guest. It is the finest ever made, or that will ever be made, so handle it with care."

Lifting it in his hand he held it tightly and felt the weight, gently he swung it in the opposite direction to Monicara and Sethbert. He smiled as he studied it. "It is truly a beautiful weapon. But what about the balance?"

"No!" shouted Monicara, but it was too late, before she could say anymore, he had it balanced on the palm of his hand and was moving it up and down to find its centre of gravity. Just then the fine metal edge caught a tiny piece of skin on his palm. Feeling the mild pain, he realised what he had done and looked into Monicara's eyes. "Oh shit!" And with that he let the sword fall back onto the altar as he tumbled backwards onto the marble floor. Dead before he had even hit the ground. Then his entire body started to change. First it started to take the form of fine sand before even that transformed into a finer mist that then disappeared into thin air.

Monicara sighed as she raised her eyes up to the heavens. "What did I just say? WHAT DID I JUST SAY? Some people! Well I suppose you can fix stupid after all." Then looking Sethbert directly in the eyes, with an expression as if she was now talking to a little baby and with a voice to match, "Anyway, as I was saying, perhaps one person to guard a sword that can destroy whole armies? Probably totally inadequate, but perhaps you can avoid cutting yourself, manage to hide from angry demons and avoid confrontation better than a whole army of angels? But personally, I am not holding my breath.

Chapter 2 - Those That The Gods Would Destroy

Like it or not if you, or most people, were to walk down a busy street in any major town or city around the world more than likely you would not be noticed. Unless you were some rock musician making a music video, pushing innocent pedestrians out of the way or some person transfixed with checking, totally irrelevant, messages on their cell phone as they walked into you - any passing stranger would walk around you but not even acknowledge your presence. The harsh and uncaring civil inattention that allows people to know that others simply exist without having to interact with everyone else. Or when reluctantly forced to co-exist in a small space, such as public transport, the dead eyed stare that looks right through you is put into place. And you would do the same for them, unless of course it was you being a musician or too busy walking about while being online on your phone, in which case just grow up and look where you are going! Normally personal space respected and returned. You might make eye contact with a random stranger and unless you are English, who see such things as being socially painful and awkward, or you stare at the wrong person in an unfortunate part of town and are construed as disrespecting some low IQ gang member, it probably wouldn't be too uncomfortable of an experience. You might be met with a blank stare as the other person rushes about on their own private business or, if you are lucky, the other person might give you a brief smile. Subconscious joy transferred from their lips and into your heart, a faint candle lighting up what could otherwise be just another dull day. Much needed affirmation that you exist and hopefully have some value. In an average day someone walking on a crowded street would probably see several thousand people and it would be impossible for the normal person to remember each individual one. Why would they want to do that anyway? The brain has enough important things to process as it is without having to record everything else. That is what CCTV cameras are there for. Perhaps a man's mind might occasionally retain the image of a beautiful woman's face or, more likely, the physical scenery slightly south of that. A woman might goggle at some male beef cake and fantasise about what might happen if it were just those two stuck on a tropical island full of alcoholic fruit cocktails and sun cream. But, on the whole, the average person can come and go without causing too much of a stir in other people's private and insular universes. No traces left, no emotional footprints in the sands of consciousness – figures alone in their own lives.

Obviously, you can always go out of your way to get more attention than you would ever truly deserve. Expressions of individuality that shouts out to others 'Look at me; I stand out so I am special and important!' whether they deserve such adulation or not. Dressing in garments that look like they were made in a clown's paint factory, just as it was in the process of exploding, would usually do the trick. Another method of crying for attention being the tired and desperate uniform expressions of individuality adopted by punks or Goths - tired clichés which all too briefly grabs the eye. As for some people they just need to pull their trousers up properly but who wants to remember them? Serenading random passers-by with Bruce Springsteen ballads, as they hurriedly walk by, also works. It might even get the attention of the police, but that isn't usually something that most people seek, either consciously or sub-consciously. So perhaps garish clothing is probably a better option for anyone whose ego needs such emotional gratification and acknowledgement. But, on the whole, you are not noticed. Sorry but that is life.

Today that was not the case for Ernest Higginbotham. He was an unusual person, not because of his above average height of 6'8". Having to tilt his head slightly when walking through a doorway was inconvenient and could result in a few bruises, if he wasn't concentrating or was in a rush, but it wasn't anything special. No, what made him so different was that he was invisible. But not in the science fiction way, he didn't have to unravel a crepe bandage from his face and then undress. Then, once he was naked, he could walk into banks and relieve them of their money or even follow women into their houses and wave his genitalia in their faces without them even knowing. Unfortunately for him his form of invisibility was more down to social circumstances. He had not so much fallen on hard times as run as fast as humanly possible chasing after pound notes blowing in the wind, tripped over a tree root sticking out of the ground, and been flown head long into hard concrete times; breaking his nose and acquiring two black eyes on impact. Polite society had many names for people in his situation; tramp, bum, hobo - with vagrant being the current politically correct term. But whatever word you chose to apply to him, and also to those in a similar place, he was so far down the pile that it would take him more than just random pot luck for him to be even able to claw his way back up to ground level. His clothes were once fashionable, expensive and smart. Now they had become victim to the elements and the rough life that he led. For much of what he wore it was only the dirt that held the fibres together. The sole reason that he didn't have lice was due to the army of fleas inhabiting his skin had won the war and killed them off. The whole ensemble look was made even more complete by his odour. Not specifically urine, although that was part of his individual scent's ingredients. It was as if decay and entropy had commenced without it having any right to start. When he went into a shop, he left a lingering stench that would induce vomit in people of a weak disposition and, once he had left the premises, staff quickly went to the areas where he had been and attacked them with aerosol air-fresheners; retching involuntarily as they did it. His invisibility was the type where, despite him being there, nobody ever really saw him in an evening laid in a shop doorway wrapped in newspapers and cardboard, trying to obtain a modicum of protection from the cold nights. His only desire was to be safe from drunks that thought it funny to urinate on or kick a man when he is quite literally down and out. Any sightings of him were totally by accident and the safe and warm middle-class people moved on and told themselves that what they had just seen was not real. And in the daytime the doorway is vacated, and he disappears, a living ghost. Walking the streets but not seen. If he should be glimpsed, out of the corner of an eye, by a person that has been lucky enough not to have been cast down to such depths, then they would cross the road to avoid the walking filth - as if being on the same side of the road would make real poverty contagious. Or the shadow crossing theirs would make them unclean; a Western caste system with its own untouchables.

However today was different for Ernest. Over the last few days he had begged on the busy London streets managing to scrape enough together, from American and

Japanese tourists, for him to buy a warm cup of tea and a bacon sandwich. Not much but he had saved the largest part of his earning to purchase a cheap, but large bottle of gin. A tragic, but easy, escape from the realities of his life or, maybe, just to briefly let him forget his shallow existence.

That had promptly been drunk and he had also become drunk in the process. This state had allowed him to release the demons in his mind and he was weaving along the pavement of Tower Bridge, avoiding, or being avoided by, the tourists that were packed on the famous landmark. Avoiding eye contact with him as they fastidiously turned their heads to look at the Tower of London, HMS Belfast or just admire the grey and brown river Thames as it casually flowed to the sea. This left him to rant and shout his frantic monologue unheeded. Seemingly crazy, wild and incomprehensible, to any person that might be within earshot, but to him his words were the most important that he had ever muttered.

"God, I never betrayed you!" his voice slurred from the effects of the neat gin. "Yes, I signed it and I am sorry, but they lied, and I never went through with it." Each utterance impassioned and sincere emphasising every word by gesticulations. Arms flapping wildly in the air with the almost empty bottle waving like a glass flag. "Please forgive me. I was weak, blind and stupid." Any audience just assuming he was at best drunk or, at the worst, insane and possibly dangerous. All that meant, to them, was that it was yet another reason to avoid him. "They do not know, and I will never tell them, you must know that my Lord!"

Cars and buses sped by on the road in front of him and pedestrians did the same on the pavement behind him; a solitary, socially invisible, figure surrounded by a river of people. But today there was one pair of eyes fixed on him, knowing that he existed – for now. The demon had chosen his human form well; average height, average build and average clothing. Nondescript and the ideal figure to ensure he received the ubiquitous civil inattention. Just another ordinary face in a busy and un-noticing crowd - allowing him to do what he needed to get done. Despite the bustle of the people walking around him, all determined to reach their destinations, he was able to slip in between them unobstructed and make his casual way towards Ernest's defenceless back. As he drew nearer, he could make out the words being shouted and was the only person within earshot that knew what such utterances truly were. But he also knew that such unorthodox prayers were of no use. They wouldn't save him in this life, or the one after. Seeing a large red London double-decker bus approaching he recognised the opportunity and took it. Swiftly reaching out his arm his hand made brief, but firm, contact with Ernest's unsuspecting and defenceless back. The impact pushing him forwards, onto the road and into the path of the bus. Brakes squealed, tyres slid and there was a solid thud as Ernest's fragile human body met the far stronger metal body of the vehicle. Only then did he become visible again to the world. The sight of the crash and his broken body solicited screams from a few in the crowd. Some rushed onto the road in an attempt to help him but it was too late; assistance given in death but not in life. His once strong body, weakened by his enforced life, had become a shadow of what he once had been and the impact had resulted in spontaneous death. Seeing the body on the floor the demon could tell that he had successfully completed his mission and he casually walked away from the scene. No witnesses, so no crime. To everyone there it was just a crazy drunken tramp that had either fallen or jumped in front of a bus.

After the ambulance had arrived, the crew decided that he was beyond any attempts at resuscitation and pronounced him dead. They then took his body to the local mortuary and left it there in a cold detached way, as if they were dropping off someone's shopping. In Victorian times there had been one at the north end of the bridge but now his last journey, on Earth, was to the less prominent one in Westminster. But he didn't really care; his soul was refusing to leave the side of his body. He accompanied it and would have held his own hand if he could, solace to a figure that had received none in life and, in death, no longer needing it; sadness, slight relief, but not self-pity, at coming to such a sudden end. His physical and emotional pain was over with only one question left in his mind. Where would he go now? Normally, after death, the soul either went straight to Heaven or directly to Hell but he was still there, escorting himself as his former self was placed on a cold metal sliding drawer and slid into a coffin shaped chilled unit. Then his conundrum was answered. There was a faint whooshing noise, as if a glider had just flown overhead, and the lights dimmed slightly. Turning around he saw the figure, a man towering over him with giant gently flapping wings and blue flame flickering all over its body. All the figure said was "COME!" in a voice, inside his mind, cold enough to freeze his soul. Ernest's first instinct was to run and hide, but where could he go? Start an afterlife game of hide and seek, perhaps if he hid under the dissection table he would not be found! No,

Ernest knew that, no matter what, the apparition in front of him would follow him and soon catch up. Reluctantly he surrendered and walked towards the flickering blue light. The spirit nodded in approval of Ernest's wise choice. Then reached out his hand and placed it on the soul of the late Ernest Higginbotham. Upon contact both of them were gone, leaving the morgue room empty. Apart from all the dead bodies of course, but death had already visited them, leaving just empty shells to be grieved over by those that were left alive.

Chapter 3 - Lost and found. And Lost Again.

Many people believe that they have a guardian angel that might not exactly sit on their shoulder but follows them about and generally ensures that they come out of stupid situations unscathed. But, on the whole, most must scrape by thanks to just dumb luck rather than any great judgement. Despite this they would somehow rather believe in dead people guiding their actions or changing random situations so that they can walk away from car crashes without a scratch. Maybe hands guided so they have the luck to place their life savings on the appropriate horse in the correct race or just nudge them slightly so that they do not commit too deadly of a sin. Such things would be nice but if everyone had them then there would be no free will and Heaven and Hell wouldn't be needed. Plus, the human race has such a latent desire to do stupid things that the average angel would probably beat themselves to death from all the face palms they'd give themselves. However, guardian angels do exist and are sent to look after a few people that have been specially selected for the privilege but, even then, the purpose is more to watch them and report back to Heaven rather than pushing their designated subject out of the way of oncoming runaway traction engines or even wild bulls. One such guard was an angel by the name of Frederic, but he had always found that to be a little old fashioned and even the nickname of Fred sounded passé, so he had opted for the simple sobriquet of Bob. In life he had been raised in Alabama and then bought a boat and decided to live the wild bohemian life sailing around the west coast of America trying to avoid responsibilities and the taxman. He had lived to be in his 60's and passed across to Heaven after a particular fun night involving two naked women half his age, a lot of beer and vodka and one too many joints. The combined delirium caused him to dance off his boat and drown. But at least he died very happy indeed. No saint but still a good man. Perhaps his corpse floating on the water was why he liked to be called Bob- a happy reminder of a great way to die.

His brief, with regards to his designated guardianship, had been simple. Just keep an eye on Ernest Higginbotham, following him and if there is anything that Heaven should know then report it straight away. But unfortunately, one cold evening, Bob's attention had become a little too focused on the barmaid, at a local pub that Ernest happened to be frequenting, and not enough on Ernest himself. As a result, it wasn't until the next day that he realised that his human had disappeared. He had tried looking in all the usual places. He wasn't in his home, the local village, where he lived, or any of the numerous usual drinking establishments that he frequented. He had finally given up trying and embarrassedly reported his loss to his supervisor in Heaven. This resulted in him promptly being told, in no uncertain terms, that he had been given one simple task, mucked it up and that he was an idiot. Then he was instructed to go back and continue looking for Ernest. On returning to Earth he had spent several years carrying out a systematic search of towns and cities. Like a private eye he had taken solid human form and walked the street asking people if they had seen him. But what few friends and acquaintances he had were all of no use. It was like he had disappeared. A feat that was not totally impossible. If someone really wanted to get lost and never be found it was easy to do. But they had to truly want to do it, with money not always helping as much as most people would have thought. The search had extended further and further afield as he followed one dead-end lead after another. Until Ernest finally met his untimely end; thanks to the assistance of a demon and a London bus. Once his soul had been freed of his body an ethereal signal was released and a ripple in, what nerds might call, the fabric of time and space was sent outwards like an inaudible sound wave and finally hit Bob like a high frequency punch in the stomach. There were no words in the message, but he instinctively knew that his ward had moved on and also where the body could be found.

He had promptly got a ticket for the next train into London's King's Cross Station and made his way to the morgue. He identified the body, so that the authorities were not left with just another unidentified 'John Doe' corpse and the next of kin, for what they were, could be notified. He wouldn't get much of a funeral, but he deserved more than the anonymity of an unmarked grave or unrecognised cremation. Finding that the soul had departed he had simply assumed that his work on Earth was done and he could return to Heaven and enjoy a little bit of well-deserved heavenly downtime.

Standing in front of St. Joshua, in the clean but inspiring office in Heaven, he was finding his return to paradise less warm, comfortable and congratulatory as he had hoped. "You bloody idiot" was the key point of the Saint's welcome. "You couldn't keep your eyes off an unimportant human female, or more accurately her breasts, for five minutes and keep them on someone that is important. Then you completely failed to find him again."

Bob's admonishment was not the reward for all his hard work that he'd expected. But he stood before his supervisor and bit his lip, knowing that a failure to keep quiet, or say sorry at the appropriate moment, could result in him being allocated a mission on Earth in some cold and desolate place. Hardly a punishment akin to a place in Hell but looking after someone in Florida was more desirable than some 'one reindeer town' 350 miles north of Helsinki.

"And to make matters worse he hasn't appeared in Heaven!" continued St. Joshua. He was red with rage, the veins in his neck throbbing and Bob allowed his imagination to wander; visualising his incensed boss's head exploding. Grey matter being splattered around the room and the eyeballs shooting into his face; perhaps one last attempt to keep an eye on him? Having to suppress a snigger at that thought he just remained impassive, nodding or shaking his head at what he thought were the appropriate places. "Have you any idea why you were supposed to be a guardian angel to him?" without letting Bob answer the rhetorical question Joshua continued "He was the guardian of The Sword!" He paused to let the significance of the words sink in. Not realising that Bob had no idea what his superior was on about, but he had no intention of throwing more fuel to the flames of rage, aimed at him, so he kept his own council. The verbal tirade continued for the next half hour until the Saint could think of no more insults to wildly spit out. Spent, he began to catch his breath and think about what to do now. He realised that, even though he didn't want to do it, he had no alternative; God had to be informed. It was rare that he was forced to pass on any information to his master, guardianships tended to be simple affairs, an angel was assigned someone, despatched to Earth and their spirit could float about unseen and watch what happened. Hardly the most taxing of tasks and not requiring a great deal of skill, experience or intelligence so his department tended to be ignored. At most they needed the ability to concentrate for long periods without being distracted by any, and all, attractive humans that they felt like ogling. But when things went wrong, oh boy, how they could get messy and that was when the Saint hated his job. Passing on the information to God wasn't like a demon having to inform Satan that they had messed up; that would have been gory and painful. In Heaven there were no punishments, no naughty step to go sit on while the unfortunate person thought about what they had done, or not done. At the very worst there would be a gentle sigh of disappointment and words to the effect of 'never mind, it can't be helped' but to a loyal, loving and conscientious saint or angel the thought of failing or letting God down was punishment enough. Many sleepless nights would follow as the unfortunate messenger would relive every second in their mind; wishing that it wasn't them that had been given such a burdensome task. Many a Saint had become grey overnight after such an occurrence and only after God had laid His hands on them, to take away their sorrows, were they free to carry on as normal. Nobody liked Heaven being full of wailing and miserable angels. It was bad enough with born again Christians cluttering up the place and trying to make everyone else feel miserable without normal good people being dour as well.

No, it wasn't a chore that he wanted or relished. He knew exactly what needed to be said but didn't want to do it and he knew just the feckless angel to pass on the details...

Chapter 4 - Unexpected and Unheard Expletives

Outwardly, at least, God had taken the news, delivered by Bob, well. The information had been taken on board and He had given words of comfort to the worried looking Angel and the uncomfortable Saint that was accompanying him. 'Such things happen' and 'I suppose it can't be helped' were freely given out before both of them were dismissed and allowed to go and enjoy the benefits and pleasures that Heaven brings. Dedan, his key angel, had been sent to make preparations for his return to Earth – so that he could hopefully sort out the situation - and God now sat alone in His large and comfortable office. Elbows resting on His desk and face in His hands. A despondent look etched across His face as He allowed the magnitude of the news to fly wildly around His brain. Despite having no view of the future, He knew that a violent and miserable time was a distinct possibility and perhaps even inevitable. One wayward keeper of The Sword and Satan could have the upper hand. If not the end of days, then long nights of trouble and the end of all that was important and mattered. The precarious balance of peace gone as His ultimate deterrent was wielded by the eternal enemy. Satan had held it once before and hesitated; an error that He doubted that Lucifer would ever repeat if he got a second chance. Distant memories of the backwards and forwards flowing battles fought in the 1,063 years of the Apocalypse, before the creation of The Sword. Then thoughts of how victory followed victory after the weapon was forged and put to such effective use. With The Sword in the hands of Satan, Heaven was defenceless and vulnerable. No matter what the demons must be prevented from finding out the whereabouts of The Sword. The deterrent must remain just that.

Something to be feared and avoided, a symbol to keep them in their place and that place was Hell. They could fight the occasional battle with angels and the demons trying to storm the pearly gates, but they must always know that The Sword could be retrieved and used against them if things got too precarious and it looked like the side of good was losing the upper hand.

He knew that Ernest wasn't in Heaven, He'd got St. Peter to double check his records and there was no trace of him. He also doubted that the lost soul of Ernest would have strayed so far as to have taken him directly to Hell. If he had ended up there, God felt sure that there would be a stream of demons rushing to Earth in an attempt to retrieve the weapon. But so far, the portals from Hell were no more busy than usual and were not concentrating on any specific location. So, if Satan did have Ernest's soul and knew the location of the Sword's resting place, then he was playing it uncharacteristically cool. So, if he wasn't in Heaven and he wasn't in Hell there was only one other possible place, but that option wasn't something that made Him relax and feel comfortable either.

For humans, that try and project their role model views of how God should behave and talk, there is little or no room for accepting that He has frailties and could say or do anything that they considered being wrong, when measured against their own pompous standards. So, if you tried to tell them that their God could swear then their minds would close and their mouths would open as they damned you to Hell for all eternity for even suggesting such a heresy. It didn't fit their picture of what God would do so it must obviously be wrong and some lie put about by Satan. According to them it would be black propaganda to trick pure souls into sliding into Hell; a blasphemy not to be thought or uttered. Unfortunately for them God had no desire, or intentions, of modelling His true self on the dull or self-righteous deity that they wanted. Heaven was first and foremost a place for good people to go and judgemental and closed-minded bigots frequently found themselves in a place far more uncomfortable than they anticipated; with Heaven being a far better place for their absence. Therefore, despite the view of some dull opinionated worshippers, God involuntarily and unconsciously released a couple of loud and extremely coarse expletives that related to the sexual act. Even when they came from His mouth, they still were not acceptable in polite conversations with geriatric grandmothers or, far worse, toddlers that tended to pick up such language and repeat the words ad nauseam; the smile on their faces growing bigger as embarrassed and frustrated parents try to stop them from saying the coarse utterances. The profanities unheard by anybody were still powerful enough to shake the walls of His room and make the computer monitor on the desk of his secretary, Angelica, sway slightly in the office next door. Realising that the words, that He thought had been just in His head, had escaped from his mouth God got up from His chair and walked to the door. Opening it slightly He put His head around it. Angelica was busy typing away but stopped to look up at her Boss and give Him a wide and warm smile. She looked immaculate, as she always did. Her smart and elegant clothes were tight and highlighted her figure. He knew that Dedan had designs on her, but God had no plans to make it easy for his emissary. Assistants, as talented and beautiful as her, were hard to find and He had no intention of losing this one if she fell in love and went off to spend eternity with Dedan. Obviously, He wouldn't prevent her, her happiness was important to Him, but He refused to let her become just another of his casual conquests.

"Yes, my Lord?" she asked. From the look on her face He could tell that she had not heard His utterances. She was a kind and forgiving soul that understood that such things happened, but He still had no desire to shock or upset such an efficient and friendly assistant.

"Oh, nothing my dear. Just checking that Dedan had gone and wasn't wasting precious time standing around trying to chat you up." His voice was gentle and full of enforced playfulness; the panic in His mind hidden and far from obvious to her.

"No Sire, he was in such a hurry that he just asked me to arrange for him to return to Earth and then rushed out. He didn't even try and flirt with me or dish out any of his usual double entendres!"

"That is good, thank you Angelica. Could you please be an angel and make me one of your wonderful cups of coffee for me? Oh, and one more thing can you contact Roxy and ask her to come and see me? I think Dedan will need a bit of help." With that He went back into His office, closing the door behind him. Massaging His forehead God gave the assortment of ancient and modern fish, in his brightly illuminated fish tank, an absent-minded stare. 'Interesting days' he thought to Himself. Just then His mind was brought back to Heaven by Angelica gently knocking on his door and bringing in His cup of coffee in His favourite mug. The words 'THE Big Boss' clearly identifying it as His personal piece of crockery; not that anybody else would ever try and drink from it.

Chapter 5 – Roxy

Heaven is a fairly relaxed place. As long as you don't hurt people you are fairly free to do whatever you like. Being there in the first place means you passed the entry test on Earth, so it isn't like you will suddenly turn evil. With the one obvious exception being Satan, but he was part of a tiny minority and there are safeguards now in place. People were free and choose whatever name they liked - although picking Hitler, Satan or Beelzebub was still frowned upon. This was the case for Roxy, on Earth she had gone under the name of Rossana, a beautiful name in itself but she always found it cumbersome and liked her close friends to call her Roxy and, when she entered Heaven, she decided that she wanted to keep that pseudonym.

Having had her meeting Roxy walked away from God's office, her mind was busy going over what she had just been told and some of the more interesting details of her mission. There were parts of it that she loved. Before she died, she'd been an Italian that had ended up married to a boorish lout of a German and ended up stuck living in his country, away from family and friends, until she had become a victim of her tobacco habit. She had been knocked over by a cigarette delivery van while crossing the road to go to the shops to buy cigarettes. On reaching Heaven it had taken her a while to be able to laugh at the irony of her own demise but once she reached that point it became a story that she enjoyed telling.

She loved the country of her birth and wished she could visit it again and now the opportunity was there in front of her. However, the choice of leader was *interesting*, she was nodding acquaintances with Dedan, having spoken and joked with him when she had seen him on the streets of Heaven. She had found him a witty person that made her, and everyone else laugh. His cheeky self-deprecating humour, and casual manner, put everyone at ease and the sparkle in his eye was almost demonic; not a trait that would be expected to be found in Heaven. But she also knew him far better by his wider reputation. His, already formidable, legend had grown after his recent trip to Hawaii when he had managed to prevent Satan from wheedling his way back into Heaven. He'd participated in the destruction of the most insane demon that Hell had ever seen. Then, to top it all off, he had prevented the massed armies of Heaven and Hell from having the second Armageddon on the 18th hole of a local golf course. Such stories spread quickly around the close and comfortable confines of the afterlife and as they progressed each teller embellished on their version and the actions grew. With the actual truth having to be dug out of the surrounding words like a dinosaur fossil out of rock hardened by millions of years of pressure. But, even if all the stories were not 100% accurate, she knew that he had played a pivotal role on the mission and had the respect of virtually all that had gone to Earth with him. The one exception being St. Michael who, for some reason that she didn't fully understand, had gone on a sabbatical to one of the far reaches of Heaven and wasn't talking to anyone. But with his abrasive and overly punctilious personality that was doing everyone a favour; with many wishing that he would stay there for good.

But there was another facet of Dedan's reputation that she was also familiar with. She had lots of female angel friends in Heaven and quite a few of them had recounted long stories of his exploits on quiet and secluded clouds. Also, his noisy gymnastics on Hawaii, with Emily, an angel responsible for communicating with the demons and Bathsheba her demoness counterpart, had been told to her by impressed and jealous male angels that just happened to overhear some of the horizontal sounds. Of course, the eavesdropping was all done by total accident when their ears just happened to be leaning against the bedroom wall. Such exploits were beyond her comprehension as Dedan had never struck her as being anything special. He was hardly the tall dark and handsome type that would get a second glance on one of the many golden beaches in Heaven. To her he was more like the reliable but plain brother. Comfortable and safe but he wasn't tall, was slightly overweight and thinning on top. As sex symbols went his body had already gone in an opposite direction. Maybe going on a mission with him would be an education. But if his ego, or vanity, made him think that he had a chance with her then it would be him that would be getting a few lessons. Never mess with an Italian, especially an Italian woman.

When God had explained the mission to her, He had given her the opportunity to refuse but, even if she'd wanted to, angels tended not to decline such tasks. God knew what He was doing, and she was flattered to be chosen. However, she had heard many vague and dark tales of Limbo and the idea of going in there, trying to find some lost soul and ascertain the location of some mythical sword was unusual and dangerous. Limbo had, by definition, the ability to keep souls until it chose to release them to Heaven or Hell. It didn't negotiate, make deals or feel sorry for its residents. There were souls that had been stuck in there for thousands of years trying to prove that

43

they were worthy of Heaven rather than being sent to Hell. As she understood it there was no dust mat by the door saying 'Casual visitors welcome, please wipe your feet'- once in there you had to be processed just like everyone else, whether you were on a mission from God or not.

She continued to ponder the risks, and how to ensure Dedan behaved, until she reached her large and luxurious apartment. It wasn't anything better or worse than anyone else's. It was Heaven so it was perfect for her and just how she liked it; a large bay window with a view of paradise at the front and a garden at the back full of roses. But she would have to forgo such pleasures for as long as the mission on Earth lasted. What she needed, on the mission, would have to be taken with her and she knew that it could be hot in Florence in summer, so she decided to dress for the place. Being Italian she had an eye for, and an appreciation of, high fashion and knew that to avoid looking like a tourist she needed to make a stylish statement with what she wore. With this in mind she selected a tight black dress that had been made by Coco Chanel. Ever since the famous designer had arrived in Heaven, she'd been kept busy by lots of French and Italian residents asking her for 'just a little favour' and she always found the time to oblige. Looking at her reflection in the full-length bedroom mirror she had to admit that she liked what she saw. She was only 5' 4" but the dress made her appear taller and what was there, in such a small package, looked stunning. The elegant garment was short enough to show off her slender and tanned legs and at the top her long dark brown hair, with hints of red and light brown, cascaded over the black straps hugging her shoulders. Her dark eyes and amber toned skin making her look like the Mediterranean child that had lost the sun for too long. She decided to add to the whole ensemble by selecting a few gold and diamond trinkets made in person by Boodles, the famous jeweller. Checking herself in the mirror's reflection she had to admit that she looked good and, never mind Florence, she was ready for the cat walks of Milan. Dedan can look but he'd better not touch; or he might just find himself with broken hands. Her jewels were not for him to be touching, never mind fingering.

She packed a small bag with spare clothes, which might be more practical for any trips into Limbo, and then she left her apartment. With vanity in mind she took the long route to the dimensional portal. Roxy felt good and she wanted to know if she still had '*it*'. What had been natural in her youth on Earth, before her fire had virtually been smothered by a dolt of a husband, she had turned heads. Such flirtatious acts always seemed out of place in Heaven but now it was different. Even though she wasn't vain or egotistical, like many women, she enjoyed an excuse to look beautiful. She definitely now had an excuse and a reason for it. She needn't have worried; both male and female heads were turned all along her route. Most men threw her admiring and lustful glances, with a few just admiring her dress and shoes, wishing they had an outfit just like it. And the females gave her the obligatory glances, jealous of someone looking far more attractive than them and for receiving more lascivious glances than they did. Roxy smiled to herself at the effect she was having and savoured every step of her walk. When she got to the entrance to the portal, she was greeted by an angel that was obviously enchanted by her grace, elegance and beauty. He was left speechless which made him look like he was imitating a goldfish. As she walked past him, he finally managed to compose himself and remember what he was supposed to be doing.

"Errr, Roxy?"

"Hello, yes that's me." The sultry Italian accent and bright smile she gave him did nothing to help the poor angel to concentrate on his task.

"I have a bag for you. It contains a pistol and an assault rifle". He handed her a compact and heavy suitcase and Roxy thanked him. As she took possession of it the unexpected weight made her nearly drop it but she ensured that her lack of control was not obvious.

"The rifle is dismantled but if you need any help re-assembling it Dedan knows how to handle a weapon!" He added helpfully.

As she walked away, she just turned to face the angel and with a smile responded "Yes, so I have heard!"

At last she finally reached the silver coloured doorway that was the portal and she stopped. It looked so basic and simple, step through it and you disappeared from Heaven and reappeared back on Earth, at the location you wanted. No ancient writing on it, no control panel from a space movie, just a large rectangular piece of metal, safe, simple but effective. All that was missing was a physical door.

And there, stood leaning nonchalantly on it, was Dedan a casual smile on his face as he took in the sight of his new assistant. Dressed in plain blue jeans and a baggy black t-shirt, he had just one plain dark blue suitcase at his feet, ready for his trip to Europe.

Sweeping his arm towards the door frame, as if he was inviting some flirty female angel into his bedroom, "Care to join me and have some fun?"

Chapter 6 - The Devil Doesn't Always Get His Due.

Satan was carrying out one of his occasional surprise inspection tours of Hell, busy finding work for any idle hands. Any demon that looked like they were not filling their working time productively, and making the souls in their charge suffer, would find themselves quite literally in a whole world of pain and hurt; often swapping places with one of their victims. Instant demotion for them and a promotion for what used to be a victim, with the punisher becoming the punished, receiving what they gave out. They even had the right of appeal, and Satan, as sole judge and arbitrator, had the right to ignore their pleas and, depending on his mood, inflict greater suffering; which he invariably did if anyone was ever stupid enough to complain to him.

Today he was ensuring that painful discipline was being kept to its maximum effectiveness in the seventh ring of hell. There was no such thing as pain being beyond human endurance there. Screams met his ears and he loved the sound. His happiness usually meant someone else's unhappiness. His concentration and focus were currently aimed at a random lost soul that he had found cowering in the far end of a tank of volcanic lava. His sins, on Earth, were returned to him with interest. Like Emperor Valerian his greed, during life, was being punished by having Satan pour liquid gold down his throat. Satan's glee was interrupted by a Demonoid running up to him. Despite the creature's tiny stature his courage was respected throughout Hades, being the bearer of news to Satan could be an excruciating experience to any demon that delivered it in the wrong way. And this particular messenger recognised that the news he bore was probably not going to gain him smiles, a friendly hug and plentiful rewards with invites for him to marry one of Satan's seven daughters - even if he'd been stupid enough to want to. A high degree of diplomacy was needed if he was to avoid being less than accidentally pushed into the lake of fire that was flowing past him. "Majestic Lord, I bring you news from Earth!" His voice clear and not betraying the fear that was gripping his heart like the fingers of Satan; that he could quite possibly literally soon be feeling.

Casually Satan dropped the tormented damned soul back into the flames, as if it were a piece of paper being consigned to the flames, or of no more importance than garbage. Turning to the messenger he slowly looked at him, a sneer of contempt on his face. Rigidly stood to attention the underling resembled a short soldier that had been arrested for being drunk and, now sober, was currently waiting for his admonishment from his commanding officer. Without words Satan could tell that he was not about to receive good news.

"YES, what do you want you maggot?" He growled menacingly ensuring that he got his usual unpleasantries out of the way straight away.

"Sir," snapped the Demonoid crisply, as if even the word was stood to attention. "Ernest Higginbotham has finally been found and killed by a hunter demon!"

The news didn't seem to have the effect that the Demonoid had expected. Satan just looked at him, head tilted slightly in bewilderment. "And who in Hell is Ernest Higginbotham, and why should I care?"

"Well…. He is, or was, the guardian of The Sword of Uncreation. Several years ago, you despatched a Hunter demon to destroy him and despatch him to Hell."

"Oh, *the Guardian*." Satan's voice now lighter, thanks to a sudden realisation that the news was good. "Why didn't you say? Alright, take me to him. I would very much like to meet our new guest."

The diminutive Demonoid's eyes widened, knowing that the punch line to his tale was not going to solicit a smile, never mind any laughter. "There is a problem Sire. He isn't exactly *IN* Hell!" Swallowing hard and wishing that he could have a glass of cold water; his thirst not helped by the surroundings. "After death he didn't materialise here."

The rage in his voice taking on a sharp edge "So after all that we did he still ended up in Heaven?"

"No sire, the Hunter demon followed the body to the local morgue and seeing the *blue flamed one* from a distance he believes that his soul is currently being held in Limbo."

With those words Satan fired a ball of flame at the already dehydrated Demonoid's head, scorching flesh and searing orifices in the process. As punishments went, he had received a mild, metaphorical, slap on the wrists. He would heal, eventually. "Okay" Satan casually said, his brief outburst of fire having released a modicum of his frustration. "Not great but we still have a chance. I am sure that judgement will be in our favour, but just in case I think it would be prudent to send down a few demons to tip the scales in our direction and ensure that he is personally escorted into my presence."

"Very good my lord" responded the messenger through a scorched mouth. The top of his head still illuminated by a small flame; like an evil and ugly candle.

"Now get out of my sight you pathetic worm, I have things to plan." With that he strode past the Demonoid and out of the punishment chamber.

Walking purposefully with his hands clenched behind his back he passed grovelling demons, which were determined to prove their adoration and elegance to their evil master by supplicating themselves as he went past them, un-noticing and caring even less about their postures or demeanour, his thoughts were elsewhere. At last the opportunity to finally win was tantalisingly close. He could almost feel the grip of The Sword in his hand once again, and this time he wouldn't get it wrong. Victory would be his. No hesitation, no pauses and no doubts, just sweet vengeance. On he went, past chamber after chamber of screaming agony until he finally reached a part of Hell out of bounds to most demons, without valid reason; a place that was a comparative Heaven for the souls being punished. His own domain was a decaying and crumbling palace with seven towers manned by loyal demon guards protecting him from less than loyal occupants of Hell that might want to sit on his throne. No matter how many repairs he made to the place decay and entropy's destructive grip quickly took its effect and began the process of destroying what had been built or fixed. Such was the all- pervasive power of Hell itself. Everything could last for all eternity, but it wasn't allowed to exist without a price.

On entering the office, outside his inner sanctuary, he glanced at Stuart, his private secretary, personal spy and, when the mood took him, foot stool. There was no love or respect for his weasel like assistant. Satan knew that there was no loyalty in Hell and if Stuart could gain some sort of benefit from stabbing him in the back then he would. On Earth he had been a cowardly and spineless accountant and pedantic bureaucrat that had happily swindled, stole and poisoned his way into a mediocre but comfortable life. In Hell Satan knew that he had little to fear from such a snivelling character. Subservience was what Stuart was best at and knew that ambition was a slippery path which usually ended up with people falling from a great height onto rocks, spikes or both. "Stuart" he barked without pausing on his progress towards his office. "Send for the head of the Marching Horde, NOW!" Although such words could easily be misconstrued by a demon that was a too literal in understanding instructions, and a decapitated head had been accidentally proffered in the past – but Stuart knew better. With those words still in the air Satan had pushed the reluctantly stiff door, leading into his office, open and was through it; leaving Stuart to unquestioningly follow his orders. Too many questions could lead to a painful demotion, so he knew his was not to reason why. His was to do and not to be dissected!

All over Earth, in many nations, there are elite Special Forces. Military specialists trained to be the best there is, hard as they come and able to handle any dangerous situation without batting an eyelid. The British army has the SAS, the USA has the Special Forces Group, the French have the Foreign Legion and the Russians have the KSO. None of which you'd want to mess with as they are all trained so that they could creep into your bedroom at night, defecate on your pillow then leave. And it isn't until you wake up in the morning having rolled over and found yourself with a very sticky, and smelly, substance on your cheek do you realise that they have left their calling card. And along with stealth they would think nothing of charging a much larger force armed only with a bottle opener and a rolled-up newspaper. And they would invariably win the ensuing battle.

The Marching Horde, in so many ways, are absolutely nothing like any of those Special Forces. They might leave a brown calling card on your bed linen, but they wouldn't be subtle or discrete about it. They'd more than likely aim for your wide-open snoring mouth. They might also be outnumbered and attack an army of far superior numbers, but they would seldom opt for everyday household objects but, if they did, they would lose. Their weapons of choice would be ideally thermo-nuclear or if they were not available then heavy artillery with armour piercing rounds. Anything less than that would be seen as a compromise and losing an unfair advantage. They might not all have been intellectuals, but they were however, for demons, courageous, brave, resourceful and cunning. Like many an ordinary squaddie the average one might not have had degrees in anything unless some obscure Universities did PhD's in drinking and swearing, in which case they'd all have the highest honours going. However, as in life, there are often exceptions to rules and the Marching Horde were definitely no exception. As a human Finley had been a duplicitous, cunning and versatile subaltern in the British army during WWII and his ambition was such that he could easily have risen highly and rapidly had it not been for the Geneva Convention holding him back. It frustrated him that the enemy flagrantly committed war crimes yet his ability to see the benefits of ignoring them was frowned upon by his short-sighted superiors. Why couldn't they just see, and accept, that in battle prisoners of war were an impediment? So, an example of his idea to deal with them, more creatively, involved first attacking an exhausted platoon of Volksdeutsche Hungarian troops, accepting their surrender then finally summarily executing them against a church wall. This blood lust extended to several civilians that just happened to be in a captured village and he was only stopped in his wild killing frenzy when a Captain, in his regiment, calmed Finley's excited nerves by fatally shooting him in the head. This sent the eager lowly officer to Hell and also saved several innocent women and children from his indiscriminate executions. On arriving in Hades his skills and talents for evil were quickly recognised and he was promoted to membership of the Demon Marching Horde and, through several strange incidents of demons being *accidentally* locked in punishment chambers, he rose to what he saw as his rightful place - High commander. As with all demons he was given the opportunity to select a more imposing shape while he was in hell, however he opted for his human form and it was in this guise that he stood before Satan. Tall and slim he stood smartly to attention. His officer training still kicking in despite the lax view of army protocols amongst the Horde. His polished black and yellow plated body armour adding the aura of power and authority that came with his rank. The Samurai sword attached to his belt more than just a ceremonial embellishment. He had used it on several occasions to maintain discipline. It is amazing what effect severing the arm from a soldier, giving you the eye, had. It inconveniences the demon, until it grows back, and also sends out a clear message to the other troops. 'I am in charge, and don't you forget it!' It was also useful for maintaining law and order in cases of the occasional demon insurrection. When those happened, he knew which side he needed to be on - loyalty to Satan had its rewards and definitely fewer punishments.

Satan looked at the leader of his personal bodyguard with a mixture of respect and suspicion. He knew from experience that underlings could easily be tempted to make a play for supreme power, after all he had done it himself once, he also knew that Finley was happy with his rank, authority and, for the time being at least, had no wish to sit in Satan's chair. And even if he did try anything Satan felt sure that he would be able to win any battle, irrespective of who took the wrong side. But the soldier he saw before him was definitely an asset that could be utilised and was ideal for the task in hand. His intelligence and flexibility allowed him to distinguish himself, as a man of many resources amongst the rest of his peers, so a mission needing the ability to think on his feet and adapt was just what was needed.

"At ease Soldier!" He barked. Deliberately taking on the tone of a superior officer and therefore ensuring the instructions would be received correctly. "I have a mission for you, it is fairly simple and of critical importance. And failure is an option, but it would be an option that you might not find comfortable and certainly not desirable!" He paused to allow the full magnitude of the threat sink in. Not that he needed to pause for long, Satan's idea of a carrot and stick approach was one of hitting someone with a carrot and if that didn't work then using a stick. If that failed there were harder and far pointier things to use for encouragement or, perhaps more accurately, discouragement. "I need you to go down to Earth and go through the gates of Limbo and retrieve a soul for me. Take three of your best soldiers with you and do what you need to do to bring him to me. And, of course, it should go without saying that you will need to stop any possible Angels from getting their hands on him; should they cross your path."

"Sir! I understand exactly what you mean." his voice clear, loud and respectful with his chest out and chin up; in true British officer style. "I will not let you down."

It wasn't possible for Satan's left eyebrow to rise any higher on his forehead, but if it could it would have rested at some point just north of the nape of his neck. But the look of condescension worked despite the fixed limits of his brow movement. "Oh, Finley, Finley, Finley, let me assure you that letting me down *is* definitely the LAST thing that you would want to do. Stuart will arrange for you to get to Italy and once there a special emissary will contact you, giving as much assistance as he can. Dismissed!" There were definitely worse things than death and, in Hell, that was just the beginning.

Finley snapped smartly to attention, he made an about turn and marched out of the office leaving Satan watching him go. Engrossed in his own dark thoughts he contemplated how he would yield The Sword in battle, allowing himself the sin of hubris at the thought of becoming the ruler of all Heaven and Earth. But he knew that such a plan would not be easily achieved if he didn't get his taloned hands on the wayward soul. But he had a chance and such an opportunity might never knock on his door again, so he had to act quickly to answer it in case it just posted a card through the figurative letter box and drove off in a hurry so that the delivery man could go to somebody else's door. And Satan knew exactly which other door would get knocked on if he wasn't ready. There was no prize for second place when God was involved.

In Satan's outer office Finley stood glaring imperiously at Stuart, who was sat at his desk craning his neck to look up at the tall officer in front of him. He had been on missions to Earth before so knew all about portal transportation back down to Earth and the physical discomfort and haphazard nature of returning to Hell, so much of Stuarts routine instructions were just formal and pointless. However, he did pay full attention when the details of his help on Earth were passed on. Although the description of the contact was vague the location and timing were specific. He balked when he was told what clothing he'd have to wear to fit in but realised that a Catholic Priest's black soutane robe was the ideal camouflage for four demons, in human form, walking around Italy. Besides the idea of pious Christians showing them deferential respect tickled his funny bone. He could see himself giving them a satanic blessing, with them not knowing any differently and being happy for it. Not quite converts but unknowing sinners.

Finally, Stuart finished his dull and monotone lecture and the silence brought Finley's wandering mind back to where it should be. He hadn't heard the last few sentences but looking at Stuart he saw an expectant face as if a question had been asked and was awaiting an answer.

There was the assumption that the talk had finished with the final, almost obligatory 'Any questions?' The standard question at the end of most such talks, but he couldn't be sure so he just gave Stuart a look of disdain as if whatever he had just said was contemptible and not worthy of an answer. Stuart recognised the look and shrugged. "Just asking!" he said, taking the silent rebuke at face value. Stuart knew Finley and had no desire to be decapitated by the blade at his side. Losing your head in Hell had a totally different meaning to what it did to Earth and walking around with a loose head waiting for it to reseal with the neck, and become sturdy again, was embarrassing, awkward and uncomfortable. Plus, it made nodding in agreement to everything Satan said nigh on impossible.

You could spend an eternity trying to find anything to like about Satan's private secretary and, at some point, you would realise that you were wasting your time as he had no saving graces. Even in Hell there were demons that could have good flaws in their characters but not Stuart. He was oilier and slimier than a politician making promises just before an election and less sincere or believable. If you trusted him then you'd end up regretting it. Fortunately, there was no pretence about him; he didn't try to ingratiate himself into your life so that he could stab you in the back. But, if there was any stabbing to be done, he would be the first candidate. Finley had little time for him, sensed Stuart's unease and enjoyed it. He turned and left the assistant, a dark smile on his face. He knew that his mission was important and failure was not an option but in his own mind the concept of not returning with the wayward soul was outside of his comprehension. He had plenty of troops in his army that had been to Limbo and

ended up in Hell anyway. How difficult could the mission
be for him?

Chapter 7 – Unnatural selection

The trio of demons, who had been handpicked by Finley to help him on Earth, were lined up before their commander. The battle armour did nothing to stop Finley from thinking of an evil version of the Three Stooges. Despite being in demon form none of them could be accused of looking frightening. Rutherford, the tallest of them had a gaunt face, stubbly beard, twisted horns, and buckteeth. Banks wasn't as tall but was stockier, however the whole appearance was spoilt by his fierce and fiery red eyes being crossed so that any terror you could feel at his appearance was lost as you were never sure if he was looking at you or someone in the distance just over your right shoulder. Then there was Collins, he was the shortest of the three and looked more like a bulldog that had learnt to walk on his hind legs all the time. Many a demon had, on first meeting him, made the mistake of taking the look to be a reflection of the demon's character. One foolish Agares demon had even tried to pat him on the head and give him a dog biscuit. His hand grew back eventually but the demon was reminded that a dog can bite; even a hand can feed it.

"Right you three, listen up, you have been chosen by me for a special mission. You are going to become Catholic Priests!" This news wasn't met with much shock or resentment. Thanks to the lip service given to the concept of rich men and needles going through eyes of camels, there were plenty of priests that didn't quite meet the expected standards for entry into Heaven. Despite all the last rites they had found themselves in a place with less air-conditioning and comfortable furniture. Saying sorry at the last minute didn't expunge a lifetime of cruelty, greed or forcing themselves on innocent children. "We are going for a little jaunt to Italy and are going to stroll up to Limbo and save a lucky soul from any risk of it being sent up to Heaven. Thus, ensuring he comes with us back to Hell. Willing or kicking and screaming, it is all the same to me."

"Not a problem chief" chipped in Collins in a chirpy London cockney accent. "Why would he want to go to Heaven anyway? As Mark Twain once said, 'you go to Heaven for the climate but Hell for the company.' I am sure that he will be glad to come with us – whether he likes it or not."

"Oh, yes. Because the brochure for Hell, as a holiday destination, is so glossy and appealing" interrupted Banks.

"However, wasn't it Oscar Wilde that said…" ventured Rutherford but he was cut off by Finley before he could continue.

"Alright, alright! Thank you, but I have no desire for this to turn into a nerd parade where you all end up debating Wittgenstein or quoting people that had nothing to say in the first place. I know what you three are like. I have been drinking with you remember? I have seen you all drunk and, despite what you might think, you are the most boring company imaginable." He paused to give himself a face palm at the recollection of a dull few hours he'd rather have spent with more interesting demons. "You are the audio equivalent of listening to paint dry, magnolia paint at that."

He could sense their desire to argue and contradict him about his opinion of them and their social skills. In their minds they were always the life and soul of any and all parties. Their repartee bringing culture and sophistication to what were normally just tedious anti-social get togethers. Events where all the Marching Horde just spent their downtime getting drunk and fighting before eventually, but inevitably, entering into unconsciousness. In their minds all they did was raise the intellectual level of the conversation so that there was sophistication and witty banter in amongst the general inebriated vulgarity. Strangely enough there hadn't been many parties for a long time. Or, if there had been any, the other demons had somehow forgotten to invite them.

Finley looked at his three would be companions and was beginning to have second thoughts about his choice. They were definitely the most intelligent members of the Marching Horde. And, after what he had heard about the demon army that last went to Earth, he was positive that the ability to spell their own names without having to stick tongues out, due to the perspiration inducing concentration, would be an asset for this particular mission. But had he gone too far? If he didn't put his foot down, and continually steer the conversations in directions that suited him, he would have to spend his time listening to them drone merrily on about politics, comparative religions or philosophical conjecture on morality. Perhaps he had found his own unique private mobile punishment chamber for Hell, having to listen to those three prattling on for all eternity.

With the Marching Hordes Finley never bothered to pry into a demon's background and what things they had done on Earth to deserve their entry into Hell. In his reserved, upper-class English mentality, he always thought it was rather rude and bad form to enquire into another's deeds, or misdeeds. Each one of them was evil and that was all he needed to know. The acts and deeds that they committed were immaterial to him. But for the highbrow version of Curly, Larry and Moe that were stood before him he was definitely curious. They just seemed out of place in Hell and were not the usual military types. Despite all his reservations about their ability to prevent him from falling asleep after 30 seconds of conversation he had seen them in action in battle and they had proven themselves to be vicious and tenacious fighters especially during a recent demon insurrection. Watching them fight was barbarity made into an art form. The enemy's arms and legs were severed with a precision that any surgeon would be proud of; if they could stomach watching it. And heads were removed from torsos with single blows and sent rolling across the floor like footballs during a world cup match. On more than one occasion he had wanted to shout, 'IT'S A GOAL!' as he fought alongside them and glimpsed the sight out of the corner of his eye. Plus, they had the added capability of being able to think not only for themselves but as a team as well. Most demons were focused on just one objective, get into battle destroying as many of the enemy as they can in as short of a time as possible. Usually good stratagems but there were times when the ability to assess a battle, and realise that other tactics were available, were boons. Those three could think on their feet and adapt to changing ebbs and flows in circumstances. They never ran after retreating enemies to be caught in traps or fought until they couldn't fight anymore; only to be hacked to pieces by the opposition. They were ideal for his job on

Earth and when dealing with Limbo. They would, hopefully, prove to be three aces up his sleeve if he came across any angels that just happened to be on a similar mission and wanted to stop him.

"Alright lads, time for us to go. Our disguises and weaponry are waiting for us at the dimensional portal so the sooner we set off the better."

He led the way along dimly lit corridors, yellow from the sulphur that pervaded the air and black from the eons of flames that occasionally occurred thanks to the combustible nature of the atmosphere. The three soldiers close behind him discussing Nietzsche quietly, in case Finley heard them and told them to shut up, or simply slapped them to obtain silence. On their way they came to the strange shape of a naked bottom half of a human form sticking out of the rock wall. Legs stood straight, buttocks protruding and chest disappearing into stone. It was a demon called Carsten that had been killed in battle on Earth and returned in the haphazard way that happened to demons that meet an untimely and unplanned death on Earth. He had re-materialised in that position and none of the demons had it in their character to dig him out. So, there he remained with his hands and fingers stuck in the wall gently moving and wearing away his stone stocks. The subtle attrition would eventually allow him to dig himself out but that would be a slow process. And the opportunity for the other demons to find amusement at the expense of this unusual piece of modern art had not been missed. Carsten's clothing had quickly been removed and his delicate parts had been the source of much fun and amusement to many a depraved demon. However, once that source of entertainment had been utilised and become boring, as opposed to being bored, a legend had very quickly grown and spread around Hell that it was good luck, for any passer-by, if they gave the partially imprisoned demon's bottom a smack as they walked past. This story was quickly, and willingly, accepted by the sadistic demons and a new tradition had begun. It had started with the demons using their hands to deliver the blow but some industrious demon had somehow managed to find an old cricket bat and had left that standing by Carsten's free rear end and that was now used for the demon equivalent of rubbing a lucky rabbit's foot. And like the rabbit, it was certainly unlucky for Carsten. The four soldiers were sticklers for tradition and knew that luck might play a part in their trip to Italy, so they felt it their duty to administer the requisite blows. Four loud thwacks could be heard echoing down the corridor before they resumed their walk to the portal that would take them to Earth. The transportation process was not the most comfortable of experiences and left the demon feeling nauseous, so it was always good to have a bit of a laugh at another's suffering before going on a long journey.

Chapter 8 – Buena Sera Terra.

The idea of two people suddenly materialising, out of nowhere, in front of the doorway into a locked and unused shop, and not being noticed, might seem ludicrous and incredible to most humans that didn't know any better. Even more so if the area is a busy underground walkway and shopping area full of late afternoon shoppers and commuters that are using it as a thoroughfare to get home along with tourists getting lost or just taking in the sights. But that is exactly what guaranteed Dedan and Roxy's anonymity and obscurity. A mass of preoccupied people being far too busy to stop and take notice of anyone else, especially two ordinary looking people that might have been there all the time for all they knew; or cared. They could have appeared wearing gorilla suits singing Black Sabbath songs and it would have been doubtful if anyone else would have given them a second glance or acknowledged their existence. Such was the way with humans, too busy to notice two angels filling previously empty air with solid flesh and blood.

On arrival both Roxy and Dedan looked around, taking in the strange surroundings. Roxy had been to Florence before and it wasn't what she remembered or expected. Being surrounded by shops and having an enclosed concrete roof took her by surprise. But being Italian she could tell straight away that she was in Italy. It was in her DNA and she could feel it in her soul. The smell in the air and the vibrancy of the place sung to her inner being and made her feel at home. The Italian signs announcing '50% Verdita', or 50% sale, in all the shop windows, to entice the tourists to spend, confirmed it to Dedan that they were at least in the right country.

They were on a corner of the arcade that led to their left and ahead of them, while to their right were escalators and steps where they could just make out the bright glare of daylight at the top. Deciding that they were more likely to get an idea of where they were, precisely, Dedan gave Roxy a slight nod in the direction of the escalators. They rode up them and came out at the top where they saw yet more people busily walking about and then they saw an Iveco 4x4 armoured car with two heavily armed Italian soldiers casually stood next to it, chatting away as they watched the people go by on their daily routines. The extra security a symbol of the fear generated by terrorists that thought that they could prove that their god was worthier of worship if they planted bombs and killed innocent people. The belief that 'God told them to do it' totally inaccurate unless Satan was their deity of choice, in which case even he never instructed anyone to be such idiots. Looking beyond the troops they saw a sign announcing that they were in front of the entrance to the Florence Santa Maria Novella train station. At least Angelica had arranged for them to appear close to the centre of the city. The bags full of clothing, guns and ammunition were too heavy to be carried for great distances, especially in the oppressive early afternoon heat of Italy in summer. Dedan had grown up in the desert and was used to the burning sun but the sudden burst of heat made him sweat and his t-shirt quickly became wet from the perspiration.

"Wait here a minute" Dedan casually instructed Roxy and two minutes later he returned carrying a small pocket map of the city. "A small €2 investment, I think we might need it."

Unfolding it they looked from the map to their surroundings and quickly got their bearings. Ahead of them they could make out the massive church of the Sacred Saints and diagonal to that was the cenotaph in the Piazza dell'unita Italiana, the square celebrating the unification of Italy in the late 19th Century. From the map they could work out that the Via Saint Anthony was leading off of there, and that was the location of their initial destination, their hotel.

The walk was not too long but crossing Italian roads was always a treacherous thing to do so they had to do that with care and caution and that delayed the journey, making their eventual arrival at the Hotel San Antonino, and its welcoming air conditioning, a much needed relief. Roxy had opted for style but her elegant high heeled shoes were perhaps, in hindsight, not the best choice for having to manoeuvre around hot busy streets while carrying heavy suitcases. But sometimes fashion and style took precedence, especially to an Italian.

The hotel concierge greeted them with a happy smile and the obligatory "Ciao" but he didn't continue as his perceptive senses, honed by years of hotel work, were giving him confusing signals. He saw a stunningly beautiful woman dressed in the most stylish of clothing, so he automatically assumed that she was Italian, but she was accompanied by a man that didn't give off any Mediterranean aura. Even men in Italy had pride and gave their appearance due care and attention, the heavily sweating man that was stood before him didn't appear to have bothered with mirrors or expensive clothes shops for that matter. His plain clothes would have been at home in the aisles of a supermarket and never in a top branded designer house, a rich American he assumed. He'd have to be. How else would he be with the beautiful creature stood by his side?

From his many missions to Earth, carried out over the centuries, Dedan had learnt and spoke hundreds of languages, some long dead and forgotten and many still spoken today. His ability to swear in at least 656 different tongues had served him well over the centuries. He was able to tell jokes, mostly dirty, in virtually all as well. This usually undiplomatic and highly inappropriate talent had proved to be a precious ice breaker and way of de-escalating many would be dangerous, and confrontational, situations. The main exception being German, he had struggled many times to find a joke in their language but had always failed abysmally. But at least he wasn't alone, humour wasn't something that Germans were famous for and most Germans couldn't help him with his search. Italian was also a language that he could get by with, but he was always wary that he never spoke it like a native, so he gladly opted to speak to the member of the hotel staff in an English with an accent to match. "Hello, the name is Walters, Mr. and Mrs. Walters. I believe you have a reservation for us?"

The concierge had watched the couple walk into the lobby and had been trying to guess at their nationality. On hearing the voice, he was able to stop his conjecture on the origins of the man. English - say no more! Style, to most British, was what they climbed to get over a wall into a farmer's field while they were hiking. If clothing ever conveyed a message it was just to say that 'I want to stay warm'. Élan, panache and sophistication were just words to be met with suspicion in England, a sign that any clothes

69

in a shop would cost more than they were willing to pay. Those that did try to pull it off were usually rich women and the more money they spent, in the attempt, the cheaper they looked. Quickly checking his computer screen for the reservation records the Italian felt comfortable welcoming them. "Yes sir, the best room in the hotel."

False passports were handed over for him to copy and then returned as they signed in. Then Roxy started a polite conversation with the hotel receptionist in Italian, glad to be able to converse in her native tongue. However, Dedan was still drenched in sweat and aware that they had a lot to do and was in no mood to hang around in the small lobby while his 'wife' chatted. "Roxy?" he interrupted her conversation, his voice tired and tinged with a hint of frustration. "I think we need to get to our room, unpack, get changed and freshen up." Roxy took the hint and said her goodbyes to the concierge. It had been a long time since she last talked with an Italian, or at least a living one, in her mother tongue and she had enjoyed it. Home at last.

As the hotel staff member watched them walk into the lift, and go up to their room, he sighed. If he had a wife like that, he knew exactly what he'd be doing in their hotel room with her on such a gloriously beautiful afternoon. But unpacking wouldn't have been the first of his priorities. "English and their *wild* passion!" He exclaimed out loud, followed by another sigh of despair.

Oblivious to the Italian man's jealousy, and contemptuous view of his adopted undercover nationality, Dedan arrived at the door of their room on the fifth floor. He opened it and gallantly swung his arm in a gesture so that Roxy knew that she could go in first and put down her heavy bags. Once inside the spacious room they both did the first thing that most holiday makers do when the walk into their room, they went to the balcony overlooking the tops of the rest of the medieval part of the city. Unlike far too many modern city centres there were no ugly bright steel and glass tower block monstrosities spoiling the view. Instead there was just the magnificent domed top of the majestic Duomo Cathedral standing gracefully above the rows of tiled roofs. If this had not been a mission, and his companion had been more receptive to his charms, then he could have turned this trip into a romantic and passionate event that would have certainly gained the concierge's respect and admiration. If only the clerk had known how frustrated Dedan felt about his inability to take such a pleasurable course of action. There was no lack of passion or desire, just the total absence of opportunity and the right willing person.

Roxy gave Dedan a seductive, but teasing, smile that left him with the uncomfortable impression that she had just read his mind. If she had he knew what he could expect, and deserve, a slap across his face but fortunately for him the blow never materialised. Instead she just went to the suitcase containing her clothes and opened it up. She quickly flicked through the contents and bundled some of the varied garments into her arms. "I am just going into the bathroom to get changed. Why don't you do some unpacking of clothes, get your firearm sorted and get packing that."

"Of course, my angel, anything for you." his voice full of mirth as he watched the bathroom door close. "Can I help you with anything while you're in there Mrs. Walters? Undoing the zip on your dress perhaps? I am no expert but happy to jiggle it about for you and then see what happens."

"Why thank you" she shouted through the closed door. "That is very kind of you but there is no need for you to jiggle anything of mine. I can manage quite adequately. Any jiggling will have to be done by yourself, on your own." her dark Italian accent making his heart flutter and his groin wish for a bit more than a quick fluttering. "I am a big girl now, so can handle such things myself!"

"Jeez" he whispered as his imagination allowed him to create a less than professional, working relationship, mental picture of his colleague in a state of undress. "You are indeed and I bet you can." the voice louder this time; allowing her to fully hear his words.

Eventually she opened the door allowing him to see her in her chosen new attire. Clothing that would, all being well, be far more appropriate for dealing with Limbo. Black trainers, black denim jeans and a black long-sleeved top all of which were figure hugging and would do nothing to help him maintain his concentration while on the difficult part of the mission. He thought that she might feel the heat on the way from the hotel to the gates of Limbo but conceded that you can't have everything and better to dress practically for there. He doubted that their objective would be as warm as the streets of Florence.

"However, did you get into Heaven?" she enquired casually.

"That my beautiful angel is another story, which I do not have time for right now." pointing his arm in the direction of the unopened suitcase on the bed. "Now your turn, if you would like to get your hands on a weapon, we can be on our way."

She gave him an '*Oh really!*' look of chastisement and let out a sigh of contempt at his double entendre. "You never give up do you?"

"Certainly not, I was just hoping that you would. I never give in but I often surrender, to the right person of course!" a cheeky twinkle in his eye. Despite her desire to keep a stern expression a smile broke out on her face melting the icy look in her eyes.

Opening up the case and, ignoring the rifle, she pulled out a SIG Pro 9mm semi-automatic pistol. She balanced it in her hand and turned it to give her a better look at it. Nodding appreciatively at the choice of weapon, light polymers with a comfortable grip. She liked it.

"Are you sure you know how to use that thing, I don't want you shooting yourself, or worse accidentally shooting me?"

Without turning to him she withdrew the magazine from the handle, checked the rounds and slid it back in. Then cocking it she pointed it at Dedan's head. "Don't worry Dedan, if I shoot someone it will not be by accident! And I never shoot too soon. I hope you don't have that problem either." Then raising the gun, so that he was no longer the target, she de-cocked the gun and slid it into the back of her trousers and covered it with her top leaving no trace of it being visible to any casual observer. "And...?" She asked, looking him in the eyes and leaving him with a puzzled look on his face and an active mind contemplating her sexual innuendo. "…What are you taking to defend yourself?"

"Oh, that." He put his hand behind his back and revealed his weapon of choice, a Smith and Wesson M&P9C pistol. It looked similar to Roxy's choice, compact and matt black. "There you go, light and effective. In addition to this I have couple of spare clips of ammo in my pockets and two hand grenades about my person. Just don't ask me where, but if you hear a metallic clinking noise when I walk just ignore it!"

"Good choice but I'd have thought you'd have had a bigger weapon." Smiling as it was her turn to increase the double entendre quotient. "Shall we go? We had better set off just in case Satan has sent any of his demons on a little vacation."

Before leaving the room Dedan closed and fastened all the cases and placed them in the wardrobe. Room service wasn't due until the morning but he didn't know when they would be back to pick up their bags and there was no point in leaving suitcases full of guns in plain sight and for them to be met by heavily armed members of the Carabinieri, a branch of the Italian police, and have to answer some awkward questions relating to possession of illegal firearms.

Chapter 9 - Not All are Dust or Shadows

Irrespective of their individual traits in their appearances the vast majority of demons were not overly unique, simply variations on a twisted theme. If Satan were to walk about Hell and sneeze, he'd probably donate a bucket of green and sticky lubricant to any number of Incubus and Succubus practicing their particular skills on each other. The same went for most of the other types of demons, there were legions of demon's, devils and miscellaneous other maleficent creatures going by strange names often with too many J's, Z's or Q's in them for the average game of scrabble. All would give young children long lasting nightmares along with quite a few adults as well. However, the Umbra Demon, that was currently hovering 6" off the ground in front of Satan's desk, was one of a kind. His translucent dark grey body took human form, but he looked more like a distant brooding storm cloud compacted into a small area. All the threatening menace pushed into a single space. Although there were many myths and rumours surrounding it there were little hard facts and even Satan wasn't sure where it had come from. The Umbra Demon, and his ever-present squire, had just appeared one day during the busy, disgusting and messy part of the 1800's. The creature had soon proved his worth to Satan with his assassination skills and ability to avoid any form of destruction while on Earth. The creature had never spoken but when anybody spoke to it, they were left knowing that their words had been taken in like a black hole capturing light; never to be released again.

Satan had just finished explaining the Umbra Demon's mission to Earth and was now silent. He doubted that it would be allowed through Limbo's gates, but he could at least prove to be an unexpected and handy ace to have in the game, should any angels suddenly appear and try to get the upper hand. He didn't trust angels. They were all too often devious, tricky and underhanded and that was surely the demon's job. The floating demon slowly nodded its vaguely shaped head and, turning, headed for the door closely followed by his obedient squire. The sound made, as he went through the air, was like the noise of a breeze blowing through trees in the distance; almost imperceptible yet there if you were listening hard enough. The squire, on the other hand, had human form but wouldn't have stood out from the crowd if it wasn't for the array of short spears, daggers and Japanese ninja throwing stars attached to various belts wrapped around his body. None of which would have made him inconspicuous in a social gathering. His walk was louder and far less graceful than his master, but he managed to keep up as they both left Satan's office.

When he was alone again in his spacious, well furnished, yet dilapidated and ever decaying room Satan gave the demon some thought about where the creature's dimension really ended and the realities of Earth truly began. He speculated on what the Umbra Demon truly was but found no answers. Even if they were just barely tangible echoes of lost souls, ghosts existed on Earth and they could be either harmless or downright nasty depending on the type of person that had managed to avoid completely entering Heaven and Hell. They eventually faded but, in the meantime, in the dark and lonely hours their presence could be seen, or sensed, by the weak, vulnerable and frightened. But as their physical presence on the earthly dimension was so weak, they could never be witnessed by anybody that ever deliberately looked for them. That was why ghost hunters were always treated as a joke by the people that didn't believe in such apparitions. The more you looked for them the less likely you would be to ever see any. The irony for any ghost hunter, that claimed special psychic powers or spent a small fortune on scientifically designed night vision goggles, motion-sensitive cameras and hand held RADAR devices, was that the more you looked for a ghost the more likely you'd be a liar if you ever claimed that you'd seen one. But they did exist there, trapped and waiting to disappear like dry ice on a slowly warming sunny summer's day. However, such things shouldn't be able to exist in Hell or Heaven. The lost parts of the souls were re-united and the person could either enjoy paradise or endure Hades as a single, complete and solid entity. The form that the Umbra Demon took was counter to all the rules of both God's realm and his own. Even on its numerous missions to Earth it shouldn't be any good at its job. Holding and utilising such silent but deadly weapons with such skill and dexterity would be impossible for any normal ghost. Even poltergeists, with their penchant for picking things up and using them as projectiles, were clumsy and were as likely to hit a target as a villain that is shooting at the hero in a spy film. Bullets could fly everywhere as guns were emptied, reloaded and emptied again leaving the main character ducking and diving his way to a safe vantage point where the bad guys could be finished off. In the process of the battle they'd have left the good guy barely out of breath, without a hair out of place or a speck of dirt on his clothing; ready to run into the warm and welcoming embrace of the waiting heroine. With the female character being the one that the films always make too dumb to pick up a gun and rescue herself. No, whatever it was, the Umbra Demon couldn't be any sort of ghost. All the speculation of what the Umbra Demon truly was were academic in Satan's mind anyway. No matter what it was he had something that could hurl a fighting star at someone's chest in such a way that the unfortunate victim wouldn't feel any pain and not realise they were dead until they opened their eyes and found their soul reclining on a sun-lounger in Heaven or feeling a greater heat elsewhere. Why should he care about the rest of the strange creature's resume when it had skills like that?

Chapter 10 – Hot in the City, but There are Hotter Places to be.

The arrival of the quartet of demons in Florence was just as inconspicuous and unnoticed as their Angelic enemy counterparts at the opposite end of the city. Apart from a lone old lady, preoccupied in taking her small black poodle for a walk, there was nobody else around to witness their sudden and inexplicable appearance. Four clergymen stood before the Florence Art School situated in the Peace Park made an unusual site, but Catholic priests were not an uncommon thing to see anywhere in Italy and wouldn't have been cause for any suspicion -even if anybody had been there to greet them. The disguises were almost totally perfect and unless you were paying close attention it would have been unlikely that you'd have noticed the complete lack of any crucifixes hanging from their necks or about their persons. It wasn't unknown for certain types of demons to spontaneously combust on contact with holy items such as rosaries, sacred water or crosses so they didn't want to risk that. People be they members of the Catholic Church, or otherwise, running around the place screaming in agony while doing unwilling impressions of human torches did tend to get people's attention and make them a focus for unwanted scrutiny.

So, on they casually strolled across the grassy park like four large black and ominous crows. Even though he had served in the Italian campaign during the Second World War Finley had never bothered to pick up much of the language over and above the words needed to order food and drink and then ask the way to the nearest brothel. None of which would be of much use on this mission. But perhaps, he thought, they could be very useful afterwards if free time permitted. Despite their high IQ's none of his three assistants had used their time, as humans, to become polyglots either so they had less of a grasp of the modern language than Finley. When they were alive, they had all resorted to the traditional British way of communicating with foreigners. Speak English very slowly and loudly as if they were talking to a deaf idiot. Done in the firm and unshakable belief that the whole world did actually speak English, but they always pretended not to and chose to babble away in some strange gibberish just to annoy the civilised tourists. However, as they had no idea where they were, or which direction they needed to take to get to their destination Finley decided that he had best try and communicate with the sole human occupant of the park. Casually carrying the dull brown cloth carpet bags, containing their weapons, they approached her. On seeing them she gave them a broad smile, genuflected and crossed herself. Racking his brain Finley tried to muster as many Italian words from around his brain as he could but the collection of genuine words that appeared would hardly have filled a page of a tourist's phrase book and even if they did nobody could have been able to string them together to make a cogent sentence. All he could do was think of the second option when speaking to Italians. In his politically incorrect opinion almost every word could be English as long as a vowel was added to the end of it, even if the word already ended in one.

"Skewzee" He began, with a false and forced accent that would have made anyone that was politically correct put up their hand and politely interrupt in protest. "Signora, whereo iso the-a Pizza della-o Limbo-a?" Even if he had spoken Italian moderately well the response he got would still have been incomprehensible. Her words sped out of her mouths like rolling and bouncing verbal bullets from a machine gun. Like many Italians they have two speeds for talking, excited and 'runaway train'. Slow and calm is an alien concept to them and no way to talk. Whatever she was telling them was reinforced by frenetic gesticulations as if her hands were directly linked to her jaw and either her mouth moving made her hands fly wildly about or the other way around. But either way the blur of words and gestures left the party of pretend priests none the wiser as to which direction they needed to go. Deciding that combining the two linguistic skills Finley tried again. "Da Pizza della-o Limbo-a?" This time his voice louder and each word spoken slow enough for a tortoise to beat in a 100m race. Once again, the woman, in his opinion, refused to be able to comprehend what he thought was a simple and plain question. Instead she rapid fired yet more unintelligible words back at him, accompanied by enough swinging arms to knock out a heavy weight prize fighter. Pausing he racked his brains to try and remember at least something that Stuart had told him during his inattentive briefing. Then it came to him, there had been some sort of directions; something about a bridge. As he dug deep into his memory, he unknowingly screwed up his face in concentration giving the woman, stood before him, the impression that he was either constipated or suffering from diarrhoea, but she wasn't sure which. But either way she had no desire to find out. Eventually it came to him. "Yes, yes, yes. That's it!" He exclaimed out loud, startling the old lady and making the pet dog hide behind her legs, with its tail between his legs. "Bridgeio? Pontio Vekkio? Where-o isa da Ponti-o Vekkio-o?" On hearing what she could only assume was the words *Ponte Vecchio*, the world-famous bridge, the penny, or in her case Euro, finally dropped. She maintained her vocal speed so that what she told them remained akin to a secret code to their stiff English minds but this time her hands were able to be the better form of communication. Pointing towards the gate at the far end of the park and beyond she was able to direct them in the right direction.

"Gratsio, gratsio, bella donna." Were Finley's last words to the bemused and confused woman as the four loud, slow speaking and mono lingual demons set off towards their destination, or at least in the right direction of it.

In demon form they were used to heat, outside of a few specialist punishment chambers, the fires of Hell ensured that nobody ever shivered and could complain of the cold or moan that they had to sit in a slight draught. It was eternally hot and most demons quickly acclimatised to it. Yes, the flames could tenderly lick their thick flesh and they could experience the agony but on a day to day basis they accepted the heat as normal, like a teenage holiday maker in Ibiza accepted the sunshine there despite the painful sunburn. Only there was less alcohol, drugs and casual unprotected sex in Hell. Unfortunately, for them, when a demon took on a human form, they lost their tolerance to extreme heat and had to deal with temperatures in the same way that every other human had to. If it was cold, they put on more clothing, shivered or sought out a building with functioning central heating. If they were too hot, they looked for shade, took clothes off or sweated. Once the demons were away from the shaded protection provided by the trees in the park the evil quartet had the same choices as humans. However, the mission made the removal of their holy garments unwise, the route to their destination was unlikely to be air conditioned and the sunny streets gave little shade so all they could do was sweat. But they certainly managed to do that well. The black cloth covering their bodies absorbed and trapped the heat so that they quickly became drenched in sweat. Anyone with a sensitive nose, walking too close to them, would have quickly decided not to walk so close and give them plenty of room. The sweat running down their foreheads would have put a runner, just completing a marathon race in the Sahara, to shame. The discomfort was made worse thanks to the heavy and bulky bags they had to carry along the narrow sidewalk. The other pedestrians, that were not engrossed on their phones and were therefore looking where they were going, politely moved onto the road to let the priests pass by unobstructed or impeded but even so the progress was slow and uncomfortable. Eventually they reached a wide but busy piazza with shops at one side and a large imposing museum on the other. Seeing a tourist map vending machine outside a shop Finley inserted his money and removed the map. Opening it up he studied it as Rutherford, Collins and Banks attempted to take a look at it over his shoulder. Hands curling around him trying to point at key features and their chatter filling his ears.

"Look, look, that is where the Birth of Venus painting is!" offered Banks.

"Wow, and that is where Michelangelo's David sculpture is on display" added Collins, pointing to a spot at the far edge of the map.

"Finley, do you think that when the mission is over, we might get the chance to go see them?" requested Rutherford cheerfully; his voice full of misplaced optimistic glee.

Turning to face them Finley was conscious of his surroundings and knew that some swear words were universal and transcended language barriers so an explosion of expletives escaping from the mouth of one priest loudly aimed at three others might seem a little odd to any humans that happened to witness such an occurrence. So, instead, he decided to take a deep breath and remain silent. However, the look of combined anger, contempt and disgust that he gave them was sufficient to convey the swear words he wanted to say out loud. The words, if spoken, would have given any elderly nun a heart attack and probably made a brothel madam take in a sharp breath in surprise and shock. She might even have had to look a couple of the words up in a dictionary. On seeing their mission commander's face, the three of them immediately put their arms to the sides of their bodies, went silent and began to stare guiltily at the ground, feet shuffling as an extra signal of their discomfort. "Thank you!" he hissed contemptuously. Returning to the flimsy paper map in his hands he ran his finger around it until he was finally able to reference the big building he could see, by his side, to his location on the map. Grunting he allowed his forefinger to follow the line from his location to the Ponte Vecchio on the winding Arno river. Eventually he saw what he was looking for and lifted the map so that his silent colleagues could see where his finger was pointing. "Bingo!" he exclaimed happily. "Come on chaps, time to go. Tally ho." Without waiting for any response, he was off striding purposefully away along the route he had identified on his map.

As they got closer to the bridge the massed throng of tourists meandering aimlessly around the streets got denser. There were so many beautiful and ancient buildings to be taken in and photographed that stopping and blocking other people's way was a common occurrence. The people stood trying to take pictures were an inconvenience but mostly were accepted by the other tourists and were treated patiently. Often stopping to remain out of camera shot or taking a slight detour so that they could walk around them when they could. But such niceties were not an issue for the four impatient priests' intent on getting to their destination as quickly as possible. Unsuspecting tourists had their precious pictures photo-bombed as priests ignored social convention and barged past. Magnificent architecture was obstructed by black clothed bodies causing the frustrated photographer to take even more pictures which they might never even look at when they returned home. Where there was a crowd that had slowed down, to circumnavigate other pedestrians that had stopped, Finley was not averse to simply pushing them out of his way as if he were pushing open heavy double doors. Their immediate reaction to such unexpected rudeness was for them to turn and look at the person carrying out such coarse and impolite actions. On seeing that it was what looked like holy men doing it any swear words, that were about to be distributed, were held back. Irrespective of faith people recognised that likening a man in holy garbs to a certain fun part of a female's anatomy was inappropriate no matter what the location or circumstance. And Italy was definitely not the right place to release a barrage of profanities aimed at people dressed in Catholic vestments. Employing such direct tactics, they were able to quickly get onto bridge. It had originally been built so that butcher's shops spanned both sides, from end to end, but with tourism came the more lucrative trade in precious designer jewellery so the meat shops were replaced by exclusive jewellers eager to part rich American or Russian visitors from their cash in exchange for either tacky bling or discrete good taste, but even for those without the disposable income the bright shop windows were a popular attraction and made the bridge even more compacted than the road leading to it. The unfortunately named shop called 'Golden Shower' was particularly popular with, mostly British, photographers with a smutty sense of humour and, as they congregated there, it made that section almost totally impassable. Therefore, any attempt to push people out of the way would have been futile so they were forced to slow their pace and just follow the flow of tourists as they casually crossed from one side of the bridge to the other. The impatience and frustration making Finley angry but he knew that there was nothing he could do about it. The river of humans, moving like golden syrup over pancakes, eventually released itself on the far side with people spreading out to explore the many sights in the old part of the city. The freedom from the constricting crowd instantly lightened his mood and the desire to massacre everybody that got in his way decreased. Although his demon instincts remained, so a small massacre of a few loud and annoying tourists would have been enjoyable. However, the two armed police officers stood on duty by the side of the road might have objected and intervened in his fun and games. Perhaps, he mused, he could possess someone later on and have some fun that way instead.

Finding a quiet spot on the kerb the four demons huddled together to look at the map one more time. Their location wasn't exactly high on any tourist's bucket list so it was hard to find and if you took your finger away and briefly took the attention from the map the search for the small insignificant dot and place name would have to be repeated. After a brief democratic discussion over the best route to take, which Finley carefully listened to and weighted up the pros and cons of each person's suggestions before he showed his leadership skills and totally ignored everything they had said and opted go the way he had planned to go all along. His three companions were not too worried about being overridden by Finley, even if the heat was oppressive, they were just enjoying the cultural atmosphere and ambience of the city and after the stench and darkness of Hell it was their idea of bliss. Just being in the vicinity of so many works of art, by a long list of renaissance artists, gave them a level of happiness that would have caused them to be severely punished if they'd experienced such emotions in Hell.

With a firm "Come on then!" Finley set off once again. As usual he didn't even bother to check if his mini platoon of armed demons were following. They walked behind him eyes darting in all directions as they admired the buildings along their way. They might be demons on a mission, personally given to them by their boss Satan himself, but that didn't mean they couldn't enjoy themselves.

Chapter 11 – Limbo, How Low Can You Go?

According to historical records, created by monks of the early Christian church, the tiny square going under the name of the Piazza Della Limbo was so called because infants that had died before being christened were buried there and their souls could never enter Heaven. This was of course a harsh rule that didn't actually exist. God was never a stickler for worrying about a soul being baptised or not, sprinkling a body with a bit of water didn't make a person good or bad, it was usually just something people did because they didn't understand what good and evil really was. If a soul was evil the person could dip themselves in a swimming pool full of water blessed by the Pope and urinated in by the Dalai Lama and it still wouldn't expunge one single bad deed and give them a better chance of entering Heaven. Babies tended not to have the opportunity to carry out sinful acts so those that died entered Heaven whether any human church had given them permission to do so or not. God liked to think it was His decision and not theirs. But still such superstitious claptrap persisted in many people's minds and many a grieving parent was left thinking that they would never be reunited with their lost child in Heaven. That was one reason why the naming of the square was woefully inaccurate. The other reason, that the history of the place was not totally correct, was because the cosy piazza housed the gateway into the dimensional void where souls went if there were uncertainties about whether they should go to Hell or Heaven. Sometimes the scales of justice were finely balanced, or got stuck, and more analysis was required. And so, they went to see Limbo, or more accurately Limbo saw them.

The Umbra Demon's mere presence in front of the controller of Hell's dimensional portal was enough to make the other demon feel uncomfortable and break out in a colder sweat than was presumed to be possible in Hades. Although no words were spoken and the Umbra Demon didn't have any discernible eyes, in which to convey any messages, it was made clear that anything less than a perfect materialisation in exactly the right place would result in severe, yet unspecified repercussions. Taking far more care with the most miniscule of detail the cowering demon checked and rechecked co-ordinates and ensured that the spectre hovering before him, along with his squire, were sent to the correct location without any errors.

In the shadows, that the high walls surrounding three sides of the square provided, his ethereal form was almost invisible. It was like looking for a jellyfish in dark water. It was there but you'd have to know that and be looking hard for it. The only physical tell-tale signs that he was there were a collection of ninja throwing stars in one hand and a short spear in the other. If you happened to see them in the gloom, you'd have thought that, at first glance, they were hovering unaided in the air. Before leaving hell, the Umbra Demon's squire had donned a large and seasonally inappropriate coat and wrapped it around himself. With the purpose of the coat being to hide the vast amount of assorted weaponry which he carried for his master. Then once the painful adverse effects of the transfer to Earth had caused his intestines to stop inflicting agony internally, and flatulence externally, he positioned himself inconspicuously in the far corner of the square standing with his arms tucked inside his jacket ready to remove any battle implement that his master might need in a sudden fight. His eyes darting as he scanned the road at the opposite end of the square, looking out for any visitor that might pose a threat or as a target. Many tourists walked by, but few even turned to take any notice of the historic little square. There were no magnificent statues or imposing buildings to demand attention or require photographing. There could have been a Shakespearian play being performed there but it would have gone unnoticed by the visitors to the city rushing past on their way to more interesting locations. To any onlooker it was just a square with a few un-noteworthy back doors perhaps leading into boutiques or pizzerias facing onto more attractive, and tourist friendly, locations.

Suddenly the relative emptiness of the square was removed with the arrival of Finley walking quickly into the centre resolutely trying to block out the inane chatter of his three closely following foot soldiers. Despite being told to be quiet on several occasions the excitement of their location, and the city itself, made them continue with their wild jabbering streams of consciousness. Talk of artists, poets and philosophers but as far as Finley was concerned their stream was just carrying pretentious turds out to a polluted sea. Stopping abruptly, he looked around, taking in his surroundings, he could sense that something wasn't quite right. First, he saw the squire, suspiciously dressed in his large coat and then he strained to make sense of what else he was seeing, or more accurately, not seeing. The Umbra Demon was like a shadow in a shadow. It was almost lost like a whisper released in the corner of a vast hall, or like looking for an honest politician at a political party convention. Trying to focus on the vague creature and seeing the floating weapons he realised who his unexpected ally was. He had seen the Umbra Demon from a distance in Hell and he also knew him by his reputation.

He'd always thought that the elusive, and enigmatic, demon would have been a great asset to the numbers of the Marching Hordes, but the Umbra Demon was too much of a loner and besides the uniform wouldn't have fitted him.

"Welcome Finley, my Master has been waiting for you and is at your service!" The Demon's Squire's voice was deep and loud as if he was shouting from the bottom of a well. He and I may not enter with you but can guard the door and if any angels appear, we can prevent their entrance; assuming, of course, that they are not already in there!"

Unsure who to address Finley turned his head back and forth from squire to demon before settling on looking at where he assumed the demon's eyes would, or at least should, be. With demons it wasn't always guaranteed that any part of the anatomy was where it would be in relation to a human body. Finley had once innocently shaken what he thought was a demon's hand only to realise that he was performing a sexual act on them. That is one of the many reasons why demons usually avoided too much casual physical contact with each other. With his stare fixed on the demon his voice was aimed at the squire. "Thank you. The Umbra Demon's reputation precedes him, and his presence is valued." giving his three annoying soldiers a quick glance before returning his eyes to the demon "I think that if there is any trouble his legendary fighting expertise will be critical."

Placing his carpet bag on the floor he opened it and pulled out a Heckler and Koch MP5 sub-machine gun and cocked it. On seeing their leader's actions, the companions did the same, holding the weapons in readiness and looking around, assuming that their boss had seen something suspicious. Straining they saw nothing to be alarmed at, but they maintained their defensive stances.

"On Earth such weapons are useful, but if you take them through the doors of Limbo you will find them useless and, more than likely, a liability. Use of force or actions made due to anger and hatred will just bring judgement upon your heads and send you back to Hell before you even have the chance to find the lost soul." The Squire's voice maintaining its deep resonance and leaving Finley wishing that he had a throat lozenge to offer to the cloaked figure. "We will look after your arsenal while you are away."

Finley didn't feel comfortable walking into a strange, and quite possibly hostile, environment without any weaponry but he accepted the instructions. "Okay lads, give your weapons to our friend with the vocal cord problems and follow me."

Although all the doors around the square were the same shape, size and of similar dirt encrusted pollution grey colour Finley was easily able to identify Limbo's door. Faded but still there and with a barely discernible inscription carved into the lintel above one of the doors. 'Nosce te ipsum, et nos cognovimus melior tibi'. Although he had hated his upper class up-bringing, and the forced lessons which that entailed, he was finally glad that he had received a rudimentary classical education so that he was able to translate the Latin words. 'Know thyself, but we know you better'. Ominous words for any would be house guest. Although he doubted that the entrance itself had ever been used by any living person, or voluntarily walked through by a demon for that matter. There was no handle, keyhole or any other normal door furniture that could have given him any indication as to how to open it, so he just placed the palms of his hands against the door. Then, as he pushed, he seemed to cease to have a solid human body. He just fell through it as the old wooden door maintained its thick and robust solid form. Then, once he was on the other side, he regained his material form and continued the free fall so that he landed face first on the dusty yellow marble floor on the other side. Before he could push himself up out of the dirt he was joined by Collins, landing on his bosses back, quickly followed by Rutherford then Banks. Seeing the method of entry that their boss had discovered they had quickly tried the same thing and suffered the same results. Although his head was now pressed against the cold floor and his jaw had difficulty in moving Finley was able to speak "Will you idiots jus ger off mi!" he mumbled. The three of them quickly rolled off their human shaped rug and promptly stood up, simultaneously apologising; hands helping to both pull him to his feet and dust him off. Sighing he felt like a dog being petted by some over eager kindergarten children, so he pushed them back in an aggravated manner. "Now stop it." He snapped harshly. "Remember where we are. We might be on a mission for Satan but that will mean nothing here. Do NOTHING that might make you the focus of judgement, otherwise you are straight back into Hell and be of no use to me at all. Do you understand?" The sharp and angry tone of his voice was an ironic contrast to the message of calm behaviour that he was trying to pass along to his subordinates.

"Yes sir!" They all snapped smartly.

"Good, come on, let's go and retrieve a lost soul and find a way of bringing him back to Hell. Satan wants him dead or...." Pausing to think of a pertinent end to the saying "... well dead I suppose." With that the four of them set off along the long hallway that they had discovered.

Chapter 12 - The Horse and the Hoarse Whisperer.

In Florence there are many modes of transport; for example, trains are relatively cheap and exceedingly reliable. If you like to take your life in your hands, and experience near death experiences, buses were even better priced, but they tended to be best for going in and out of the city and not used for manoeuvring around the narrow tourist filled streets of the old town. So, one of the methods of transport popular with tourists, having enough money to pay for the experience, are horse drawn carriages. If you have the spare cash you can sit in comfort and stare at a horse's arse in front of you and gaze at the more edifying sights as the historic, and beautiful, city all around as you travel.

The particular horse, that Dedan had chosen, was a chestnut mare with a red hood covering its ears to keep out the flies. The way it was worn made the animal look like the equine version of Satan, only on a sad day - but that was more because of the long face. And he knew that if he told *that* joke to Roxy, he risked her darkest sarcasm. Horses have a primitive sixth sense and irrespective of the form taken they could always feel when a demon, or angel, was close by. The closer that Dedan got the more it began to try and move in the opposite direction whinnying loudly in panic and frustration. It only calmed down when Dedan was able to hesitantly place his hands on the creature's neck and offer it some placatory words into its ear. "There there, easy boy. It's alright. We're not going to hurt you." The words alone did nothing as, despite what some humans think, horses can't speak English or any other language for that matter, except horse - of which they are proficient in. However, the sense of goodness and kindness that ran from Dedan's angelic hands into the horse's flesh had a soothing effect. Instantly it calmed down and turned its head slightly so that it could look at the strange human fully; getting extra reassurance that it was safe. As if in agreement, or as a show of greeting, the horse casually nodded and then faced forward again. Relieved Dedan looked first at the carriage driver and then at Roxy. "Excellent, this horse is ideal. Roxy, show him the map" indicating towards the driver, rather than the horse, "and tell him that he will be well rewarded if he takes us along the Borgo *whatever it's called* street and drops us off at the Piazza del Limbo."

Roxy explained what was required but the driver was a man of tradition and he had always seen his mid-afternoon lunch break as sacrosanct. However, when a large wad of high denomination Euro notes was waved in front of his face, he decided that perhaps he could forgo a sacred tradition, just this once. Eagerly stepping down from his seat, opening the small door to the rear of the open topped carriage he flamboyantly gestured for Dedan to climb aboard. The he gallantly took Roxy's hand, kissed it, and helped her climb into the carriage. Had it been some American tourist, that had tried to haggle a lower price, then he'd have grabbed her bottom and helped her up in a less than chivalrous way. But he sensed that such an action could have lost him this fare, and probably got him a slapped face as well, so he decided that discretion was the better part of profit.

Retaking his seat at the front of the carriage he shook the reins and the horse obediently began its ambling gaited walk. The driver attempted to start a conversation with his two passengers, first in broken English then in fluent Italian aimed at Roxy but their responses were brief, perfunctory, and he got the unspoken message that they were not interested in a tour guide or someone to just chit chat with. Shrugging his shoulders in ambivalence he focused on navigating along the narrow streets and avoiding running over inattentive tourists. Not always an easy task as they often thought that they had right of way on roads and that if they were run over by a horse and carriage they would somehow, miraculously, walk away from it unscathed. The Florentine tourist authority took a dim view of visitors to their city being run over but, being Italians, they were a pragmatic and sanguine people and accepted that sometimes accidents happened and couldn't be helped.

Taking a quick glance behind him he saw that Dedan and Roxy didn't appear to be his usual and average fare. When there was a couple in his carriage, they usually behaved in either two ways, they spent the whole time embracing each other, mouths tightly pressed together with tongues often exploring the other person's dental work and tonsils, with the second type excited at all the magnificent sights that met their eyes and greeting each ancient building with coos of amazement and admiration. But these two didn't fit any such category. They didn't seem to be appreciating the ride for a start. Despite the beauty of his female passenger the man didn't seem to be taking any notice of her; and that was a sin in itself in his eyes. But worse than that, both of them seemed pensive, distracted and more interested in tracking their progress on the map against the street names and prominent statues than they were with actually appreciating the magic of the place. Never mind, he thought, casually dismissing their strange demeanours and body language. They had paid him more money than he'd make in a busy week so why should he care how they behaved?

On the horse went and, as directed, it turned onto the Borgo Santi Apostoli street that led past the Piazza. Dedan saw that they were close to their destination and tapped the map gently and nodded to Roxy. Face stern she nodded back at him, acknowledging the unspoken warning. Casually stretching he innocently scratched his shoulder then moved his hand behind his back, as if to continue the scratching process, but instead he carefully withdrew his pistol from the back of his trousers and moved its position so that it was tucked into the front of his clothing, hidden under his t-shirt. Ready for easy access, should it be required. Seeing the action Roxy followed suit, ensuring that the driver was busy avoiding pedestrians and not likely to turn around while she was in mid process of moving her weapon. Once the gun was safely repositioned out of sight, she gave Dedan a feeble smile and a slight nod of her head to confirm that she was also ready for whatever might arise when they reached their destination. They didn't have to wait long. As soon as the horse had got onto the small stretch of road that ran along the edge of the Piazza its ancient instincts kicked in and it could sense the tidal wave of primordial and raw evil emanating primarily from the Umbra Demon and partially from its squire. Fear beyond anything the animal had ever felt before gripped it. Pure unadulterated terror coursed through its body and permeated its soul. Instincts took over and it reared up front legs kicking at thin air as if to defend itself from some invisible, yet horrific, attacker. White froth forming around its mouth it realised that there was nothing in front of it, so assuming the source of the panic was somehow behind it the animal changed tactic and began to kick with its hind legs. Fortunately for the driver he was far enough behind the seemingly possessed horse to be safe from any wayward blows from the metal shoed feet but, unfortunately, he was not saved from the additional basic by product of most frightened animals. Thanks to the regular diet of straw and oats the texture of horse excrement is fairly firm and unlikely to spread over a large area and, being fairly dry, not liable to drown somebody if it landed in the mouth. However, the fact that it maintained its form was of little consolation to the driver as large round lumps of the stuff arced from the animal's rear straight into his face. The relatively dry substance was softened thanks to the horse piss that was also released at the same time and adopted the same trajectory as its more solid counterpart. The poor driver was having the problem of calming a horse that had suddenly become crazy while he was being assaulted by digested horse food and drink.

"Things are about to turn messy, get out!" shouted Dedan above the noise of the horse.

"Messy?" queried Roxy in a loud voice "all that is missing is a fan and we'd be covered in shit as well!"

"Don't argue, just get off the carriage and take cover" with that he dived to the ground rolling, as he went, to break the fall. Seeing Dedan's actions, and not needing to be told a third time, Roxy did the same from her side of the carriage. Just in time as the horse finally realised that whatever it was that was there was would not be kept away by wild kicking of either its front or hind legs. With that knowledge it decided that flight was better than fight and it ran off along the narrow street scattering startled tourists as it went. Looking up Roxy saw that Dedan was stood, gun in hand, with his back tight against the corner of the wall leading onto the Piazza Del Limbo. Without hesitation she ran across the road and joined him, adopting the same position next to him, pistol in her hand, raised to her chest, in readiness. "What is it?" She whispered breathlessly.

"I don't know, when I jumped from the carriage, I saw *something* but I don't know what." Dedan's voice full of pensive uncertainty, as if he wasn't sure that he saw anything other than his own fears. "But whatever it was the horse sensed it and sensed it big time! There's someone, or something, in the square and it is not an angel sat reading the Bible." He rapidly glanced around the corner, into the small square, and withdrew it just in time as a shiny glistening fighting star travelled past the space that micro seconds earlier had been where his head had been. The force was such that it carried on with its flight and only came to rest when it had lodged half of its metal body into the wooden window frame of the leather shop on the other side of the street. Seeing something whiz past his field of vision he attempted to see what it was that had so nearly given him a fatal case of sudden death syndrome. He could just see the metal object even if, from that distance, he couldn't work out what it was.

"What did you see?"

"Nothing but that nothing REALLY wants me dead!" The humour in his voice masking a deep fear that would have had many humans turning their underwear brown. "I have heard stories, but I have always hoped that I would never have to be part of one of those tales..." With that he readied his gun and moved his body around the corner just enough so that he could fire three rounds at the shadowy space across the square where there seemed to be a faint mist holding ancient weapons several feet off the ground. The bullets went straight through where the apparition's heart might have been, if it'd had one, and came to rest in the wall behind it, releasing dust and pieces of brick in the process. Dedan managed to regain his place of safety, just in time as two more fighting stars followed each other in quick succession, missing him by mere fractions of inches.

"Well done sir, I am impressed!" The voice of the Umbra Demon's squire was deep and hoarse. "I have never known my master to miss before. You are indeed charmed. Now might I suggest that you keep your lucky streak and leave before my master's aim returns to normal and he kills you? I assure you that you can't win."

Dedan lowered himself to his knees and leant so that he could face the demon again. Three more shots were fired in rapid succession, this time aimed at the position of the head of the shaped mist. Once again, the bullets were ineffective at destroying the demon but did manage to chip the wall behind it. He swiftly returned to his position of safety avoiding further flying objects that hit the road behind him and ricochet harmlessly across the ground. "Does that answer your question demon turd?" Shouted

101

Dedan angrily, frustration boiling in him at the demon's simple but annoying refusal to die.

"Very well," croaked the squire. "As they say in the crude modern parlance 'Bring it on sunshine'!"

"I could say the exact same thing to your master" responded Dedan loudly. "A few toy cowboy stars that you get with a child's costume? Ooooooh, hold me mummy, I am frightened!" Turning to Roxy and speaking quietly "here, hold this" passing her his gun. "When I give the signal cover me. But be ready to duck back into cover."

"Alright Dedan, but what are you planning to do? It might help if you give me some sort of clue!" Just then she saw him pull a small round M67 hand grenade from the front of his trousers. "Oh, that!" As if the movements were second nature to him, he removed the safety clip with his free hand and then pulled out the firing ring. Roxy then stepped back slightly, aligning herself with where the demon stood and fired shot after shot at the space semi occupied by the demon. As she did that Dedan turned and released his hand grenade. His aim was true but as there was nothing solid for it to make contact with it hit the wall and bounced off it so that lethal fragments of sharp and jagged metal ripped through the air but did no damage to the ethereal figure. Back in the safety of their original positions Dedan sighed. "Oh crap!" He muttered. "I have one grenade left and even fewer ideas left once that is gone!" Looking Roxy in the eyes he gave her a weak smile. "I am sorry, but we need to do that once more, but this time with feeling!" Roxy nodded slightly, accepting that it was one desperate, and possibly fatal, act for one of even both of them. This time she dived to the floor and fired her fingers tight on the triggers on both guns; letting loose round after round of angry metal. Dedan turned to face his adversary but this time the demon was ready for him and had one of his metal stars already in the air. It found its mark, embedding itself deep into Dedan's chest. The pain and impact were sudden enough to cause him to lose his aim and for his throw to fly wide of his target. Instead of it hitting the demon it reached his squire and impacted on his chest just as it exploded. His shredded body thrown back and falling to the floor just as the Umbra demon evaporated and disappeared leaving the remainder of its fighting stars, and its unutilised spear, to suffer from the natural effects of gravity and drop to the floor letting off tinny sounds as they impacted on the hard stone ground.

Getting up Roxy laughed; more due to nerves than from joy. "We did it." She screeched excitedly. "We did it!"

Walking cautiously to the space which the Umbra Demon had, until only recently, taken up she curiously kicked the weapons laid at her feet. Dedan's route was slightly different to Roxy's. He went to stand, awkwardly, over the body of the squire, rubbing his chin and holding his side as he looked at the corpse.

"Is he dead?" Roxy enquired.

"Yes, he's gone back to Hell!"

"Are you sure? He might be playing dead. You could always put a few bullets into him if you want. Why don't you check his pulse while I cover you?"

"Pulse?" Dedan responded as if his mind was elsewhere.

"Yes, you know. The thing in his neck, just below the side of his chin!" The light-hearted sarcasm thick in her voice.

"Oh, I know what a pulse is," pointing to a round object several feet away "but as his body is here and his head is over there, I am not sure where to go to even search for one."

Seeing what he was pointing at "Yes, good point, well made. I think we can safely say that he isn't likely to get up and carry on the fight with us."

Just then Dedan fell to his knees blood from his wound trickling through his fingers. Seeing him fall Roxy ran to his side and knelt next to him; holding him in her arms to give him support. "I'll go get medical help, you just…"

"We don't have time for that. Just find the door leading to Limbo and get me through it. I'll be alright once I am on the other side." He could see the hesitancy in her eyes "Just do it!" he barked. Without waiting for the order to be repeated she got up and started to run around the outskirts of the square looking at each doorway as she went; finally stopping at the door with the inscription. "I think I've found it. Either that or someone really likes pithy Latin inscriptions." Turning to Dedan she saw him laid face down on the ground. "Dedan!" she cried loudly, running to him and kneeling once more by his body. Rolling him over so that he was facing upwards she saw that his eyes were open. "Why Roxy, you DO care!" Forced humour in his voice trying to hide his pain. "I know you want me, but I don't have the energy at the moment. Perhaps later?" The laughter at his own weak joke causing him to cough up bright frothy blood.

"You're an asshole, you really are."

Lifting him up and draping his arm over her shoulder she dragged him towards the door. "You really need to lose weight. If I'd known I'd have to carry you on this mission I'd have come alone!" The joke made Dedan smile but he no longer had any energy for laughter. "How do we get in?" She asked; her voice now serious and tinged with panic.

"I don't know" Dedan's voice quiet as he fought the pain that was coursing through his body. The sharp metal still embedded deep in his side; piercing and ripping vital organs as he moved. "To my knowledge no one has ever been through it before. As it pre-dates doorbells I suggest we try pushing it."

Chapter 13 – The Hall of the Dead Gods.

First Roxy's hand touched the door then, putting their combined weight against it, they both fell through the portal and landed on the floor, Dedan laid on top of Roxy, his face embedded in her chest. Raising his head and looking into her startled eyes with a massive smile on his face. "See? I told you I'd be alright! And a soft landing too, who could ask for anything more?"

Quickly pushing him off her she looked at him with a concerned look. Lifting up his torn t-shirt and inspecting his flabby stomach and chest she could see that his wound had disappeared. "It's gone!" She exclaimed in surprise and bewilderment.

"Hey, steady tiger. As I said we don't have time for you ripping my clothes off and ravishing my body. If you play your cards right you can have me after the mission. But you've got to say please first!"

"You really are an egotistical…" she paused to try and think of a suitable insult, her default Italian language searching for the right words to use in English. Finally settling on "…shit!" Both laughed, releasing the tension of battle. Standing Dedan stretched out his hand offering it to Roxy so that she could pull herself up. She paused, looking at it, then put her hand in his and allowed herself to be pulled upwards to her feet; her face close to his. "Thank you Dedan, but you're still full of shit!"

"Oh, I know that. Always have been and always will be and I assure you that you are not the first person to tell me and probably won't be the last."

Looking around them they were able to take in their new location. It was a long and wide hall with a yellow marble floor patterned with mosaics depicting some ancient scenes of winged, sharp toothed, demons battling angels armed with swords and spears. The light came via an opaque glass ceiling high above their heads and along the full length of the hall, on both sides, stood stone statues of men and women in various postures raised high above the ground on plinths. As they walked towards a gold encrusted door, at the far end of the hall, they casually looked at some of the figures.

"Who are they?" Roxy enquired as she idly brushed her hand against the plinth of one of the statues. "There are inscriptions at the base of them, but they all seem to be in different languages and I don't even recognise some of the letters never mind make out the words."

Taking a closer look at couple of them Dedan smiled a wry smile; chuckling quietly to himself. "Well, I never thought I'd get to see this. If I am not mistaken this is the legendary Hall of the Dead Gods."

"Dead Gods? What do you mean dead gods? Gods can't die." Roxy's voice full of confused puzzlement and an expression to match.

"My fair Roxy, let me assure you that they can, and all too often do, die. Many gods are created by the simple act of enough humans actually believing in them. Not just a belief akin to 'I believe that the sun will come up in the morning' or 'I believe that I will have boiled eggs for tomorrow's breakfast'. But believing as in *knowing* with their whole heart and soul that something more powerful is out there shaping their destinies and that thought can be so powerful that it triggers the actual physical creation of what they believe." Pointing at the nearest statue to him, a man who appeared to be sat on the toilet, robes lifted up over his waist as he strained to relieve himself. "For example, allow me to introduce you to this chap here with the pained, or more accurately straining, look on his face. This here is a god that you might know, or more likely will not know, as Tivr. He was a sun god around when I was alive in early Biblical times and I met him on a few occasions when he tried to convert me. I always wondered what happened to him. From the looks of it his last adherent on Earth passed away while poor old Tivr was trying to take a dump. Then, lacking any believers he automatically turned to stone and ended up here; just another discarded and long forgotten religion." Then pointing excitedly to another statue, this time of a tall and slender female stood running her fingers through her hair, with a resigned look on her face. "This stone beauty is Dione. A Phoenician goddess blessed, or perhaps cursed, with the power of prophesy. From the look on her face she saw what was in store for herself. What a woman, what a body and what a pity. She had a great sense of humour, even if she saw all the comedy punchlines far too early. But such is the life of a deity that doesn't have good PR and can't run advertising campaigns. They are left on the shelf and get past their sell by date." He patted her gently on her cold stone legs. "Sorry old girl. You were more fun when you were softer and warmer."

Roxy turned and looked up and down the hall moving her arms in an act of gesticulation encompassing all the stone forms. "So, these are ALL ex gods? There must be hundreds of them."

"Hundreds? More likely thousands. Despite the strength of ardour belonging to their believers, at the time, gods can come and gods can go. This is their final resting place. A grim mausoleum capturing their final poses as their religious flame ran out of holy oil and flickered to a final lonely death, never to be re-ignited. No more worshipers means no more of that particular god."

Turning they continued to walk along the hall in silence. Roxy pausing occasionally to look at some of the ex-gods and wonder at what they were doing in their final moments and Dedan stopped intermittently to gaze at some half-remembered name or face. Occasionally there was sadness in his eyes at seeing a good god and at other times there was glee at seeing some evil character forever deprived of the opportunity to make humans suffer. Suddenly his mind was brought back to the present. Reverie expelled from his mind as a thought took its place. "Roxy, have you still got those pistols secreted somewhere against that beautiful body of yours?"

"Yes, why do you ask?" Her hands slowly moving behind her back, as if waiting for the instruction to pull them out and start shooting.

"Where we are going, they will not be needed and could in fact be more a liability. We might end up getting stuck in the judgement process. So, I think it is best if you simply leave them here. Just stick them behind that statue there, and we can maybe collect them later if we return this way. And, if not, they will do no harm where they are. I doubt that…" He paused to look at the inscription on the plinth supporting a statue of an old bearded man, in a strange hat, sat on a chair resting his chin in his hands "…Ekeku here is likely to come back to life and start using them."

"If you say so Dedan." Reluctantly she removed the two pistols and gently placed them on the floor tight against the back of the obscure Pre-Columbian god. Rejoining Dedan they both carried on with their walk. Deep in their own deep but private thoughts, Roxy thinking about the new concepts, relating to gods, that she had just been told about and speculations about existing belief systems. While Dedan, on the other hand, was letting his mind go 'off mission' and wonder that Roxy looked like laying on the silk hotel sheets naked except for chocolate sauce that needed licking off.

Yes, Roxy might not have known Dedan for long but she certainly had him sussed, he could be a real lascivious shit at times. He might be an angel but he had plenty of human faults, frailties and weaknesses and could easily have found himself in Hell had he not, despite all his inappropriate talk, had a strong sense of decency and fought his own inner demons so that he always ended up doing the right thing. Fortunately for him, and despite what many humans wanted to believe, perhaps because they were not getting any themselves, sex in itself was not a sin. But if it had been Dedan would have been in big trouble long ago.

As they finally reached the golden door, at the far end of the hall, Roxy stopped and looked along where they had come. Suddenly she laughed and looked at Dedan. He looked at her with bemusement. "And...?" he asked.

"I was just thinking of the coach driver. I bet he needed a shower when he got home. At least he got plenty of money, so he could buy some new clothes!"

"Well I did say that things would be messy!" returning her laughter and smile

With the mental image of flying faeces in both their heads they reached out and grabbed hold of the ornate door handle and it turned, causing the giant door to open freely and easily.

Chapter 14 - How to Destroy a Shadow

The squire hadn't always been the attendant to the ethereal knight. He had been, in his years before his death, a magician and conjuror. He was a skilled illusionist that went under the stage name of 'The Magnificent Marcus Von Kinder' but his real name was Johan Röh. It was under the assumed identity that he travelled mid-19th century Europe performing his tricks. As the fame grew so did the class and quality of his audiences so he rapidly went from doing shows for farmers that paid him in corn to better paying Lords and finally receiving large fees to show off his amazing skills to the political leaders and crowned heads of Europe and the Far East. Nobody could work out how he performed all his tricks as women would disappear from behind a screen on the stage and then appear again in glass cases hanging by a single wire from the centre of the theatre's high roof. He could make underwear of dignitaries vanish from the wearers and re-materialise in the orchestra's instruments and he always left his most curious and mystifying trick until last. He would have a member of the audience - usually a bishop or cardinal, if they were available, come onto the stage and hold either a spear or some metal throwing stars. The cleric would inspect them and the surrounding stage closely, ensuring that there were no wire or mirrors, and then he would be instructed by the Magnificent Marcus to throw the objects at a target placed in the sparsely lit recesses at the back of the auditorium. The audience would take cover and the holy man would insist that he couldn't do it but eventually he'd be persuaded to let the projectiles loose and off they would go flying wildly over the audience's heads, across the eye line of the balconies and Royal Boxes and finally hit the target dead centre. This happened every time and no matter how hard people looked they could not find any wires or contraptions to make it possible. He was even offered, progressively larger and larger, fortunes if he would just privately whisper his secrets into the ear of a Queen, Prince or Archduke desperate to know how it was done. But every time the offers were made, he simply maintained an enigmatic smile and politely declined saying that he had made a solemn oath to a Tibetan monk never to reveal his secrets. No amount of gold could ever persuade him to break his word. Although if the truth had been revealed he might not have got the treasures that he had been offered. The simple fact was that he had no idea how he did it. All he knew was that if he thought it then he could make objects move just by the power of his mind. Size and shape were not an issue, only distance. After about 150 yards he couldn't make it work. As he got older, he began to lose his full mental faculties and with that decline followed the ability to perform all his tricks. As they reduced in number so did his audience and the money they paid. He eventually saw himself on the brink of being paid chicken feed again so decided that he had to adapt his tricks and create a unique and bespoke act. He managed to cling onto the flying weapons trick and also developed a new illusion of making an apparition appear by just willing dust or moisture in the air to coalesce into the form of a shadow like figure. It was with these combined abilities that he began a new career as an assassin. He, or more specifically his Umbra, would be paid considerable sums of money to convert some titled living person to somebody that could no longer use the title of *living*. The floating particles were an efficient decoy; weapons would be fired harmlessly at the strange apparition whilst he could safely stand in whatever shadows he could find and send sharp blades into his target. Then, once the target was despatched, he could direct the Umbra in one direction, hotly pursued by guards, soldiers and police while he casually made good his escape in the opposite direction.

This lucrative side-line managed to keep him gainfully employed for another decade until finally his lavish lifestyle took its toll and he was killed by a narrow wooden bridge, going over a tributary of the Danube. It gave way under his ample weight and he fell into the water, smashed his head on a boulder and booked himself a place in Hell. Once he had reached the other side, he found that he still had the skill of creating his creature out of the dust in Hades so he decided that he would continue with his charade. He created the Umbra Demon and assumed the role of the lowly squire. The reputation of the demon grew and the squire was left in peace. The talent for murder was quickly recognised and Johan, and his creation, were sent back to Earth for special missions where blades were required to ensure a suitable death for some human that had been contracted to donate their soul to Satan but refused to do the right thing and die when they were supposed to.

In all the years since then the Umbra Demon's reputation and glory had grown within Hell and, further afield, Heaven had learnt of it and created many unfounded myths as well. It had somehow, but inaccurately, been given the extra ability to reach into a human and rip out their soul or it could destroy an angel just by looking at it. As a collection of aging shoe makers might be described, it was a load of old cobblers but the demon was never seen so how could they be sure?

Despite all the damage that the Umbra Demon had directly received on missions the squire had consistently been ignored and hadn't even received a single scratch during the wild gun fire thrown at his creation. It wasn't until the injury induced by Dedan's poorly thrown hand grenade that he had calmly lost his head and been killed in action. Used to returning via a relatively uncomfortable but direct hell-gate portal the resultant return to Hell, via the death path, was a completely long forgotten experience. His soul was wracked with indescribable agony as it was pulled into the Hell dimension and dumped unceremoniously in a totally random location. In this case he found that he had appeared in a sewage punishment chamber where the damned were either hung by their neck, or if they were really evil souls, by their feet into a lake of demon excrement. His screams for assistance aimed at the demon guards in charge of punishments were met with derision and manic laughter; after all they had never taken any notice of the lowly squire so had no idea who the unexpected guest truly was. To them he was just another demon that had been killed on Earth and dumped back in Hell. As he trod water, or more accurately churned the poo with his arms and feet, he attempted to make the Umbra Demon appear, so that they would know who they were dealing with and help him out of his smelly and sticky predicament. But thanks to the foul vapours that filled the air the Umbra Demon was not formed out of dust or water vapour but from the particles of faeces that permeated the whole chamber. The resultant shit demon didn't have the same fear and menace factor of its Umbra equivalent. The insults it received weren't stopped until it threw perfectly pitched balls of crap at the demon guard's mouths, causing them to choke on their own words. Only then did they stop and take the squire seriously and help him out. The squelching sound he made, on his release, just seemed to add insult to injury for the humiliated squire. The flies that occupy hell soon found a new base as they followed his dejected form out of the chamber. Trudging to Satan's office in the central ring of Hades he was ensured that he was given a wide berth by any other passing demon. He wasn't looking forward to reporting his failure to his satanic leader but perhaps his wet and brown ersatz armour would give him some protection from any resultant flames he received as punishment.

"No matter what, I don't care how long it takes but I will get vengeance on those two angels!" He snarled to himself through gritted teeth. The Umbra Demon, and his ever present squire, would have vengeance.

Chapter 15 - Galileo, Not so Magnifico.

Once through the imposing door and out of the Hall of the Dead Gods, Dedan and Roxy were met with the sight of a long narrow corridor stretching out into the distance. Flickering overhead strobe lights bathed it all in the false headache inducing light that only that type of lighting can provide and along each side were equally spaced faded white doors set into magnolia painted walls. They gave each other a puzzled look and interpreting his female colleague's unspoken question Dedan shrugged his shoulders and spread his hands, palms upwards, in the universal gesture of 'Don't ask me. I haven't a clue either!'

"Shall we?" he asked casually while he pointed to the first door.

"Why not?" replied Roxy with an equally relaxed ambivalent tone in her voice.

Walking to the first door they opened it and looked in. The sight that met their eyes was not what they expected. It was a long and wide room full of people leaning against walls, sat around on rows of plastic seats or, where there was insufficient seating they were just sat on the floor. Against the far wall were plate glass windows and outside they could see commercial jet airliners stood waiting on a sunny runway and, further away in the distance, they could make out a tall air traffic control tower.

"Righhhhhhht." Dedan Mumbled as he closed the door again. Then they both walked across the corridor and gingerly opened the door directly opposite to the one they had just looked past. Apart from the appearance and positions of all the people the room was identical to the previous one; similar crowds of people, the same chairs and the identical view out of the window.

"Interesting" said Roxy scratching her head. "I see."

"YOU DO?" demanded a surprised Dedan.

"No. Not really." sniffed Roxy, a puzzled sneer on her face.

They walked along the corridor repeating the same exercise, with various identical doors, and were met with the exact same thing each time. Gently closing the latest door Roxy looked Dedan in the face. "I think there is nothing else for us to do but go into one of these rooms and investigate."

"Alas, I think you might just be right" sweeping his arms along the corridor "Alright my beautiful angel, care to pick a door. Any door you like. Open it wide and I will enter!"

Roxy raised her eyes to the ceiling and sighed and strode across the floor to the door diagonal to where they were. Opening it she walked into the large room closely followed by Dedan. Once inside they closed the door after themselves and, on its closing, all trace of it ever having existed disappeared leaving a wall with a board displaying an advertising poster for a car hire company written in Italian. Dedan briefly tried to find a way to open it again but realised that it was futile, no such door existed at the side they were now on. They were stuck there; wherever 'there' was.

"Okay, this way." Dedan suddenly pronounced the words as if he had planned everything in advance and knew where he was going. Stepping carefully over luggage, outstretched legs and people strewn all over the floor he began to walk to the far end of the hall. People ignored him as they chatted with each other, played on cell phones or sipped coffee while reading books. He walked past a long line of people lining up by a small café against the wall. It had pictures on the back wall and overhead, displaying images of large portions of appetising meals and sandwiches, there were also adverts showing photos of large steaming cups of black coffee. As he walked by the people that were being served, he could see that what they were paying for, and being given, bore no resemblance to the pictures. Small and limp sandwiches, small burgers wrapped in soggy tissues and small cups of coffee that smelt so cheap and nasty that the all-pervading odour made him retch as it invaded his nostrils.

Walking further across the room he reached the far end of the hall and saw an exit barrier with two TV display screens, attached to the ceiling by large metal rods. The message on both of them, in white letters on a bright blue background, was informing anybody that cared to read them that all departures were delayed by 1 hour. But despite the words there was still a long line of people waiting to go through the gates. Some faces looking frustrated, others cross but on the whole sheer boredom was the overriding emotional default setting. Any talk was in hushed tones between small groups, brief friendships made when people are stuck in lines with nothing consequential ever discussed; the weather, holidays or how much they all hate standing in lines.

Looking at the windows he found something not quite right, although what he saw was three dimensional it had a frozen quality, no wind moving the trees at the edge of the airstrip, no planes landing or taking off and ground crews, attending the planes, were idly stood stock still as if they were cardboard cut-outs. Although he wasn't sure that the last feature was that unusual for many airports across the globe.

Roxy gently touched Dedan's shoulder to get his attention. "What is this place?" Her voice hushed as if she was in a library and she would be told off for speaking too loudly.

"If I am not mistaken this, and all the other identical rooms, are purgatory; oblivion. The place where souls, which do not tip the scales to fall into Hell or fly up to Heaven, go to be assessed. Their actions here are judged and they are then dispatched, up or down as it were. No right of appeal and no re-trials. Every day the same for them, wallets always with money in for what might, laughingly, be called food and always the same faces. They checked out but no guarantee that they will ever leave."

"So, this is Limbo?" Uncertainty and confusion etched on her face.

"Limbo?" Giving her a surprised look? "No Limbo isn't here. This is purgatory, but I am sure that he isn't far away."

"But I am sure that I know this place, I think I have been here before."

A shocked look appeared on Dedan's face. "You went through judgement? I am sorry, I didn't know that. I thought you…"

"No, no I went straight to Heaven and I am shocked that you could think otherwise" a mock hurt look briefly lighting up her face, "I mean that I had been here when I was alive. This looks just like the departure lounge of the Galileo Galilee International Airport at Pisa. Look at the mountains in the distance, those are the Tuscan Hills. I am sure of it."

"You are probably right." Relief in his voice at not having put his foot in his mouth regarding the presumption he'd made about her life and where she went at death. "I suppose an airport departure gate is the closest thing to purgatory that a human will ever encounter, while they are alive anyway. Get impatient and they join the highway to Hell or show compassion, and kindness, to their fellow would be travellers and it is the stairway to Heaven. Just stand and wait doing nothing and you could be here for a very long time."

Biting her lower lip Roxy adopted a pained look on her face as if she was doing a mental double take on something in her mind and finally decided to speak. "He?"

"What?"

"You said 'He'. When I asked about Limbo you said *HE* isn't far away"

"Oh, that." Casually looking around as if to check that there wasn't anybody in the hall paying undue attention to what he was saying. "Didn't you know? Limbo

121

isn't the place. He is a person. He runs this place and is judge, jury and executioner; although the term *person* might be a bit of a loose term for him." Scanning the ceiling as if he were looking for hidden cameras or some supernatural being floating somewhere above their heads, he took a deep breath. "Limbo!" he shouted, his call attracting curious glances from some of the nearby lost souls. "Limbo, we request an audience with you. We are on a mission from God and He seeks a boon of the highest importance." Looking at Roxy as if he was uncomfortable with continuing and therefore forced to confess something of such great importance in a public place. "The future of Heaven and Earth are at stake!"

His words were met by a silence that seemed to appear from nowhere, as if thick ear defenders had been placed over both their ears. The gentle buzz of conversation, movement and general background noises suddenly ceased as people stopped and looked at Dedan. Surprise on some of the faces but the rest of them staring at him as if he were insane; some deranged lunatic that had managed to get through security. A crazy rant aimed at the ceiling. Then, as abruptly as the silence had started, it ended. People went back to what they had previously been doing, the soft background noise returning unnoticed by the throng that had grown accustomed to it and deemed it to be natural.

Suddenly there was an announcement over the public address speakers. Being unexpected its details were missed by both Roxy and Dedan but the other inhabitants of the hall all stopped to listen attentively but finding that it didn't relate to them they returned, disappointed, to what they had previously been doing.

"Will the two passengers for Limbo please make their way to the departure gate?" The soft Italian accent of the female voice repeated the message. "Your connection is available now".

Dedan gave Roxy a triumphant smile "I think that means us." Pointing towards the gate "Shall we go?" They wove in between the people stood in line waiting for what they assumed would be their turn to go through the gate. Obvious looks of resentment thrown at the two angels like daggers showing contempt for the two people that were getting to leave on their 'plane' before them. Despite the instructions that had been broadcast to the contrary they were perceived to be pushing in. "Excuse me. Excuse me please." The requests politely, and patiently, given by both of the angels; conscious that most of the souls in front of them were in no mood to make way for them. Both angels knew that there was no need to push and shove so remained calm and unhurried; they would soon be able to see Limbo. Finally, they got to the gate and were met by a man in the livery of an airline steward, a man with immaculately coiffured hair and a seemingly impossibly smooth and clean shaved chin. All polished off with smart trouser and jacket uniform. "Good afternoon Sir, Ma'am." His smile as forced as a synchronised swimmer, with sunlight thrown through the window glistening on his polished white teeth. "If you would care to walk this way, I will escort you to where you need to go." With that he impatiently strode off with flamboyant steps without even waiting for them to acknowledge his instructions or to check that they were indeed following him.

"If I could walk that way, I'd go see a doctor" Dedan whispered to Roxy conspiratorially; a wry smile on his face. It seemed that angel humour didn't change over the millennia.

Roxy laughed guiltily and playfully slapped him on his arm. "Shhhhh." She muttered. "He'll hear you." They smiled briefly at each other and then took their places behind their guide. They walked silently with the air steward, just in front of them, emanating an air of disdain at having such a menial task disrupting whatever tasks and chores usually took up his time. Along long winding corridors and down flights of stairs they went until eventually they reached a large white painted steel door. "Right sir and madam. We are here" his voice full of insincerity and undisguised contempt. Opening it for them he ushered them through and once they were in, and no longer his responsibility, he slammed the door closed again and minced off back the way he had come while, under his breath, he cursed everybody that had ever distracted him from his set duties. Although, despite his high sense of self-importance, his normal routine usually involved walking around the departure lounge trying to appear important while checking his reflection in any available mirror. The availability to learn how to love oneself was not a skill achieved by everybody. Self-doubts or self-knowledge often got in the way, but it wasn't an issue for him. He had turned self-love into an art form that should have had its own chapter in the Karma Sutra and there was no threat of anyone else stealing his heart. Despite his vanity and ego, he had been released for Heaven long ago but, this was his idea of paradise, so he decided to stay. As they say, it takes all sorts...

Chapter 16 – And Behind Door Number…

Having had a similar experience with opening doors as their angelic counterparts Finley and his trio of philosophical killing machine had also reached the same conclusion that all the rooms were pretty much the same and that they might as well choose one at random, go inside and see what they could find. Finally selecting one 50 yards along the corridor, on the left, they had walked in and began their investigation as to what the hall was and its real significance. They all had encountered souls before that had been here, been judged and ended being despatched to Hades. But they had never seen fit to interrogate any of the damned as to what the place was like or what had happened there. In Finley's mind the damned were the damned and had to be made to suffer, they weren't in Hell for the intellectual conversations and friendly one to one chats to ensure that they were happy in their punishment. He'd rather hear them scream in agony than hear their pathetic life stories about how they never meant to do wrong, or if they'd have known what Hell was really like then they'd have been good. His response to any lost soul, that tried to strike up such a conversation, was invariably 'Too late idiot' which was then usually followed by the infliction of some excruciating punishment reinforcing the point that he wasn't interested, and it was in their best interests to just shut up. If he didn't nip such things in the bud, he was worried that they would get to the point where they thought he was interested in small talk. But in Hell there wasn't much scope for that. 'Oh, isn't it hot in here?' was usually as imaginative as it got but what sort of answer did they expect, it was Hell. Hot was usually an understatement and there wasn't usually much variation in the climatic conditions. It wasn't as if they were holidaying in Finland or Ireland and could expect snow or rain.

Lacking any background information, as to what to expect, they stood in the hall by the wall, where the door used to be but was now replaced by an advertising board. Bemused they looked around trying to figure out how they had suddenly been transported to some airport departure lounge and where the all-pervading smell of awful coffee was coming from.

"My goodness." Ventured Rutherford, with a smug smile. "Maybe we are back on Earth in a manmade Hell?" Then adding "Well, wasn't it Jean Paul Sartre that said Hell is other people?" With that he laughed bellicosely at his own weak witticism, which was a character fault of most pretentious intellectuals. The joke was greeted with knowing laughter by his two fellow troopers but all mirth was rapidly banished when Finley gave Rutherford a sharp and harsh look and raised his hand as if to strike him. Making Rutherford involuntarily jolt his head forward violently in expectation of a blow that never came.

"Any of you annoying hyenas want to share some similar hilarious humour? Perhaps you'd like to find some way of impressing me by quoting Nietzsche so that some tenuous comedy sketch can ensue? Or you want to talk about Schrodinger's parrot?" He looked at Banks and Collins challengingly.

"No Sir!" They both mumbled with pathetic voices; avoiding eye contact with him and each other. One demon intently gazing down studying his feet, as if he were looking to ensure that they were still there, while the other looked around as if scanning the place for any Archangel flying towards him.

"Good!" Snarled Finley trying, but failing abysmally, to keep calm. "Rather than you lot starting up an improvisational comedy group why not go and have a look around? See if Ernest just happens to be here and then report back to me." He paused to look at the three demons in human form. "Well?" He snapped, his patience wearing thinner by the minute. It had been a long day and he was no longer used to the strains and aches of having a human form. "What are you waiting for - Christmas? GO!"

Without waiting for the verbal chastisement to be up-graded to the physical type they separated and began to walk around the hall. Banks went to the left; Rutherford chose to go to the right, towards the area containing the departure gate, leaving Collins to mingle with the people directly in front of where they came in. Busily they went about their designated task. Stood, sat or kneeling as they talked to what they assumed were normal human passengers waiting for their release from the dire place so they could catch their appropriate flights. Questions were asked but no responses were given that indicated that they were either Ernest Higginbotham or had ever even heard of him. Suddenly Finley's attention was grabbed as he heard a loud and threatening voice at the far end of the hall. Rutherford was stood lifting a man off the ground by his neck and was shaking him roughly. Although Finley couldn't quite make out what was being said by his soldier, he could see that softly-softly approach had suddenly started to solidify and the gentle touch had turned into a boxer's hard punch. Recognising the risk of making such a scene, in somewhere that on Earth was notorious for its traditionally high security, Finley began to run along the hall in an attempt to intervene and prevent any escalation that would result in a human being sent on a flight to Heaven or Hell and the resultant incident causing armed police to turn up and shoot them while not trying to resist arrest. As he ran towards the demon the sight, he witnessed, made him stop in his tracks and pause and look around in panic. One second Rutherford was shouting and venting his frustration on the poor body by tightly squeezing the muscles around the neck of the unsuspecting human and the next minute the demon had disappeared. No blinding flash of coloured light. No strange noises to indicate that something out of the ordinary was in the process of being witnessed. It was as if a movie maker had simply paused the film process, removed a character as everyone else in front of the camera stood still and, when he resumed filming, the actor was gone. Thanks to Rutherford's sudden disappearance his victim found himself briefly defying the laws of gravity 6" off the ground. However, gravity quickly noticed the mistake and pulled him rapidly back to the floor. Not expecting the fall, the legs crumpled on impact with the hard surface and he landed like a scalded petulant school boy throwing his wet duffle coat onto the kitchen floor; only without the accompanying squelching noise. On picking himself up he just returned to his former seat, picked up his newspaper and resumed reading it as if nothing had happened. The neighbours sat next to him also acted as if nothing unusual had happened and people suddenly disappearing from existence was a regular and common occurrence. Then Finley suddenly remembered his own instructions just before entering through the doors leading to the hall full of sculptures. "Shit!" He whispered to nobody in particular.

"Banks, Collins stop what you are doing and come here NOW!" His shouted order carried easily across the relatively quiet room. It attracted indignant looks from a few of the chamber's inhabitants, but they quickly returned to their apathy to all that was happening around them. On hearing the instruction, the two remaining team members immediately stopped conversations with the humans and started moving towards Finley. As they walked all focus was on their superior, so they didn't notice that Rutherford was no longer visible. Almost running they zigzagged around waiting passenger's luggage and jumped over people that were laid on the floor until they finally reached their destination. As soon as they got to him Finley hesitated to gather his thoughts and ensure that Banks and Collins were giving him their full attention.

"Right lads, you might, or might not have noticed that Rutherford is not joining us. In fact, if I am not mistaken, he has been sent, against his will, back to Hell." He paused again to allow them to look for themselves and see that their friend was no longer anywhere to be seen. "I have a theory that this is purgatory, but I just need to carry out a quick experiment to confirm it. Banks…"

"Sir!" Banks response was accompanied by a sharp military snap to attention, or a sharp one by Marching Horde standards.

"Just one quick thing I need you to do. See that lady sat on the chair just there?" The question was accompanied by a pointed finger aimed at a middle-aged woman sat on a chair intently messing with her mobile phone.

"Yes sir."

"Just run up to her and kick her a dozen times."

Although such instructions were not particularly unusual Banks was surprised at having to carry it out in such a public place and in a casual way. It might be fun to be sadistic, but it just seemed to be inappropriate. But orders were orders and he saw no reason to refuse to carry it out. Taking a run up he released his first kick that impacted on the side of her head knocking her to the floor. Instantly Banks disappeared in the same manner as his colleague, his unscheduled return to Hell assured. Instead of lying on the floor unconscious or, more likely, dead after receiving a blow that would have pole axed a bison she simply stood up, rubbed her head as if it had a mild ache and returned to her seat resuming her intent and full focus on her phone.

"Riiiightttttt." Finley exclaimed as the final piece of the jigsaw puzzle in his mind finally slipped into place revealing a metaphorical picture of a female tennis player scratching a cheek of her pantiless bottom. At last he had what he wanted to see, it now made sense and the realisation made him happy. "Collins, I want you to listen to me very carefully. Whatever you do ignore everyone. Under no circumstances show them anger or hatred and especially do not inflict any form of physical violence on them. And just for good measure I would suggest that you do not show them any kindness either. I think it is unlikely, but I don't want to risk you suddenly disappearing up to Heaven either. Imagine the problems and paperwork that would cause by someone having sorting that mess out."

"If you say so" responded the nonplussed Collins. "Sir, what IS going on? Where exactly are we?"

"We are exactly where we are supposed to be. It might be hard to believe but we are in purgatory."

"Hard to believe?" looking around him at the room with the soul-destroying ambience of a real airport departure lounge "I can't think of a more appropriate place for people to go."

Looking around Finley saw what he was looking for - someone that seemed out of place, a character that was like an anachronism, akin to a spaceman appearing in Shakespeare's Hamlet. There was an attractive blonde stewardess with enough make up on her face to paint a battleship a bright shade of radioactive orange. But that in itself wasn't the give-away that she was out of place. It was the inane grin on her face that was the true indicator. Her eyes were vacant as they seemed to stare at some imaginary line a thousand yards away, but they had a joy-full glint to them and the smile, despite the vapid appearance, made her look like she was walking around with Ben Wa Balls correctly fitted between her legs and working their magic with every step. He thought that she could orgasm at any moment deafening anybody standing too close to her and leaving a slippery floor where she had stood.

"Quickly. This way." Was all he said as he rushed towards the gleefully vacuous looking stewardess. Even though he hadn't the opportunity to ask questions, even if he had wanted to, Collins obediently followed his master; careful not to accidentally push or shove any of the people stood in his way. Eventually they caught up with the woman and Finley was able to gently tap her on the shoulder to get her attention. "Excuse me miss." His voice polite and calmer than he truly felt. She turned to look at him - her eyes maintaining their glazed stare as if looking at some invisible object in the middle distance; with his head being directly in her line of sight having no effect on where she was focusing. "Yes sir, how may I help you?" Her chirpy and insipid Californian Valley Girl accent immediately made the hairs on his arm stand on end. Her voice seemed to match her appearance perfectly.

"Look, I know where we are. We have been sent by Satan and we need to talk to Limbo as a matter of urgency. Do you understand?"

"Of course, sir." The smile on her face unchanged. "If you'd care to wait here, I will make a call and see if you have clearance to go through the departure gate." With that she walked calmly to the desk at the end of the departure gate, picked up a telephone and began to talk into it. Once the conversation had finished, she replaced the handset and returned to where Finley and Collins were stood waiting. "Yes, Mr. Limbo is just busy at the moment but if you follow me, I will escort you through the gate and take you to his chambers. He will see you as soon as he is free. This way gentlemen." Turning crisply, she led them past the people lined up and they went through the metal gate. They followed an identical route that Dedan and Roxy had taken, along corridors and down flights of stairs until they finally reached a big white metal door. Opening it for them she ushered them in. "Please make yourself comfortable, help yourselves to drinks and cigars while you wait and have a nice day." With that she closed it again once they were through.

Once out of the imitation departure lounge and fake airport they found that they were in large room with oak panelled walls and a large Persian carpet on the floor. To their surprise there were also comfortable looking tanned brown leather arm chairs that were positioned in groups of four circling small wooden tables with crystal cut tumblers and decanters full of whisky and brandy. There were also unopened boxes of Montecristo cigars placed next to them waiting for someone to break the seal and enjoy Cuba's finest. "Well," ventured Finley as he selected a seat and sat in it "I think it would be rude to decline such hospitality, don't you?" then he picked up a decanter and held it up to the light, studying its label and contents. "Fancy a drink Mr. Collins?"

"I don't mind if I do Mr. Finley" replied Collins as he took a chair next to his boss's. Then he proceeded to open up a cigar box, remove a cigar for himself and pass the box to his superior officer. There was a brief moments silence as they both poured drinks, lit cigars and took appreciative puffs of them. Allowing the smoke to linger in their mouths before finally exhaling; blowing smoke rings and watching them drift away before gravity finally broke them up.

"This is the life, or it is possibly an afterlife, and I could certainly get used to it." Finley sat back in his chair with an appreciative grin; drink in one hand and cigar in the other. All of a sudden, he wasn't in such a mad rush to complete his mission. Priorities had changed and as long as the expensive spirits and cigars were available, he had no desire for his old priorities to return. Seeing Finley's relaxed and carefree posture Collins decided to follow suit and he too reclined in the chair, finally receiving a benefit from being involuntarily volunteered for the mission.

Chapter 17 – Drinks Anyone?

Although Dedan and Roxy had absolutely no preconceived notions as to what Limbo's private quarters would look like the room, that they were currently stood in, would not have been what they would have guessed at even if you'd have given them a thousand attempts. If Roxy didn't know any better, she could have sworn that it had been designed by the same person that decorated the front room for the parents of a man she once dated when she worked, for a brief time, in London. Expensive cream coloured patterned wallpaper covered the walls, a chandelier hung from the high ceiling and thick red Axminster carpet covered the floor. There was a brown crushed velvet three-seater sofa, with throw cushions and at either end. Facing the main sofa were two matching sofa chairs. All that was missing were the windows with lace curtains. Sat in one of the chairs was Limbo. His blue flamed skin shimmering but cold so that it didn't burn the upholstery. His legs were casually crossed, wings tightly folded against his back and his head was resting on his left hand with his elbow placed on the arm of the chair. His dark blue eyes emphasised by his pale blue iridescent flaming flesh. "Welcome, it is rare that I get guests and such lovely ones in your case my dear" looking directly at Roxy. His voice was soft and more like a whisper in their minds than anything entering their heads via the ears. "Please be seated" he gestured to the large sofa. "Could I offer you a drink? I have Earl Grey." He pointed to a glass topped coffee table by his side. On top of it was a white with gold trimmed Royal Doulton tea pot with delicate matching milk jug, cups and saucers.

"That would be lovely, thank you." Roxy gave Limbo an appreciative smile. "Could I have milk and one sugar?"

"Of course, my dear. And you sir?" looking at Dedan.

"I am not really a big fan of tea. Do you have any coffee?" requested Dedan hopefully.

"Well, it isn't something that I partake of myself but I am sure that I could phone up to one of the departure lounges and they could bring you a cup of coffee from there."

"No thanks" responded Dedan quickly, making no attempt to hide his look of revulsion at the thought of the airport's idea of what coffee should be. "I'd rather drink piss!"

"Really?" A surprised look on Limbo's face. "I must say tastes have certainly changed since the old days. But I can see what I can do. Do people take it neat or with milk and sugar?" Limbo's ability to deal with sarcasm and irony was none existent so he took the request quite literally.

"Err, no. No thank you." Deciding that trying to explain would only confuse things and waste time "I will be fine, I am not that thirsty after all. I'll be fine."

"Oh, alright, as you wish." A pleasant smile on his face, different shades of darker blue defining the position and emotional state of his mouth. His teeth a paler blue giving him the appearance of somebody that had just eaten a joke sweet. "Now how can I be of assistance? Your message made it seem all rather jolly urgent."

"As we understand it you have a soul here awaiting judgement and it is critical that he be sent to Heaven." Dedan leaning forward, his face stern and voice serious.

"Really? And what is this person's name?" as Limbo passed a cup of tea, and accompanying saucer, to Roxy.

"Ernest Higginbotham, he died in London."

Back in his chair Limbo was about to take a sip of his tea but, on hearing the name, he paused with the cup just before his lips. Replacing it onto its saucer he looked directly at Dedan and the shade of flaming skin seemed to take on a darker hue. "I know him, but I am afraid that I can't release him into your custody. He is a special case and can't be processed in the same way as those souls in the departure lounges. I must try him in person and balance his actions. His sins are great but there are technicalities which have to be investigated."

"But surely…" Dedan attempted to make a point but Limbo raised his hand to silence him.

"As I said, he is a special case. Most people can be judged by their own actions and eventually tip the balance of justice and they either send themselves to Heaven or end up in Hell. In Mr Higginbotham's case his sins, actions and extenuating circumstances, are such that he must have a special tribunal." His voice a mixture of apologetic politeness and iron resolve.

"But…" Interjected Dedan.

"BUT?" Limbo's voice louder in their heads this time, as if it were bouncing off various parts of their minds; hitting the frontal then the parietal and finally the temporal lobes of the two angel's brains. "Let me assure you dear boy that there are no 'BUTS' here." his tone suddenly returning to a more acceptable level, having firmly made his point. "There are no exceptions, no twisting or breaking of my own rules. I do not turn a blind eye or allow for grey areas creating some sort of benefit of doubt. If they are judged that they need to go to Hell then that is where they go. You can't come here and dictate to me. You have absolutely no dominion here."

"My apologies Limbo. I meant no disrespect." Dedan's hands clasped together, in front of him, as a sign of supplication. "It is just that if you knew his role and service you would clearly see that he doesn't deserve to go to Hell."

"Are you St. Peter?" Limbo asked casually.

"No sir. I am…"

"I know who you are Dedan. I know St. Peter and there are only four people ever allowed to see the book of souls in the eternal registry. God, in special cases Satan, Peter and myself. And you might have noticed that your name does not appear in that list. So, you do not know Mr. Higginbotham's true sins. I DO!" Limbo studied Dedan's face and realised that despite his position of authority and trust the angel had no knowledge of the eternal registry in the secret library. The repository of all sins and good deeds carried out by every human being during their lives and quite a few angels had additional chapters added when they went on missions to Earth. Dedan's had grown so much, after his death, that it had an entire row to itself. The location was so vast that it took up an entire dimensional plain and its mere existence was one of the most closely guarded secrets in Heaven. Limbo knew that even angels had their faults and peculiarities, but he had seen both Dedan and Roxy's records and knew that despite their imperfections they had no ulterior motives for being in front of him.

Roxy sensed that the conversation was not heading in the right direction and it was running the risk of turning into a male ego trip with Dedan trying to argue rather than find an alternative solution. Seeing him about to speak again she placed her hand gently on his arm, as a signal to remain quiet, so that she could try to obtain what they need to know. She was about to speak when there was the sound of a telephone ringing.

"My apologies. I wait decades and the thing never rings, but today it seems to be making up for it. Please excuse me." Reaching down the far side of his chair, furthest from Dedan and Roxy, he picked up an old-fashioned candle stick type telephone. "Yes?" he enquired into the phone. "Really? … What a coincidence…. Two gone you say?" he chuckled gently "Well I suppose that I had best see them before they end up being judged and sliding back to Hell. Please can you escort them to my reception room, invite them to make themselves completely at home and inform them that I am currently occupied but I will see them presently? … Yes, thank you. Goodbye." The conversation over he returned the antique telephone to its original position. Looking directly at

Dedan he smiled. "Interesting, very interesting indeed, but hardly unexpected. It would seem that Satan would possibly also like to make representations and take charge of Mr. Higginbotham's soul. He has sent a couple of demon representatives and they would like to, as a matter of some urgency, see me."

Finally, Roxy took the opportunity to speak "Sir, may I speak bluntly?" giving Limbo the most disarming of smiles that she had in her repertoire of facial expressions.

"Be my guest sweet lady, but I assure you that in my experience speaking bluntly and talking pointedly seem to be the same face on different coins. But please speak what is on your mind. I admire straight talk and honesty. Not that you would be able to lie to me without me knowing it."

Unfazed by Limbo's warning Roxy continued. "I am sure you are aware of his sins, perhaps more than we are. However, he was the keeper of The Sword of Uncreation and if he should fall into the hands of Satan then I am sure that he would end up revealing its location to him at some point. I am equally sure Satan can be very persuasive and has many ways to make people talk. Surely you can imagine what could happen if the demon army get their hands on such a weapon?"

"Yes Rossana, I mean Roxy, I can easily imagine what would happen. Battles would be a far less protracted and the results would be very one sided, leaving Satan to party in God's office and do as he pleases on Earth. But once again I must re-iterate that I simply can't just hand him over to you just like that. It is quite impossible. Even if it meant the destruction of Heaven, and the eventual end of humanity, I simply have no way of breaking the rules and procedures. I wish I could but it cannot be done." His voice was sad but full of genuine sincerity. They could tell by the look in his dark blue eyes and the changing shades of his flaming skin that he wanted to help them but such things were beyond his powers. "You may not be fully aware but he sold his soul to the devil. At the time he was feeling betrayed, ignored and lost. He didn't know that he had a guardian angel for company and he was planning to give The Sword to Satan in return for immortality and eternal riches. However, he quickly realised what he had done and first attempted to cancel the agreement and, when that failed, he then tried to hide from the devil. Going under everyone's RADAR by adopting the guise and habits, both in clothing and actions, of a destitute and living on the streets. However, despite all that, a demon found him and pushed him under a bus, assuming that would buy him a one-way ticket to Hell. Fortunately, for you two, Ernest's earnest attempts to reverse his wrong doings and the breach of contract, and good faith, on both his and Satan's side, meant that he ended up here waiting my judgement." He paused and stroked his chin, the flames from fingers and face merging into one, creating what looked like a rippling blue beard where they met. "Perhaps… there might be a way that you can, if not obtain exclusive knowledge of the location of The Sword, then at least you could steal a march on your enemies and get there first."

Both Roxy and Dedan leaned forward on the comfortable sofa. "We're listening." Roxy added redundantly as if Limbo might have thought his words had lost their full attention.

141

"I am sure that neither of the two demons, currently sat outside waiting for an audience with me, will be as charming as you Roxy but when it comes to purpose, they will probably put forward a very solid case for the custody of the lost soul to be passed over to them. Obviously, it will hold no sway with me and I will tell them the same thing that I have told you. However, I can allow you to talk with Mr. Higginbotham and attempt to persuade him to reveal the location of The Sword to you. I can delay the demons for as long as required, but I must warn you that this will form part of his judgement process and the demons will be given the opportunity to talk with him at some point as well. What he says to both parties could possibly decide his outcome, one way or the other. Or it could just prolong his judgement. But be warned, if you try and tell him that his answers are part of the process you will automatically send him the other way. Do you understand?"

Even though they didn't like the idea of fair play when it came to demons, after all they knew that such niceties would not be extended to angels if demons had their way, they comprehended what they were being told. All they could hope for was that Ernest would freely open up to them and not spill his guts out to the demons. "Splendido!" exclaimed Roxy with a resigned smile on her face. The Italian word involuntarily released. "I am sure we will be able to show him the light without having to shine it in his eyes."

"Marvellous" added Limbo. "I will entertain the demons for as long as necessary and, when you have finished, it will then be their turn. I will see you when you have finished and ensure your safe return. Dedan, good luck and to you Roxy arrivederci bella." With that he snapped his fingers and they vanished from the room, leaving an empty tea cup as the only indication that they had ever been there.

"Oh well." Sighed Limbo, despondently. "I suppose it is time to give the devil their dues."

Chapter 18 - The Hell is Alive with the Sound of Music.

When Satan was having a bad day everyone else in Hell had better run and hide or take cover because when the proverbial hits the fan it goes everywhere. Even the best hiding places are no guarantee of coming out again with clean clothing. No demon, or soul in torment, is safe. And as bad things went today could never have been described as being good or even bad. Today was plain ugly. If Hell had a thermostatic switch, he would have turned the heating up in the entire place. If he could change it so that he could reset everyone's pain threshold to a lower level, so every agony was felt with greater depths, then he would have done that so screams might have crossed dimensional vacuums and be heard in Heaven and Earth. Satan always wanted suffering but today he needed it to be exquisite. Even the term suffering seemed an inadequate word for what he felt others should be feeling. He wanted to create a word beyond any human comprehension to describe what he'd inflict on anybody that he saw. In his dark mind he had toyed with a few ideas for portmanteau words. His first idea of putting pain and agony together and getting 'Pagony' had been dismissed as it sounded like an Italian composer of operas. Then he rolled the idea about and thought of mating torment with anguish around in his head but 'Tanguish' sounded like a one-horse town in North Africa. Although such word play was immaterial it helped him to divert his mind from the rage that made his head feel like it would explode and scatter his brain all over his room with bits of it landing in the fireplace where it would boil and eventually burn away; although such punishments were not precluded from being inflicted on others. Roasted brains were an option if he felt peckish later. Finally, he settled for the contraction of the words torment and suffering deciding that 'Suffermenting' would do and if anyone didn't like it then that was all the better.

The catalogue of anguish that had led him to such an emotional state was not long, it didn't have to be, but it was just the right amount to send him over the cliff's edge and into the chasm of incandescent rage. And, thanks to his ability to create fire, incandescent was the appropriate word. His morning had begun with the sound system deciding to wind up Satan by playing Barry Manilow's 'I write the songs' on a constant loop. Not a bad song but after hearing it fifteen times on the trot it could have been enough to test the patience of a diehard Manilow fan, never mind the master of Hell. In his long running battle with the possessed music system he had tried, on numerous occasions, to simply remove it and drop it into a burning lake of fire, in one of his punishment chambers, but the infernal machine had simply re-materialised again. Still in pristine working order, in the same place it had previously occupied; enthusiastically continuing with playing a medley of Barry Manilow's prolific tracks. He had tried muffling speakers, but the songs managed to permeate any such sound suppression. He had even resorted to obtaining a state of the art music player and stack of heavy metal CD's, from Earth, and tried to beat his mechanical nemesis by playing Black Sabbath, Iron Maiden and Megadeath at full volume, therefore drowning out the sound of the easy listening hits. This had worked for about a day before the new music player developed a fault and changed all the CD's, piled up next to it, into the entire back catalogue of Barry Manilow and the sheer number of albums in his discography was enough to make the music system's table buckle under the weight. So that attempt at outsmarting a musical public address system was promptly abandoned and the new state of the art device was consumed in the flames. Much to his relief that player didn't re-materialise like the other one kept doing. Today's assault on his ears had caused him to attack the main body of the Amp and controls with a hammer large enough to make Thor suffer from penis envy. Satan's workout was long and thorough. Each blow resulting in more and more of the machine to take on the appearance of tiny pieces of splintered wood and squashed unidentifiable slithers of flat metal. By the time he had finished all that was left was a mess of fused metal and powdered wood. However, such minor inconveniences were nothing to the belligerent music device. Despite the total lack of any physical method for creating the sounds it simply ignored such minor details and carried on with the provision of a musical background, only increasing the volume as if to make a point to Satan. With Barry's beautiful accompaniment it began the process of reassembling itself like something out of the Sorcerer's Apprentice. Eventually Satan had given up that battle for the day and decided that ignoring it might be for the best. He thought that work would be enough of a distraction for him to blot out the background noise.

The rest of his day didn't go to plan. First, he'd had the sight of Johan Röh, the squire, who was for some reason trying to disguise himself as a giant turd with limbs. The demon had come into his office and explained the full history of the Umbra Demon and provided the account of his mission. Included were the details of how he had failed to despatch a couple of angels back to heaven and ensure that they didn't interfere with his plans. What made it worse, from the description he had just been given, he strongly suspected that one of the angels was Dedan. 'One of these days…' Satan thought to himself, as visions of the meddling angel being flayed alive, and given a slow death, flew across his mind. The trembling demon finished the recounting of his experience at the Piazza Della Limbo and stood waiting in trepidation for whatever punishment Satan decided to inflict on him. The sweet voice of Barry Manilow doing nothing to sooth or assuage his fears, he knew that Satan's rage could be sudden and was far worse if you weren't expecting it.

However, despite seeing Satan's eyes turn a burning ruddy colour and sensing the imprisoned anger behind them, the expected, but undefined, punishment simply didn't appear. That seemed to just make the tension and expectation even worse. A fierce and painful fire bolt aimed at his groin straight away would have been better than the anticipation of an unknown torment. All Satan did was sit behind his desk, his elbows resting on it and his fingers steepled as he listened to the words, asking occasional questions for clarification but the violence bubbling under the surface remained internalised. When he had finished talking the silence seemed to take over the room. Even Barry Manilow decided to add to the atmosphere and pause from his melodic description of his inability to smile. Slowly Satan leant back in his padded leather swivel chair and absent-mindedly played with his horns in a phallic manner that would have had Sigmund Freud pointing at him and exclaiming "A-ha" in a thick German accent.

"Get out of my sight you pathetic excuse for an excuse. I will think up a suitable punishment for you and will administer it at some point when I see fit." Satan's voice was cold and sharp as a Viking's sword. Seeing that Johan was not moving, his eyes narrowed "Are you deaf as well as stupid? I said GET OUT!" Spittle accompanying the words as they both flew out of his mouth.

When previously told what to do his focus had been on The Sword of Damocles menace that was revealed to him, however the lack of subtlety and nuance in the instruction that had to be repeated and emphasised brought the creature back to the present better than any slap in the face. He decided that cowardly discretion, in the form of running away and getting as far from Satan's office as possible, was preferable to a casual stroll out of the room. His human Teutonic instincts briefly revealed themselves as he clicked his heals together and curtly bowed but as soon as that was done, he turned and ran to the exit door, opened it as fast as the heavy groaning wooden edifice would allow, and he was gone from Satan's sight. Leaving the Demon Lord with the satisfaction that at least four of his demonic Marching Horde had made it into Perdition before the pesky angels and that Finley and his troops outnumbered the angels two to one.

His smug satisfaction was not to last long. The private dark brooding thoughts were interrupted by a firm knocking on his door followed by the obsequious face of Stuart, his smarmy personal assistant, appear at a horizontal angle, neck and body blocked from sight, as if it were suspended in mid-air half way up the door itself. Looking at his servant with undisguised contempt and loathing Satan could tell by the oily and arrogant grin on his face that there was yet more bad news on its way and no matter how it was presented he wouldn't like it. "Yes?"

he growled, the letter S seeming to emanate from deep within his throat before joining the other two letters.

Unperturbed by the tone, in his master's voice, Stuart kept his rictus like grin. In fact, his eyes seemed to increase their level of glee. If Stuart wasn't so resourceful and devious in his uncanny ability to spy on other demons and obtain information quickly then Satan would have certainly sent him to one of the worst punishment chambers in Hell. However, until the time his uses ceased to exist, he knew that, as much as he hated to admit it, Stuart was a valuable asset. But it still didn't make the presence of such a vile creature any more bearable.

"Sire," the single word dripping with sadistic pleasure, like honey glazed poison. "I have two of the Demon Horde here to see you. They have unexpectedly returned to Hell after a brief visit to Purgatory." If, at that moment, Stuart's tongue could have slithered like a snake tasting the air it would have done.

The metaphorical mercury level in the thermometer of Satan's inner rage started to rapidly move up the glass tube. Satan's shark like teeth clenched tightly enough to have bitten through armoured steel. His fingers clenched his desk and his talon like nails sank into the mahogany surface. Thoughts of the ramifications of the news spinning into focus in his mind like a newspaper headline in a 1930's movie, only in vivid and lurid blood red hues. Releasing the tension in both his jaw and his hands he composed himself just enough so that he could speak. He couldn't hide his rage but at least he was able to talk. "Show them in." No other words were necessary, even if he'd had the calmness in his being to express them.

Stuart opened the large door wider, it groaned angrily at the forced movement, as if it felt that allowing anyone into Satan's inner sanctum was not part of its job description. When there was enough room for them to enter Banks and Rutherford marched solemnly into Satan's office and, on reaching the front of his desk, they halted and brought their feet down to sharp attention. Arms rigidly by their sides in poses that were not always the strictest of Demon Marching Horde fashion. All that was missing, from their military positions, were crisp salutes.

Satan raised himself from his chair and walked around his desk so that he could stand closer to them. He positioned himself first in front of Banks, his hot foul-smelling breath running over the soldier's face, the creature's original demonic appearance having now returned. Swallowing back the urge to vomit his eyes remained fixed, looking forwards and trying to avoid any direct contact with his dark Commander in Chief. He knew that throwing up over him would not have helped his predicament. After the silent scanning of the stiff form before him Satan moved to repeat the inspection of Rutherford. Again, no reaction was received so he just stepped back and sat casually on the front of his desk, arms supporting him as he leant back. Finally, he decided to break the ominous silence "So? Tell me what happened. As I understand it you managed to get access into Purgatory and after that...?"

Banks briefly turned to look at Rutherford and then returned back to his position. He wasn't sure if it was wise to speak first or remain silent but he knew that one of them had to say something so decided that he would take the risk. "Sir, we wish to report that we entered Limbo" the mental image of the literal meaning of that sentence made Satan smile despite his anger "and encountered a long passage full of doors, all leading to what looked like identical airport departure lounges." This piece of information made Satan lean forward, an expression of intent curiosity on his face. Seeing the slight movement Banks paused in anticipation of a question, but none came.

"Proceed." Satan said quietly as if he didn't want to alter the mood that filled the room.

"Well, we errrr, went into one of those rooms" the confidence in Bank's voice draining away and attempted to find the confidence in his soul that he wanted; but it wasn't there. "Then Rutherford here" he quickly nodded his head in the direction of his colleague "he attempted to interrogate a random soul in the terminal and, as he started to persuade the person to talk, he suddenly disappeared right in front of Finley's eyes and apparently he returned here to Hell."

"Really?" enquired Satan. "Very interesting, and what happened to you?"

"Well sir, Finley instructed me to run up to a female sat close by and kick her a dozen times. When I started to carry out the instructions, I found myself in a punishment chamber on the 5th ring of Hell and had to explain the situation to the demon in charge there so that she would release me, and I could come here and report directly to you."

Satan inhaled deeply. "So, you two morons inflicted violence in one of the judgement halls of Purgatory? You just acted first and left thinking completely out of the process?" His knowledge of the Purgatory process obviously far greater than that of the two soldiers stood before him.

Seeing that Banks was doing all the talking Rutherford decided that it was prudent to contribute something to the reporting process. His rational being that the more details given might be inversely proportional to the amount of punishment inflicted. "Sir. I wish to report that we were in fact only obeying direct orders given to us by Finley!" A proud, but out of place, smile at having clarified that minor detail. However, the smile didn't remain on his face for long or, more accurately, his face didn't remain on his head for any period of time. Taking a single but powerful swing of his arm Satan's hand, with long claws drawn, impacted with the front of Rutherford's head. Finger nails digging deep, cutting flesh and travelling through his skull bone and not stopping on its journey until it had gone across the whole of the head. The face, removed from the front part of the skull, flew across the room impacting on a side wall leaving part of the brain and the back part of his jaw muscles visible. The space where his face had formally been, framed by white bone matter, quickly turning red by the still circulating blood. All the while the rest of his body attempted to remain at attention but even in Hell gravity usually has to be obeyed and the un-dead corpse fell to the floor in a heap. Being a demon, death's release was not found that easily. His face would eventually grow back, but until then he had to walk around Hades and be a stark reminder to any other demon, that saw him, that failure had its painful price to pay.

"Only obeying orders?" Satan snorted derisively at the words. "Even feeble brained humans learnt that wasn't an excuse for stupidity and carelessness so what makes you think that it would be accepted by me?" The question was totally rhetorical as the status of Rutherford's face meant that he was in no state to answer. It was hard to talk without a tongue, jaw or even a mouth for that matter. Although ironically, even if the excuse might not be something that Satan wouldn't accept as an excuse, or even justification for failure, he would not have looked too kindly on any demon refusing to obey or even questioning an order, or instruction, that he gave. War criminals on Earth might give that story to judges and juries at the Hague in an attempt to delay their inevitable trip to Hell but as far as Satan was concerned it was a case of there being two rules, his and anyone else that failed him.

"So," turning his attention to a now very nervous Banks "as they do not appear to have returned suddenly to Hell, I take it that Finley and the other one is still in Purgatory and hopefully are having more success than you and the useless pile of flesh currently making a mess of my carpet?"

"Collins? Yes, sir they were still in the departure lounge when I... sort of departed."

"Well I can only hope, for their sakes, that they have more success than you two." Growling at nothing in particular he gave Banks a hard stare. "Now get out, I am sick of the sight of you!"

"Thank you, sir. Straight away sir." With that Banks turned and started to quick march towards the door, but he was not marching quickly enough to make his boss happy. Satan decided that he needed to vent some of his still tightly pent up frustration, so he raised his arm, pointed his fingers at the back of the retreating soldier and fired a large ball of fire. It hit Banks squarely in the back, continued its searing path through his chest escaping out the other side hitting the door before finally exploding in a ring of fire. "Stuart," he shouted through the partially open door, well aware that his assistant would have been eaves dropping and heard every word. "Come and dispose of these two demons. Oh, and arrange for somebody to clean my carpet, it seems to have somehow got some blood on it!"

Chapter 19 - Good Angel - Not Totally Bad Angel

Being dead definitely has its pro's and con's. On the plus side you tend to stop getting letters from the tax man demanding money. Or, if you continue to get them, at least you can safely ignore them. No matter how large the amount they there are now somebody else's problem and not worth losing sleep over; even if sleep was an issue in the afterlife. You also no longer have to worry about an enemy's threat to kill you. Unless they are the cause of death then they are far too late and should have acted sooner or just shut up. The job that you despise and all the daily chores, which made existence a dull and seemingly soul-destroying routine, are now over with.

The other side of the coin is that you have to leave those that you love, or love you, which is never a happy thought. The clandestine knee tremblers with a work colleague in the office stationery cupboard also have to come to an end. At least that will allow the soaking wet and stained photocopier paper to dry out. And also, the casual words 'Over my dead body' said to a detestable person, that was making unwelcome and possible inappropriate advances to you, might now be seen as a contractual agreement and not an instructional synonym for 'Go away'; only using an Anglo Saxon word starting with 'F' and ending with 'Uck off' instead! So that could lead your lifeless cadaver to have far more, and possibly, much kinkier sex than you ever had while you were alive.

Then, of course, there is the afterlife to be considered. If you have been good then all your troubles are a thing of the past, an eternity of bliss and happiness awaits. Relax, put your feet up and enjoy yourself. If you have not been a good person then choices, which you can make about future happiness, become far more limited. In fact, they become zero squared. In other words, you could be in the same state as the person that was flippantly said the words 'Over my dead body'. Involuntarily screwed! Although the word *option* denotes an element of choice - there is a third path and that is the path to Perdition. But, despite the possible long processing periods, that is just a temporary stop gap and sooner or later you will find yourself judged and despatched one way or another. This waiting station was the case for Ernest Higginbotham. Despite the possible foolishness of the agreement he made with Satan he did earn himself a respite from going straight to Hell by his good deeds and trying to cancel the contract. Limbo had to give him special treatment and judge him personally and somehow, without the assistance of any external guides, Ernest had managed to work out that he had ended up in Purgatory. He knew he was dead so, his logic deduced, he wasn't in Heaven or Hell, so where else could he be?

Although in Perdition there were no opportunities for people to self-harm, or end their own lives, after all where they are already dead and any pain would come freely if they were judged to deserve it. However, despite this, Ernest Higginbotham was incarcerated in a brightly lit plain white padded cell. As Limbo could pluck him out of the room, at any time he chose, there was no door to spoil the contours of the cloth lining the cell walls and floor. Despite his accommodation he was not confined in a straight-jacket, death had improved his physical state so that he wore a clean, smart and new tweed suit and polished brown shoes. He was permanently clean shaven and most importantly of all his personal hygiene had significantly altered for the better. Gone was the strong bouquet of au de dirty toilet, which could have knocked flies off a bucket of cow dung at ten paces, to be replaced by a fresh and clean smell. As a human he had become an untouchable or, if you did touch him, you'd have to wash your hands afterwards. But, now that he waited for judgement, he had been handed back an element of self-respect and humanity that he had lost, or been deprived of, as a living human.

Loneliness wasn't really something he noticed or cared about. His whole life had left him isolated and a loner. Being an emissary of God, and having a special task, meant that the path he took in life was mainly a solitary one. Now, lacking any form of mental stimuli, he spent most of his time pacing his room or sat on the floor, legs tucked into his arms, staring fixedly at one of the plain walls deep in thought contemplating the long catalogue of unfortunate events that led him to his current situation. Such thoughts were hell enough to someone that was, on the whole, a decent man that had just made a few bad judgement calls. All he had left was the hope that his judge would make better ones than he did.

His deep inner soul-searching was abruptly distracted by the sudden and unexpected appearance of Dedan and Roxy right in front of him. Taken out of his introspection he blinkingly looked up at his two visitors. Realising that they were not some apparition, created by his mind to destroy the loneliness, he stood up and offered his hand to the unexpected guest. "How do you do?" The English in him letting him get away with the greeting that confused the rest of the world. "I am Ernest, pleased to meet you."

"How do you do." Responded Dedan, familiar with the strange start to any conversation. "I am Dedan and this fair creature here is Rossana." At that Ernest grabbed Dedan's hand and shook it vigorously, as if he were pumping water from an old-fashioned water hand pump, and then repeated the process with Roxy. He hadn't realised how much he had missed interaction with other people until they suddenly turned up in his padded cell. "Ernest, before we start talking do you know where you are?"

"Oh, yes, I think so lad." Ernest nodded sagely at the idea of having to say it out loud. "If I'm not mistaken this is Limbo."

"Well..." Dedan was about to explain the grammatical error and common misconception when Roxy quickly interrupted him. Aware of wasting precious time and of Limbo's warning of saying too much and tipping the scales of justice the wrong way.

"Yes, you are. And will be judged at some point. Your soul will either go to paradise or end up in Hell. I am sorry but that is how it works." Thanks to her inherent kindness Roxy had genuine sadness in her eyes, and voice, at having to confirm his fears. "God has sent us to try and get you to Heaven or at least find out a piece of critical information from you."

"Oh, I see. Interesting." Ernest's voice far more casual and resigned than either of the two angels had expected. "I presume the information that you are looking for relates to a certain Sword of Uncreation?" pausing as if to realise something important. "Where are my manners? I know I lack all the comforts of home but please sit down. It feels rather awkward stood talking like this." He gestured to the floor, just in case they had any doubts as to all the options available and where they would be able to sit.

They all sat on the floor, Dedan and Ernest had crossed legs while Roxy adopted the lotus position. A feat that made Dedan briefly look at her lustfully, his creative and lascivious imagination diverting him momentarily from the task in hand, but he quickly re-focused as he realised that such graphic and erotic thoughts could quite possibly send him to Hell. "I must admit," ventured Ernest "that I was not expecting this. However, I find it a most welcome diversion. Have no fear, there is no need for any persuasive tactics, either gentle or otherwise. Although I am sure that Rossana would have made a wonderfully kind interrogator to your hard-line counterpart. Isn't that right Mr. Dedan?"

"No Mister, just Dedan please. My time on earth was long before surnames took the form and prominence that they have today." Dedan smiled reassuringly. "And as for me being some sort of iron fist in a velvet glove to persuade you, all I can say is that such methods would probably not be permitted and prove to be counterproductive to our mission. So hopefully you will talk willingly to us."

"Of course, of course Dedan." His smile broad and his voice betraying his eagerness to confess all and tell them everything that they need to know. "I presume that you are seeking the location of The Sword? Of course, I am happy and, in a way, relieved that I can tell you where it is hidden. It is…"

Chapter 20 - Suddenly No Longer Thirsty.

Although, on a day to day basis, it was a big part of his job to judge, as a matter of principle Limbo didn't prejudge people. Souls came to his domain because they had to prove that they were deserving of the final location that they would end up in. Past sins might have been large but so must the good elements to have caused them to be here. Looking at Collins and Finley he didn't have to maintain his unbiased and fair manners or attitudes. Their holy garb did nothing to fool him, the evil of their past, present and future seemed to mix together and emanate a foul stench of all that was vile. His disgust, for his two guests, created flames that made his skin turn a shade of blue that was darker than his eyes, making them almost disappear, imperceptible in the surrounding darkness. If they had sat on real scales of judgement, they would have tipped them so far down on Hell's side that it would have taken three angelic elephants to sit on the opposite side just to make them find equilibrium. He wanted to send them straight back to Satan empty handed but he knew that he had to show a fairness that was beyond their comprehension or capabilities to ever give to others. As Roxy and Dedan had been allowed the opportunity to present their case fair play meant that, at the very least, the two demons currently sat on his couch must be extended the same courtesy.

"Can I offer you a drink?" Limbo might not have liked his new guests but he believed strongly in good manners and, no matter what, he intended to extend his hospitality to the two members of the Marching Horde. "I have tea, but I can arrange for coffee or piss to be brought; if that is your choice."

Thrown by the final option Finley looked at Collins with a confused look as if to seek clarification that he had heard correctly and to try and seek guidance as to whether they were expected to choose that beverage. Perhaps urine was a popular and traditional beverage in Purgatory and it might be rude to refuse it. Collins was just as perplexed as Finley so just shrugged. "Er, no thank you Mr...."

"They call me Limbo"

"Limbo? Okay" understanding finally breaking through the outer wall and making its way into Finley's brain. "No thank you Limbo, we had plenty of your exquisite brandy and scotch, so I think we will be alright."

"Very well, as you wish." If his eyes had been visible amongst the dark blue flames Collins and Finley would have seen sheer contempt for them. He regretted passing on the instructions that they should make themselves at home and help themselves in the other room, they didn't deserve to experience such quality. But he liked to be the perfect host - so his own character wouldn't have allowed him to do, or say, anything else. But sometimes he wished that he could be just downright rude.

"So, gentlemen, I see that at least half of your party managed to make it without throttling or taking a running kick at anybody. What self-control you displayed. I'd like to say that I am impressed but I would be lying." The veneer of Limbo's usual hospitable demeanour wearing thin and showing in his cynical tone "your souls are evil and you have no place here. You belong in Hell but unfortunately the rules here are such that you have to be judged either by your actions, as your two friends were, or

I have to judge you. Something I am more than happy to do. However, the rules of balance also dictate that I do not do that. YET!" His voice, in their minds, colder than the flames on his skin. "What is it that you want here?" The question was pointless, as he knew exactly what their purpose was, but he was in no rush. He could sense that Dedan and Roxy were still amiably talking to Ernest and he, in return, was telling them all they needed to know. Limbo's word would be kept and only when they were finished would he pluck them out of the padded cell and allow the demons access.

"Sir... Limbo, we are here on a special mission and we want a soul released to us. It belongs to Satan and he has sent us to take possession of it." Began Finley calmly.

"You want!!!" Limbo's voice like a sea storm in their minds. "Want? Take? Those sound like orders. Do you think you have any domain here? Your powers and authority mean nothing to me. As far as I am concerned you are two evil and irredeemable demons and that would be judgement enough."

Realising that he had adopted the wrong tone Finley bowed his head in an act of supplication. "Limbo, my humblest of apologies. I realise that I took the completely wrong tone but unfortunately time is not my greatest friend and neither is my master. His impatience and desire for a speedy and successful resolution of the matter made me speak out of turn. I am sure you can appreciate the punishment Satan could cause me if I fail him."

"And I should care about the suffering of a demon because...?"

Smiling deviously Finley nodded. "I suppose you are right. But you have a reputation for fairness and justice irrespective of who, or what, you are dealing with. You do not give favours and are unbiased in your actions. That is all we ask from you."

"All you ask? State your case and I will listen and then judge fairly."

"Thank you, mighty Limbo. Ernest Higginbotham is currently a guest of yours awaiting your judgement; however, we have documentary evidence that his soul belongs to Satan. I have in my possession..." Finley moved to reach inside his Catholic clothing as if to retrieve a document.

"Yes, I am well aware of the contract. One of Satan's standard forms I believe. Basic terms and conditions with small print that would need an electron microscope to make it visible. Written in blood and bearing his authentic signature. I am well aware that it exists, so you can keep it in your pocket. If it didn't exist Ernest would currently be having a leisurely time in Heaven, what you seek would remain secretly hidden and we wouldn't be having this conversation." Limbo's voice was terse but he was trying his best to calm down in the presence of the devils, but he wasn't succeeding. He could manage to sooth the frustrated and angry part of his mind and his blue tone would brighten but as soon as he had to process anything that the demons said to him, he immediately changed and the shade went from powder

164

then sky through denim before his skin was a raging flame of dark sapphire blue. Forget fifty shades of blue, Limbo might not have names for all the different tints, but he could take the nuances of the colour into triple figures. In his domain he had plenty of people available to play cards with, but he learned long ago that he made a terrible poker player. If he found himself with a Royal Flush, or four of a kind, his uncontrollable excitement would make him glow dark and the darker he went the better the hand. If he ended up with cards fit only for folding, or ripping up and burying in a deep hole, he would go the opposite way and turn almost white with disappointment and apathy for the complete lack of any pretty pictures of matching royalty. Such blatantly visible *tells* meant he lost a small fortune before he realised his problem. When dealing with the two demons, sat in front of him, he was aware of his external emotional display, but he just couldn't care less about them seeing it.

"Excellent, that will save us a lot of time. I am glad that you are not contesting our claim. So, if you'd be so good as to hand him over to our custody, we will be out of your hair..." Pausing Finley corrected himself "flaming head." They stood as if to prepare to take immediate possession.

"Not so fast *gentlemen*" the word almost sticking in his throat. "Please be seated. It doesn't work like that." Sensing that Dedan and Roxy were still preoccupied with Ernest he thought that he could take his time with his dealings with Satan's mouth pieces. Nonchalantly he picked up his tea cup from the small table and casually took a sip of his drink. Savouring it, before swallowing, then letting out an exaggerated sigh of appreciation; the gesture a deliberate and calculated ploy to annoy his impatient interlopers. "For demons you seem to be rather intelligent chaps, not the average type from Hell that scrapes the skin off their knuckles when they walk. So, I am sure that the relevance of where you are has not gone unnoticed? This is Purgatory, perdition and although I dislike it and risk accusations of vanity; the eponym of *Limbo*. Souls do not come here for storage until some angel or demon comes and collects them. They have to be judged and that decision is final and irrevocable."

"But..." began Collins.

"Buts?" Limbo raised his hand to silence him. "There are NO buts, no IF's and no HOW ABOUT's. There are facts, actions, processes and finally judgement. No legal loopholes or extraneous debates. Mr. Higginbotham's sin and action are indeed heinous, deplorable and stupid but, as he is here, I am sure that you realise that there is much in his history that was good, thus placing him where he is."

"So, Limbo, can I ask when he will be judged?" Collins asked; his mind racing ahead and envisioning the possibility of their goal being thwarted.

"Judged?" If Limbo had possessed eye brows, he would have raised them in surprise at the question. "Judgement starts as soon as souls enter my domain. It is not like some earthly court where some paid lawyers stand up and tell lies, then the defendants plead their cases, all done with sadness in their eyes and remorse in their voices. I do not sit imperiously listening to excuses and then bang some big wooden gavel when I have spent my time in deliberation. Souls are put in situations which they have to deal with. Do the right thing and they do well. If they do not so well then... well..." ending the sentence by pointing his extended thumb to the ground, like a Roman Emperor passing his judgement on a gladiator that had failed to entertain.

"Is there nothing we can do then to speed up the judgement process?" Finley's voice tinged with a hint of despair. A despair caused more by the thought of his own plight, if he failed, than any concerns for the soul of Ernest.

Leaning forward, as if revealing a closely guarded secret, Limbo's voice in their head was matter of fact "Well gents, as it happens you are, or more accurately, will be, part of the judgement process. As we speak two angels are currently talking with the suddenly extremely popular Mr. Higginbotham."

At those words both Finley and Collins's faces took on expressions of alarm and fear.

"Relax." Limbo assured them, on seeing their faces. "As I keep trying to explain, balance is important here so if he is to be judged fairly you must also be given the opportunity to see, and talk, with him. Whether he chooses to make the conversation two sided is entirely up to him." He deliberately paused to allow the words to sink in; taking the opportunity to take another sip of tea. He knew what they were going to say next, but he had no intention of making it easy for them by finishing their sentences for them before they had even been spoken. Finley and Collins were thinking about Limbo's words and sat waiting for him to volunteer more details and instructions as to how and when they would get to see Ernest. Long seconds passed and still nobody spoke. Collins gave his commander another quizzical look, unsure as to whether he should break the silence.

Finally, Finley decided to end the impasse. "Limbo, can we see him now? Time is of the essence and I am sure that you have better things to do than judge such a person and sit here talking to us."

"Well, you are certainly half right with that sentence." His flame becoming slightly lighter, as if to applaud his own witticism. "I do have better things to do than sit talking with you two. You can see him shortly. I will despatch you into his presence once Dedan and Roxy are finished. I doubt that you will have to wait much longer as I sense that their conversation is coming to its natural conclusion and possible fruition."

At the mention of Dedan's name Finley sat upright. "Dedan? Did you say Dedan?"

"Yes, an interesting mess of contradictions which is unusual for an angel. But, if you pardon the simplistic expression, he seems to know 'his stuff'. Are you and he acquainted in some way?"

"No, not as such. We have never met but I know him by reputation and would very much like to have the opportunity to meet him face to face." Finley's intent being less of a friendly handshake, accompanied by a few polite platitudes, and more a release of snarling swear-words - as he stabbed the angel in the throat. He had heard all about Dedan's escapades in Hawaii and felt that God's personal assistant needed knocking down a peg or ten. Plus, he was sure that Satan would reward anyone that made Dedan suffer before giving him a sudden, and unplanned, premature return to Heaven.

"Oh, Mr. Finley! And they say that I am sometimes transparent. Let me assure you that I do not need telepathic abilities to know your intentions towards Dedan, but you can leave such thoughts alone for the moment. You and he will not be meeting in my domain. Besides, even if you did bump into each other here, any violence would immediately send you straight back to Hell well before you could inflict any real damage to him!"

"Let me assure YOU Limbo, that I would only need one small window of opportunity." Finley's face full of a casual menace that failed to impress Limbo.

"Perhaps Mr. Finley, perhaps. But such things are academic as I control all things here and know that you will never meet him here in my domain. You will have to arrange a rendezvous on some other dimensional plain."

"Yes Limbo. It can wait." Demons do not let go of hatred easily and Finley was no exception; for an immortal soul time was irrelevant.

Across his kingdom Limbo was sensing Dedan, Roxy and Ernest. Not so much listening or watching, like some supernatural CCTV spying on their every move, rather more of senses being aware. Distinct words couldn't be heard and for all he knew they could be stood naked hitting each other with pillows. It was a feeling, a connection with their inner humanity. Their emotions spoke to him and that was the only stimuli he needed to know that they had finished. The angels were happy with what they had been told and Ernest's intentions were good. All he needed was for the demons to repeat the exercise so that he could be certain, and also tick the box in his own moral code ensuring balance and fairness.

"Right, if you are ready, I shall now send you to talk to Mr. Higginbotham. I would wish you luck, but my own moral code will not allow me to lie."

"There we are then!" said Finley, just as their bodies disappeared to be replaced almost instantaneously with the surprised forms of Dedan and Roxy, looking slightly confused by their sudden change of location and the disappearance of Ernest. Blinking as they took in their new view they turned and saw Limbo sat in his usual chair, teacup and saucer in hand, smiling a pale blue toothy grin at them. The flames on his skin now a calm tranquil ocean blue. "Hello, you two, how lovely to see you again. I believe that your little chat went well. Please no need to stay sat on the floor; you are not talking to Ernest anymore. I have far more civilised furniture options. Please, be seated." Dedan rose first and offered his hand to Roxy as she went through the undignified and low-level gymnastics that everyone must endure to get out of the lotus position. Pulling herself up she gave him a brief smile of thanks and they made themselves comfortable on the sofa.

"Can I offer you a drink? I still only have tea but can always phone out for some fresh urine if you are thirsty."

"No thank you Limbo." replied a smiling Dedan as he absentmindedly ran his fingers through his thinning hair. He wished that he had just accepted the awful coffee, when first offered, or at least kept his contempt of the stuff quiet. "We are both fine. We are just eager to return to the earthly dimension and then we can pick up our things and return to Heaven."

"Oh." Exclaimed Limbo, his voice sounding ill at ease inside their minds. "I am terribly sorry Dedan, I thought you'd have realised. You can't return to Earth."

Thinking that he had somehow managed to get trapped in the purgatorial process, and would need judging, Dedan's face dropped. He knew that he needed to return to Heaven as quickly as possible and didn't want to be stuck where he was.

Sensing his guest's change in mood Limbo chuckled softly. "No, oh no Dedan, I do not mean that you are to be judged. You have your many, and interesting faults but you are far from being a devil. Besides I suspect that your final question will prove, without a shadow of a doubt that you are, despite yourself, a good, kind and caring person. But the reason you can't return to Earth is that, thanks to the injuries that you received outside my gates, you are technically dead... Again! Or at least wouldn't survive ten seconds back there." So, I have no option but to send you straight up to Heaven. But thanks to you coming here you will also be able to return to Earth whenever you wish, rather than having to wait."

The news was met with initially relief and then joy as he realised that he would be able to report everything to God straight away without wasting time going via Earth and opening a dimensional portal. "That is great. Then please can you send us there as quickly as possible?"

"Alas my friend you must go alone. Roxy's body still lives on earth and as such she can't get to Heaven via here and I will have to return her to the earthly plane before she can return her soul into God's graces. I am terribly sorry, but I do not make the rules. Besides, I doubt that delay will not be too inconvenient."

Looking at Dedan with a warm smile, but sad eyes, Roxy spoke. "It's alright Dedan. I'll catch you up." Then, returning her attention to Limbo. "I take it that I am not to be judged either?"

"No, my dear lady. You are goodness personified, your biggest faults, as a human, were smoking and your poor taste in men and neither of them are hardly sins in themselves. But a bit of advice to help you break one of those terrible habits; when you get back up to Heaven, keep away from people like Dedan." He gave her a broad smile and a conspiratorial wink that was not lost amongst the shimmering blue flames. "Goodbye my dear it has been a true pleasure making your acquaintance. Next time you are in the area please feel free to drop in for a cup of tea and a nice catch up, it has been charming." With that Roxy was gone, leaving Dedan looking pensively at Limbo.

Standing, Limbo moved towards the angel and gave Dedan a friendly slap on the shoulder. "Don't fret dear boy, it's nothing personal, just giving the wonderful lady a bit of sound advice, you might be an angel, but I am sure you'll admit that you can be a bit of a cad and downright scoundrel at times."

Raising his eyebrows, as if surprised by Limbo's last comment he replied. "That's alright Limbo," returning the genial slap onto Limbo's shoulder, making the cold flame ripple as if a sea on fire. "I can't deny it; even if I wanted to - especially not here, or to you. As you might say I can be an absolute bounder. But I never hurt people in that way, or at least try not to."

"I know Dedan, I know. You hurt yourself more looking for something which you fear that you may never find or are afraid that you might find it and discover that it isn't what you want. But the past is not always something that is repeated! In a place based on love even happiness isn't always guaranteed. I hope you find that which you yearn for above all else. Some walls can only be removed by the builder!"

Dedan nodded. With the accurate summary of his soul, his inner soul was pierced deeper than any spear ever could. He paused and looked at his host pensively. "Can I ask you something before I go?"

"Fire away dear boy. Fire away. I am expecting it and I'd be disappointed if you didn't ask it."

"Ernest, he might be a fool, but I know enough to recognise evil when I see it and he is certainly not that. Yes, he sinned, and it was a whooper and it could still bring about the downfall of Heaven and, in turn, humanity but…"

"But? But his soul is not evil in itself? Yes, his action was indeed foolish, and the repercussions even now could be serious, but he is still being judged. I have never before wanted to bend or break the rules however, in this

173

instance, I wish I could throw away the rule book, turn a blind eye and let one slip through the net and go to Heaven. Unfortunately, I am like a railway train. I am on tracks and must follow them no matter how much I desire to change the route. Hopefully soon he will prove himself and I can release him."

"Thank you, Limbo."

"It is alright. I am glad you asked me the question though. For all your faults I hope you know that your scales are definitely leaning steeply towards Heaven." With that he gave one last blue smile and Dedan was gone. Turning to return to his chair he shook his head, his voice full of disgust. "Piss? What a strange fellow."

Chapter 21 – Sanctus Stercus

It didn't take long for Finley and Collins to acclimatise to their new location. However, Ernest's shock at seeing two catholic priests suddenly appear before him took a while to dissipate. He somehow guessed that he would get further visitors, but he was expecting demons not men of the cloth.

"Errr, hello. I'm Ernest. Please Father's I am afraid that I can't offer you any chairs, but the floor is padded so it is quite comfortable to sit on."

Finley quickly realised the confusion their clothing had caused in Ernest's mind and decided to make the most of it and perhaps benefit from the subterfuge. "Why bless you my child. Thank you. We are all the same in the eyes of God, so we do not put ourselves above others, so, if the floor is good enough for you then it is good enough for us. Isn't that right Father Collins?"

"Why yes of course Father Finley." The fellow demon immediately recognising Finley's tactic. "The floor is ideal and comfortable. So, let us sit and talk. I am afraid we are a little pressed for time, so I think a little informality is more than welcome."

They sat; the demons with their legs stuck outwards a stark contrast to the cross-legged compact figure of Ernest. "I must admit" began Ernest his voice soaked in bitter despair, like a sponge dipped in lemon juice "that I was expecting demons but seeing you I think that I have made a terrible mistake."

"Really my child? Tell me more." Finley's soft, oily, tone soothing Ernest.

"Well I have to confess that I have only just had a couple of visitors and they tricked me into thinking they were angels. But I think they were actually demons. They must have been." His arm pointing to their priestly garbs as if to emphasise his belief in their piety. "I have been a fool yet again." Tears welling in his eyes.

"Please do not worry, devils can be tricky and take on many forms to please the eye and trick the soul. Do not dwell on it. Please, what did you tell them? Please tell us word for word." He turned to Collins and gave him a sly wink that could almost have been taken to be a twitch to an outside observer, but Collins fully understood the signal. Success and it was easier than they had anticipated.

"Please, please can you forgive me?"

"Of course, we can. We can forgive you everything but first tell us where The Sword is!"

"It is buried…"

As Ernest Higginbotham unburdened his soul the two demons sat listening intently taking in every word. No detail escaped them and by the time Ernest had finished and they had asked a few minor questions, to clarity a few grey areas, they knew exactly where The Sword was and how to get it.

At last Ernest's strange confessional came to its end with the confessor happy in the assumed knowledge that he had finally done the right thing.

"So that is everything?" Finley's voice kind but firm. "You haven't left anything out?"

"No, I promise you, that is everything I know." His voice almost pleading "Please, tell Limbo that I did the right thing and that I didn't mean to tell the demons anything. I do not want to go to Hell."

Finley stood up first and Collins quickly followed suit. "You might not want to go to Hell, but we do, and we need to get there quickly. Thank you for all your assistance. I am sure we will see you in Hell very soon." With that he raised his arm and punched Ernest squarely on the nose, breaking it with a cringe inducing crack and sending him to the floor clenching it as blood instantly started to spurt out of it. As soon at impact was made Finley disappeared; his evil action, and intent, instantly activating Perdition's very own Hell-o-meter and instantly dispatching him back to Hades. Seeing his senior officer's action, and Purgatory's equivalent of Newton's Third Law, Collins decided that his action would cause an equal and metaphorical opposite reaction. He swiftly swung his leg back and let it fly towards the prostrate figure laid on the floor in front of him; his foot impacting on Ernest's stomach with a loud thud. And Collins, just as Finley had done a few seconds earlier, disappeared; leaving Ernest alone with his pain, both physical and emotional. The final realisation of who he had just told the holiest of secrets to taking him further from the peace he craved.

Chapter 22 – This Sounds Like a Job For…. Jimi Hendrix?

"Ilkley? Ilkley Moor?" God said the words with bemusement as if He was remembering something but the picture in His mind was forming slowly and the image wasn't as expected. He repeated the words several more times, slowly, His voice sounding like it was having an echoed conversation with itself. Then He smiled broadly at Dedan. "So, after the demons looked in the first and most obvious place the Guardians decided to put it back there. Clever, very clever."

"Sire? I'm sorry but I don't understand."

"Oh, yes, you had been killed in the battle prior to that and missed the final conflict." Referring to the fact that if a demon, or angel, were killed while on earth they returned to their respective dimension and couldn't return straight away to Earth and resume fighting – the wait could be several years. A mutually agreed rule and blocker created by God and Satan so that battles didn't turn into an all too real version of a video game. Get killed and return straight away to carry on the fight where they left off, they were not Italian plumbers or people trying to avoid bombs dropped by alien space ships. Souls might be eternal, but every battle has to end at some point.

God stood up, sending His plush chair gently rolling backwards on its wheels like someone slipping on black ice. "In Yorkshire, England, there is a Moor, full of heather, bracken and rocks. Quite beautiful really, even when it rains, which happens quite a lot. Sethbert, one of my knights, had returned, exhausted and almost insane after a long journey. In his possession was The Sword of Uncreation. A weapon that I am sure you know by reputation, or at least by legend. It is all that they say it is and more."

"And?" Dedan watching as God walked around His large and exquisitely decorated office and inner sanctum.

"There were battles at the gates of Heaven, corners of Hell and all over Earth. The war had raged on for over a thousand years, ever since Satan had first tried to take my throne. Back and forth, numbers ever increasing as humans were killed in the cross fire and swelled the ranks on both sides. There seemed to be no end in sight; just a bloody stalemate for the rest of time. Killing each other only for the slain to return a few years later and pick up their weapons again." God's eyes looked sad as he recalled the carnage and destruction. "Something had to be done so, shall we say that, I called in a favour from an ally and they made The Sword. It took them decades but when it finally arrived it stopped the ebb and flow of the waves of battles. A beautiful and exquisitely crafted weapon that was light but powerful. As soon as we used it demons started to run and cower back in Hell. Victory was in sight. Then, one night, one of their demons somehow sneaked into our camp and stole The Sword. Suddenly it was our turn to fall and not get up. Even the smallest of seemingly insignificant cuts making angels and saints disappear, gone, lost forever. Satan is a skilled swordsman and he did a lot of damage. Over the years the weapon changed hands a few times until finally he had me within reach. I had my back to him, distracted, planning the next battle and he raised it ready to strike and then…"

179

"Then?" Dedan muttered, rapt as he listened to the story. The slight pause, as God thought, adding to the suspense. If there had been any pins around, to be dropped, he'd have been deafened by the sound.

"And then… He hesitated. I don't know why but he just stopped. Sword held tightly in both hands raised high ready to administer the ultimate coup de grace. I'd have been gone and his path to Heaven, and all his desires, would have been his. I just happened to turn at the right time and the look in his eyes. I will never forget it. Not hatred or anger but…. Never mind." God shook his head as if to remove the rest of the sentence from his mind. "My sword swung around and impaled him sending him back to his domain. I picked up The Sword of Uncreation again and finished the day's battle. After that the demons seemed to lose heart and by the end of the week, they had all gone. The war was won. I saw the weapon and realised that its power was too great even for me. It had its uses as a deterrent. As humans say, these days, the ultimate Weapon of Mass Destruction. But it was too dangerous to ever be used again. If it fell into a demon's hands, we might not be so lucky next time and Satan might not pause. I decided that I needed The Sword, but it should be kept away from both angel and demon."

"So, you enlisted humans to be the guardians?" Dedan's voice unable to conceal his surprise.

"Yes, humans and…others! I made The Sword invisible to Me. I couldn't track it while it was on Earth. There as a last resort so I could find it if I asked the right human but on the whole, it was left with them, as I understand it there have been several resting places. The last one that I was aware of was Germany but that got moved in 1933. I had thought that it'd gone to America and suspected it to be on Mount Rushmore, but it seems that I was mistaken. It had been continually handed down from one lone guardian to the next until today, the chain of possession broken. There have always been several false guardians, with guardian angels to add to the smoke screen, but I was never sure who the real one was. And despite his efforts Satan was never able to discover any Guardian that was willing to talk."

"Until today? Ernest Higginbotham sold his soul to them and has paid the price. Why didn't you just use it to destroy Satan and Hell?"

"We shall see about poor Ernest. His apostasy was due more to a misunderstanding as to what his reward would be for his loyalty. He felt lost, alone and in despair and a devil whispered in his ear. You saw him yourself, he isn't a bad man. Just.... misguided!" He allowed the word to disappear into Dedan's mind before he continued. "As for destroying Satan; has your visit to my friend Limbo taught you nothing? It isn't just Purgatory that must have balance. Earth has many variations of Yin and Yang and even Heaven must have its Hell. Without it there is no threat to humans. Just a promise of glory if good or obscurity if bad, freedom of choice between two diametrical opposites is gone. No, my dear friend, as much as we might not like the place, Hell has its purpose." God walked to His ornate brick fireplace and stood with His hands clenched behind His back looking into the flames; seemingly lost, deep in His private thoughts.

"So, Satan now knows where The Sword is?" Concern in Dedan's voice, as he watched his Lord from where he was sat.

"Perhaps he does, perhaps he doesn't, but we must assume that he does and make plans accordingly. You must go to Ilkley and stop him from making any archaeological digs and historical discoveries."

Rising so fast from his chair Dedan accidentally sent it tipping over backwards. "Great, I'll go find St. Michael and sort out an army. Hopefully I can get feet on the ground within the day."

"Not so fast Dedan." turning to face His eager angel. "I already have an army down there."

"YOU HAVE?" his voice full of surprise.

"Oh yes, you'll see them when you get on the Moor. They might look harmless, but I assure you that they are better suited to the terrain than any soldiers that St. Michael could ever muster. I think that you will just need to take two people with you. Perhaps three if Roxy makes it back here in time." Moving back to his desk he pushed a button on his intercom. "Angelica, would you be so kind as to contact Bob, or Fred or Frederic or whatever he likes to be called today, and ask him to come to My office? I have a chance for him to redeem himself."

"Of course, Sir" came Angelica's calm and efficient voice via the device.

"Right Dedan, off you go."

"Err Boss, go where?"

182

"Oh, quite right. Jimi Hendrix is the other member of your small band of brothers. I will let you go see him and explain the mission to him."

"For Fuuuuuuu…" The overriding desire to swear stifled due to who he was talking to. "No, please God, not Jimi Hendrix - anyone but him. I'd rather fight shoulder to shoulder with that pompous prick St. Michael, and that is saying something."

"Yes, I know that there is bad blood between you two, but you will just have to make peace and get on with the mission." God gave Dedan a look that made it clear that argument would not be tolerated.

"Very well Sir. But may I ask why Hendrix?" Dedan's voice full of frustration.

"Simple, he actually knows the place quite well and besides he has military training, so I am sure that he will prove himself to be useful to you. Now please do not make me give you an order. Trust me. Now off you go, Jimi still lives in the same place."

"Okay, he has army training but is he experienced? Never mind…Yes Sir. On my way." With that he walked to the door muttering the word 'Hendrix' repeatedly under his breath. His mind full of mixed emotions, a desire to obey God without question but also contempt for his designated companion. 'Anyone but him, please anyone but Jimi, bloody, Hendrix' he thought to himself as he walked through the doorway out of God's office.

Chapter 23 - A Guilty Pleasure.

Roxy's exit from Limbo's presence, and her subsequent return to the tourist filled streets of Florence, was just as spontaneous as Dedan's trip back to Heaven. She found herself standing in the end of the Via della Bombarde, a relatively quiet street directly opposite to the Piazza della Limbo. She saw past the parked police cars and ambulance that the whole square was cordoned off with yellow police tape and guarded by heavily armed anti-terrorist soldiers. The use of guns and hand grenades in a fire fight, during broad daylight, had them alert and dangerously edgy as they looked out for any suspicious figures that could have been the perpetrators. Whereas before, when she saw them outside the train station, they had held their guns casually as someone would carry an umbrella on a dry but cloudy day, now they clasped them tightly in anticipation of having to use them at any unexpected moment. Fear of the unknown clearly visible in their eyes. Was the next person to walk past them going to be a terrorist or a tourist? Woe betide any unfortunate bearded Muslim looking man that crouched down to tie his shoe lace or woman attired in a full black Niqab that happened to sneeze too loud as she meandered by. It might be racial profiling, and scorned upon by politically correct politicians, but to soldiers and police officers it was all they had in their mind's directory of what a possible threat to their safety was. They might not be nervous enough to shoot first and ask questions later, once the bodies were in the morgue, but it kept them alert and sharp. Scanning the street, a guard saw her and looked her up and down assessing any possible threat that she might pose. Seeing the tight black trousers and compact body alluded to under her t-shirt he quickly decided that she was sexy but not a threat so he, reluctantly, removed his eyes from her and continued with his lookout for sights more dangerous than Roxy's. Relieved that her sudden appearance hadn't been noticed and caused overly curious glances she stepped into the street, that led away from the piazza, that was the cause of so much attention and began to walk back in the direction that she had early come; gingerly stepping over horse dung as she went. She knew where she needed to go, the hotel to pay the bill and ensure that all weapons were collected. No point in leaving such loose ends laid about the place. But first, and most importantly in her mind, she had something important that she had to do - her own private mission.

A detour that wouldn't take long but it was something that meant that all other priorities could move down her list. Side street after side street she went, keen eyes searching. Past the large, and stunningly elegant, shop windows of Tiffany's, Prada and Gucci. When she had been human, before her death, she would probably have spent a long time window shopping and admiring all they had to offer but, now that her time in human form was limited, she knew that she had to focus on what she saw as being most important. Such designer labels were no good to her, after all she was close personal friends with many of the designers, now they were in Heaven. Eventually she came to a busy road intersection and saw there in the distance, on the opposite side of the road, the target. Her personal and private object of desire, an inconspicuous small shop front with a big blue and yellow sign attached to the wall above the door; the giant white letter 'T', on a blue background, advertising the fact that it was a 'Tabacchi' or a tobacconist. No E cigarettes for Italians, cigarettes were still the phallic symbol of adult independence. Carefully crossing the busy, and chaotic, road which was the only way to cross any Italian street, she went into the shop. Then a few minutes later she re-emerged, onto the bustling street, with pockets full of packets of cigarettes, a hastily opened packet in one hand and a lighter in the other. Manoeuvring one of the white sticks, from the container, straight into her mouth she lit it and took in a deep appreciative breath, allowing the smoke to fill her fresh and clean lungs. Cigarettes were available in Heaven, but like so many things there they were sanitised and harmless and lost so much in the translation from the original vices on Earth. A great single malt Whisky tasted like manna from Heaven but there was no 'glow' in the throat when it was sipped. You could get drunk but never too drunk and there was no such thing as a hangover in Heaven; no matter how hard an angel might try. Pizza's tasted lovely in Heaven, but where was the full pleasure without the guilt at consuming so many empty calories? And the same applied to cigarettes for the smokers. No true nicotine kick that humans could always appreciate. Heavenly cigarettes had the same boost and emotional impact that eating a plain baked potato had. It was okay but not something to get excited about. No, this was one true earthly pleasure that she was going to cherish while she could. The rest of the journey for her was like a walking steam train. Plumes of smoke emanated from her mouth as one depleted cigarette was discarded and immediately replaced with a full one and ignited in a single smooth movement. The joy from each breath triggering synapses in her brain causing an almost sexual pleasure. A really good Earth shattering orgasm and a cigarette were two of the things that she had really missed during her time in Heaven, but alas she only had time for one of them.

Recognising that perhaps a non-stop shag, as she walked through the streets, might have been frowned upon, even in Italy. So maybe another time she thought! She knew Italian men and she also knew that there'd be no shortage of them willing to oblige her on that score as well.

But with smoking she knew that her time on Earth was far too finite and short so, other than the unlikely risk of being run over yet again by a cigarette delivery van, the health risks from smoking didn't apply to her, leaving her totally free to puff away with impunity.

Reluctantly she finally reached her hotel. Pausing she threw down her half-smoked cigarette and extinguished it with a quick twist of her foot. Smoking is prohibited inside all public building in Italy so she obediently, but sadly, complied with the law before walking inside to collect her room key and pay the bill to the surprised and bemused concierge. He wasn't used to people paying for rooms and then booking out the same day having not even spent the night there. With the price of rooms, it was hardly the type of place that you paid by the hour for a clandestine rendezvous with people that measured their friendship in hours and how much someone was willing to pay for their company.

Once the money was handed over to the concierge, she took the small elevator up to the top floor and went into her room. Removing all baggage from the wardrobe she placed them on the bed and looked at the clock on the wall. She just had time, she thought, so opening the shuttered door leading to the balcony she went outside and sat casually on the plastic and metal chairs, still hot from the warmth of the sunny day. There was always time for one last cigarette, or two, or three, or even four. Eventually, after losing herself in the moment, she found herself an hour later still sat in the chair still smoking. She also found that her once full packet of cigarettes was now an empty packet. She was tempted to open another but decided that time was no longer on her side and that she really should be heading back to Heaven and reporting in. She was sure that Dedan would have got there before her and have everything in hand, but even so she must get back. Finally, she got up from the chair, tapping her pockets to ensure that she still had some packets in them, went back into the hotel room picked up the heavy bags, opened up a dimensional portal and walked through it. The smokes in Heaven wouldn't be the same, and they certainly wouldn't last that long, but at least she had a souvenir of her trip. When she had gone the room was left empty and forlorn. Apart from a slightly crumpled bed and a lot of cigarette butts on the balcony floor there was no sign that two angels had ever been in the room. Any astute police officer, trying to trace the whereabouts of an English and Italian tourist, that just happened to be at the scene of a possible terrorist or mafia related crime, would draw a complete blank if their investigations led them to that room. Lots of possible clues but all leads would be dead ends, in more ways than one.

Chapter 24 - A Distraction

In Angelica's office all was busy efficiency, as it always was. Heaven's sound system was playing ambient music to fit her mood and was currently playing what sounded very much like Santana. It was quiet but still audible and gave the room a bright and cheerful feel. The buoyant guitar solo seemed perfect for that moment. As for the room itself papers were filed away. Records and reports were in the correct places ready for immediate retrieval should anyone ever request them; which nobody ever did. As for God's personal assistant she was dressed in her usual tight black skirt and clean and figure-hugging white blouse with the top three buttons undone revealing enough to entice and intrigue any male angel that just happened to be passing. Whenever she was in her office, dressed like that, there always happened to be a lot of angels passing. She was sat primly typing some information into her computer and giving all the indications that she was totally oblivious to Dedan's quiet presence. An intense stare dedicated to her screen and fingers a blur as she typed. Dedan stood quietly watching her, his back leant against God's now closed door. His right foot raised and resting on the wood, giving him an almost predatory appearance, or the impression of a lazy and misshaped sprinter about to run 100 meters, a coiled spring ready to be released. The angel's eyes carefully watching her, appreciatively taking in every movement of her curvaceous features. The longing and yearning like a plump child with his nose stuck against a bakery's shop window, looking longingly at the succulent and delicious buns on display. Wanting to hold them in his hands and taste them in his mouth. But despite all of Dedan's shallow lust and desire for something, he just couldn't have, there was something more than her body that he was struggling to put his finger on; there was a respect and admiration for God's secretary. He knew that she could be stand offish with many and tried not to mix business with pleasure but her smile and the glimmer in her eyes showed that there was genuine kindness, which wasn't surprising for an angel. But there was warmth there wanting to get out. Perhaps she had been hurt in her past life and put up tall castle walls to keep out unwelcome intruders? But never the less he wanted to storm the walls and get to know her better than the funny double entendre filled repartee that they occasionally shared. But he was getting the messages and reading the signs. And all the signs read 'No Entry!' Dedan finally decided that the silent impasse had passed over to an awkward and embarrassing silence as he wasn't sure whether she was actually aware of him or not. But either way he felt that he had better say something. "Hello Angelica, how's things with you?" Perhaps not the most scintillating of conversation starters but at least he had opened up a dialogue.

"Hello Dedan, I am good. And you?" Speaking without looking up from her computer, keyboard and steady and rhythmic typing. An air of busy preoccupation making the words seem forced and as if her question was rhetorical and she couldn't care less how he was right now.

"Yes, I am fine thanks, look Angelica after this next mission, if all goes well." His voice anxious and hesitant, like a plain looking teenager about to ask the most beautiful girl in the school to the prom.

"Yes Dedan?" Angelica's voice giving the impression, to Dedan, that she was preoccupied and only half listening.

"Angelica, when I…. If I get back from the next mission…"

Just then he was interrupted, mid date request, by the outer door opening and Roxy walking into the office. On seeing Dedan and Angelica her face lit up with a broad smile and her dark eyes seemed to be electric. Although she still had the same clothes on from the mission, she had left the cigarette smoke stink, which had accumulated on her clothing during her brief but intense smoking session, behind on Earth as she entered the portal that brought her back to Heaven. "Sorry I am late, I had to settle things at the hotel and tie up some loose ends. All is done and dusted now." She looked quizzically at Dedan's face; a physical canvas full of emotional anguish that was lost on her. "What's up? Sorry, have I interrupted something?" Looking self-consciously back and forth between the two angels, hoping to get an indication of what was going on.

"It's alright Roxy. I think that Dedan was either practicing for the inarticulate speaker of the year award or was trying to ask me out on a date. If it was the first, he was doing brilliantly and, if the latter, then he was coming across like a bumbling ass. Sorry Lover Boy," looking at Dedan "but you were."

"Well?" asked Dedan.

"Well what?" replied Angelica coyly. Enjoying the embarrassed discomfiture, she was causing.

Sighing deeply, he looked first at Angelica's face which was taking on a look of complete, but fake, innocence and then looking at Roxy and her look was of somebody trying too hard not to laugh. "Angelica, when I f...."

But before he could speak further Bob entered the room and stood next to Roxy. A look of total and complete obliviousness on his face. "Hi. What's up?" He enquired to the room in general.

"uck it!" Dedan decided that discretion was a better part of making a complete fool of himself in front of a growing audience. "Hello Bob, we have a little mission back on earth. We have to retrieve The Sword of Uncreation from some god forsaken bleak moor in Yorkshire."

"Brilliant!" Exclaimed Bob more enthusiastically than Dedan expected. "I love their beer and there is a pub I'd like to visit if I get half a chance. A little off the beaten track, but the barmaid there is…"

"Yesssss Bob, I am sure there is. But I doubt that we will have time for that. We suspect that Satan managed to obtain the location of The Sword from a certain human that you were supposed to be protecting. So now we need to clear up your mess."

"Oh, sorry about that. But, in my defence, I did try." The contritional tone in Bob's voice heavy, but genuine.

Realising that he had been a little too harsh on the angel who had, after all, done all he could to find Ernest. "It's alright. Shit happens."

"Damned right, exactly. Shit happens man!" Bob instantly taking heart from Dedan's leniency.

On the use of the word 'Man' Dedan reluctantly returned his thoughts back to the next part of his mission. "Speaking of 'man' we need to go and collect one more person for our little jaunt back to the wild and windy moors. Do you know Jimi Hendrix?"

At the mention of the name both Roxy and Bob looked at Dedan with open mouthed amazement. Although it is hard to believe that there are some people that don't like Hendrix, Dedan was one of them, however Roxy and Bob were both massive Jimi Hendrix fans, and as humans they had listened to the albums. On more than one occasion Roxy had made love while his albums played in the background and Bob had found his music to be a great seduction aid and occasionally a musical aphrodisiac. Other times he had just got stoned out of his mind while playing his CD's and LP's far too loud. But those occasions had been a life time ago. Or at least had been when they were alive. In Heaven they knew where his mansion was but neither of them had ever had the courage to go and ring the bell at the massive iron gates and ask to have a chat with the not so living, but still a, legend. They had both heard that he got lots of fans visiting him and had assumed that they'd be seen as a nuisance.

"Okay, from the looks on your faces you have either turned into goldfish or you have heard of the hippy git." Contempt wrapped every word. "Well it appears that in His infinite wisdom and for reasons, that I can't say that I agree with, God has decided that Mr. Hendrix should come with us. I personally think that we'd be better off with a lobotomised baboon than that stoned, preening psychedelic clothes horse. But it seems that we are all out of apes missing their prefrontal lobes, so it appears that we are stuck with him. Mine is not to reason why, mine is but to do and hopefully not die because of some self-absorbed guitarist."

Bob and Roxy looked at each other in surprise. Shocked at Dedan's uncharacteristic public outpouring of contempt for a fellow angel; someone that must by default be good. His dislike of St. Michael was well known throughout Heaven, and shared by most, but he never made such a public show of his feeling. The dislike of Jimi Hendrix must be deep for such vitriol. Ever the one for blunt speaking Bob spoke up first. "Call me psychic, but I get a subtle vibe coming from you. In fact, I get the distinct impression, correct me if I'm wrong, that you are not a big fan of the great Jimi Hendrix?"

Dedan narrowed his eyes and chewed on his bottom lip as he considered his answer. "Let's just say that he and I have had our differences in the past and my opinion of him as a person is not very high and I think he would be a liability on this mission. Or any mission for that matter."

All three looked at him waiting for elaboration. Silence was all they received. Whatever it was between Jimi Hendrix, the legendary rock musician, and Dedan, the obscure character from the Bible, he was not going to tell them.

"Oh well, I suppose we can't stand here all day reminiscing about the past we have a mission to complete." Shrugging his shoulders and raising his hands in resigned acceptance of the situation. "Roxy, Bob, shall we go? Au revoir Angelica." The trio of operatives then left Angelica's office, leaving her to muse over Dedan's cryptic words. Then she realised that she had access to Heaven's records. Perhaps if he wasn't going to tell her the story then they would.

Chapter 25 - What's the Difference Between Hell and Work?

Finley's sudden physical transmission from Ernest's padded cell to Hell had left him with a strange feeling in the pit of his stomach and his head. A sensation as if he had eaten too much rollmop herring that had then decided to have a knife fight with his intestine rather than just settle on disagreeing with him. Then, as if he had reached inside a medicine cabinet for some indigestion tablets, somebody had metaphorically kicked him in the stomach. To stop himself from falling he had grabbed hold of the cabinet and it had come off the wall and landed on his head. Smashing and sending shards of broken mirror into his skull. On the whole it could be said that the whole sensation had left him in a delicate state. The location for his random return to Hades had also left a lot to be desired and the ice forming on his nose was not what a demon, who had become accustomed to the boiling heat, particularly liked. Despite the old human adage about cold days in Hell, or the presence of snowballs, such things did exist there in a select number of punishment chambers. Although the snow filled landscape was not a place of childhood fun and games with snowmen, sledges speeding down hills or pretentious people skiing down mountains prior to sitting around a big log fire, eating melted cheese and getting drunk. This frozen realm was designed to provide exquisitely painful punishment to those damned souls that were deemed to be most likely to suffer from the experience. In Hell the punishment always fitted the sin. So large and jagged snowballs were not for playful throwing and were more likely to be used as iced suppositories or as weapons to be fired at high velocity towards people's heads. The punished were more than likely be used as sledges and ridden down steep slopes by the demon guards and as for the skis you do not even want to know. Such are the stuff of human nightmares. All that could be said was that the circumcised sinners were the lucky ones.

Finley had appeared buried in a snow drift, a disorientating process and had spent the first 20 minutes just trying to work out which way was up. Finally, after digging his whole body out, he then had the difficult task of finding a demon guard and explaining who he was and why he had to get to see Satan straight away. Upon finding a giant fur coated Yeti demon he had attempted to tell him the full story. However, his main points were first met with scepticism and as Finley had persisted the meeting of the words became more physical as blows were issued. As far as the demon was concerned everyone in his domain was scum and should be treated as such; the actual act a damned soul trying to lie, so that they could escape their punishment chamber, was not unusual and had to be dealt with harshly. Therefore, the furry creature had decided to treat the story, given to him, in the same casually violent manner. One blow had the effect of sending Finley arching up through the air and making him land on a hard and unsympathetic snow bank, burying him deeply in it. Leaving a body shaped indentation as the only evidence that he was there; the limbs and head tracing out a life-sized snow devil. He had extricated himself for yet another punch and icy burial but persisted in his attempts to explain to the unreceptive Yeti. After managing to dodge further blows he had finally found an argument that seemed to make sense to the belligerent and intellectually stunted guard. If Finley was who he claimed to be, and the information he carried was so critical to Satan, what punishment would the Yeti get if Satan found out that he'd been the cause of it not getting through to him? Being a snow-based demon, he was sure that any punishment meted out to him would more than likely involve pits of fire rather than strawberry flavoured snow cones. Finally acquiescing to Finley's demands to be released, and allowing him to go visit Satan, the demon materialised a door out of the chamber and, once the Yeti had seen his latest guest leave, he promptly closed it again, hoping that there would be no unwelcome repercussions for him carrying out his duty. Then he decided to rid himself of such thoughts by taking his anxiety out on the first damned soul that he encountered. All he needed was a pair of skis and a damned soul with a prepuce. Anger management in Hell could be a painful experience, especially if you just happened to be in the wrong place at the wrong time.

Once in the corridor Finley's senses were filled with the reassuring sights, sounds and smells of Hell. Screams of pain and suffering could be heard echoing off the sulphur and dark blood lined walls. Brimstone filled his nostrils and the blistering heat was a pleasant sensation after the cold of the ice chamber. Demons of all shapes and sizes walked past on their own specific tasks. With the ever-present suspicion and distrust ensuring that he received guarded and untrusting glances but, other than that, they showed the commander of the Marching Hordes no undue interest. 'There's no place like home.' He said to nobody in particular and began his walk to Satan's inner sanctum. Not a place that many demons ever visited, or wanted to, but Finley had good news and could envisage rewards for his diligence.

Thanks to the totally random nature of the process of travelling from Purgatory to Hell, Collins's return had been far less traumatic and complicated. He had the similarly painful feeling in his body, that Finley had experienced, but he had landed feet first in a dimly lit solitude punishment chamber. The ensuing loud chattering that ensued from the soul that had long been deprived of company had quickly attracted the attention of a demon guard and Collins had been promptly dragged out of the small room, leaving the damned soul to suffer its torment again; once more eternally alone and ignored. Back in the corridor Collins saw lots of demons busy with the daily routine, fighting each other or scheming. Slightly ahead of him there were a couple of ancient Chaldean demons fighting each other with chainsaws. He wasn't sure if they were serious or just trying to relieve the other of a limb or two as a bit of fun. With Chaldean demons it was hard to tell and their idea of a good time usually involved chainsaw and decapitation. Thanks to the deafening noise of the saws in the confined corridor there wasn't any opportunity to get past them, or ask them to move out of the way, so he just stood watching them and waited for the game to come to its natural and obviously bloody conclusion. They both swung wildly with spinning blades impacting spinning blades and instantly pushing themselves apart in a display of grinding noises and metal sparked pyrotechnics. Swinging them with the dexterity of samurai swords one creature would sweep it high to be blocked by the other. Then there would be the turn of the other demon to aim for his opponent's midriff only for that demon to jump backwards, missing being eviscerated by mere inches. Then there would be leg sweeps athletically jumped over followed by more random sweeps with the deadly weapons. Sometimes aimed horizontally, others diagonally or vertically; all in the attempt to better the other. The chainsaws wielded with more artistry and skill than any lumberjack. On the deadly game went with exhaust fumes, from the petrol driven motors, filling the area around them with the sickly-sweet overpowering smell, reducing visibility and adding to the enjoyment of the now growing crowd of demons, all hungry for the sight of blood and perhaps the chance of a piece of flesh caught after being sent flying into their possession. A little snack to keep a peckish demon going until a winner was finally decided. Although, to the other demons, both Chaldean demons looked identical, the crowds quickly chose sides and began to get into the spirit of the event. Like a rowdy crowd of football hooligans cheering when their champion made a valiant attempt to destroy the other and booing angrily when the protagonist opponent made some cowardly and underhand attempt to win. Baying for blood the audience were enjoying the free show. They neither knew, nor cared, what had started the conflict but they were definitely getting their money's worth. Back and forth the demons battled but neither could get the upper hand. At one point a fighter stepped too close to the crowds blocking both ends of the corridor and swinging his heavy chainsaw back for an attempted sweeping headshot that would manage to bisect one of the demons in the audience; splitting his head in two neatly down the middle, between the eyes, only stopping at its neck. The additional spectacle adding to the crowd's frenzy as blood was sent splattering over walls, floor, spectators and competitors.

Eventually the pace began to slow as the weight of the weapons began to sap energy reserves. Sensing that the end must be near the crowds seemed to increase their volume; shouting support as if the only outcome acceptable would be for one of them to end up in small pieces. With victory the winner swinging its, still buzzing, saw above its head in triumph. Finally, one of them seemed to draw up a final egg-cup worth of stamina from its reserves and briefly drawing its elbow back it then shot it forward again managing to take advantage of a slight gap in defences and get his chainsaw inserted deeply into his opponent's stomach. Muscle, blood and intestine were dragged out of the body by the spinning blades and spread over the victor. The vanquished eyes looked down at the new addition to his stomach and collapsed to the ground. The winner switched off his weapon and fell to his knees, his energy level totally depleted and no longer able to stand. Forgetting previously allegiances to one fighter or another, the crowd gave out a giant combined cheer. Then as the corridor was no longer blocked, by sweeping and indiscriminate whirring blades, the demons walked past the exhausted victor. Patting him on the back and giving him words of congratulations and then they were back on their way. The sport they had witnessed just another random event that happened occasionally in Hell. Seen and then quickly forgotten. And the pleasure given to the unappreciative crowd was the only reward for the winner. The loser would recover eventually, organs would re-grow and wounds would heal, over time, but until then he was just another pile of flesh littering the floor of Hell and providing light snacks to some hungry colleagues.

As he set off for Satan's inner sanctum, and private office, Collins gave his thanks to the surviving Chaldean demon, a 'Great show, well done' seemed hardly sufficient praise for such a colossal battle but it was all he was willing and able to give. Eventually he managed to navigate the winding paths and get past the countless demons without further hindrance and reached Stuart's office. Without knocking he entered and saw Stuart sat with his feet casually on the desk.

"So, you finally decided to join us Collins. Well done, very kind of you." Stuart's voice the verbal equivalent of foul smelling, vomit inducing, pond-slime. "Did you enjoy the fight?"

"Fight? How did you…"

"It is my job to know everything worth knowing in this place and don't you forget it." The implied threat of severe repercussions for any amnesia on that point was clear. "Finley has already arrived and is in with the Master now. He has told him all about the location of The Sword. It seems that you were more cunning and resourceful than I thought. Well done."

"Thank you." Collins was uncertain how to respond to such courtesy, especially coming from such a vile example of evil. In Hell compliments were seldom genuine and were often a precursor to knives appearing in people's backs; either figuratively or, more likely, literally. Machiavelli had previously held the post now occupied by Stuart but thanks to a string of coincidences he had made lots of mistakes and annoyed Satan, all of which just seemed to happen after Stuart had to, just coincidentally, visited his office.

"Go straight in, he's expecting you. No need to knock." The instruction accompanied by a casual sweep of his arm in the general direction of the door into Satan's office.

Collins was surprised at Stuart setting such an obvious trap for him. The knock he gave the door was extra firm, just to make a point to Stuart. Only when he heard Satan's booming and terse voice, telling him to enter, did he begin to push the big and heavy door and go in. Once inside the inner office, the epicentre of Hell, he used all his body weight to close the resistant door behind him and went to stand next to Finley. He stood silently listening to Barry Manilow's voice singing quietly on the sound system, waiting for Satan to speak. He waited and he waited, sometimes, in Satan's presence the silences could be just as painful as the words and physical punishments that accompanied them. Ever since the earliest days of his chosen career path, as the Prince of Ultimate Darkness, Satan had learnt the valuable lesson that being on maximum anger and rage all the time was a powerful weapon to use but it soon got blunt as the damned and the demons quickly switched off and let the vitriol and rage pass over them like a buffeting storm. In their minds they tied themselves to the masts until it was all over. And also, even for him, it was completely draining to keep up that level of intensity all the time. By the end of the day he was hoarse from all the shouting and the ensuing headache didn't help his mood when he was alone in the evening and just trying to relax, with a large glass of single malt whisky, and just blot out the incessant easy listening music. Currently Collins had caught Satan in one of his vocal troughs. Silence mingled with gentle speaking keeping the listener attentive and on tenterhooks while they waited for the inevitable peak of his wrath to hit them full on. Knowing it was coming was one thing but draining when you knew it will strike suddenly but no idea as to when. In the quiet zone Satan smiled almost graciously at

Collins. If it weren't for the red skin and wildly twisted horns sticking out of his head, he would have looked like any human high-powered executive sat at his desk. Elbows resting on his blood-stained antique oak desk absent mindedly looking at the palm of his hand as he gently rubbed it. Finally, bored with that distraction, he looked up at the two messengers, his face a mix of confusion and calculation as if he were looking at a pet rabbit and expecting it to calculate a quadratic equation and tell him the answer to 8 decimal places. When he finally spoke Satan's, voice was calm and almost friendly. "You two have done very well and I am happy with your work. You didn't bring the Guardian back here to face me and fulfil his contract properly, but such things are academic, you got the information that I needed and that is more important. I remember the Moor that he told you about. God threw a massive rock onto a handful of my best warriors. A dirty trick if you ask me. I wish I'd have thought of it first!" He smiled to allow his audience the opportunity to laugh at his mild joke which they did obediently but with little sincerity or enthusiasm. Satan scowled at them contemptuously. "I want that Sword." His words quiet but carrying more implied menace than any shouting fit could have achieved. "Muster sixteen more of your finest Marching Horde troops and make sure that they have brains underneath their helmets and not just muscle. I do not want them to sound like broken vacuum cleaners when they try and speak."

"Yes SIR!" Finley's voice snapping sharply with an efficiency that had been beaten into him as a human and was always instinctively activated when his troops were being discussed.

"Also, I want you to muster a battalion of Demon Cows. I know that Jon, the leader of the herd, still isn't walking properly after getting deeply attached to a bull during his last mission and most of his fellow cows, that went to Hawaii, were eaten in the line of duty but I am sure there will be enough of those dumb bovine knocking about Hades to be able to go to Earth and be of use."

At the mention of the Demon Cows Finley's face lost the pride it had acquired from telling Satan the good news about the location of The Sword. The Marching Horde had an infinite well of contempt for the cows. Whenever they had gone into battle with them, they had always failed to prove their worth for anything more than main courses. Admittedly the cows had the pent-up rage of true demon warriors and could quite possibly herd together and crush to death an unwary human but when it came to actual battles they were about as much use as a bullet proof vest made of wet two ply toilet tissue paper. He had yet to hear of any fighting angel that suffered from *Bovinophobia*, so they never struck fear into the enemy and when attacking their waddle wasn't exactly fast. The only weapons that they had were sharp but short horns. Capable of possibly injuring an angel if the blow was lucky and was in between plates in the protective clothing but on the whole the demon cows with their war cry, and unimaginative motto, of 'MOOOOO' were not a force to be reckoned with, more a force to be laughed at, a bit like the human equivalent of going up against the Bolivian navy.

"Sir, may I just…"

Finley's objection had been anticipated by Satan and immediately blocked. "No, you may not!" his voice sharp and gaining volume. "The terrain is not conducive to human combat and is better suited to less… Human forms. Besides, it is Yorkshire, famous for its farms. They will be fine. What could go wrong?"

In an act of self-preservation and knowing that the kudos from his earlier good work could soon be forgotten and replaced by punishments, Finley's desire to respond with words to the effect of 'Everything' were stifled and kept unspoken. He just stood to attention, nodded curtly and then spoke "Of course my Master. Your words are my actions!"

Smiling Satan nodded back at the two members of his personal bodyguard and law enforcers. He knew loyalty could always be relied upon, or at least most of the time, from them. "Good, I am sure that once this is all over, I can think about doubling your salary, now get out of my sight." Just as they turned, and started to head for the door, he spoke again "And bring me that Sword. Do NOT disappoint me." The last four words carried enough threat and menace so that they were left in no doubts as to what he meant. Failure was an option but, as they didn't get paid, the loss of any bonus was immaterial, but it would be an infinitely painful time for them if they upset Satan.

As they walked out of the office Collins whispered to Finley "I think I know just the demon to take with us as one of the sixteen. He even has his own chainsaw."

Chapter 26 - Refusing Heaven

Limbo sat in his usual chair and sipped his cup of tea. It was his favourite drink and, having experienced the coffee served in the many departure lounges in his domain, as far as he was concerned tea was the only drink. And in Purgatory, if you had any working taste buds, he was totally correct. Unlike the human perception of super beings there was no need for theatrical actions to make their will become manifest. No heavy blinking, strange twitching of noses, snapping of fingers or even saying gibberish words as magical incantations. The thought made it happen. Anything else was usually just garnish for any possible tourists and, in Limbo's mind, rather too showy and ostentatious. Deciding that he had waited long enough and, without any physical movements to make it happen, he made Ernest Higginbotham appear in front of him. On appearing in the private chamber Ernest's reaction was far more visible. He looked around the room in confusion at his sudden and unexpected transference from his padded cell to the delicately, tastefully and conservatively decorated room. He turned to look at Limbo, his suddenly healed face deep in concentration trying to remember where he had seen his host before - An action which was strange as most people would probably remember seeing somebody with wings and flickering blue flames for skin. "You're the one that took me from the morgue after I died in London!"

"Yes, allow me to introduce myself properly. My name is Limbo. I run Purgatory. And I know that you had already worked out your location so thankfully that saves a little bit of explanation. You'd be amazed how some people just find it so difficult to grasp the concept." He smiled disarmingly or as disarmingly as somebody with blue teeth and flaming lips can manage. "You are probably also aware that you have been judged and I have finally been able to come to a verdict. A judgement; if you wish."

Although he no longer had one, or at least one that a human would accept as one for purposes of digestion, Ernest's stomach churned in fear. He knew that his sins on Earth were great but having to be tried he also understood that his good deeds were numerous and noticeable as well. He had hoped that he would have been able to prove his eligibility to enter Heaven but knew that the demon's trickery had made him freely tell them the whereabouts of The Sword of Uncreation and he had yet again jeopardised the existence of Heaven and the fate of all mankind. Not great and memorable actions for someone trying to show that they were stuff that angels were made of. "Sir…"

"Please, just call me Limbo. I am not one for such formalities and titles."

"Limbo, I know that you have your job to do and as such I am damned but before you send me to Hell, I'd…"

"Hell?" Limbo's voice was full of surprise. "Who said anything about you going to Hell? I know it is almost unheard of but not unprecedented for me to actually have a chat with one of my domain's guests before they depart but you are one of the exceptions. Let me assure you that I weighed your soul as you talked to the demons and you believed in your heart that they were real men of the cloth. Had you known the truth you would have remained silent. So, have no fear, you can go to Heaven if you wish."

"Wish?"

"Yes, there is an alternative that isn't Hell and you facing Satan's displeasure at you breaking his contract. I see that your sins still weigh heavily on your soul and that is your punishment that you are not willing to be free from. A prison cell that only you have the key for. Heaven would be too much of a temptation for you to forget your past and allow yourself to move on before you are ready and able to forgive yourself."

Ernest nodded sadly, recognising that each word was true. He wanted to say more but words seemed reluctant to appear and try and add to what he was being told.

"Therefore, Ernest I would like to offer you a third option. You can stay here and work for me in Purgatory. Not exactly Heaven but far from Hell and you will find that I am, on the whole, a fair and good boss. You can stay for as long as you wish and if you ever feel that you are ready to go up to Heaven then I will not stop you. I can give you time to think about it, if you so wish."

"No." Ernest replied without hesitation. "No, I would love to stay here, it would be an honour."

"Good, I think you have made a wise choice. Now what are you like with paperwork? I have always thought that I could do with a personal assistant."

"I am sorry Limbo." An apologetic look on Ernest's face. "I can't stand the stuff; my idea of filing involves a waste-paper bin and a box of matches."

"Excellent, a man after my own heart. You're hired." The words accompanied by a raucous laugh. "Now that is settled, and you are staying, can I offer you a lovely cup of tea?"

Chapter 27 - Manual Ladyland

Heaven, just like Hell, is its own independent and infinite dimensional plain. Like the human universe which expands, only with the determining factor being the population not the result of some big bang making it expand. As more people enter the gates the realm grows. But there is no shortage of land or overcrowding, in Heaven at least. The good get their heart's desires and are happy. Greed tends to be frowned upon, but such an abundance of that deadly sin usually sends people elsewhere anyway. Therefore, if someone dies and their idea of paradise is a log cabin, by a stream in the woods, then that is where they can be. Want a penthouse suite in a tall metropolitan city tower block? Not a problem either, if it makes you happy then so be it. Many just know that happiness is with those that they loved, and lost, in life so they end up being in a heavenly facsimile of the home they had in the happiest times.

Hades has its rings that could expand as new punishments were created and occasionally extra rings were added, but room to roam and enjoy the stunning vistas were not part of the holiday package so a little over crowding of the damned souls was far from uncommon. Dark stinking corridors ran through the circles like spokes on a bicycle wheel and after a long walk you would eventually reach the ring you wanted and follow that circle and you would find the torment chamber you were looking for. Admittedly all the corridors, rings and chambers looked pretty much the same in Hell and signs tended to be more for gothic show and horror effect than to direct lost souls. There might be a Roman numeral engraved somewhere on the wall of an intersection, identifying which ring you were on, but that was usually scorched or sulphur encrusted. Signs above doors were often in Latin saying things like 'This Way To The Sorrowful City' or German 'Work Makes You Free'. But do not expect any signs saying, 'Welcome to the flaying alive chamber' or simply '42nd Street'. If you wanted either of these signs it might be better to try differing areas of New York.

Despite the infinite space concept of Heaven, the way to get from one place to another was far simpler, and easier. Infinity didn't mean that you'd have to spend an eternity walking. You could choose any method to get to your desired location and the duration of travel was also up to you. If you wanted to get to Diogenes's spacious barrel on the side of a dusty road then you could fly there and take a week, you could take a car and be there in a day or hop on a wispy cloud and be sat, asking him about his love life, within minutes. And so, it was with Dedan, Roxy and Bob's trip to go to see Jimi Hendrix. Dedan had things to discuss and plan with his two colleagues and he deemed that they could talk, walk and enjoy the views as they went. Although he'd never had the desire, or inclination for that matter, to visit Jimi's mansion Dedan know exactly where it was so he ensured that they reached their destination just at the right time. They casually walked by the side of the long, and high, white stone wall surrounding his home. The occasional tree could be seen growing, rising high into the sky, with branches overhanging and giving the path shade in the bright and sunny heavenly day. It was never too hot or too cold in Heaven but the breeze and ambience of the surroundings seemed to make it seem perfect. On they walked until they finally reached the tall wrought iron gates, painted black apart from the tops which had rounded spikes painted gold. Along the front were the words 'Lady

Land', each metal letter welded on and painted white. Dedan stopped in front of them and sighed heavily. 'Why me?' he thought again, to himself. Looking at both sides he saw no doorbell, button or buzzer switch for guests to announce themselves or gain access. "Bob," his voice stern and serious "we'll need to climb the wall. You come with me and help me over the wall. Roxy, you stay here, and I'll see if there is a switch to open the gate from the other side". Dedan and Bob walked to a part of the wall that had an overhanging branch, of a tree growing on the other side of the wall. Bob bent forward slightly and cupped his hands while Dedan awkwardly put his foot in Bob's hands and pushed himself up on the other's head. He flew up into the air and just managed to miss the branch by inches, causing him to fall onto the ground. Dedan swore gently under his breath while Roxy gave herself a frustrated face palm. Her urge to heckle and poke fun at them was stifled, for the time being. She could see the expression on Dedan's face and knew that here and now was not the right time and place. Even angels in Heaven could blow their top and whatever the problem or issues between him and Jimi Hendrix it was not conducive to a happy atmosphere. She just hoped that they could either settle their differences soon or be able to focus any animosity and aggression on any demons that they might encounter during the mission. "Right, let's try again." Dedan's voice was full of determination. He deliberately didn't turn around to look at his female colleague; he could imagine the expression on her face, and what she was thinking, so he just looked from Bob's equally determined face to the branch overhead. Bob and Dedan were sharing the same male ego emotion. A fixed and possible task where they refused to be beaten by something so relatively minor as tree branch being a little higher than they had wanted. As if he was reading Dedan's mind Bob assumed the same position as before and waited for Dedan's bulky frame to use him as an angelic spring board. This time the timing was slightly better and Dedan's fingers touched the branch but were unable to wrap themselves around the rough brown bark. Even in Heaven gravity is needed to stop the domain from being just a surreal place full of floating spirits so Dedan succumbed to its all-encompassing effects and fell to the ground once more. He released another expletive under his breath. Even though the word was in the long dead language of Akkadian and would therefore have been undecipherable by either Bob or Roxy. Even if they had fully heard it, they probably would have guessed that he was swearing and would have also assumed, correctly, that the word used referred to a sexual act. Getting up and brushing himself off he gave off a deep guttural growl that emanated from deep in his lungs. If he'd looked back and seen Roxy's face, he would have seen her covering her mouth in an attempt to stifle a smile which was in grave danger of turning into wild laughter. But, despite deliberately not looking at her, his imagination was accurate in picturing the look on her face. The thought made adrenalin surge in his body and the resolve in his mind stronger than any tempered steel. 'This time, you bastard, this time.' he thought to himself. Once more Bob assumed the position and braced himself for Dedan's weight. Foot in his hands, Dedan's hands on Bob's head as both pushed upwards and this time his trajectory and timing were spot on. Up flew his arms and his hands managed to wrap around the thick and sturdy branch. He hung there briefly shuffling fingers slightly so that they could obtain greater purchase and avoid slipping and therefore providing Roxy with any further excuses to release her pent-up laughter. He swung his legs a couple of times and launched them upwards. They wrapped around the wood and with the extra hold he'd gained he was able to wrap his arms around the branch and swing himself around so that he was on top of the tree's limb rather than hanging from it like a rather plump and odd shaped fruit that had been missed at harvest time and left to rot or like a giant deformed piñata for people with severe anger management issues. Carefully he pushed himself onto his knees, all the time maintaining his grip on the branch. Inch by inch he shimmied himself along it, closer to the tree trunk on the other side of the wall. "Bob," he shouted down to his assistant, slightly out of breath, "go and join Roxy, I shouldn't be long, and I'll see if I can open up from this side."

"Sure thing man." Responded Bob before setting off towards Roxy, hands in pockets softly whistling Hendrix's 'Little Wing' song. He was bubbling with excitement at the idea of finally meeting a hero from his time as a human.

Dedan finally reached a point on the other side of the wall that he deemed to be safe enough for him to let himself drop without too much of a fall. The grass looked short and neatly cut so there were no rocks to make it an uncomfortable impact. Embracing the branch like it were an ugly naked woman that was somehow hovering 12' off the ground, he swung himself around and allowed himself to dangle. Taking a few deep breaths, in anticipation of the sudden impact, he released his hold and fell. As his feet touched the soft ground, he instinctively allowed his knees to relax so that his body fell to the ground, rolling to

215

dissipate the force across a greater area. He lay there, briefly, on his back looking up at the leafy branch and tree overhead. He took a few more deep breaths and then rolled onto his side and lifted himself up. After a quick brush of clothing, to remove the brown dust left by the branch, he flexed to loosen his shoulders and turned, ready to walk in the direction of the gate; in expectation of opening it up for his retinue. On turning he was met by the sight of Bob and Roxy stood a few feet away from him. Both with hands clamped over their mouths, capturing the laughter that was valiantly attempting to escape. They looked like wise monkeys that would have easily received a long verbal train of abuse and expletives from an embarrassed and frustrated superior monkey if they had taken their hands from their mouths to laugh.

Finally, Roxy felt brave enough to lower her hands from her mouth. "Hello Tarzan, had a good workout, have we?" The teasing broad smile on her face making the whites of her beautiful dark eyes appear to sparkle with mischief with her seductive accent helping to take away some of his frustration.

"How the…." Dedan searched his memory banks for a suitable Akkadian swear word that would fully encompass his surprise at seeing Roxy and Bob already in the grounds of the mansion; with both, seemingly, without any signs of physical exertion or strain. Despite finding a few good old default Anglo-Saxon words he couldn't find any in the chosen archaic language so decided to forgo the catharsis of swearing, especially as there was a lady present. "How did you get in?"

Turning slightly Roxy pointed towards the now open metal gate. "It wasn't locked, I just pushed and eccoci qui." Pausing as the realised that she had broken into Italian and sounded like she was about to ask people to put their left leg in and their left leg out, before shaking it all about. "I mean 'here we are'." There was no electric switch just good old-fashioned hinges and muscle strength."

At first Dedan wanted to be angry but the continued disarming look on Roxy's face quickly calmed him down and the uncertain look on Bob's face also helped to break the tension and Dedan eventually gave into laughter. Freed of any risk of rage fallout from their boss they followed suit. "Well, I suppose that will teach me a lesson. Try the gate before de-evolving back to an ape."

"You had a few falls, anything hurt?" Roxy's soft voice full of mild, but genuine, concern.

"Pah, nothing hurt but my pride!" melodramatically rubbing his bottom as if it were sore. "Shall we go and see the owner and invite him on a trip? I am sure he is used to those."

"What is it with you and Jimi?" asked Bob casually as Dedan joined them.

"I don't want to talk about it. Come on, let's go." Dedan's body language making it clear that that story book was officially closed; for now, anyway.

On they walked along the cobbled road leading to Jimi Hendrix's mansion. Past ornate marble fountains with sculptures of Roman gods spewing water out of their mouths. "I hope they are not dead gods." Muttered Roxy, more to herself than either of her companions.

"Nope, they are just creative embellishments; Jimi's over the top rock and roll decorating tastes." Dedan replied casually.

"Never mind that I just hope that the Big Boss doesn't object. False idols and all that." Added Bob with a smile.

As they continued their walk they chatted amiably, discussing the neatness of the verdant lawns and the elegance of the views. In the distance a hill ran down to a lake surrounded by Willow trees, branches bowing down and leaves dipping into the water. Swans and ducks were gracefully swimming on the clear blue water and seemed to be basking in the glory of the day. On they walked up the gentle incline towards the imposing white building that passed as a simple *house* to the legendary guitarist. Finally, they reached the stone steps leading up to the imposing light brown wooden front door. Getting to it first Roxy gave it a firm 'Shave and a hair-cut' knock. She paused and waited for someone to answer. Looking at Dedan for instructions he simply shrugged. Turning the handle, the door opened easily at her touch. Turning to face Dedan again "Do you want to use the door, or would you prefer to smash a window and climb through that? Bob and I can always meet you inside if you want."

"Thank you, Roxy, let me think about that for a second." Making a dramatic show of rubbing his chin as if he was in deep thought. "I think that, just this once Roxy, that I will use the door. Less fun, but perhaps a little easier."

Once inside they closed the door and stopped to take in the view of the hallway. There were four doors spread along the walls at either side, a double curved staircase just to the left and right that met in the middle just above large, closed, double doors before separating again to go to the top floor and a curved balcony with more doors. Hanging from the ceiling was a giant Mechini crystal glass chandelier and on the walls were paintings in ornate gilt-edged frames. Bob moved closer to inspect one of them, a picture depicting a well-proportioned naked woman laid by a river with an old-style ghetto blaster music system next to her head and two cherubim's flying above her feet. A quizzical look appeared on his face as he pointed at the bottom right corner. "Dedan? It says here that this was painted by Rubens!"

Dedan stepped closer and peered studiously at the signature. "Yes. So what? Just because a painter dies doesn't mean that they have to put down their paint brushes and give up their art. No offence to the old master, as he is a really nice bloke, but I always found his style a little over-powering. But I do have a couple of Claude Monet paintings in my home. A wonderful painter but if you ever invite him around for dinner lock up the wine cellar!" They casually inspected the other paintings and found more recent works of art by Mantegna, Bellini and Dali and even Dedan had to reluctantly admit that Jimi had exquisite taste. Although he found Titian's large portrait of their, as yet, unseen host to be overly flamboyant and pretentious; just like the subject, Dedan thought to himself.

Eventually they finished admiring the mini art gallery and decided to actually try and find the owner of the building. They walked to the double doors below the curved stairway and Bob put his ear to one of them listening intently. "There sounds like there are people through here. Here goes…"

Swinging the doors outwards they looked into the room and saw wall to wall naked women laying casually on the floor, sat on soft cushions chatting or just walking about with glasses of champagne in their hands. On seeing the three new guests those closest to them smiled and greeted them with offers of drinks and invitations to help them to take their clothes off and come and join the party.

Bob's mouth dropped in a mixture of surprise and lust. "Well bugger me!" he exclaimed. "I've walked into a living album cover. Now why didn't I think of this when I was choosing my paradise?"

"Close your mouth Bob. You look like a train tunnel!" Roxy was not stirred at the strange sight in the same way that Dedan and Bob were, and she certainly had no desire to remove her clothing and join the display of flesh.

Despite his own private stirring in his trousers Dedan tried to convey an air of dignified indifference at the orgy that, given half a chance, was waiting to happen and decided to try to appear as if he was totally in control. "Good day ladies. Sorry to disturb you but could you please direct us in the direction of Jimi Hendrix? I believe that he lives here."

A dark skinned and full bosomed woman, stood closest to them, gave him a seductive and alluring smile. "Sure honey." her voice a soft south Mississippi drawl that would have been enough to arouse him if he hadn't been in a mission. "He is through that door. I think he's jamming with Miles Davis. He's been in there for the last three days." She pointed to the far end of the room, gave them another smile and returned to drinking her champagne and chatting to the woman stood next to her.

As they walked towards the appropriate exit it was only Roxy that seemed to be focused on the door itself. Other than ensuring that she didn't step on any of the unclothed women that were underfoot she tended to keep her eyes on her destination. Dedan and Bob, on the other hand, were being extra vigilant and were taking excessive care to look where they were going so that they didn't inadvertently tread on anyone. Although they were more than willing to provide medical assistance to any woman that might happen to need it. As they gingerly stepped between the warm bodies, they were met with sporadic invitations to strip off and join them but despite their unspoken wishes to acquiesce to such charming requests they politely declined all temptation. But both of them made a mental note to return here once the mission was over. Eventually they got to the door and Bob gave the room one last sad look, like a diabetic child in a chocolate factory that had been invited to have his fill but knew that he wasn't allowed any of the delicious and mouth-watering treats. "What a way to spend an afterlife. Jimi Hendrix, what a guy!" He muttered to himself.

Inside the adjoining room they were met by the sight of a large glass window and banks of knobs, dials and sliders all illuminated by blinking green and red lights. They walked towards the studio mixing desk and squinted to see into the comparative gloom of the darkened room on the other side of the glass. They first saw numerous large candles, placed around the room, their flickering flames casting dancing shadows on the walls and floor. Then, as they got accustomed to what they were looking at, they were able to make out several large cushions and bean bags, embroidered with Indian and oriental designs, strewn across the floor by the far wall. And there, on one of them, they could see the unmistakable gaunt face of Miles Davis, the candlelight on the sweat of his ebony skin making him look like a carved statue, only his movement giving him any impression of life; his black suit with gold patterned stitching dancing in the subdued lighting. His trumpet stood by his side as if it was a pet waiting to be petted. Then they saw Jimi, sat three cushions away from Miles. His hair wild and bushy, the same doleful eyes he had when he was alive but the thin and feathery moustache now part of a thick and full-grown beard. He had a Fender Stratocaster half in his hands and the other half resting on his lap as his arms moved casually back and forth up and down the neck teasing the strings as they went. Bob searched the banks of dials, quietly reading the few minute labels, until he finally found what he was looking for and reaching out he slowly slid one of the controls upwards. As he did so the booth was filled by the sound of frenetic but rhythmical guitar playing. It seemed to possess a magical property so that it was both invigorating and relaxing at the same time. It somehow managed to embrace the spirits of all three of them and make them want to just remain stood there admiring a true craftsman at work and enjoying their own private concert. Notes flowed like a soothing river through the room's speakers. Roxy found a swivel chair and sat down resting her elbows absent-mindedly on the desk before her and placed her head in her hands transfixed by the guitarist's every move. Bob leant against a side wall, casually stroking his chin as he watched his hero. Even Dedan was momentarily lost in the moment, but his reverie was short lived. On focusing on the busy musician, the anger and resentment that he had bottled up started to bubble and fizz like a drink that had been shaken too much and was just waiting for someone to innocently open it and get covered in a sticky mess. Gritting his teeth, he looked at Roxy and Bob, despite his own negative emotions he recognised the rapt admiration and love that they had for the artist and his work. He didn't want to spoil their brief pleasurable moment, but he knew that God had sent them on a critical mission and that must take priority.

Taking a deep breath Dedan spoke softly, with sadness in his voice. "I am sorry Roxy, sorry Bob, but we have a job to do. We need to break the spell and talk to him. I am sure that once the job is over, he will be more than happy to give you a private concert. But for now..." his voice trailed off as Roxy and Bob both looked at him with eyes that conveyed reluctant agreement with what he was saying. But the look also told him that they wished that the circumstances were different and that they could stay and enjoy the improvised jamming session. Maybe even hear a bit of Miles's playing as an extra treat. "I AM truly sorry!" repeated Dedan apologetically. Walking to the volume control he slid it downwards to, almost, its previous position, returning the booth to relative quiet. Then reaching over the control desk he clenched his fist and gave the toughened glass several firm knocks. Inside the candle lit studio, the unexpected noise dragged Jimi out of his daydream like state. As the concentration on his instrument had been removed, he looked up at the control booth, eyes blinking to get accustomed to the brightness of the room compared to where he was sat. Craning his neck forwards, and screwing up his eyes, in an attempt to see who was knocking on his glass window. "Who is it? What do you want man?" His soft Seattle accent calm and relaxed, aided by the inhalation of the type of tobacco that was still illegal in many American states but now, on the whole, welcome in Washington State.

Dedan bent over and put his mouth next to a thin microphone on a wire stand and pressed a wide black button, activating is. "Hello Jimi, its Dedan. God needs you for another mission. We need to talk."

"Oh, hi man, long time no see. Sure, not a problem. You're not still mad at me, are you?"

"Can we come in and talk?" Dedan's voice impassive and cold.

"Yeah, why not. Make yourself comfortable." Then, as his eyes finally got used to the brightness of the control room, he was able to make out the figures of the two other inhabitants. "And please bring your friends. We might as well make it a party. I have some grass."

Dedan, Roxy and Bob walked through the door leading to Jimi's room. Navigating around candles, tall but thin microphone stands and cushions they reached the still seated guitarist and sat either side of him; all the while being watched by the still and unspeaking Miles Davis.

"Jimi, this is Roxy and this is Bob. They are, shall we say, bigger fans of you than I am."

"Bob. Roxy. Cool to see you both." With that he reached across and shook the hands of them both. "Okay man." Looking at Dedan. "How can I help? Always happy to help the big G and who knows? Maybe you can learn to forgive me."

"I seriously doubt that but who knows?" In the darkened room nobody could see the expression on Dedan's face but if they had they would have seen a poisonous mixture of anger, resentment and frustration.

They sat on the unbelievably comfortable cushions and talked. Well, Dedan mainly talked. Miles sat there quietly listening and taking it all in. Roxy sat watching Jimi's reactions with undisguised respect; mesmerized by every movement of the once living, but now dead, legend. Her father had been a massive fan and played his albums often and always loudly, so she had grown up loving every long note that he had ever recorded. Bob also sat transfixed watching his all-time hero. He also admired Miles Davis but had his own musical hierarchy so Jimi was getting his full and undivided attention. Occasionally he would realise that his jaw had dropped down, with his mouth was wide open in awe, and when he noticed he would quickly close it - hoping that his hero hadn't seen him drooling. He had so many questions that he wanted to ask but knew that such things would have to wait. The words 'This IS Jimi Hendrix' kept bouncing around his brain like a pinball machine. Bells ringing and lights flashing as the sentence hit synapses after synapses. As an angel Bob had the body of a man in middle age, although he had modified it in

Heaven so that he was slightly taller and far more muscular, but in his heart, at that moment, he felt like a teenager at his very first rock concert consumed by the sheer enormity of the location and the aura of the flaming star on stage. 'This IS Jimi Hendrix' he said to his mind once more, in case his brain wasn't aware of the fact. Although his cerebrum was also well aware of who it was in the presence of and was equally impressed. If his brain had happened to respond it would have said 'Yes, I know. Cool isn't it?'

Dedan, on the other hand, was the only person that was not overawed by the person he was talking to. He remained detached and professional supplying as much information that he had to hand but impressed was not a word that could have been used to describe any of his emotions. He had his orders and would obey them, but the overriding words that kept swimming through his mind, as he talked, were 'Why the hell did it have to be him?'

As he talked Jimi occasionally asked for clarification on a few minor points but on the whole his demeanour and facial expressions, or what could be seen of them through his beard and in the subdued light, were perfect tranquillity and calm as if he was being asked to go shopping and Dedan was telling him what to buy. As the possible scenarios, and their various strategies, were put across to him he just nodded sagely and reinforced them with the occasional "Yeah man, cool." Words that did absolutely nothing to fill Dedan with confidence in the guitarist but eventually the briefing concluded with the usual asking if there were any further questions; which there were not. Then they all stood up and prepared to leave.

"Hey man can I come too?" Miles Davis's low pitched and mellow voice taking Dedan by surprise.

Taken aback by the request Dedan paused and looked at the trumpet genius, considering the options. God hadn't told him that he could take extra troops but on the other hand He had not specifically told Dedan that he couldn't take anyone else. However, he had serious doubts about what Miles could add to the expedition. Reveille, Taps or Last Post would probably not be needed and blowing the signal to charge any demons might just lose them the element of surprise. Plus, he saw no benefit of having free form jazz played as they walked over the Yorkshire Moors looking for the notorious Sword. But there was a part of him that just thought 'What the hell! Why not?' Surely Miles couldn't be as big of a liability as Jimi Hendrix. Maybe any demon on hearing jazz would be frightened away? Unlikely but it could happen.

"Sure." Was all he needed to say to the musician for Miles's sallow face to light up with happiness. "I know you two were supposed to have recorded Bitches Brew before Jimi died so perhaps you can work on it as we walk."

"Yeah, man. We can do that." Growled Miles casually.

"Right then, that is all sorted. It will be England so expect rain and please dress accordingly." Dedan paused and looked from Miles to Jimi, taking in their current flamboyant, gregarious and loud clothing. "And for God's sake you two, will you please wear something more conservative and suitable for the occasion and location?"

Both gave him broad smiles but there seemed to be cheeky glints in both their eyes which didn't exactly fill him with confidence.

"Hey man, you know me." Jimi's voice a mocking serious contrast to his happy facial expression.

"Yes Jimi. That is the problem!" Dedan lowered his head and walked out of the room rubbing his temples, closely followed by Bob and Roxy. "See you both at the dimensional portal station in an hour. Don't be late!"

Chapter 28 - If At First…

Some people find spelling difficult especially the word consternation, but it could have been written all over Angelica's face in illuminated manuscript. A monk spending a month with quills and coloured ink couldn't have created a more pronounced letter C. She was staring at her screen and not getting the answer she expected, or wanted, as if a fixed stare would change the unhelpful information that it was giving her. She tried tilting her head and giving the monitor a quizzical look but that didn't work either. Then she retyped in the search again and waited patiently for the little timer symbol to disappear and reveal what she thought would be different information. But no matter how many times she repeated the same question, or tried to change the wording slightly, she always got the exact same answer. The words were there in big black letters, 'CONFIDENTIAL'. They were in block capitals as well which in computing terms made it even more confidential than if it had been lower case. The initial mild curiosity, about why Dedan had such a loathing for Jimi Hendrix, was not mollified by the system's insistence on not elaborating on any part of the truth. After all she was God's personal assistant and as such was privy to all records and data relating to angels and what they had done on Earth. There was much that she had no desire to know, especially when it came to some of Dedan's exploits but, regarding this issue, her nose was so far out of joint it could have been on her forehead and made her look like a baby unicorn. She had tried the ultimate IT support trick and switched off the computer and switched it back on again, then repeated the search. But yet again her quest for knowledge was blocked by that one word. Deciding that taking a no for an answer was not an option and

'CONFIDENTIAL' wasn't technically the same word as NO, Angelica decided to change her approach. As she had access to God's own private password, which she had been given with the strict instructions that it should only be used as a last resort and an emergency she decided to use that. Using deductive reasoning the curious angel concluded that she could use as her finding the information was an emergency and, as her password hadn't worked, it was a last resort. Carefully she entered each character slowly to ensure that it was right. Then swiftly her screen flickered and the information on it changed. The message now read 'STILL CONFIDENTIAL!!!' the three exclamation marks adding to the veritas of the block capitals. She felt the uncharacteristic urge to swear but, having been brought up in a strict Catholic home and getting an education to match, she was unused to using such language and only had four such expletives in her vocabulary. One related to the sexual act, two were vulgar synonyms for a certain female part and the other was a popular but mild term for faeces. Out of those few choices she wasn't quite sure which one to use. So, lacking any firm favourite, she decided to avoid it completely and just say "Bottom" gently under her breath. After all someone in her high-profile position was not expected to use the same language as someone in the US navy and God might not totally approve; although she doubted that.

Reaching across her desk she picked up her telephone and pressed a couple of short form auto dial numbers. She heard it ring a couple of times before someone at the other end finally answered, a deep but puzzled voice spoke.

"Helloooooo?"

"Hi, St. Peter?" Angelica recognised the voice but still thought it best to check.

"Yesssss. Who's that?" a hint of impatience in his tone.

"Hello Peter, its Angelica ringing from God's office. I have a document related query."

"Reallyyyyyy?" After so many centuries of dealing with new arrivals and not being part of the 21st Century there were two things St. Peter was not fond of. Firstly he had stopped liking people long ago and secondly he had nothing but disdain for modern devices, and technology in general, always feeling awkward on the rare occasions when he had to use the telephone, so he always elongated at least one word per sentence in an attempt to make him sound like he was preoccupied in deep thought, rather than letting on that he was wishing that whoever had rung him would just go away.

"Yes." Angelica was already getting fed up with the conversation and was regretting it. St Peter always came across as having a mind like a three wheeled car where one of the remaining wheels had lost its nuts and wasn't too keen on staying attached either. "I have been trying to access some data on a mission that Dedan once went on."

"Sooooooo?"

"Well I am wondering if you can check your library of souls and see what is there?"

"Noooooo. Sorryyyyyy. You know I can't do that. Only four have access to that information and the library. You are not on the list, so you do not get in."

"But St. Peter please," Angelica's voice soft and gentle. "I am getting a message on my computer screen."

"Yessss?"

"It says it is 'CONFIDENTIAL'." Her voice managing to capture the block capitals as she spoke.

"Ohhhhhh, I seeeeeeee. That is simple."

"Really?" Angelica's voice rising an octave in anticipation of finally getting results. "And....?"

"It is simple Angelica. It is coming up with that because it is confidential and nothing to do with youuuuuuu!"

"Oh, cheersssssss St. Peter. You have been a great help." With that she put the phone down and returned to her computer, and uncooperative monitor, wishing that her vulgar thesaurus was larger so that St. Peter could be given a suitable word that fully conveyed her exasperation. Somehow, she would find out the truth, with or without the cantankerous Saint's assistance.

Chapter 29 - Cry Havoc and Unleash the Cows of War.

If someone, that hadn't already been briefed on the mission, had to guess the specific purpose of the assembled demons that were tightly packed around the cramped hall they'd probably be wide of the mark. Retrieval of mythical artefacts might be the idea of a quest to a romantic dreamer, but Hell wasn't particularly full of those. Magic rings, cloaks of invisibility and super swords did exist, but they tended to be ineffective against angels and devils so, on the whole, they ended up being left alone by both Heaven and Hell. After all who needed an antique piece of jewellery when going into battle? Demons knew from experience that human resourcefulness in the field of self-destruction had developed far better ways of killing each other. An AK47 might have been created in the 1940's but it was still far more effective at returning a spirit to its respective dimensional realm than a gold amulet or some potion created by some mad old hermit stuck high in some inhospitable mountain range. Weaponry had moved on even further, so the demonic weapons of choice tended to be even more powerful and indiscriminate. If the assembled troops had been given free rein, they would have liked to have gone to Ilkley Moor equipped with GB14 nerve agent or perhaps even a few small thermonuclear weapons. Thankfully Finley knew that such things would definitely come under the category of overkill so he had issued strict instructions that nothing deadlier than assault rifles were to be carried.

As for the demons, that were present for inspection, Finley was experiencing mixed emotions about them. First in line was Collins. Stood to attention, in green fatigues and carrying an M16 assault rifle. Finley gave him a knowing nod of hard-earned respect. Next the 15 members of his own detachment of Marching Horde made him feel proud. They had transformed from their assorted demon forms and adopted human bodies. The shapes were tall, muscular and menacing all covered by the same Marine Pattern camouflage fatigue uniforms. Their heads and chins were clean shaven and each of them had a look of psychotic anticipation in their eyes. A few were so psyched up that they were breathing heavily and sounded not unlike raging bulls after they had won their round in a bull fight and had the heart of a toreador still stuck on their horns to prove it. Finley was left feeling that any pre-battle speech worthy of Shakespeare would have been unnecessary for them. The blood lust was already there and the thirst was just waiting to be quenched. Thanks to his instructions limiting their instruments of death they had all, to a man, opted for the FN SCAR assault rifle. They knew that the weapon had been specifically designed by the American government for their special forces and it was the most powerful gun imaginable. If ever a demon truly needed to kill an angel then these were the toys for the boys. The M203 grenade launchers attached just underneath the short rifle barrels made them even more formidable and effective. As Finley surveyed them, he nodded in approval at the fine examples of military muscle and demonhood. Next in line was Collin's personal recommendation, the Chaldean demon. Although Finley had never seen him before, and didn't know what to expect, the demon in human form, was definitely nowhere near to what he had envisaged. The 4' 4" tall 'man' that was in the parade line seemed as wide as he was tall. The uniform that he'd been issued appeared to be struggling to keep the body inside the material and if he'd suddenly sneezed then the stitching might not have proved to be fit for the purpose intended and left him looking like a dwarf version of Conan the Barbarian. For weaponry he had a double barrel shotgun with a piece of old brown twine as a strap and it was hidden somewhere behind his compact and stocky back. He was casually leaning on his other weapon of choice - a brand new yellow and silver petrol driven chainsaw, which despite its own height being almost equal to that of the *trooper*, the Chaldean Demon was still able to rest his elbow on the downward pointing lumberjack's tool. Finley gave him a casual greeting and was given an incoherent but angry growl in return. His type of demon was generally well known for being bad tempered, vicious and anti-social and he was no exception. He was looking forward to the opportunity of going to Earth and hopefully inflicting some serious carnage, mayhem and destruction so anything that seemed like dull small talk was just wasting time and should be avoided. He had a chainsaw and what was the point of having one of those if you couldn't kill people with them? Obviously, there weren't that many trees in Hell needing felling, so its other possible use was not something he knew, or cared, about. It was unknown for any Chaldean demon to go into tree surgery and by the looks of this example it was unlikely that they would in the near future. Any trees cut down would either be by accident or because there was an angel hiding up one.

Next in line was a far less edifying sight. Finley looked at them and visibly shuddered, not so much from fear but from despair. If he'd have known about Dedan, and his resistance to having Jimi Hendrix as part of the Angel military force, he would gladly have swapped that one guitarist for what he saw in front of his eyes. Stretched to the far wall, and making several rows behind, were over 100 black and white Holstein Friesian cows. However, he didn't know the breed's name or even less care. As far as he was concerned, they were just dumb and useless bovines and even if they were demons, and had the evil souls to match, they were just dim, dull and monochrome cattle that were about as menacing as residents of a geriatric home on a day trip to the coast. In fact, he suspected that the old people would probably be more versatile and useful in the heat of battle. It was fair to say that Finley's view of the cows, as being anything more than a liability, couldn't be lower even if he'd formed it at the bottom of a deep mine shaft. However, Satan had specifically directed him to take them along, so he had little leeway to argue.

Reluctantly he walked up to the nearest cow and officiously looked it up and down with a sneer on his face. He felt no compunction to hide his contempt from his enforced herd of troops. Depending on the situation, and mood, the eyes of a demon cow could either be the usual vacuous and dumbly inscrutable black or, if they were in a sinister mood and were planning some mischief or devilment, they could turn a fiery red that was visible in the darkness of any farmer's field. Many a drunken field-hand, navigating their way back home via a short cut across a desolate field, had experienced such a sight. The cows liked to play such tricks and knew that the inebriated would never be believed; Demonical red eyes in the pasture? As if! Cows didn't have many facial muscles, and those that they did have tended to be specialised and used around the mouth for endless chewing. So, they were not equipped for laughing. But if they could they would have.

At that moment Finley was being observed by their black eyes. No feelings were conveyed but the lead cow was not oblivious to the negative vibes being sent to it by its commander. Well aware of the Bovinophobia that was prevalent within much of the demon community the cows had learnt to be sanguine bovines. They did their work and kept out of the way of others as much as they could. But it was hard for black and white creatures that could weigh a ton, and walked like their anus were chewing boiled sweets, to play hide and not go seek and be any good at it.

"Alright, who are you?" Finley demanded of the lead cow.

"Mooo." Relied the cow. "Mooooooo".

The vocabulary of the demon cows was not massive, even by the standards of the most inarticulate of demons. They had one single word but there was an infinity of subtle nuances within that single sound that enabled them to have long and in-depth conversations or convey even the most complex of ideas to the other demons and, for some unknown reason, they were always understood. Nobody understood how or why but it was simply accepted and left unquestioned.

"Okay, so Paddy, you are in charge of the herd." Finley's mind briefly contemplated asking the cow if it had its own field of expertise but decided that the humour might be lost. "Where's Jon?"

"Mooooo, moo, mooo, mooo."

"Oh, yes that's right, he had a romantic experience with a very amorous bull and is still *recovering*."

237

"Mooo."

"Yes, but from what I heard he quite enjoyed the experience. But does the bull call, does he write? Not a word!"

"Mooooo" almost making a laughing sound; with that being the only indication that they found the joke funny. "Mooo?"

"Don't worry about that. I was about to explain that." Finley then went on to respond to the request for more information relating to the mission. He carefully described the object that they were after, its history, purpose and current location. All the while the herd watched him with undivided and intense concentration, many casually masticating on their pervious meal that was making its slow progress around their stomachs via several chewing sessions before all the nutrients were no longer there. Where they got the grass from in Hell was a mystery, to most demons, but somehow, they managed to maintain the chewing, no matter what the occasion or situation. Once he had finished, he paused briefly to let his words sink in.

"Mooo, moo, mooooooo. Mooo!" Paddy was concerned.

"Yes Paddy. You know that, I know that but unfortunately Satan doesn't and it is by his special, and specific, orders that you, and all the rest of the herd, are here to assist with this, the most important mission in thousands of years."

"Moooo. Mooooooo!!!"

"I certainly hope not, at least there will be a few Marching Horde troops there so you shouldn't be, unless there are some randy bulls about; in which case you certainly, well and truly, will be!" Finley laughed but this time the cows didn't see the funny side of the joke. Having seen the nervous condition that their leader, Jon, seemed to be permanently in, since his return from Hawaii, they had no desire to be ravaged by a horny bull.

He continued his inspection of the rest of the cows that were lined up in formation. A totally unnecessary act as they were not carrying any weapons, other than their horns. As for uniforms they had the normal black and white leather hides which were standard issue to monochrome cows. Any general worth his salt would, when inspecting troops, have to occasionally stop and speak to any random soldier that happened to be unfortunate enough to be in front of him and Finley was no exception. He stopped every now and then to chat with a cow. Each inane question met with some equally dull and none descript 'Mooo', 'mooooooo' or even 'Moo' as a response. When he had finished his tour along the ranks of bovines, he felt that he had shown his little army that he was not totally aloof and was moderately approachable. And of course, like all generals, he had neither of those two qualities; a self-deluded officer was nothing new, not even in Hell.

Stepping back a little he surveyed his troops for one last time. He felt comfortable about the Chaldean demon and his own troops and was sure that if there was a battle, they would be ideal. However, for the demon cows, he had resigned himself to the fact that they were possibly more of a liability than an asset. If there was a battle then they were on their own and were expendable. Any angels could focus on aiming at cows while the demons could fire at better targets. Besides, on the plus side, if the real troops got hungry, they had their own food source willingly coming along with them. Demons, after all, were mainly meat eaters so a bit of beef was always welcome; the fact that it was donated by, or forcefully taken from, a colleague was of no importance.

Walking to the edge of the room he picked up his own weaponry. An old-fashioned WWII British army service Webley revolver and Uzi submachine gun. Then he returned to his original position. He knew that there was one unwritten military law which had been utilised by many of the greatest and most successful generals, from Alexander the Great, Caesar through to Patton and Rommel. That was the rousing speech to the troops, prior to any engagement. It was a tactic also used by the less successful generals, but history tended not to record their possibly great, but in the end futile, words. The soldier that, on Earth, had only risen to the ranks of second lieutenant was now a General in the afterlife and he was going to make the most of the role. He'd never given such a talk before, but he'd learnt enough about other leader's words during lessons at Sandhurst, the British Army's officer training school, and felt confident enough to cobble something together. After all his audience were demons so if he just repeated the words 'Blood' and 'Kill' enough times they'd be whipped into a wild frenzy anyway. Standing before his troops he lifted his head proudly and stuck out his chin, ensuring that those before him were silently hanging on his every word, before finally speaking. "Men…" He paused and realised his errors. "Marching Hordes, Chaldean Demon and Unholy Cow

Demons!" his voice loud and full of arrogant pride. "Soldiers, all demons love to fight, they love the clash of battle. The very idea of losing is hateful to us. And after all we have enough hate as it is!" He nodded at the presumed power of his own words. "If there are angels then they will see us and fear." Looking at the cows he paused and began to silently question his own words. "Do not hesitate and simply know that victory is the only option. Death to the enemies and victory to us!" He felt that he was getting their attention. "All right you bastards, we're not just going to kill the angels, we are going to rip out their guts and feast on them, real food of demon-kind. Then, when we have The Sword of Uncreation, it will be our turn to be on top. Wielding it to vanquish them and follow Satan back to Heaven. With him on the throne of God none can stand against us and those that did stand on us and kept the boot of tyranny pushing our faces in the heat and dirt of Hell, shall pay." Demons of various shapes, sizes and colours began to cheer, shout and *moo* loudly in support. In their mind's eyes they could imagine the final battle where they no longer killed and got killed only to eventually return or see their enemies return to keep on the eternal battle; no winners or losers, just fighting. They saw, in their enraged imagination, angels falling and never returning.

Seeing that Finley had his audience in the palm of his hands he knew he was running out of inspirational words but momentum was still pushing him forward. Struggling to think of coherent sentences he decided that random words would do just as well, as long as they were the right random words. "Kill, blood, death, chaos, mayhem, kill, blood and more blood!" whereas, before, his words had been close to the mark the lack of flowery and creative oration allowed the final points to hit the bull's eye. They were words that the massed demons could understand completely without having to process them. They could visualise the impending party and they knew that they were invited.

Marching Horde raised their rifles and began shooting blindly into the air, dislodging sulphur encrusted rocks from the ceiling and showing their heads in dust and rubble. The Chaldean demon pulled the cord to set his chainsaw spinning and in turn span his weapon above his head, narrowly avoiding the untimely decapitation of the Marching Horde demon stood next to him. And even the Demon Cows got into the spirit of the occasion. Their own red mist rage making blood course through their bodies and rage enter their minds, pushing any other thought, or emotion, callously out of the way. Dull and lifeless black eyes had been replaced by enraged glowing redness. Loud Moo's of agreement and general eagerness filled the room, drowning out the cheers and shouts of the less bovine shaped demons in the room. The reaction that he received made Finley smile confidently and nod his head several times as the adulation engulfed him. All that was missing was an enemy at which they could focus their hate and sate the thirst for blood. But he knew the time would come, and probably soon. The angels could be already there, ready and waiting. But, despite the presence of the cows, he felt that victory would be assured, he would retrieve The Sword, hand it to his master and then take the seat, which he saw as rightfully his, at the left-hand side of Satan's throne. Raising his arms triumphantly he pointed to the corridor leading to the dimensional portal. "Troops… We go to war. This time victory will be ours."

Chapter 30 – Hard to Pull Yourself Away.

Dedan and Bob had reluctantly manoeuvred their way through Jimi's main reception room, and the multitude of naked women, casually letting eyes drift and admire the views as they lifted foot after foot avoiding the tempting flesh that was strewn all along their route. Soft and seductive voices inviting them to divest themselves of their heavy and warm garments then lie down and enjoy the party. Although the casual t-shirts and jeans were not really that heavy, they had to admit that they were feeling distinctly hot and would have appreciated the opportunity to remove a layer of clothing, or two. Although, in this instance, the taking off of clothes would have made them sweat even more. So, knowing the time constraints, they decided to be gallant and turn down the polite invitations to enjoy the obvious pleasures available to them. But they simultaneously made yet more mental notes to find an excuse to return here once the mission had been completed and they had plenty of leisure time available to stretch and get their various tired, stiff and battle swollen muscles massaged.

Despite the same invitation being willingly extended to Roxy she was less interested in the scenery and more than happy to decline all requests. She wasn't prudish but, unlike most men that she had encountered, she wasn't a prisoner to a wild libido that drowned the brain in testosterone, making any thoughts, which somehow managed to survive, to make their lonely way to the genitalia; a strange battle headquarters. There it was no place for vital decisions to be made so that, when they did get made, they'd usually be wrong, ill-judged and came too soon. After the sixth refusal to strip off, and swim in the sea of flesh, her voice began to harden and acquire a terse edge to it so that each "NO THANK YOU!" seemed to rise by a decibel at each repetition. Eventually the trio made it to the room's exit and were free of the temptations. The irony being that if sex was really a sin then that room would have been Hell for them. Closing the doors behind him Dedan leant against it and released a loud sigh. "Yay though I walk through the valley of delights!" he muttered quietly.

"Amen brother, amen!" replied Bob with a look of loss in his eyes and defeat in his voice.

Roxy just looked to the floor as she walked ahead of the two men and shook her head despairingly. "Men!" That was all she needed to say; one solitary word covering a whole dictionary of disappointments, bitter experiences, lies and being let down. She was beginning to think that all the demons needed for winning any battle would be several battalions of naked women, armed with bayonets attached to rifles, making the first charge. Faced with such an enemy all the male angels would be so distracted that they wouldn't even notice the firearms and the angel's swollen ranks could be skewered within the first two minutes of the engagement, ensuring a demonic victory with absolutely no losses to their ranks

Turning she looked back at the two men, who were still leaning against the doors, seemingly unwilling to move away from it in case it was all just a dream that could never be retrieved. "Are you two coming? Or have you already done that?"

The sarcastic double entendre seemed to have the effect of being a verbal slap in their faces, dragging them out of mental orgies and into the real world where battles had to be fought, demons conquered and a sword retrieved. Returning her stare Dedan smiled sheepishly like a guilty school boy but his eyes acquiring an impish appearance. "Have no fear Roxy my angel, I only have eyes, and other parts, for you. I am ready to fight the fight and if I am to see action then there is no one else I'd rather see action with."

"Yes Dedan, I am sure of that, but shall we go to war first?"

Bob laughed, enjoying the verbal sword fight. Each thrusted word was parried and followed by counter strike. Neither one seemingly willing to lay down their invisible rapiers and allow the other to win. "As fun as this is shall we go? I think we need to get ready and Dedan's clocking is ticking so I don't want to be late. You two can continue this oral engagement at another time!" Laughing, Bob strode casually past them and out of the front door. Happy that he had been able to fire the final shot and have the last word in the game of innuendos. After all, he thought to himself, he wanted to come first.

Each of them made their own ways back to their own heavenly homes. Roxy had planned to change out of the clothes that she had worn on her visit to see Limbo but, when she looked in her spacious wardrobe, she realised that she had nothing in there that was suitable. There were plenty of dresses by top designers, jeans with labels that would have made owning them beyond her financial resources on Earth and high heeled shoes that looked amazing but were agony and impractical to wear and walk in at the same time. And that was applicable to perfectly smooth and flat surfaces never mind the uneven grassy fields and mud of a remote Yorkshire Moor. Picking up the phone she hit a single speed dial code and waited patiently until it was answered. Recognising the voice at the other end she spoke, allowing her Italian accent to come to the fore. "Hello darling, this is Roxy. I have a little favour to ask. I am in a hurry, but can you quickly create a little number for me? I am on a special mission from God and need to turn heads while I go un-noticed on earth!" She listened to the response and with gratitude and excitement in her voice she responded. "Oh, thank you, grazie, grazie mille. Ciao bella!"

Thanks to Bob's prolonged stay on Earth, as a guardian angel, and then an angel searching for his lost ward, there wasn't much in his wardrobe. His clothing was limited but upon opening the slim mirrored doors he saw exactly what he thought would be suitable and pulled the clothes out and laid them on the floor, allowing himself a satisfied nod of approval.

Dedan, of all the three, had the most experience of fighting on Earth and his wardrobe was full of uniforms from a wide range of historical periods. He had, over the millennia, managed to acquire a range of clothing that would have made any historian, or movie costumier, green with envy. Pristine white ancient Egyptian clothing with matching sickle sword hung next to a heavy metal and leather Roman centurion's breast plate and long *cingulum militare* – the belted groin shield - a piece of uniform he had reason, on more than one occasion, to be thankful for having. Then there was the stylish blue of Napoleon's

Imperial Guard's tunic hanging next to the dull khaki brown of a WWI American 'Minute Man' uniform. All still in immaculate condition and each single one would have made him a wealthy man if he'd have sold them to any reputable antique dealer on Earth. Nostalgically he flicked along the long row of military garments pausing occasionally to look at a particular piece of clothing and reminiscing about the time that he'd worn them in battles along with the fun and games he'd had in them. Oh yes, he thought. Many a woman loves a man in uniform and he had frequently enjoyed their enthusiastic, and physical, adulation.

At last he found what he was looking for, the pale green and brown camouflage pattern of the British Army number 8 field battle dress uniform; warm, comfortable and ideal for the weather conditions and terrain of where they were going. Removing it and holding it up to the light for closer inspection he nodded approvingly and laid it on his bed. Noticing the beige beret protruding from the jacket pocket he removed it and placed it carefully on his head. It had been a few years since he had last worn it but thought that it was appropriate. The dull brass cap-badge showing a winged dagger and the motto of 'Who Dares Wins' clearly visible when he looked at his reflection in the mirror. He had trained hard to pass himself off as a member of the world famous Special Air Forces, or SAS regiment. The demons might not know what it meant but he hoped that they'd find out the hard way!

Quickly changing clothes, he checked himself out in the full length mirror on the wardrobe doors. Despite his not very trim, and far too bulky, build - from his beret down to his highly polished boots, he looked every inch the hardened trooper reader to go into battle.

Chapter 31 - A Blocked Passage

The primary route from the chamber, where the demon army met for their muster, to the dimensional portal room was direct but it wasn't convenient, comfortable or safe. But, being Hell, the alternative paths were not particularly any better either. Thanks to the fact that to one side of the long corridor was a volcanic fire punishment chamber and on the other side of the passage was a sewage chamber there were problems not normally encountered on Earth. The entrance doors were secure, so escape for any damned soul was difficult but, like most things in the place, the fit was not perfect. The gaps between door and frame allowed for a certain amount of escapage of substances used for tormentation. The resultant combined mixture of released methane filled liquefied body waste and tongues of flame didn't make for a great atmosphere. The additional fire radiating through the walls not only made the corridor unbearable for those that were nimble enough to avoid the natural flamethrower and the resultant extra heating of the adjacent chamber ensured that brown geysers shot out from that side as well. Making the whole place a hot and foul-smelling path and one to be avoided by all but the most determined, foolhardy or just plain stupid. Thanks to the time taken for inspection and the motivational speech Finley had become conscious of time constraints and decided that the best way to get from point A to point B was a straight line, or as straight as the existing winding corridor would allow. Any detour would have taken several hours and he didn't want to take that easier route in case Stuart just happened to be spying on him, via some unknown method.

As they grew closer the front line of troops, which happened to be Marching Horde demons, intent on being first in everything, were quickly seeing the errors in their eagerness and slowed down. The sudden deceleration resulted in the problem that the demons, of various forms, that were behind them were using their momentum to push them forwards. As more and more of them saw first the stationary front rank, then the flames and what looked like a dirty steaming water spout, the trepidation turned to resistance. With the bovine contingent afraid that they might become flame grilled prime beef before they had even left Hell. In such a large contingent of them this fear began to manifest itself in a very cow related way. The noxious smell in the confined and hot corridor was not improved by the sloppy brown source of methane that was emanating from the end of the cows that didn't make a mooing noise. It was also fortunate that the cows were at the back of the line otherwise the Marching Horde, and the Chaldean demon would have had their light brown camouflage uniforms turned a much darker, stickier and damp shade and, even if they'd have escaped being hit directly, their boots wouldn't have remained black. Fortunately for Finley and Collins, who were bringing up the rear, they were far enough behind the cattle to avoid anything that was famous for hitting fans. Despite footwear discolouration the mess remained on the floor and would quickly congeal to a hard crusty carpet in the heat.

Finley attempted to push in between the unprocessed wall of steaks, in order to get to the front and find out what the holdup was, but the cows were wedged solid between the rough walls. He soon gave up on that approach and undignifiedly climbed onto the back of the nearest cow - not that there is ever a dignified way to climb onto a cow. Once he was there, he proceeded to walk precariously to the front. Body bent forward awkwardly as he went so that his head could avoid making sudden and painful contact with any of the various sized rough, smoke and solidified sewage encrusted stalactites hanging from the ceiling. Thanks to his weaponry strapped to his back his unconventional gait gave him the appearance of Quasimodo after he had been conscripted into the British army. When he reached the front of the unmoving troops, he displayed an unanticipated turn of gymnastic agility by placing his hands on a Marching Horde demon's helmet and vaulted himself forwards. Flying through the air, with more grace than a demon should, he landed perfectly just a couple of paces in front of the lead troops. If Olympic judges had been there, they would have given him at least a score of 9's. Thanks to his position he was facing his own troops so was able to angrily push his face close to the nearest soldier; eyebrows furrowed as he looked the soldier in the eyes. He took a couple of deep breathes, so that he could catch his breath, and instantly realised that the air he was eagerly filling his lungs with was far from being fresh and healthy. The coughing spasm managed to fill the lower ranked demon's face with projectile spittle. But despite the unexpected liquid he maintained his stoic appearance and kept eye contact with his spluttering superior. Any compunction to defend his face from the phlegm onslaught, or desire to wipe it off, was resisted. He felt certain that whatever words were about to be aimed in his direction would not be taking the form of positive reinforcement or encouragement so wiping his face clean would not be seen as conducive to kind words.

As quickly as the coughing fit had come on it was gone, the worst of the sewage enhanced air had been forced out of his lungs and he was able to regain composure; although the breakdown of his commanding poise and demeanour did nothing to calm his mood. Returning to his position, before the phlegm speckled trooper, he resumed his accentuated facial expression of anger. "Right, why have you stopped? What in SATAN'S name are you waiting for? A boy scout to help you across the road perhaps? Maybe you would like me to give you all piggy back rides so that you don't tire out your dainty little toesies? Well? Is there a reason for stopping?"

Uncertain how to react to the sarcasm of Finley, struggling to remember all the questions and their order the demon hesitantly spoke. "No, sir. No, no and err no Sir." Pausing as he allowed his answers to sink in and confuse his frustrated superior. "Sir, look, there sir." He pointed along the corridor in front of him. Finley followed the outstretched arm and turned to look in the direction of its forefinger. At first all he saw was a dimly lit passageway full of thick smoke and steam. He was about to turn back to the soldier and demand greater clarification when the gap in his knowledge base was filled. He first saw a jet of liquid fire shoot out of a fissure in the rough wall and fly across to the opposite wall. The resultant temperature increase caused a super-heated jet of brown steam to take to the air before it started to cool, coalesce and then fall to the floor with an uncomfortable squelching noise; leaving in its wake a fine particled mist of russet coloured waste product. The liquid that landed on the volcano chamber's wall created more steam and cooled it down, briefly, pausing the eternal flame and steam cycle.

"A-ha, I see what you mean. Gas masks were not on my list of required military hardware. But we do not have the time, and I do not have the inclination, to go back and find a more salubrious route. It would take us a couple of hours and that is time we do not have. We'll just have to time it correctly, hold our breath and run. If we get it right then we should all be okay. If we don't then…" He left the sentence end there, adding to the foul mixture already hanging in the air. He was sure that his troops would be able to finish the sentence in their own heads. Positioning himself he made ready to run. "When you see me start to run just take a deep breath, hold it in and don't stop running until you see me stop. Understand?"

As one his entire regiment gave him an instantaneous shout of yes/moo. They were brighter than most regular demon troops and could easily comprehend the notion of running and holding their breaths at the same time. Even the cows were able to grasp that concept without it being explained. Suddenly the volcano wall had returned to its optimal temperature and released its mini lava flow into the air. That in turn caused the same reaction as before and the foul smog was replenished. It was at that moment that Finley inhaled deeply, resisted the urge to cough it out again and began his sprint. Lowering his eyes and keeping one hand over his nose he ran. Legs pounding through the deep and warm thick brown mud, sending up splashes onto his formally pristine officer's uniform trousers, but such niceties were not important when compared to the risk of being incinerated before he even had the chance to leave Hell.

On seeing their pacemaker set off the front row quickly followed their leader and row after row they saw the way forward to be clear and took the opportunity to join the short race. Despite his diminutive height and the cumbersome choice of weapon the Chaldean demon had unexpectedly powerful legs that were well suited to running so he quickly overtook the rows of troops in front of him. He then caught up with Finley and sped past him. Reaching the far end of the corridor, and its relative safety and comfort, he stopped and turned to watch his colleagues. Thanks to his head start Finley soon caught up and leant against a smoke blackened wall as he caught his breath. The remaining Demon Horde then joined him and moved to the sides to allow the herd of cows to waddle inelegantly past them. Collins had managed to pass most of the cows and he jumped out of the way of their stampede and took his place next to his General. Just as most of the cows had reached safety a flame was released burning the tail of one of the cows, causing it to release a pain filled scream of 'Moooooo' and the same flame thrower blast gave a full broadside to the final cow. Instantly the side nearest the eruption was cremated adding the smell of singed leather, burning hide and well-cooked beef to the already repulsive atmosphere. Knocked over by the blast the unfortunate demon cow fell into the vile brown carpet of mud. The wounds not fatal to the eternally damned demon but sufficient to prevent it from going on the mission, disable it for a long time, as its flesh re-grew, and making it useless for anything but a giant ready meal to the remaining troops if it'd been able to join them on their mission on Earth. Looking at the downed member of his detachment Finley sighed. "Oh well, never mind." The words muttered casually to Collins. He wanted to comment about it being no great loss but thought that it wasn't prudent with so many of the creature's fellow bovines within earshot. Looking at his remaining forces he saw that they were darkened from the exposure to the unusual fog, uniforms were more naturally camouflaged and hides now had the appearance of brown Jersey cows rather than the black and white breed they really were. But other than one burnt and still smoking tail and the communal colour changes there were no other injuries. They may not be clean, or have an elegant bouquet, but at least they were battle ready, willing and able.

"Right men....errr...Right Demons." Quickly correcting himself. "Let's get a move on, we have wasted enough time as it is." With those words he marched forwards and took his place at the front of the line, determined not to allow the front rows to stop again. "Come on, follow me. Quick, MARCH!"

Obediently the game of follow the leader began. On they quickly marched, apart from the cattle as they were not famous for their ability to keep military marching time or formation, so they quickly shambled behind the, mainly human like, demons.

Eventually they reached the living landmark that was Carsten. His sore and red rear end stuck out of the rock wall with the old cricket bat handily resting against the wall by his side waiting for the next person to utilise it and gain the perceived good luck that was obtained by using it correctly. Despite the self-imposed time constraint Finley decided that they had enough time to uphold that specific tradition, and besides he had found it very therapeutic the last time. He had successfully completed his previous mission, so who knows, he thought, perhaps there was something in it after all. Grabbing hold of the bat with both hands he swung and made contact squarely with Carsten's already beaten and tender buttocks. Then he passed the bat onto Collins who promptly repeated the demonic equivalent of rubbing a lucky rabbit's foot. This was repeated by the Marching Horde and the Chaldean demon. However, lacking opposable thumbs, or even any hands for that matter, the cows were not ideally suited for playing cricket or handling a bat, but they had dexterous mouths so were able to grip the handle in their mouths and repeatedly issue their singular coups de grace. Any screams emanating from Carsten muffled and lost in the solid rock that held him. Once everyone had completed the striking of the bottom the well-worn cricket bat was carefully placed back where it had been before and the, now happy, troops carried on their journey to the large room containing the dimensional transportational portal. Once there Finley gave the signal to the awaiting controller and, in pairs, the soldiers walked through the ethereal door and were gone. Once all the contingent had disappeared Finley and his second in command, Collins, jumped through the door and were also gone, leaving the room empty except for the device's controller and an over powering smell of shit.

Back in the brown fog filled corridor there was movement against the far end wall. It seemed to move and separate, as if a large portion of it was coming loose from the main part. Slowly limbs became discernible amongst the black, darkened yellow and ochre reds. Then the shape began to change colour and it adopted a more human like form and appearance. Stuart, now easily recognisable, stretched and shook his shoulders to get circulation flowing through his body after such a long period of keeping still and observing the troops and their irregular march past. He nodded pensively as if he was reluctantly agreeing with the situation and then began to walk back to his office, along the corridor, a clear path through the solidifying mire creating by the sprinting troops. With lightning like reflexes, he jumped forward just in time to avoid a stream of fire and the echoed liquid outburst, but once totally clear he stopped and looked down at his formally immaculately clean shoes and shouted to the empty passageway. "DAMNED COWS!!!"

Chapter 32 - We Happy Few, Well a Few Happy

Thanks to Heaven being, well Heaven, its dimensional portal was better designed with access, convenience and space some of the key elements that made it a far better experience than Hell's version. Also, although the purposes were exactly the same, Heaven's method was far smoother. It didn't leave the transported angel feeling like they had been beaten up by a troop of bad-tempered Mandrill Apes suffering from severe hangovers and armed with hob nailed baseball bats. Instead, once on Earth, it left the angels refreshed and comfortable as if they had just had a soaking in aromatic oil infused bubble bath while listening to Mozart and sipping a glass, or three, of fine wine.

When Dedan considered the most appropriate method of transportation to take him to the portal, and the rendezvous with his assorted team of fighters, he weighed up the options but rejected all but one straight away. To him there was no contest, it had to be a motorbike, but not just any one it had to be something iconic and have a trailer full of cachet. In his mind there was only one choice and that had to be the Harley Davidson WLA 'Liberator' bike. He walked outside and went to his garage. Opening the doors, he perused the collection of assorted vehicles that he had grown attached to, and decided to keep, after various missions of Earth. There was a sleek black Porsche 911 Carrera sports car but that was as far as any of them came to being top of the range fashion statements or male penis extension type cars. No BMW's, Rolls Royce's or Ferrari's. However, amongst the collection that was lined up before him, there was a rusty old red Mini Cooper which had proven its worth during a chase along a jungle track in South America, along with an orange VW camper van that had been the accommodation for several convenient but brief trysts with both human and angelic females. It was deceptively spacious and comfortable although the suspension had seen better days. Walking along the cars he paused at some so that he could briefly reminisce on past adventures and he patted a few as if they were old and loyal pet dogs. Then, finally, he found what he was looking for and smiled at the sight of the green motorbike. The robust WWII design far less showy than later, but much better designs, that were rode in the 1970's and later decades. The 1941 machine was pristine and still had the military white star livery and 'US Army' stencilled onto the fuel tank, olive drab finish, higher handlebars and louvered blackout light. This time, when it came to him touching it, his fingers made it more like a lover's caress than the touching of a pet animal. The old leather seat felt soft and the metal cold against his skin. The memories of his mission on Earth filling his mind, vivid images of him taking the form of a member of the American 101'st Airborne Division and how he had destroyed a demon masquerading as a Major General intent on sending a regiment of allied troops to their destruction.

Coming out of his reverie he sat on the waiting motorbike and pushed down the starter peddle. Thanks to years of inactivity it failed to start first time, but after several more attempts he persuaded the engine to fire up. The engine's loud growling like a hungry tiger, in a circus cage, that had just seen its meal taken away from it and given to a dancing bear. The initial vibrations of the machine running up his spine making him feel centuries younger than he actually was. Turning the throttle, he slowly navigated his way out of the full garage, passing larger and more imposing vehicles, then, once he was out of the confined space and outside, he quickly sped up. With the roaring engine startling and deafening other angels who just happened to be on the street as he sped by. In his military fatigues and with the assault rifle strapped to his back he knew that he had made the right impression, he looked badass with a capital *bad*! To some vanity was seen as a deadly sin but here and now Dedan just didn't care, it was a last hurrah before he went into battle; a conflict where the demons might already have The Sword and they could use it on him. So, if he wasn't going to return, he wanted other people's memories of him to be exceptional - A rebel without a clue but having a true cause.

However, if truth be known, thanks to the loud roar of the bike and his attire, most of the angels that saw him were less than impressed by the heavenly easy rider and more annoyed at their peace and quiet being not so much broken as unceremoniously smashed. The general consensus was to think 'Oh, there goes that tosser Dedan showing off again, what a pretentious git!' He might have been a hero to many but that didn't make him perfect in their eyes and let him get away with disturbing the peace of the place.

He soon reached the entrance to the dimensional portal and dismounted his bike, leaving it at the side of the heavenly road. He knew it would be safe, after all who in Heaven was going to steal it? Even if someone took it for a joy ride, he knew that, of the most likely candidates, James Dean had his own motorbike and Marlon Brando wouldn't have fitted on it. Thanks to all the manna in

Heaven he had eaten he now needed a truck to move him about. So, it was alright being left where it was.

Walking into the large room he finally saw his valiant band of brothers, and sister, stood around casually talking with each other. The sight of the assorted ragtag bunch of misfit pseudo soldiers brought him crashing back to reality. Despite his inherent optimism he couldn't stop his mind from screaming 'If the world does come to an end, then it starts here!'

"Alright Gentlemen ... and lady." Dedan's voice firm and just loud enough to cut through the private conversations without him having to shout. Despite his role and position he didn't want to come across as some officious leader intent of sounding far too superior and aloof. After all he might not completely like the makeup of his group but they were a team and if they had any chance of success then they needed to be able to work together. Like it or not he knew that he would have to ignore his differences with Jimi Hendrix and trust God's better judgement. He might not have much of a plan but Dedan knew, from long experience, that God usually did. His supreme master tended not to risk the future of Heaven and the continuance of all of humanity on wild whims, gut feelings and a desire to annoy Dedan by making him be in the same room as someone he despised. "Let's get the show on the road. Can you all please line up with all your kit so that I can see what we have and ensure we are not missing anything?" The command was issued, and the entire army of four people casually picked up their equipment that was laid on the floor by their feet and went to stand in a short line in the centre of the room. Roxy, feeling the magnitude of the occasion, felt that she ought to be stood solidly to attention but when she tilted her head slightly forward, and looked at her colleagues on either side of her; she saw that they were standing casually as if they were waiting for a bus. Arms folded or hands in pockets. Not wanting to appear out of place she adopted a compromise at ease position with her arms behind her back and legs shoulder length apart. Dedan took one look at the strange quartet and began to question God's presumed infallibility. He wanted to give them the command to stand easy but if they were any more at ease, they'd be sat on the floor sharing a joint.

First in line was Jimi, his interpretation of a military uniform was a modern state of the art American army advance combat helmet with a night vision device attached to the front of it. And as far as up-to-date went that was as good as it got. As a jacket he had a 19th Century French Hussar's tunic, black with elaborate gold braiding zigzagging across the front and silver buttons which were unutilised as he had it open revealing his bare chest. For trousers he had tight black leather ones with the whole combination finished off with big black laced up boots. Dedan closed his eyes, held his breath and counted to ten. However, it didn't help as when he opened his eyes again Jimi was still stood in front of him and Dedan still felt like punching something, or more specifically, someone; and he had a good idea who that someone should be. Leaning against his right leg was a large black and red guitar case and an M16 rifle. "Jimi?" Dedan's voice was slow and deliberate. "Why the hell have you brought your guitar? Do you think that if we bump into any demons that you'll be giving them a concert? Play a bit of Voodoo Chilly and they will all just sit down, become mellow and forget what they have come for?"

"Relax man, trust me, everything's cool. It'll be alright. I know what I am doing." ignoring the cheap shot at the expense of one of his most famous hits.

Looking at Hendrix's clothing and chirpy face did nothing to persuade Dedan that the anything was cool or that anything would be right. However, he decided that correcting Jimi would be like arguing with a sherry trifle. The trifle would still be sweet but unchanged and he'd left out of breath, frustrated and wanting to demolish the whole thing in one sitting. He decided to let it go and just hope that, if there was a battle, Jimi got killed early on and didn't get any of his blood or brains splattered onto anyone else. That sort of thing was terrible to wash out.

Next in line was Miles Davis and that sight did nothing to raise Dedan's flagging spirits. The uniform bore no resemblance to any adopted system of clothing that Dedan had ever come across. His M1 type US Marine helmet was more Viet Nam than modern conflict but at least it was tested and practical, however there were three sticks of celery sticking out of the cloth band that was wrapped around it. If it was some form of anti-war message it was lost on him and if it was some form of foliage camouflage then it wouldn't have worked even if they were hiding in a field of celery. Any attempts at blending in were also lessened by the rest of his attire. His dark blue turtle neck sweater was finished off with a stylish red and yellow paisley patterned cravat. Dedan wanted to make a sarcastic comment about blending in and not being seen but thought better of it. Then he looked at Miles's trousers, light brown casual ones with shoes of a similar shade. Ideal for a stroll through a cosmopolitan city centre but there might be some obvious drawbacks when the smooth sidewalks ended and the less than firm ground was the only option. He tilted his head to get a better view of what was behind the casually attired soldier and was relieved to see that there was no sign of trumpet, cornet or a music case of any size or description. At least any guitar playing would be done as a solo. Instead he saw that Miles had also opted for the good old fashioned and reliable M16 assault rifle. Thank goodness for small mercies, he thought, at least Miles might be able to take down a few demons before he ended up returning to Heaven. "One question Miles, why the sticks of celery?" He was sure that he wouldn't like the answer but felt that he had to know.

"I like celery." Miles's deep gravelly voice showing no hint of sarcasm or irony.

At least Dedan had been right, he didn't particularly like the answer but there wasn't much he could say about it. "Okay Miles, seems legit to me!"

Roxy was the next smiling face he encountered in the line. He couldn't fault her for adhering to the spirit, intent and theme of his original instructions. She was stood there in appropriate British Army helmet and boots however the clothing between the two, despite its correct appearance, looked far too good. Collars, pockets and epaulets looked far too pristine, smart and perfect, as if a rich billionaire had been conscripted and not been able to escape military service. If it had been a dress uniform for parades, in front of the Queen, it would have been ideal, but it somehow just made him pause and wonder what exactly was wrong with the whole picture. Then it suddenly came to him. It wasn't the body that was filling the clothing out. Although Roxy did that perfectly the only way that so much subtle and discrete panache could be carried off would be if the uniform had been created by a master clothes designer. After all Hugo Boss designed the Nazi's uniforms so why should it be only the evil that were dressed in style? Dedan was no expert on fashion, after all, when he was a human, living on Earth, the idea of urbane sophistication was a dirty robe that could also double as a sack to carry dead fish. But he had seen later humans develop clothing over the millennia and could sense clothing taste even if he didn't have a taste buds honed for such things.

"Nice one Roxy, you look absolutely stunning. But then again you always do." The last comment made her tilt her head slightly and give him a coquettish smile, her eyes playful and bright. The army helmet and military camouflage doing nothing to hide her prepossessing good looks. She was about to give him a sarcastic response, but he continued before she had the opportunity to speak.

"Go on then, it is obvious that you haven't gone for some ordinary off the peg generic ready to wear uniform. Who's the designer, and more importantly, how did they manage to get it get it all stitched together in such a short time?"

"Oh, this old thing?" she put her hands to her chest as if to imply that she was wearing an ancient and ordinary dirty cooking apron. "My good friend Oscar de la Renta knocked it up for me. He always loves a challenge and said that for the right model he could work miracles. So, here we are. Amazing what can be done with a sewing machine in Heaven."

"Impressive but I hope that he has had it double stitched and is for more than just catwalks. The last thing I'd want to see is you stretching suddenly while in battle and all your clothes falling off. Going into battle against the Amazons was fun but this is modern times and the climate is not conducive to the Spartan style of naked fighting." He paused to allow that mental image of Roxy, in only her battle helmet, to run through his mind. He had other things to concentrate on, so he filed the pictures in his memory for retrieval and studying later.

"Don't worry Dedan. I'd hate to expose such a battle-hardened trooper like you to such a sight. You'd be amazed at what lithe gymnastics I can do and still keep my clothes on." Her smile full of mischief.

Dedan allowed that picture to develop in his mind as well then stored it in the mental cabinet with the other images. Some art was too good to be allowed to be lost. Once again forcing himself to focus on reality, rather than the private erotic exhibition that was his mind, he completed his inspection of Roxy, focusing on the practical rather than the aesthetic. He saw that she had the British Army standard issue SA80 assault rifle strapped to her back. At least she would look authentic when she was trekking along the moors. Any human seeing her would, hopefully, assume that she was a member of 'Her Majesties Forces' out on some manoeuvres. Taking a quick glance at Bob he wondered how they'd react to the sight of the other three. Unenthusiastically he positioned himself in front of the last member of his small squad. If Roxy's uniform had been the height of military sangfroid, then Bob was the antithesis. Oblivious to the emotional frustration that his appearance was having on Dedan Bob gave his superior a chirpy smile to signify how proud he was of his appearance. He looked like a survivalist that had a limited budget but had found some bargains at an army surplus store. His helmet was made of Kevlar and covered with a dirty brown cloth material that Dedan suspected had been used as a dishcloth or cheap dinner tablecloth in a previous life. His jacket and trousers were the same faded brown and green camouflage pattern and looked like they too had seen better days. The footwear was tight lace up black boots and they were the one part of his chosen wardrobe that looked appropriate for someone trying to look like a British soldier. If only any random human that saw him would only look at the footwear and ignore the rest. Strapped around him were several thick cloth bags bulging with unknown objects and in addition there were two further straps pulled tight around his shoulders that were supporting a large, heavy-duty back pack. It also appeared to be full but Dedan had neither the patience nor inclination to make too many enquiries into its contents. Bob was the person that had to carry it, and not him, so as far as he was concerned there could be lead weights, a small piano and a sheep dog in there for all he cared. And considering the odd collection of soldiers, and their choices in garb, he wouldn't be surprised if there were some truly odd things in there. Then, to round off the hillbilly look, Bob had a heavy looking belt fed machine gun laid on the floor. Dedan was not familiar with the make or design but he was sure that he didn't want to be in front of it when Bob pulled the trigger. It looked like it could not only fell a tall oak tree but deforest a whole wooded hillside in the process. But that was not a problem, when it came to killing demons there was no such thing as overkill.

Stepping back slightly, and positioning himself centrally to the motley foursome, he decided to give them one last briefing to ensure that the team knew what they were doing and didn't decide to go wondering off and getting lost amongst the heather and gorse of the rolling hills.

"Right, listen very carefully, I know you have been told this before, but I want to ensure that you KNOW exactly what we are looking for. There is a stone on the ridge of one of the hills which has an ancient swastika carved into it. It was done by druids so is more the symbol of peace and love than the sign of hate that is often synonymous with it these days. Anyway, it is surrounded on three sides by a metal fence but is accessible from the front. Buried underneath it is The Sword. We need to get there and dig it up before the demons do and then return to Heaven as quickly as possible. Once we have it, and if the demons turn up, I do not want to waste time with any battles. If they happen to get hold of it, we are all well and truly screwed." He paused to allow the words to sink in. He felt sure that Satan would be sending more than five demons to get hold of The Sword so even with the earthly assistance that was already there he was sure that they would be heavily outnumbered. "And remember, no matter what happens, do NOT touch or even go anywhere near the blade of the thing. One cut, or even the slightest scratch and it is all over for you. Goodbye to the good afterlife and hello to total oblivion and there is no coming back from that. Alright, pick up all your stuff and let's get going. We have some archaeology to be done!"

He walked purposefully to the dimensional portal, gave everyone one last smile, stepped through the aperture and was gone. No whizzes, sparks or flashes - just there, then a fraction of a millisecond later, he was gone as if he had never been in the room at all.

The rest of them quickly followed suit, one by one they passed through the simple empty doorway. Wishing the next in line good luck before they went and then they were all gone leaving the brightly lit and warm room empty and silent as if the former inhabitants had been just ghosts passing through; which, to some humans, was what they could seem to be. Just dead people returning to Earth; only these five were spectres with some serious fire power.

Chapter 33 – First Build the Barricades.

The rumours about the actual existence of The Sword of Uncreation, its whereabouts and Dedan's mission to retrieve it, before the demons could get their hands on it, had started to spread throughout Heaven. Then the initial vague, but completely accurate, rumour had begun to metamorphosis into elaborate and complex tales that grew and took on stranger twists as the people hearing the stories added to them and then passed them on for someone else to include their own private embellishments. Until, finally, the events and details bore little resemblance to the facts. However, far too quickly, the story began to run full circle so the angels that had started the rumour in the first place heard the mutated monster of a tale and assumed that it must be true. The finished version was that Dedan and six other magnificent angels had gone to Earth and were, at the very moment, face to face with a vast army of demons armed to the teeth and suffering from some kind of blood frenzy that would make a school of hungry sharks look tranquil. However, in their minds, Dedan had a brilliant and cunning plan, which they were unsure as to what it was, and that he had some sort of ancient mythical weapon to ensure victory. Both of which Dedan would dearly have loved to have had.

Eventually Heaven was steadily turning from a paradise full of happiness and love to a paradise full of paranoia, suspicion and fear. Some, trusting in Dedan's abilities, knew his reputation and had faith that he would save the day; with him probably ending up sleeping with a few sexy angels and demons in the process. Others were less convinced about Dedan's invulnerability and invincibility. They agreed that he was great in battle but were not sure if it was just luck or skill and to win against so many demons would need plenty of both. But they kept control of their negative emotions and allowed themselves to remain calm. Then it came to the rest of the misinformed angels. Left to fill in gaps with false assumptions and images of worst-case scenarios acted out on their heavenly doorsteps. They envisaged demons rushing the pearly gates, them toppling over with a deafening clang and then horned and hoofed creatures raping and pillaging before they used The Sword to send the inhabitants to nothingness. The panic that was gripping their inner beings had fingers stronger than a vice and was making them forget reason and to start running around like idiots. Admittedly they were angelic idiots, but they were often the worst kind. In their panic they were collecting whatever assorted weapons that they could find dotted around Heaven. Vigilante angels carrying state of the art shotguns, able to fire 300 rounds a minute, rubbed shoulders with people carrying crossbows, long bows and broadswords. They were all heading towards the entrance gates and readying themselves for some war which, in their overheated and unthinking brains, was inevitable and about to start at any moment. All that they lacked were the wooden pitchforks and burning torches and they could have taken on Frankenstein's monster and half a dozen werewolves. All new souls entering Heaven were confronted by St. Peter and his staff welcoming them but behind them was an ever-growing army of angels pointing various weapons at them. Not the sort of greeting that any of them had expected and definitely not a picture of Heaven that had been painted for them in any holy books or scriptures. It was left to St. Peter to impatiently reassure the new arrivals that they had actually arrived in the happy after life and that everything was alright, they had best move on and there was nothing to see here. Neither his words, or the tone of his voice, was convincing but the souls had little alternative so squeezed past the strange welcoming committee and proceeded to go and make themselves comfortable in what they hoped was actually Heaven and not some elaborate hoax where they were in Hell and didn't know it.

Even St. Michael, in his self-imposed isolation, had also heard the elongated version of the situation, the corrupted *facts* relating to Dedan's mission and had decided that he had punished the rest of Heaven, with his absence, for long enough and it was now time for him to return and take up his rightful place in front of the armies of God. Thus ensuring, firstly, the safety of Heaven and then, thanks to his superb leadership skills, the assured victory of his army along with the incumbent glory and praise that went with it. His swift return was met with ego bruising apathy. The vast majority of his troops, once they had been called back from their normal heavenly pursuits, hadn't even noticed that he had disappeared and those that had realised that he wasn't about had not missed him at all. Never was an army better ready for combat without its leader. Now that he was back, and there was a threat, they knew that he would have them filling every spare minute with pointless drill practice and cleaning footwear. They might not be fully trained in the operation and maintenance of the modern weapons, that they were all issued with, but at least their footwear would be immaculate and that was, in St Michael's eyes, the most critical thing. That alone, he steadfastly believed, would scare away any run of the mill demon. Nobody could ever mistakenly accuse St. Michael of being delusional and quite possibly insane. They could accuse him and there would be no mistake! Once troops were mustered, inspected to ensure clean boots and smart uniforms, with those that passed muster sent to take control of the pearly gates and disperse the ill-disciplined rabble without uniforms and, even worse, possibly dirty shoes. Those soldiers that didn't get past his intense inspection process were forced to clean their footwear before they could take their places with the rest of their regiments.

The random posse of self-deputised defenders of Heaven accepted the arrival of the official army but declined to return to their homes. Instead they took up positions behind the trained, and clean booted, soldiers; setting up a second line of defence and quite possibly a dangerous cross fire situation for those angels that happened to be in front of their weapons. On the whole the pearly gates had turned into one sided battle zone. With no enemy in sight all that they could see before them was an endless cloud filled no man's, or no demon's, land. Any demon that suddenly appeared carrying a sword, be it magical or not, would have been painfully dissected, eviscerated and diced by countless bullets before its body would have hit the ground and the spirit promptly returned to Hell.

Eventually Angelica heard about the situation, rushed into God's office and notified Him of what was going on. Her words left God bemused and unsure whether to laugh at all the stupidity, be happy that security was so quickly maintained and strengthened or just be angry at Heaven's inhabitants' total lack of faith in His judgement and ability to protect them. He frowned then took a long and slow sip of coffee from His favourite mug. The taste of the strong black mixture seemed to be like a magical elixir, calming any desire to get all 'Old Testament' on anyone and allowing Him time to think about the situation. He came to a decision and casually stood up. He greeted Angelica's puzzled and enquiring look with an enigmatic smile and almost imperceptible nod of his head.

"I'll be right back." Was all He said to His assistant and then suddenly disappeared. Being God had its privileges and the ability to dematerialise and then re-materialise anywhere He wanted to in Heaven was one of them. The location of His new re-appearance site was directly in front of the massed armies of St. Michael. The troops were tense, nervous and jittery. Therefore, the sudden, unexpected, and imposing appearance of a large figure dressed in billowing white robes right before their eyes, and more importantly gun sights, caused a tirade of bullets to be sent His way. In most situations this would not have been perceived as being the friendliest of ways to greet their God. His lightning reactions were fast so that He realised His critical error and promptly used pure force of will to freeze the bullets in mid-air where they momentarily hung like glowing hot suppositories before they gave in to gravity and fell to the ground with a metallic tinkling sound. The less than friendly fire causing no collateral damage to anyone other than the soldier's pride and ego's when they realised that they had opened fire on their God. If it had been St. Michael, stood there instead of God, most of them would have feigned contrition and pretended that they were sorry and who knows? Perhaps it would have been a genuine accident, but to open fire on their Supreme Commander in Chief was the unwritten 11th commandment.

God sighed, gave them a look that a science teacher would give his pupils after asking the entire class what 2+2 was and was given the collective answer of 'fried chicken'. He then rounded off the exercise in disdain by giving Himself a face palm. And when God gives you a face palm you know that you are REALLY stupid!

Allowing the wave of anguish to leave His mind He composed Himself and looked at the now cowering troops that were stood before him. Weapons now lowered like flaccid Casanovas caught in an icy cold draught. "Gentlemen, Ladies, My angels, eager defenders of Heaven, I thank you for your enthusiastically brave and valiant keen intention to defend Heaven from any demon army or even, apparently, any deity as well." He paused to allow his joke to sink in and let them laugh. Fortunately, there wasn't any tumble weed in Heaven as it would have been the perfect time for it to blow past; the shamed silence from his audience making it obvious that He had their attention, if not their humour. "I assure you that I have total and utter faith in Dedan and his comrades in arms. Trust Me, The Sword will not fall into any demon hands and paradise will remain just that. So please go back to your homes. St. Peter and his staff have a job to do and you are frightening all the new arrivals. What sort of first impression do you think that you are giving them when they appear in front of a trigger happy firing squad instead of smiling angels?"

The soldiers, and the mob behind them, lowered their collective heads in shame and gently nodded them in agreement. There was even the odd mumble of 'Sorry'.

"Alright." He continued "So please go."

The petrified crowd remained where they were as if expecting greater details to accompany the simple instruction. Once again it was one of those moments when God wished that He could get away with swearing in public. A loud and clear crude invective hurled at them would have sent them on their way but might not have left the right impression on the new arrivals or well meaning, but hesitant, angels.

Raising his head and arms in an imperious manner He furrowed His brow and spoke "GO HOME NOW!" Three simple words but God's voice left no doubts in the minds of any of His audience that He meant business. The air resonated as it carried them to each and every ear and even St. Michael felt that he should go back to his hermitage, at the remotest part of Heaven, as soon as possible. Perhaps changing his underpants, on the way, would make his journey less uncomfortable as well.

God leant backwards slightly, folded His arms and watched His army sheepishly disperse. Not a word was uttered as they left. Many wanted to stay and guard the gates, just in case. But none of them were either brave enough, or probably not stupid enough to argue with their God. It had not been done for a very long time and the last angel that had done it had ended up running Hell. Okay it was steady employment, but it wasn't a job that any of them wanted to try, especially as the position was already taken.

Once they had gone, and he was alone with St. Peter, He turned and looked at His loyal gate keeper, His face a picture of calm tranquillity expecting His loyal but grumpy saint to say something.

"I am sure you know what you are doing but I hope that you are not wrong. I know that the pen is mightier than the sword but if it is a battle between my quill and The Sword of Uncreation I doubt I would last longer than…" St. Peter paused, racking his brains to remember a measurement of time quicker than a nanosecond. "…a picosecond!"

"Relax my old friend." God placed His hand reassuringly on St. Peter's shoulder and re-enforced the gesture of reassuring friendship with a casual smile. "The mission on earth WILL be a success. I might not be able to see the future but on this one I am positive that Dedan will return and all will be as it always was. Trust Me."

With that He vanished leaving St. Peter chuntering under his breath but trusting in the words he had just heard. After all he had little choice. If God was wrong, he would have been as effective as a giant trying to wipe his bottom with just a single piece of tissue paper. And he'd end up in the same condition as the paper as well.

Back in God's private office Angelica was in a world of her own, deep in thought trying to guess what God's unique and ultra-secret password could be so that she would be able hack the system and access the appropriate folder, allowing her to sate her burning curiosity. She had already attempted a varied selection of permutations or words that might just have worked but none of them had been successful and all she got for her troubles were lots of messages on her screen in bold block capital letters and numerous exclamation marks. Unfortunately for her the folder she wanted remained frustratingly above her security clearance level. Looking around God's inner sanctum she tried to find something that could give her a clue to the magic word. He tended to keep to a simple formula with passwords so there might be something she could see to give it away. But wherever she looked all she saw was the same room that she saw every day. Nothing jumped out at her to give her the key to unlock the file.

Absent-mindedly she began to tidy up God's large and ornate desk. There were frequently reports, which she had created, laid unread on His desk and requiring filing. A pointless task in their creation but it was what He wanted. It wasn't just Earth that had bureaucratic and worthless paperwork made for the making's sake. She suspected that He insisted on it so that He could keep her as His assistant, but she was never able to pluck up the courage to ask Him. In addition, to the housekeeping, the empty coffee mug needed cleaning in readiness for His return. He didn't need to drink coffee and when a warm drink was required one could be created whenever He felt like it but God claimed that Angelica always made a better cup of coffee than He ever could create, out of thin air, so who was she to argue?

Suddenly God re-materialised back in his office right in front of the unprepared Angelica. It made her jump and the reaction resulted in her dropping His precious mug. Fortunately, for her and the mug, His reflexes were fast enough for Him to catch it before she had even realised that it was no longer in her hand.

"Butter fingers, I am sorry if I startled you, but I did say that I'd be right back. Anyway, as you are here, can you be an angel and make me one of your wonderful coffees?" He handed her the mug and gave her a reassuring smile.

"Certainly sire." Then, as she was walking to the door, turned to face him again "Sire, I have a confession to make. I have been trying to get access to one of Dedan's files."

"The one pertaining to him and Jimi Hendrix by any chance?"

"Yes, but every time I try to access it, and I have used various passwords, I get blocked. Can you please tell me what the story is between them?" She gave Him the most innocent look that she could muster.

"Well my beautiful angel, not much to tell but please close the door, sit down and I will tell you all about it, or as much as I can…"

Chapter 34 – The Lesser of Two Evils?

There are very few similarities between dogs and demons. Other than the teeth, occasional social sniffing of other's bottoms and the ability of some of the more agile devils to lick their own genitals there is nothing to link them. The expression 'Hounds of Hell' was more of a human literary creation than any reality. Demons tended not to fetch sticks and any tail wagging was done in a totally different, and less friendly, way. And in their defence canines, no matter how poorly trained or how large a beef steak they were offered, never sold their souls to Satan, sacrificed virgins at midnight or ever deliberately tortured someone else for fun.

However, the one metaphorical personality trait that they have in common is their blind enthusiasm. For reasons, that are still a mystery to scientists, dogs often see someone riding a bicycle and go wild and chase after it. However, even if they do catch up with it, they still have no idea how to ride it, but it is believed that most scientists just want to have a laugh and watch them try. The same mentality exists in the average demon mind. Give them something to get excited about and they will join the nearest mob and not stop running blindly about until someone with a higher IQ asks them to explain what they are doing and what they hope to achieve. They then might stop, scratch their heads and confess to not having a clue before they resumed their running. Unless, of course, they happen to be chasing someone on a bicycle, in which case one or more of them might know how to ride it. So, Demons 1, Dogs 0! This was currently the case in Hell. Just like Heaven the rumours about the mission to capture the mythical sword had started. In this instance the instigator was the dimensional portal operator. He had mentioned it to a couple of four headed Craaan Demons that just happened to be passing by. They had gone their own way and each head had taken it upon itself to deliver a slightly altered version of what had happened. Often one head would get everything completely wrong and the ensuing argument between the other heads resulted in a lot of head butting, spitting and biting. And any listener was left confused, optimistic but free to add elements to the story so that it kept sounding even better and could make the teller of the tale sound more interesting. The resulting demonic version of Chinese whispers grew faster and larger than any heavenly version of the story. The army of vicious demons, sent to Earth, doubled with every recounting and the number of demon cows decreased so that by the end of the telling there was a token smattering of cows there with the sole purpose of providing lunch if the proper fighting demons got hungry. Eventually, according to the rumour, there were fifty times the numbers of Marching Horde on the Earth mission than ever existed in Hell. Some demons even added the confusing fact that they were also on that mission, despite being stood in Hell telling others the 'facts' at the time.

The excitement and optimism, surrounding the spread of the news, also changed the whole emotional atmosphere of Hell. Grudges and deep-seated hatreds, that demons grasped with both hands and were reluctant to let go, were if not exactly freed then at least they were filed away for later and a form of peace was declared. Both the figurative, and literal, back stabbing stopped and the wary suspicious glances that were part of the fabric of Hell ceased as the demonic thoughts were focused firmly on the imagined images of the metaphorical shoe being on the other foot; or hoof, depending on the type of demon. Fanciful visions of The Sword in the unceasing and merciless hand of their leader at his most maniacal and vengeful; whoosh and no more saints, swipe and angels were gone, and then the final victory. The tip of the weapon piercing God's chest and, even before it had the chance to reach His heart, He'd be gone; a simple action turning their eternal enemy into a piece of history with their nemesis gone forever and giving them something that they all could boast about. Demon fancies of how they'd be able to tell any other demon, that was in earshot, how they were there and saw God's final humiliation and demise; even if they didn't happen to have been there or actually seen it. As there were many journalists in Hell and their often fictionally creative mentality had permeated the place many a demon's philosophies was one of not letting minor details, such as the truth, get in the way of a good story. The current tale had reached its most mutated at the outer rings of Hell and, thanks to the remoteness of the locations; their desire to be part of the action was most marked. In the atmosphere of almost giddy excitement, that was taking over the place, their punishment duties were temporarily forgotten as chambers were vacated by the demons and locked shut behind them. All with the unspoken expectation that the damned souls trapped inside would carry on with their punishments without the demon's intense, thorough and sadistic supervision. The souls, on the other hand, had different plans. Once they were unattended, where they could, they took the opportunity to remove themselves from the lakes of fire, sewage or other uncomfortable substance or remove whatever objects had been inserted into their various orifices. Once done they rediscovered the long forgotten sensation of being free from pain and torments. Several ingenious souls, in the Sisyphus chambers, even managed to aim the giant stones, which they were supposed to be rolling eternally up hills, at the chamber doors letting them roll freely downhill, smashing the seemingly solid and invincible doorways and managed to escape. Although, once they were out of the cells, they still found themselves in the prison that was Hell. But freedom, of any sort, was something to be savoured so they ran with the intention of finding somewhere to hid and then, hopefully, find a way of escaping. However, such urgency soon dissipated. As they attempted to evade recapture some Demons saw them but ran past them as if they were invisible, the evil minds fixed on more important things than a few wayward souls blocking up the narrow passageways. Realising that stopping their break for freedom was not a priority to the demons the spirits of the deceased slowed their running pace down and decided to take stock of the situation. There was always safety in numbers so, as and when the demons did decide to try and round them up, they had more chance of evasion if they were not the sole focus of any enemy's attention. They decided, wherever possible, to unlock the rest of the punishment chambers. Keys left in locks were turned, draw bolts were pulled back and doors were opened. The ever growing number of freed souls quickly began to fill the already busy corridors and exact their revenge on any demon that they could get their hands on. Even the strongest, or largest, demon was quickly overcome and defeated, like a bull elephant succumbing to the onslaught of an army of soldier ants; the sheer force of numbers on their side, dragging their prey to the ground. The demons couldn't die but they could be mutilated and the painful injuries sustained would take a long time to heal. Vengeance enacted as swiftly as they could.

Many of the outer ring demons had moved well away from the corridors containing entrances to punishment chambers, and freed prisoners, and were currently raiding armouries and arsenals. Arming themselves as if The Sword of Uncreation were already in their possession and they were just about to set off to war. State of the art weapons were strapped to backs, tucked into belts, stuffed into boots and carried in as many hands as the particular demon possessed. The propensity for greed was such that the stores were soon emptied and those demons that found themselves unarmed had to set up their own private little battles as firearms were wrenched from those that had them. Despite all the minor scuffles, there were very few injuries. The overriding desire was to be able to participate in the, presumed, forthcoming apocalyptical war and they knew that if they were injured and incapacitated then they would miss the show. The idea of killing angels was more appetising than having a small fight with a fellow demon over a gun or two. As long as they had at least one weapon then they were happy; or as happy as demons could get.

Other demons, from the same area, were even more ahead in the thought process and had assumed that the battle had been won and victory was already theirs, and the fight was just a formality. Those optimistic ones had circumnavigated the weapon storage area and headed straight for the stores of alcohol. Thanks to the nature of demons the doors to those places were far more secure than those that kept the weaponry. But such obstacles were quickly overcome, and access gained. Solid locks were smashed with doors ripped open in the rush to find inebriation. Hell's beer and the, more literal, spirits were not the greatest quality, they all tended to have a taste which made mange ridden donkey's urine and an after taste, that quickly followed the initial taste, seem like Heaven's manna. Temporary blindness, insanity and rigor mortis – while still living – was not uncommon. But it was strong, and the pains of sobriety didn't survive long against the onslaught of the vile liquids. The promptly drunken demons began to lose faculties and what little sense that they had previously possessed. The initial wave of aggression quickly passed with minimal violence being aimed at each other and the traditional cries of 'I bloody love you mate.' And 'You're my best mate, you are' could be clearly heard echoing off nearby walls. This premature celebrations and festivities began to reduce the number of conscious demons as one by one they fell to the floor and capitulated to the soporific qualities of the demon drink. Bodies lay haphazardly next to, underneath or on top of other demons. Impervious to any discomfort or pain caused by being crushed or the, less than healthy, booze burning like acid in their stomachs. Eventually all that could be heard from the insensible multitude was sporadic sleep-talking, snoring or the loud breaking of wind.

The demons that had more militaristic priorities were oblivious and apathetic to their unconscious colleagues. Any resentment, or envy, they might have normally had was forgotten as they fantasised about the far superior and plentiful concoctions that could be drunk in Heaven. Victory celebrations as they danced in the clean and luxurious halls in Heaven so recently occupied by angels but now owned by them. All that they currently lacked was The Sword. The realisation that they were all battle dressed up, with nowhere to go, made some of them realise that they might just have been in too much of a rush. They began to wonder what they should do next when their unspoken questions were answered by a wave of freed souls charging along narrow corridors, from all directions, towards them. Their deafening cries adding to the surprise, chaos and confusion of the situation. The demons were not used to the souls of the damned attacking and they were certainly not expecting them, but the damned were not concerned about their social faux pas, or the unusual situation they had just created, they had yet more vengeance on their minds.

While the damned had been kept tightly confined and controlled in a vast number of various, and creative, punishment chambers they had been manageable. Irrespective of the number of residents a small number of demons could run an individual chamber and the only difficulties would be thinking of new and imaginative ways to inflict pain. Discipline and abject subservience were maintained mainly by threats, fear and implements whose primary purposes were not always designed for torture but had been adapted for use in Hell. The constant and unrelenting agony that was given left the victims too weak to do anything. Although Jimmy Hoffa was a resident there were no unions in Hell, so conditions remained poor, with the opportunity to strike for less pain were not an option. So, they just had to suffer in silence, or suffer in loud screams, but either way the suffering was what they did the most of. The chant of '*I'm Mad, in Hell and I am not going to take it anymore*' was never heard, especially by those unfortunate enough to be receiving a punishment which involved them having their heads immersed in noxious substances, and even if someone was foolish enough to take up the cry they would have been made to pay dearly for the impudent dissention.

But now that they were free of their specific punishments the combined numbers made the demon contingent seem small and insignificant. If you had to describe the shape of the escapees, you'd have had to just say it was poor. Emaciated bodies with broken and disfigured bones, formed from eons of mistreatment and beatings, made them look more pathetic than terrifying. Almost walking like zombies, feet dragging, and skeletal fingers outstretched, aiming to inflict injury to any demon they could get hold of; bodies broken but not their minds. The combined evil that they had practiced on Earth and the punishments received in Hell giving them plenty of ideas for payback on their former tormentors. If they could get up close and personal enough to use teeth, as part of the retribution, then even better. Demon flesh might be hard and full of poison but, to the damned, the vengeance they'd be getting would make it taste sweet.

Despite the tight and undulating corridors, limiting the demon's view of the oncoming mass, the millennia worth of souls when combined into a single group, was impressive. If the heavily armed demons had been able to completely see what was coming towards them then they would have been far more daunted than they actually were. The current appraisal of the situation was limited so they just assumed that a few prisoners had escaped their confines and were surging towards them, insignificant and would easily be dealt with by the release of a few indiscriminate rounds. Sub-machine guns, automatic pistols and semi-automatic rifles were casually raised with the first volleys of scorching projectiles released towards the frantic attackers. In each corridor the first line of approaching souls took the brunt of the onslaught. Some high velocity bullets passed through their bodies and also hit the ones behind. Flesh smashed into the living corpses, immobilised yet forever unable to die, falling to the hard and rocky ground. The next line, immediately behind them, quickly took the places vacated by the fallen allies. Seeing a new set of targets the demons pulled triggers again spraying round after round into them. Bodies fell upon bodies but still they advanced. Occasionally a damned soul would have the energy and take the opportunity to blindly rush their target but would soon, in turn, become the target for the focused demon fire and be cut down, and to pieces, without getting close enough to the enemy to harm them. Realising that they had nothing to lose, and everything to gain, the damned's advances continued. Magazines in the assorted weapons emptied and were quickly replaced with full ones before the targets could get any closer. But retreating was not an option for either side. The demons were surrounded and had nowhere to run to and the damned couldn't retreat; the sheer force of numbers meaning that they could only travel in one direction, forwards. Eventually, as the area filled with smoke, the mound of bodies grew making advancing even more difficult. The need to step over the incapacitated corpses was replaced by the requirement to climb over them as best they could. Then there were walls of cadavers providing bullet proof shields to the damned but also forming an impenetrable barrier blocking their advance. The bloody impasse allowing the desperate souls to pause and rest, demons to reload if they had any ammunition left or, for those that had run out, to just ready any available knives for close quarters combat. As the din of battle faded, and the smoke disappeared, they were able to take stock of the situation. Although no demon had been injured ammunition was drastically low, they were outnumbered, surrounded and they had no way of getting any messages out and demanding reinforcements. On the plus side some of the previously drunken and unconscious demons began to regain consciousness. In their previous state they had been oblivious to the noises, smells and sights of the war that had erupted around them but in their new groggy and hung-over condition they began to realise that they hadn't woken up to another ordinary day in Hell. The waking creatures had sharp talons, teeth and horns, with which to join the fight, but none of them had the same firepower of their fellow demons. Undeterred by that fact they quickly took their place in the battle lines ready to defend themselves against the next wave of attack, as and when it happened. Teeth clenched and eyes burning red their internalised rage was focused and tensely waiting to be released, inner emotional demons inside real demons. They had inflicted enough torments to know what to expect if they failed, so their determination was equal to the damned souls who had the same desire to provide retribution on their gaolers.

Not all of the demons, in the various other rings of Hell, had been swept away with the premature euphoria of the earthly battle which they believed was being won by Finley and, in turn, Heaven changing hands. Many had remained where they were, carrying out their set duties and routines. Discipline, or as close to discipline as a demon could get, was maintained. They had not rushed to arm themselves, get drunk or desert their posts. However, thanks to the remoteness to the scene of the impromptu battle, on a remote outer ring of Hell, they were unaware of any trouble or disturbances. Assistance could have been given if only they had known that it was required.

The only demon, outside of the encircled ones, that knew that anything untoward was going on was Stuart. His ability to spy, unobserved, on any and all areas of Hell was legendary and kept many a demon from planning a coupe. By opening mini portals, within Hell, he was able to move from one place to another and his chameleonic ability to blend into the background ensured he was never noticed, his naturally loathsome body odour also assisted with blending in. As part of his routine he regularly visited all the rings of Hell to keep abreast of any news or development. Using the knowledge as he saw fit but, always, to his own advantage.

Today he had started his rounds and had appeared in a corridor overflowing with the revolting damned. He had only just managed to disappear up his own portal before his disguise became useless in such a cramped and confined space. Then he re-appeared in the main hall containing the trapped demon force. He stayed just long enough to assess the situation and then he was gone, his natural urge to survive trumping any unnatural urges to directly assist any fighting demons. The beleaguered forces unaware of his brief appearance and, equally, prompt tactical retreat.

Rather than continuing his normal routine Stuart decided that he had best cut short his espionage work and return to his office. It was neither spacious nor opulent but being an accountant, when he had been alive, it was as exciting as his imagination could make it. An A3 sized graph, depicting the number of souls in Hell compared to the estimated number in Heaven was pinned to the wall and that was its sole decoration and attempt to make it seem unique and homely. Once in his own comfort zone he sat in his chair calculating what he should do with the piece of critical information. In his Machiavellian mind there were several permutations. He could just keep it to himself and see how the battle played out. Alternatively, he could tell the stand in, temporary, leader of the Marching Horde army so that he could quell the insurrection and gain a favour in the process. But, after slow and careful deliberation, he decided that the obvious choice was the best one. Standing up again he walked across his office and knocked firmly on Satan's door ensuring that each rap conveyed a sense of critical urgency that he didn't particularly feel.

Satan's voice was, as usual, terse. "YES?" he shouted. Enough anger in that one word to last anyone a life time. "What do you want you pathetic maggot?" Satan wasn't particularly in a rage, but he had a reputation to live down to, so he felt that a hostile voice for any visitor was always the best way to maintain his superiority. Stuart was, however, totally immune to his master's voice and all the tonal variations of rage that could be conveyed. Having to hear it every day had taken away its power to fill his heart with fear.

Acting as if he'd just been invited into Satan's room, by a kind and calm voice, he pushed the solid wooden door. It initially resisted his efforts to move it but eventually gave in and reluctantly opened just enough for him to squeeze through. The accompanying creaking noise it gave him was still not loud enough to drown out the sound of Barry Manilow cheerfully telling Satan how much he'd like to 'do it' with him. The thought and image skipped across Stuart's mind, but he resisted the urge to smile at the idea. Satan didn't have much of a sense of humour at the best of times but when it came to Barry Manilow, he had no sense of humour at all.

"Sire," hissing like a hungry viper tasting the air with its tongue. "I bring you important news."

"The Sword? It's here?" as if a switch had been used to change his demeanour Satan's voice was suddenly full of light and cheerful anticipation.

It was at that point that Stuart realised that his choice of action might not have been the best after all. Satan's expectation of good news had him in a bubbly mood but that would quickly evaporate like spilt beer on a hot desert floor. The reaction could be excruciating if the news wasn't delivered in the right way. A fire ball to the head was more painful than it might sound, and the head wasn't always the target, with neither destination appealing to Stuart. He valued the abilities of speaking as much as he liked being able to sit on a chair. Briefly he pondered the best way to proceed. He'd had years of experience of manipulating Satan's reactions but this time he wasn't sure what approach would work. But, no matter what, he had rolled the dice and could do nothing to get out of passing on the news. "No sire, The Sword isn't here *yet,* but I saw the army set off safely and I am sure it won't be too long. It is about the damned souls. They're revolting."

"Yes, I know they are. But so are you. What is the problem?" totally losing the point of Stuart's simple statement.

"No, no, no Sire. I don't mean that they are... repellent." Disliking the idea that his boss thought of him in that way; but accepting it as he was hardly able to stand up for himself and argue with his boss. "I mean that some of them in the outer rings have broken out of their chambers and are currently engaged in a battle with the demons. Our troops are armed but trapped in an intersection. The sheer numbers of souls have made it a stalemate." Turning his head slightly he tensed his body in anticipation of the sudden impact of a searing ball of flame that, thankfully for him, never came. Relaxing his body, he looked at his boss trying to gauge the effect the news had had on him. But the face was giving nothing away. Even Satan's breathing seemed to give the impression of being normal and calm.

"Very well, get in touch with the temporary head of the Marching Horde, whatever his name is, and get him to send in the whole army. He can conscript in any demons he finds on the way as well." Satan's voice was monotone and almost ambivalent; leaving Stuart bemused. He'd seen Satan fly into a bloody rage if his bottle of single malt whisky ran out and he didn't have a replacement to hand but when it came to this important piece of information, he seemed uncharacteristically sanguine and almost apathetic.

"Yes Sire." Bowing he backed out of the office and giving the door a concerted pull managed to close it. Once in the relative safety of his own office he released a sigh

293

laden with relief. He had avoided Satan's full rage; he had no idea why but didn't care. For now, he was safe.

In the privacy of his room Satan went to stand in front of his fireplace and its roaring log fire and stared, deep in thought, into the flames. Like many of his demons he had allowed himself to get carried away with the idea of imminent and total victory. The mood had lifted him and even the bad news had, initially, done little to destroy his emotional high. But slowly he thought about the full ramifications of what was happening in his own domain and he began to allow the rage to return to its rightful place in his heart. While maintaining his fixed and concentrated stare at the fire he raised his right hand, pointed it at the ceiling and released a super-heated fire bolt that was about the size of his head. Up it flew and exploded on impact with the blackened and stalagmite filled roof. Red and yellow flames spread out horizontally before receding leaving thick black smoke in their place. The ceiling was used to being the brunt of Satan's petulant and hot outbursts so any explosions had long since loosened and dislodged any unsecured stones. Once over the blast had had little effect, other than additional blackening of the already soot encrusted surface and giving Satan's head and shoulders a black and grey patina of ash, as if he was suffering from an extreme case of dandruff.

Satan turned and walked towards the door, he had made a decision. His army was vicious and had dealt with innumerable insurrections in the past so some damned souls should not be a problem. But he needed as many demons to be ready for action, once The Sword arrived, so he was going to ensure that the battle was swift, one sided and decisive.

Meanwhile Crush, the temporary leader of the marching Horde, had already had his instructions and directions. He understood the magnitude of the task before him but remained undaunted. For decades the diabolical army had been training for just such an occasion and they now welcomed the opportunity to put all the practice into action. He had sent out his lieutenants to muster the troops, close to the assembled damned insurrectionists, with instructions to rendezvous armed to the teeth and in full battle armour so that they would be ready for battle. To ensure that there were no misunderstandings he had also made it clear that this was not a drill.

Satan's personal bodyguard had not wasted anytime with getting to the designated meeting place. Adorned with thick black and yellow striped armour, tall rectangular metallic bullet proof shields, with long spikes on the front of them, and wielding various axes, short swords and spears they were an imposing sight. Hardly camouflaged and inconspicuous but that was not their purpose, inspiring fear and making the enemy want to feel abject terror was what they wanted and usually got. Crush was not used to being the Field Marshal but he was ambitious and knew that success wouldn't do his promotional prospects any harm, especially if Finley failed in his mission. 'Dead men's boots' was the standard way of obtaining betterment in Hell and one demon's failure was another one's opportunity. The new found power seemed to suit him; he had his army line up for a brief inspection, ensuring that they were all fully armed and psyched up ready for the forthcoming fight. He could tell, from the look in their red and anger filled eyes, that they were pumped up and wanting to destroy anything or anyone that got in their way.

Marching noisily, the sound of feet hitting the ground in unison, the army advanced. Like a single unit, a giant killing machine they moved towards the massed ranks of the mainly unarmed opposition. Pure numbers were not on their side, but physical strength, training and tactics were. Into the corridor they went, having to thin out the line to take into account the narrowness and curving walls that prevented a fully disciplined march. Soon the tumultuous clatter drew the attention of their prey. The damned heard the approaching force, and unaware of the Marching Horde's reputation just assumed that it was just another opportunity to dish out vengeance on their horned captors. Thinking that having their foes in the same confined spaces would give them a better chance to advance they began to run towards the approaching demons. Emboldened by the lack of gunfire, mowing them down, they picked up their speed and began to scream loud incoherent battle cries, the echoing din giving courage to both sides. Suddenly the damned turned a corner and could see the Marching Horde steadily heading towards them. In their coloured uniforms they looked like a giant swarm of heavily armed wasps. Any hesitant souls at the front of the running mob were not given the chance to pause. The sheer mass on bodies pushed them ever forward.

Seeing the approaching enemy Crush inhaled deeply and shouted one single word "Testudo!" Even over the din of both armies it was loud and clear. Without further instructions the Marching Horde stopped, lifted their shields, and thanks to a small groove along the right edge, interlinked them to the shield of the soldier stood next to them. Following a tried and tested tactic, which had been polished to perfection by the ancient Roman army, they brought the shields together around all sides and overhead. They adopted the shape of a very long, bendy and spike covered misshapen tortoise. There were small gaps in the almost totally impenetrable shell but those holes were there for a purpose and the possible weakness was not something that the unarmed foes could take of advantage of. Like a semi living avalanche the damned souls engulfed the elongated rectangular solid box. Over the top and around the sides they swarmed. Soon even the rear of the formation was reached, and the entire shielded creation was invisible under the attackers. Only then did the highly trained soldiers, secure behind their shields, begin to utilise the small slots in their armoured formation. Thrusting sharp swords and spears through the apertures they were able to strike at vulnerable and defenceless flesh. Bodies taken out of the fight, laid limp either upon horizontal shields above or on the floor at the side of the far from reptile shaped fighting device. Those that were around the fallen trying to pull the limp cadavers out of the way; fresh hands grasping the gaps trying to yank the shield apart. Had the holes been slightly bigger it would have been sufficient for them to gain an advantage and turn the tide of the battle, but, as soon as fresh targets presented themselves to the demons, simple sword and spear movements repeated the killing spree and dispatched the next wave of attackers. Inside the protective walls Crush issued a further single instruction, his voice deafening as it filled the confined space. "Advance!" With that command they began to slowly resume their march forwards, heavily booted feet walking over the bodies of fallen attackers. Arms moving back and forth as weapons were pushed through holes into fresh targets. Yet still the damned came. They knew that surrender or retreat was not an option.

Fighting was their only chance of freedom, desperation their source of energy.

Eventually a few of the damned managed to pry some rocks from the wall and were able to beat them against the shields but it was futile. They were far too weak and the shield's interconnecting walls were too secure. As their turn came to be cut down the rocks fell to the floor. Eventually the sheer mass of the oncoming souls made further advance impossible. The front rows of soldiers were just pushing their sharp and blood covered weapons into already incapacitated bodies that were unable to fall to the floor due to the pressure built up behind them. Realising that forward movement had stopped Crush knew that it would just waste time and energy pushing in that direction so decided to move back so that he could let the enemy come to him. Issuing another simple instruction, his shouted order filling the inside of his shield, 'animal'- "Slow retreat!" Like a giant juggernaut, with the brakes firmly applied, all attempted forward motion stopped. Legs briefly still then, without turning around, they began to walk slowly backwards. The space that was made at the front of the colossal fighting creature allowed the previously wedged damned, who had been *killed*, to fall to the ground. Once on the floor they were walked over, with their places filled by damned souls more able to fight; each new line meeting the same fate as the preceding one, bodies no longer able to join the fight. Destroyed but unable to die and, over time, their bodies would recover with the single purpose of perpetuating their suffering.

Unlike every war fought by humans, on Earth, this was one battle where neither army could claim to have any god on their side. Two sets of evil unable to hide behind the claim that they are on the side of good. But taking the Marching Horde's tactical withdrawal as some sort of retreat the oppressed souls took it as a form of victory. The front lines stopped pursuing the metal clad leviathan and let off a united, but premature, cheer of victory. Picking up rocks they gave it a leaving present that ineffectively rained down on it. Slowly the Testudo formation backed its way along the narrow corridor away from the celebrating enemy. Eventually it reached a wide-open circle where four corridors intersected. Manoeuvring in between the demons inside the exoskeleton Crush looked through various slots to ensure that they were away from immediate danger. Satisfied he continued the laconic set of instructions that would have made even Spartans seem talkative. "HALT! Four-way skirmishing positions!" With that, like a well-choreographed dance routine, the entire army disengaged their shields from the ones next to them and split themselves into four similar sized units and took up positions in front of each of the corridor entrances, forming into two lightly packed lines with every second man three steps behind the front line. The gap giving each soldier his own killing zone to their side and in front of them, arms able to swing freely and despatch anyone, or thing, that got within reach. Given the space to swing it was an ideal formation for axes, swords and spears to be fully utilised. Now, on his own, Crush took his position in the centre of the guarded circle ready for the inevitable enemy advance. He knew that when they came there would be no rest until either side had won. Mercy was not in the nature of wars in Hell, so he knew none could be given or expected. There was no Geneva Convention in there and even if there had been it would have been ignored.

Then he heard it, the slow and uncertain movement along the aisle that they had only recently vacated; they were coming. As soon as the front rows of the damned saw the brightly coloured soldiers blocking their exit they sped up and ran full on, the sheer force of numbers making up for the lack of effective weaponry. The first wave was quickly despatched without managing to do any more damage than splattering the defensive shields with fresh blood - making them look like pieces of violent pop art. The second, through to the sixth, wave fared little better, bodies making a muddy river of blood at the firmly placed feet of the demons. Finally, Marcus, one of the souls that had originally escaped his punishment chamber and then helped to free the other prisoners, managed to make his way to the front of the eager army. He easily assessed the situation and realised that just repeating the same uncontrolled and unplanned tactics would only deplete their numbers. They had vast, but not infinite, resources and they had already suffered loses that only a blood thirsty dictator, or heartless politician, on Earth would think of as acceptable. The current approach was like death or glory, only without the glory or even complete death for that matter.

"Listen to me, please listen to me." his voice full of desperation as he tried to get their attention and prevent another useless charge. Faced by an unexpected sight the crowd stopped - relieved that there was a possible leader stepping forward and hopefully willing to take charge and provide direction. Despite the massive number of former military personal within their ranks none had taken the opportunity to take the lead and bring direction, other than just loudly shouting *forwards,* to the operation. "This is getting us nowhere, we need to just pause and think. All we are currently doing is giving them a good workout, but we are not a training exercise. If we want to avoid going back into the chambers, and facing an eternity of punishments, then we must use our brains and not just our bodies."

"What else can we do?" came a voice from somewhere within the densely packed crowd. "We have no weapons and one end of the corridor is blocked by a wall of bodies and behind that is an army with machine guns. Then, at this end, we have the Marching Horde cutting us down as if they were a lawnmower and we were the grass." There was a loud chorus of agreement with the voice's summation of the situation.

"Yes" responded Marcus, his voice rising above the murmuring masses. "They have weapons but all they are doing is following a simple battle plan and we are just doing all that they expect so that it is effective and we are nothing more than useless sacrifices." Emboldened by his audience's sudden rapt silence his voice grew stronger and more impassioned. "Yes, they have the weapons and their position is a tactical advantage, but we have a weapon that their strategy doesn't allow them to use." He paused to allow his words to sink in.

"And…" a voice shouted out in eager anticipation.

"And? We have our brains!"

"Oh, them." responded the voice full of disappointment and sarcasm. As if it was expecting the answer to involve something that could give them something firmer to mutilate demons with than a large handful of squishy body matter.

"YES! If we use them then we might just have a chance. A rigid arm is easier to break than a flexible one and they have only one defence, slash and stab. We have rocks, let's utilise them. Attack but be co-ordinated, yes some will fall but we might be able to break their formation and, once that happens, we have a chance!" Emboldened by his strategy the crowd gave him a rapturous cheer.

At the entrance to the corridor the waiting formation, and their leader, could hear echoing, but indistinct, words punctuated with the sound of cheering. The lack of the anticipated next assault wave was making them restless. Their raw basic instincts made them want to break formation and take the fight to the enemy, but they knew that they had to stay where they were. Disobeying an order in Hell was, all too often, a short cut to instant and inglorious demotion where the punisher became the punished. "Hold the lines." The words almost whispered to his anxious troops. "They'll be here soon enough."

Just then, as if he had been heard by the damned, and they no longer wanted to keep him waiting, the noise of the damned souls' approach could be heard. Rumbling, like a minor earthquake, the ground beneath their feet began to shake. Then the approaching attackers passed the corner and could be seen by the awaiting soldiers stood in the skirmishing formation. Suddenly, without the advance stopping, a volley of stones and rocks of various shapes and sizes were sent through the air, some hitting shields and others making contact with exposed faces, limbs and armoured bodies. A handful of troops fell to the grounds unconscious only to have their places taken by the soldiers behind them. There was time for one more barrage of rocks, this time aimed at the roof of the corridor just before the front row of the awaiting soldiers. Ricocheting off the black and sulphur yellow surface the trajectory was angled so that the projectiles hit the heads of the front row. Despite thick demon skulls and helmets they had no defence against such impacts and fell to the ground. Before their positions could be filled the damned were upon the remaining troops. Swooping to pick up weapons and shields from the fallen enemy the damned souls attacked. Engaging the demons in close quarters combat the previously invincible Marching Horde began to fall. Their own weapons used against them and the sheer numbers of the attackers finally becoming an asset rather than a massed liability. Each defending demon soldier, that fell, relinquishing weapons to the attackers; angry victims who were already sensing a victory. Despite putting up a firm and valiant fight, which claimed far more *killed* on the damned side than the demons, the tide was turning and the well-trained army's numbers began to dwindle. Seeing the potential defeat, and subsequent rout, Crush ordered the unutilised troops, which had been in formation at the entrances to the other corridors, to move position and reinforce the beleaguered lines. The new lines slowed down the attack but didn't stop it. With arms and weapons flaying the defenders fell back allowing the attackers to encircle them. Reacting to the change in circumstances Crush tried to shout out instructions over the din of battle but his words were lost. Eventually the troop's numbers grew smaller as did the defensive circle that they had instinctively formed.

Then, as if out of nowhere, a dark shadow appeared hiding a giant figure surrounded by a blinding corona of white light. The figure's body, blurred by the shape of jagged and widely spread wings and supported by two thick legs, could be made out by everyone in the chamber. Pausing, weapons held in mid sweep, as if the combatants were turned to stone, they all paused to look at the figure that had suddenly appeared. As the wings folded behind the creature's back, they could all see that it was Satan; his angry and hate filled face surveying the scene of carnage. A reverberating growl could be heard emanating from deep in his throat. Then, without speaking, he opened his mouth and pointed his hands in the direction of the damned souls. A ball of flame, as incandescent as his rage, spewed from his mouth while at the same time blue electric arcs flew from his fingers. The fire hit a clump of the damned and immediately vaporised the top part of their bodies leaving only lower legs and feet buried amongst cremation ashes. The ten electrical sparks made contact with the nearest targets and leapt through them, striking those behind them and continued on its hopscotch journey, downing line after line of the damned until it struck the far wall of the chamber, leaving smoking corpse with holes burnt through their bodies.

The remaining souls attempted to down the Lord of Hell but spears thrown against him were as effective as toothpicks flicked at an adult rhino's hide. Laughing contemptuously at the pathetic attempts to destroy him he let lose further sets of lightning bolts and each strike reducing the numbers of his targets. Eventually there were only a few left and seeing that they had no chance of victory they ran down the two remaining corridors that were available to them, closely followed by the remained of the Marching Horde, swift strikes to their retreating backs cutting the stragglers down.

Soon the only two left in the corpse filled chamber, who were fit and able to stand, were Satan and Crush. Satan had a wry smile on his face as he surveyed the bleak scene of desolation and destruction in front of him. He enjoyed such sights, so the bloody carnage didn't offend his sensibilities in any way. He had seen and caused so many horrible deaths in his time that such things no longer solicited any strong emotional reactions. The sight that he took in could have been just dry and lifeless autumn leaves swept into a pile for all he cared. Victory was all he was bothered about. But he was not happy that he had lost so many of his Marching Horde. They would eventually regenerate; dismembered or eviscerated corpses would, over time, reform and return to their original shapes and sizes ready for action. But that process took time and his immediate plans involved them being part of his first wave of assault troops for when he had The Sword in his hand and was stood before the gates of Heaven destroying, forever, his foes. Also, their absence made him vulnerable to any set of demons that might try and usurp his seat of power. Without his elite force for the assault he would have to rely on ill-disciplined and untrained demons that enjoyed a fight but when it came to following orders, and working as a single unit, they were like blind men trying to find New York City on a map of New Zealand.

"Sire, there are still damned souls trapped in on some other corridors, if you will allow me, I will recall my troops and, with your assistance, I will finish those scum off as well." Crush's words firm but hiding his abject terror along with the thought of having been so close to failing his master. He knew the definite risk of being a target for Satan's own brand of electric shock therapy once the last of the escapees had been dealt with.

Turning his gaze to the officer stood before him Satan's expression changed to one of utter contempt. His selected commander had let him down and to him there could be no excuses or mitigating circumstances. His failure would incur a punishment that would fit the magnitude of his ineptitude but that could always wait. Satan was eternal as was his ability to remember that a penalty must be paid. Waiting for the right time was just part of the process to him. At the moment he needed someone capable of leading what was left of his Marching Horde and Crush was the best of what remained of his limited options.

"The vast majority of the insurgents have been crushed, some in a quite literal way. Why do you think I was so late? I didn't stop to pick daisies." Satan's sarcasm lost on his frightened underling. "They will be no more trouble. Follow me." Unceremoniously stepping on the bodies of the fallen, of both sides, he strode along the corridor full of slain foes. With crushed flesh and bone cracking and squelching underfoot as he went. Finally, he reached the wall of beaten enemies. Limbs and heads projecting out of the tangled and bloodied mess like branches left in a pile by a busy lumberjack. Holding his arms outstretched and in front of him, hands shaped as if he were about to fondle a pair of breasts, he released a bolt of raw energy that would have been invisible except for the shock wave it left in its wake making the air shimmer. The force hit the fleshy wall and the impact pushed it over, bodies thrown into the chamber next door making the waiting demons jump into readiness, weapons trained on the dark space of the corridor, waiting for the next wild charge of the desperate damned. Conscious of depleted ammunition stocks fingers were on triggers but no rounds were sent flying. Each target had to be visible before any precious bullets could be used. But the only shape that appeared in their rifle sights was that of their Supreme Commander. On seeing him they quickly lowered their weapons. A sense of relief mixed with fear running through them all. They knew that their premature actions had caused all this trouble and that Satan would find the right time to exact an appropriate punishment. And whatever that was they knew that they would not enjoy it. They'd probably end up sharing chambers with the damned souls that they had only recently been using as target practice. Once they were being punished the fallen demons could expect no leniency from the demons still in control and with authority over them.

Moving around the chamber he fired the same energy bolts at the rest of the blocked passages. Once they were cleared, he finally turned to look at the expectant demons. "It is a good job that, at the moment, I need all the demons that I can spare. Otherwise none of you would be left standing right now." Sweeping his arms in the general direction of the bodies of the fallen damned "Now get all these back into some punishment chambers, I don't want them regenerating while they are still free. Then, once they have all eventually grown back to something worthy of punishment, I want them in a punishment chamber that will be fit for their crime." Finally, with a sweep of his giant wings, he was gone, flying back into the darkness of the nearest corridor leading in the direction of his own private inner ring and sanctuary.

The demons knew they had their own sword hanging over their heads, they wished it were of Uncreation rather than of Damocles but they also knew that there was nothing they could do about it. So, reluctantly, they began to carry out Satan's orders and drag out the bodies of the damned. It would be a long and slow process before they became animate again, but when that time came the demons would make sure that payment, for trouble caused, would be dished out to the damned.

Chapter 35 – Too Many Stomachs.

Oblivious to the chaos and the attempted coup, that their absence had caused, Finley and his compatriots currently had other things on their minds. The process of transportation from Hell to Earth had the usual effects on all of the travellers. Irrespective of size, or fitness, all were feeling the after effects of the process. Pain and discomfort were being dealt with, by all of them, in their own way. The entire detachment of the Marching Horde was standing holding their stomachs as if they had exposed and festering hernias. The Chaldean demon was grasping his head with both hands feeling convinced that it had a stick of TNT in his brain about to explode. The cows, being deprived of hands and arms, with which to wrap around inflicted parts of their anatomy, had to deal with their temporary illnesses in their own way. Despite the urban myth cows only have one stomach, but in order for them to be able to digest the tough grass it is huge and broken into four separate compartments. A normal, well fed, cow can be carrying a lot of grass in various stages of digestion as it passes through the body and leaves the brown by product that they are so famous for. Unfortunately for the demon cows, and anyone in close proximity to them, the side-effects that they were suffering were the projectile ejection of the complete contents of all that was stored in their stomachs from one end and the evacuation of bowels at the other end. The various shades of foul- smelling green and brown viscous matter deposited by a hundred cows quickly built up around the landing site making it a place to be avoided by anyone that didn't have knee length waterproof boots and preferably a blocked nose. Fortunately, for the majority of the other demons, they had arrived first so that they didn't have to land in the liquid that would make the Ganges look like a fresh Manhattan cocktail drink. Finley and Collins were not so lucky, having chosen to bring up the rear they landed in such a way as to wish that the British army issued long Wellington boots instead of sturdy lace up footwear. The latter were ideal for marching and battle situations but were not so good when having to navigate through the combined contents of a battalion of cow's intestines. As both of them looked down at where their feet were, now buried and out of immediate sight, both of them silently cursed all cows and especially the ones that had been forced upon them for this mission.

Unlike normal Generals, on Earth, Finley could fill his mind with mental images involving some of his troops, fire pits and barbecue sauce and those thoughts quickly sprung to mind; with him wishing that they could actually become a reality. But, for now, he had to bring himself back to reality and take stock of his location and the current situation, over and above the condition of the ground beneath, and surrounding, his boots. Making a concerted effort he was able to pull his feet, one at a time, out of the bovine mud, each lifted step accompanied by a sound akin to violent wet flatulence. Eventually both of the officers managed to free themselves and reach the solid tarmac covered road that was immediately next to the arrival point. Stamping their feet on the firm ground, in an attempt to rid their boots of much of the looser ooze as they could, Finley looked around. Surveying his location, he could see that the road ahead ran up a steep incline before disappearing over the brow of a hill in the distance. To his right, rising above him was an undulating moor covered in dense bracken and heather with several rocky outcrops visible from where he stood. The largest one was near the top of the hill, close to the road. A single giant rock stood separate and alone close to a neighbouring rock face surrounded by smaller boulders. To his left the valley continued downwards where there were streets and houses growing denser as they got closer to the river at the bottom. He assumed that it must be the town of Ilkley or, if it wasn't, then they had been sent to the totally wrong place and the portal operator would have hell to pay when they got back.

Looking behind him Finley saw a long dry-stone wall separating the moor from the houses and any encroaching civilisation. In the road, connecting the gaps in the wall, was a cattle grid. Long thin strips of metal laid diagonally over a man-made pit. An impenetrable barrier designed so that the narrow hooves of farm animals couldn't cross it. Any bovine or ovine feet would be trapped, preventing animals from invading safe suburbia and eating all the tempting freshly watered lawns or munching on the flowerbeds. He realised how lucky they had been to land on this side of the grid. If they had materialised on the other side of it, they would have had to find some way of covering the gaps between the metal so that the demon cows could have progressed. Failing that the more human shaped demons would have had to carry the cows, one by one, over the obstacle and that was not something he wanted to think about. And if you have ever had to carry a cow over a cattle grid you will know how difficult an operation that can be. Cow's natural build is such that they are not naturally designed to be carried by hand. Maybe a small calf but a fully grown one was possible but not desirable. Cow carrying races, he absentmindedly mused, were not something ever to be created as an Olympic sport. And if cattle rustlers in the

Wild West had to rely on that method to remove them then there would have been fewer lynching's in those days as well.

His small and bizarre army were quickly recovering. The human shaped demons had regained their composure and were casually stood chatting to each other as they patiently awaited instructions. The cows were greedily refilling their empty stomachs by eating the rich dark green grass that was growing on the verge, by the side of the road. Despite full mouths that were busy masticating they were also mooing away to each other sharing the details of their all too recent mutual discomfort to any other evil cow, or human shaped demon, that cared to listen - of which there were none, but they carried on complaining anyway. Finley, accompanied by Collins, casually walked to the head of his lined up army. Once in position he looked down the slight slope that they were occupying and sighed. This was not going to be an easy mission, he thought to himself.

A car, passing them on the road going up the hill, tooted its horn and gave the fake British army soldiers a friendly and patriotic wave. The sudden and unexpected noise made several of the Marching Horde instinctively reach for their shouldered firearms. A defensive movement that Finley saw and quickly shouted instructions to calm them down and avoid any possible bloodbath involving human car drivers that were just trying to be friendly. "Calm down men. We are not here to kill humans. He was just being friendly. Leave your weapons shouldered until we really need them. I have a feeling that we will meet up with some angels sooner or later and, when we do, I am sure that they will not be announcing their arrival by blaring car horns. So just relax." This instruction was met with various loud words and moos of acceptance and agreement. Slowly they lowered their hands from the gun straps and assumed their previous relaxed postures, waiting for the imminent order to proceed. They had no aversion to killing humans, in fact they quite enjoyed it, but they recognised that this unique mission had other priorities and they were not here for fun.

"Right men… and cows. We will march up the hill, along the road, and hopefully we will soon find some sort of path that will get us onto the moor and to where we need to be. Remember, we are supposed to be a human detachment of British infantry soldiers on an exercise that, for some inexplicable reason, just happens to involve a herd of innocent and dumb looking cows. So, for Hell's sake, try and keep in character."

"Moooo, mooo, mooooo" responded Jordan, the second in command cow.

"Yes, I know that, I did say dumb LOOKING and not just dumb" replied Finley. "But to humans that is what you look like and I have no intention of enlightening them."

"Right, if none of you have any objections, I think we should get on with it. Troops, QUICK MARCH!"

When it comes to describing a cow's marching ability, be they demon or not, there are numerous superlatives that you could use. Coordinated, precise and impressive are just three definite examples of some of the words that would be inaccurate and far too generous. Using such terms as shambolic, disorganised or even chaotic would probably still be being far too kind. Due to their sheer bulk, and the simple fact that they have four awkward legs, any form of close order drill was out of the question. Marching, be it quick, slow, or any other speed would be as improbable as them becoming proficient at ballroom dancing. Drill them on a parade ground, for as long as you like, and they will still look like a basic herd of cows meandering towards a shed in readiness to be milked. Not as hilarious and ridiculous as the Greek army's daily changing of the guard outside their parliament but it is still a painfully embarrassing thing to witness. Luckily Finley couldn't care less about how the cows progressed, his bipedal contingents were marching two by two on the road, in close order formation and that was what maintained the outward impression when playing the game of being soldiers. Had the demon cows been able to pull off the skill then it might have actually got some undue and unwanted attention - so it was probably for the best.

As they marched, and meandered, up the steep road the few cars that were passing by gave them plenty of room and there was no further tooting of horns to show patriotism. Despite the gradient of the incline the strength of the demons allowed them to carry on without getting out of breath, they were focused, and this was like a gentle walk in the park compared to some of the training exercises that they'd had to endure in Hell. Even though they hadn't yet walked that far some of the cows were unused to such physical exertion, especially having to maintain such a fast pace of walking. There was the occasional loud *Mooo* of dissent and the odd, far quieter *Moo* as they swore at their commander for pushing them so hard, especially on empty stomachs. As is the nature of all military leaders throughout history the complaints, when heard, were fastidiously ignored by Finley.

Thanks to the fast pace they quickly reached the brow of the hill and to their right they saw a small gravel covered car park next to a wooden hut with a sign welcoming all visitors to the 'Cow & Calf Café'.

In front of the dull green painted building stood four flagpoles, all supporting weather beaten flags of various nations. Flown to add a bit of colour to the drab building and presumably to welcome any visiting tourists that might happen to be from those particular nations. The assumption, presumably, being that if a foreigner should happen to pass by, and not see the emblem of their nation, then they wouldn't take offence and would still park up and buy refreshments from the café anyway. On arrival at the turning Finley looked past the building and saw a narrow footpath leading up the hill to the moors.

Issuing the order "Right Turn!" they continued their march off the road and onto the car park that was sparsely populated by cars belonging to day tripper's intent on enjoying the breath taking scenery and get some fresh air to replace the breath that had been taken while walking on the moor. Once all his forces were clear of the road, he gave a further order "Platoon, HALT!" On hearing that instruction the soldiers came to an abrupt and smart stop while the cows ended their fast walk in a manner that was far from elegant, but equally effective. Taking the break as an opportunity to complete the process of filling stomachs they broke ranks and began to munch on the area of grass bordering the car park.

Looking at the boy who was in his mid to late teens and stood behind the open fronted café counter Finley returned his bemused and curious stare with a happy and disarming smile. As he walked towards him the demon began to speak in an authoritarian voice "Good day to you young man. Can I have 18 cups of tea please?" The knowledge that the British Army is maintained, and kept lubricated, by copious amounts of the drink helping him to maintain his cover. The demons might not like the drink, but he didn't care about that. The softly, softly approach was his main tactic for dealing with the pubescent and spotty teenager. Leaning on the hard and weathered wooden counter he watched the youth busy himself with the order.

"We are on a strange mission and I wonder if you could help me?"

Pausing from his tea brewing duties the youth turned to look at Finley, a mixture of suspicion and caution on his face. He'd not had much experience of dealing with military personnel so the request for information scared him in case he was contravening some law, hidden within the official secrets act, if he failed to answer them or gave them an incorrect answer. "Well," the youth hesitantly began "if I can help you I certainly will."

"Good man! I need to get my men to the Swastika stone as quickly as possible, but I am not quite sure where it is exactly." Finley's face a picture of polite sweetness and innocence.

"And cows?"

"Cows?" surprised by the question.

316

"Yes" pointing at the cows happily grazing behind Finley's troops. "We tend not to get many cows up here and they seem to be with you."

"Oh, *those* cows!" Finley was struggling to find a sensible reason why a small detachment of soldiers would be escorting a large herd of cows across a bleak moor. "Good question. It seems that, thanks to health and safety, modern army rations have been found to be unhealthy and not fresh enough, so we are trialling a process where we take fresh meat with use when we are posted to a war zone."

"Well I suppose that makes sense" replied the gullible teenager.

"It does? I mean yes, it does!" Finley was always surprised how people were willing to believe anything if it was told to them by someone wearing a uniform, especially an army officer's uniform. "The hardest part, when getting cows into the field, is teaching them how to pull the parachute cords."

"Really? I don't know much about cows, but I could imagine it isn't easy."

Finley rubbed is brow just below the edge of his helmet. He wasn't sure if the human was just playing along with the joke or had, at some point, swapped his brain with that of a hamster. Either way he thought he'd best get the conversation back on track otherwise he might end up being embroiled in a surreal conversation revolving around the concept of combat cattle and them ending up driving tanks. "Exactly. Anyway, the stone. Where is it?"

317

"That's easy. Just go up the hill there" pointing to the narrow path; leading away from the car park. "Follow it for about 2 miles, then you'll get to a ridge. Turn left and follow it for about 3 miles and it is just by the side of the path on the right. You can't miss it."

"Well, thank you…"

"Barry sir." replied the youth, with a broad smile on his face, pleased that he had been able to be of assistance to an army officer. He wasn't sure what rank the three pips on the officer's uniform were indicating but he felt sure that Finley was high ranking and important.

"Well, thank you very much Barry. You have been most helpful."

Once the teas were made and poured into the polystyrene cups, ensuring that whatever tea taste the liquid might possess was ruined by the unique plastic infusion of the container, Finley ferried them across to his troops then joined them leaving Barry to do whatever people, that work behind coffee counters, do when there are no customers.

Fortunately for Barry he had the mental aptitude, or lack of one, to make him ideal for the job at the remote and exposed café. He didn't have the intellect to fill his mind with ambition for ambition's sake. He had no desire to be unhappy in a better paid career, where he'd have the pleasure of a boss lording it over him and putting scorn and pressure on him. He had found a nice and comfortable niche in life, he had very little expenses, so greed or capitalism was not his mantra. To many it might not seem to be high flying or a profession with great prospects for promotion, but he had found something that many of his detractors had lost long ago. He had total and pure happiness from job satisfaction. If he'd have understood the concept of the rat race, then he'd have been glad that he was just a spectator. Relaxing from the mad rush of having to serve eighteen cups of tea he refilled the appropriate container with sugar sachet's, ensured that the display containing chocolate bars was still neat and tidy and then filled his uncluttered mind with staring into the distance. And, considering the view, there were far worse things he could have looked at.

Finley was totally apathetic and oblivious to the spiritual nirvana that Barry had found without him even having to go to Tibet, or some other remote location, and look for it. If he had been aware of Barry's state of grace, and under different circumstances where he didn't have a specific time critical mission to consider, he might have found it an interesting and diverting challenge; finding ingenious and cunning ways of tempting and then corrupting the young man's soul. Everyone had a weakness. It could be physical gratifications with an attractive, creative and more than willing and able partner that is happy to literally bend over backwards to keep the other person coming back for more. Some find that cold hard cash provides warm comfort or the good old corruption that power brings. Although with Barry's innocent and satisfied mind there was little that he wanted outside of what was already in his life.

Chewing their cuds or sipping their drinks, tinted with the delicate taste of cheap plastic, the demons listened intently as Finley gave them directions and further tactical instruction. He had serious doubts about the bovine's capabilities on the boggy ground, but he kept those to himself. He was also relieved that he hadn't seen any indications that angels had arrived yet. They would come, he was convinced of that, but being there first gave him an advantage. There were also the expendable resources at his disposal, so he could afford to set up a possible ambush for his enemies. Directing half a dozen cattle to wait underneath the porch, attached to the café, they might be able to charge the enemy. It wasn't much of a hiding place, but it gave the large, and maladroit black and white cattle, an element of cover and protection from the elements. Although anyone with a pair of eyes and a clear line of sight would be able to spot them from a mile away. But being disposable that was no concern to Finley and even if the angels despatched the first line of defence with firearms then the noise would alert his demons and take away the opponent's element of surprise.

"Right, before we proceed are there any questions?"

"Moooo, moo!" replied the Geoff, the lead cow.

"Yes, I'm glad you get the plan, but I am sure you can spare six cows." Finley warily scanning the rest of his force. "Anyone else?"

One member of the Marching Horde stuck up his hand.

"Yes?" pointing to the demon.

"Can we have some sugar for this tea?" piped up a soldier in the third row.

"No, just drink up." Finley's voice casual, treating the question as if it hadn't been asked. "Anyone else?"

"Are there any biscuits to go with this tea?" That particular demon had actually been a British soldier when he'd been a living human and some military traditions were hard to leave behind.

Finley rubbed his face with frustration. "No, there aren't any biscuits. Are there are any other questions?" With that the remaining contingent of two legged demons raised their hands. "That do NOT relate to food stuffs to go with cups of tea!" He added tersely.

With those words all of them swiftly lowered their arms. As far as Finley was concerned if they wanted any food stuff to accompany their drinks then they could join the cows and eat grass.

"RIGHT! Shall we proceed? Platoon, by the right, quick march."

The unusual procession began their unsteady march up the steep and narrow path. It was slippery from the mud and the slime covered damp rocks, so the soldier's boots began to skid, causing several to grab onto the soldier by their side for support. The cattle fared even worse, their mass and bulk allowed their hooves to dig in a little and provide a modicum of traction, but the incline was not conducive to the cow's way of walking and gravity soon began to pull them back down the hill. Looking back Finley saw that he was running the risk of losing four fifth of his force before he had even gone 100 yards and, even if they were only cows, he still felt that there might be a slim chance that they could come in handy if there were a battle.

"Horde, we are going to have to push them up the hill. It looks like we only have to go another 75 yards and we'll be at the brow of the hill." The instruction was met by a quiet but unanimous murmur of disapproval from his troops, none of them looking forward to the idea of forcing their shoulders onto the unreliable end of a cow. Despite relatively empty stomachs, and bowels, cattle were not famous for their ability to control their flatulence. Reluctantly the soldiers paired up and began the laborious process of pushing the cows up the steep incline. Conscious of time constraints Finley chose to forgo the privileges of rank and joined Collins in pushing the first cow in the line, Geoff, up the hill. All of this exertion was accompanied by various moos, groans and assorted expletives, many in long dead languages. The human hikers, that happened to be enjoying the scenery, were treated to the unusual spectacle of a small detachment of British soldiers pushing a herd of cows up a hill. There is an old and traditional English expression that sums up that nation's talent for understatement 'You don't see that very often'. And, in this instance, any of the amused, or bemused, audience would have been forgiven for saying it out-loud.

Eventually, after several slips, a few trips and a couple of instances where Finley and Collins took it in turn to fall face first into the mud, they managed to reach the brow of the hill. Free of the restricting incline Geoff gave off a loud 'Moo' of relief and walked forwards several paces allowing the two officers the chance to catch their breaths before they returned down the hill to assist with the elevation of the next waiting cow. Taking in his surroundings, as he gasped, Finley looked ahead and beyond the flat plateau, that they were currently on the edge of, he saw several undulating hills in the distance with one final steep incline that might as well have been a mountain for all he knew.

"Oh, shiiiiiiiiiiiiiiiiiiiiiiiiiiiiiiiiit!" Was all he said when he saw the potential mammoth task laid out before him and his small army. There was a lot of pushing still to be done and he hadn't planned on getting so close to any of his detachment's arses.

As each pair of soldiers joined their leader with their first designated assisted cow, and saw what was ahead of them, they echoed his exclamation of frustration and anger. There could have been a new musical called 'The Hills are alive with the sound of *Oh,shiiiiiiiiiiiiiiiiiiit!*' They could also see what was in store for them and were beginning to think that leaving the cows where they were wouldn't have been such a bad idea.

After much more struggling, pushing and falling into the mud, the entire army were at the top of the first hill. The artificial camouflage of the uniforms no longer required as they had picked up sufficient mud on their clothing to blend in and be virtually invisible if they were to lie down on the path.

An old couple, carrying small backpacks, and wearing matching red and black waterproof coats and over-trousers, gave the assembled troops a smiling nod of acknowledgement and the traditional Yorkshire greeting of "Ey Up!" as they walked past them, heading down the hill towards the café.

Puzzled either by the accents or the strange local dialect the demon soldiers just smiled and nodded back. The Chaldean demon returned the "Ey up" but coming from him it sounded more like he was angrily accepting a challenge to fight to the death. As far as he was concerned, he might have been, but he was sure that he could win any gladiatorial contest against the elderly man and woman. Fortunately for the two people they had already passed the demon and not given him any further eye contact, otherwise they could have found themselves decapitated by a berserker soldier wielding a chainsaw, and that would have seriously spoiled their day out and more importantly, to anyone from the county of Yorkshire, stopped them from having any cups of tea at the local café.

Unsure as to which direction the angels might approach from Finley was surveying the area. They might not even arrive at this side of the moor so diverting his resources too thinly ran the risk of leaving his forces spread too thinly should there be an engagement nearer their target. However, he had no desire to repeat the cow push fiasco for every steep incline. Doing that meant it could be midnight before they reached their objective and any angels would quite probably have got there first, dug up The Sword and left. Balancing the need for a greater degree of haste, than that of an arthritic sloth, against the necessity to have sufficient forces available for battle he decided on a compromise.

"Right Geoff, I want you to send half of your herd to go over there" pointing to his right, towards a rocky outcrop. "Get them to try and keep out of sight or at least try and not be too conspicuous and if any angels appear deal with them as best, they can. As for the rest of you I want you to go that way." He lowered his arm and then raised the other so that it was pointing to his left, along a narrow and muddy looking track that ran parallel to the ridge in the distance. "Same thing applies there. Any and all angels need to be engaged. If you hear any gunfire coming from our direction come running. Alright?"

"Mooo, Moooo, Moo?" Despite the limited scope for facial expressions, or the general ability to inject cow language with any deep level of emotional content, Geoff was able to inject his question with a degree of concern that was bordering on panic.

"How should I know?" giving Geoff a stern look. "Just find a way up the hill, that your cow legs can manage, and get to us as quickly as possible."

"Moooooooo, moooo, moo???" Geoff's tone now indicating that he had shown his emotional passport and just crossed over the border into the land of panic.

"In that case it is tough luck!" Finley's voice hard, doing nothing to assuage the cow's fears. "If you encounter any angels then I expect you to fight them and inflict as much pain and damage as possible. But you will be on your own. The primary mission is to retrieve The Sword not to ensure that all the cows avoid destruction. I won't be able to send any reinforcements as they will all need to stay close to me."

"Moooo, Moo!"

"Yes," responded Finley with a resigned expression on his face. "I suppose if you get into a fight you well and truly are! Good job there are no randy bulls up here or you'd be even more so."

Geoff duly passed on the orders to his underlings. With a few moo'd expletives, deep and guttural bovine grumbles and deliberate bouts of forced flatulence aimed at the Commander in Chief they split up and headed in their designated direction.

Giving the plodding herds' time to set off Finley turned to face the remaining 17 soldiers that were better designed for firing any form of weapon. Relieved to be free of the part of his army that he deemed to be more a danger than a viable force that would inspire shock and awe in the enemy; unless of course the 'awe' was part of a sentence along the lines of 'Awe, look, here comes our next meal.' Even the timidest angel, suffering from a bad case of cowardice, would have to be severely inflicted to face their fears when encountering the waddling monochrome heifers. Despite being a human during WWII Finley understood the advances in modern warfare had not developed so that a cow weighing a ton had evolved and was any alternative to a demon with opposable thumbs, a high velocity rifle and pockets full of spare ammunition.

"Alright men, keep your eyes peeled and follow me."

Chapter 36 - On England's Green and Pleasant Pastures...

Humans were susceptible to the elements; even relatively moderate extremes of climate could prove fatal if exposed to them for too long. The ability to remain standing around outside and guarding God's sacred trust was difficult. Even a simple brief break, to find a suitable place to go to the toilet, could expose The Sword to the risk of being found. The Guardian could return, busily pulling up the zip on their trousers, and find an empty hole where The Sword should have been. This danger was magnified even more if the human had to take cover or seek protection from bad weather. And of course, sleep would be needed at some point. Therefore, God decided that He needed a back-up plan; something else in place to ensure that the sacred weapon would remain safe from any demon. To many people the term 'Lamb of God' is just a phrase with even the definition varying depending on different religions. However, as a manifest display of His sense of humour and use of irony, God had created a second line of defenders for The Sword of Uncreation. Looking at all the creatures of creation he chose possibly the most unlikely animals' imaginable, sheep. Not all of them were imbued with special, holy, powers. Most of them simply lived up to their well-founded reputation of being stupid, skittish and only happy when eating grass while stood in large flocks; useful only for the provision of wool and something to be smothered in mint sauce before being eaten with potatoes and vegetables. Though there were definite exceptions; a small and select few were the chosen ewes. Over the centuries the generation after generation of the Lambs of God had obediently stood guard in the area of The Sword. As the weapon travelled the world so did the sheep, roads and ships utilised as the Guardians ensured that protection was maintained. When a new location was found the visitors bred with the existing breeds and their offspring were able to continue the mission. The same had happened at The Sword's current resting place. The existing flock, that stood guard, were the Swaledale breed of sheep. Their thick and tough fleeces gave them ideal protection from the elements and they could stay on the moor without anyone ever giving them a second glance. Also, their long, curly and sharp horns were adequate weapons when used against any unwary traveller that looked like they might be trying to obtain the weapon.

This natural camouflage was the ideal façade with which they were currently maintaining a wary eye on the unwelcome interlopers. Just like horses they had a sixth sense when it came to knowing when angels and demons were about and they could tell that there was more to the cows and soldiers than first met their eyes. Their hearts were instantly gripped by a mixture of fear, apprehension and the unspoken knowledge that they were in danger. Where there had been only the sounds of the wind and distant bird song the relative silence was not so much broken as destroyed by an ever-growing chorus of 'Baaa's' as sheep after sheep took up the hue and cry, a warning alarm call to the flock which was scattered over the moor, that danger was imminent. The un-translated language heard by the demons but just interpreted as simply the bleating of dumb animals afraid of humans. No notice was taken of the eyes intently following their every movement; rectangular pupils assessing the enemy, weighing up the opposition and planning tactics that, for centuries, had never had to be brought into practice. After long years of simply waiting they were now face to face with the dreaded demons. Their moment had come and the excited Baaaaaa's were exchanged as strategies were finalised. They saw, and recognised, the weapons that they were up against but size, surprise and the terrain were on their side. The long ferns would hide them until the time came to strike, a dirty white woollen blur as their long and twisted sharp horns, reinforced with solid skulls impacted with unsuspecting demons. They would be able to strike then disappear back into the undergrowth before the invading force even knew what had happened. Then, once the element of surprise was gone, they could bide their time, hidden from sight. Picking the right target and waiting for the appropriate moment and then strike again. Their sacred mission finally fulfilled. But first they were easier targets that had to be dealt with before valuable numbers were lost from agile, intelligent and trained foes armed with rifles and other weapons.

The ridge was narrow, and the path was not easy for the cows. Loose stones and deep mud made them walk gingerly, or as gingerly as a cow's movement could manage, to avoid slipping. Walking in single file with intense concentration, as they had little room for manoeuvring, to their right was marshy dense heather and tall ferns, impenetrable to the bulky and heavy bodies and to their left were rocky outcrops leading to the edges of high cliffs. One unguarded step and they would have fallen to their deaths; spirits returning to Hell without completing their task and along with failure came the added danger of having to face the wrath of Satan. Never mind cats; a cow in Hell's chance of gentle treatment was unlikely even at the best of times.

Then the lead cow stopped and let out a cautious and curious 'Moo' of alarm making the rest of the herd, lined up behind him, stop where they were and look up. Heads tilted to the sides trying to get a better view instead of the sight of the cow's backside directly in front of them; straining to see what he had seen. Then they all saw it, a lone sheep stood 20 yards ahead; its bright red eyes glowering at them as if to challenge them to come closer. Even though he'd never encountered the Lambs of God before Geoff could tell that there was something wrong and the sheep, that was currently eyeballing him, was no ordinary farm animal. Aggressive postures were not something associated with sheep but this one had adopted one. Whispered 'Moo's' emanated from the back of the line. Unable to see what was happening they were curious and wanting to know what was going on. A quite conversation ensued as information was passed back and forth along the line. Cautiously Geoff began to move closer to the lone sheep; hooves wobbling on the precarious torturous ground with careful steps trying to avoid any disastrous slips.

Then the sheep let out the universal war cry that he had learnt from being a little lamb but never thought he'd get the opportunity to use. "Baaaa!" Before he had even come to the last vowel, in the sentence long word, the other sheep, that had been hidden, waiting in anticipation, struck. Moving quicker than the cow's eyes could work. All they could see were flying blurs as dense white and grey clouds of wool sprang from the undergrowth. Simultaneously three sheep flew through the air, impacting on the cow, which was second in line, on the side of his body. Although cow tipping has been proved to be scientifically impossible, and was just an urban myth, nobody had told the sheep or even the cow for that matter, as the combined impact on its flank knocked its centre of gravity away from the middle of its body to somewhere just to the outside of its left legs. Unbalanced limbs flayed, trying to regain balance on the slippery surface before it lost that battle and fell over the edge of the steep precipice. Down it tumbled bouncing off protruding rocks dislodging various sized stones as it went downwards; with the body finally impacting on the rocky ground quickly followed by the freed projectiles - the jagged rocky ground dealing an instant death.

The sheep released a loud victory 'Baaa' before turning their attention to the large and undefended rear of Geoff. Two of them leapt upwards, sharp horns stabbing both buttocks. The injuries, that the assault inflicted, were not enough to cause any terminal, or even serious, damage but it was enough to startle the cow. Unable to turn around and defend himself, or even get a better view of his attackers, he lowered his head, horns pointed at the sheep on the rocky outcrop ahead of him, let out a bone curdling battle cry 'Mooooooo' and then he began his charge towards his opponent. Ungainly legs bouncing along the ground, throwing up mud high into the air as he ran. Like a bull in a ring, facing a fighter, nostrils were snorting and eyes fire red with rage as he sped onwards. Seeing the oncoming bovine, the sheep widened its legs to give it better purchase on the ground and then lowered its head, hard skull and sharp horns aimed to meet the oncoming charge. Closer and closer Geoff ran to the sheep. Ten yards, five yards and then just as heads and horns were about to make impact the sheep sprang to its left, away from the cliff edge. Seeing his target move out of his way Geoff attempted to stop and turn at the same time. The momentum not working for him so all that happened was that he flayed his legs uselessly and he sped past the former location of his adversary and tumbled over the edge of the cliff. With a long and desperate "Moooooooooooo!" he shared the same fate as the other cow had experienced just a few seconds earlier. There was a loud thud as his body struck the ground then a brief silence that was broken by the four lambs releasing a chorus of "Baaahaaahaaabaa." laughter at the cow having fallen, in both meanings of the word, for their obvious ploy.

Despite the language problems and the inability of either side to understand the 'words' of the other respective enemies the cows could tell that the noises were aimed at them and it was mocking mirth. Although they were incensed and wanted to wreak vengeance on the diminutive assailants the narrow area didn't allow for turning and as they were stuck in single file reversing was not a real option either. Had they been able to move freely they'd have positioned themselves so that they could meet the enemy head to head but all they could do was offer undefended parts of their bodies to the scoffing sheep. Angry 'Mooo's' were sent out in reply daring the sheep to do their worst. Then, suddenly, the sheep's taunting laughter stopped, leaving the cows wondering what was going to happen next. They didn't have to wait long for an answer, there was a brief "Baa" accompanied by the sudden noise of heather being trampled, bracken parted then boggy and muddy ground being disturbed and the sounds were accompanied by a long line of sheep launching themselves from their cover. The formation of defenceless cattle was given an ovine broadside as if the attackers had been shot from a row of cannons. In a single instant the remaining forty four cattle were struck by the combined force of a hundred heavy and well-aimed sheep. Horns perforating their leather hide and muscular flesh, stab wounds not deep enough to seriously injure but the force of the impact sufficient to send them stumbling over the edge of the cliff. Legs slipping as they futilely attempted to maintain some semblance of grip on the ground and keep upright. Their own hysteresis corrupted so that their state of equilibrium was moved. Heavy cattle, unable to defy the laws of gravity, were inexorably dragged down towards the rocks. The bodies of their two fallen colleagues, far below, instantly becoming even more tenderised meat by the increasing number of dead cows; their spirits already returning to Hell and forced to face the rage of their evil master at having failed on their mission and been defeated so easily. They were sure that Satan would not be impressed when he heard that they had all been killed by a flock of cunning sheep. Death might sting but it wasn't as painful as what he would do to them.

A long line of sheep faces appeared, looking over the lip of the cliff, surveying their slaughtered foes far below. Horns red and dripping blood and, just like the cows, they didn't have the facial muscles to smile or gloat in the same way as a human could, in such a circumstance, but that didn't stop them from savouring their victory. Eyes no longer glowing red they turned, gave out a light red flash and, as if in chorus, began to give off a resounding and undulating "Bahahaha." Further contemptuous laughter released a mixture of relief, at having no casualties on their own side, and contempt for their enemy. The joke at the expense of the cows who had allowing themselves to be trapped and killed so easily.

Their self-indulgent reverie was soon broken by another sheep coming up to them and giving them a questioning "Baaa, baa, baaa? Baaaaa, baaa!" Then, when he looked over the cliff, he could see what they were all laughing at. He had to admit that he was impressed. A great result for a squad that had trained for a long time but never seen action. But, as for the second part of the statement, that had a more sobering property on the jocund sheep. Being advised that there were an equal number of cows in the opposite direction made them regain their composure and focus. They knew the terrain would, again, work to their advantage, but the paths were wider and facilitated a greater degree of movement to the cows. So, once the element of surprise was gone, they would have more of a fight on their hands or, in their case, cloven hooves. Also, the irony was not lost on them that the cows, that were stood waiting to ambush any unsuspecting angels, were congregated around a famous landmark called the Cow and Calf rocks. Perhaps not the most auspicious of names but they thought that, perhaps after the battle, it could be renamed the Sheep and Lamb rocks? Sheep might not be large, but they had egos and could dream big.

Wiping the blood off of their horns, as best they could, on the nearby heather, the victorious Lambs of God began to leap back into the dense foliage; disappearing amongst the rich greenery as if they'd never been there. Stealthily they weaved their way around the clumps of plants, feet sinking into marshy areas but thanks to their light frames they didn't sink too deeply into the water-logged ground. Legs easily removed so walking remained unhindered. Any noise made lost in the wind that swept the moor. Then they were at the edge of the tall plants. Before them was the path where the demons had stood when they had reached the top of the hill overlooking the café and car park and, after that, grass and rocks. All cover to hide in was gone, leaving them with just their appearance as their only element of surprise. Not many expect to be attacked by a flock of sheep, and the cows were no exception, but after any initial strike it would be a case of locking horns and seeing who came out of the fight alive.

A party of students, tired but full of the cheerful energy that only the young, or drug addled, can maintain, clad in brightly coloured warm padded jackets, waterproof over trousers, sturdy boots and carrying back packs were heading to the car park after hiking across the moors. Their inane and happy chatter was briefly paused as they were all surprised to hear such loud baa'ing coming from the undergrowth by their side. Out of sight it sounded like the bushes, where the sheep were hiding, were busily in conversation with each other. Then a flash of white gave a sheep's location away. Hardly a tiger's camouflage in the jungle but still surprisingly hard to spot. Despite the initial thoughts, about sheep talking to each other, the walkers discarded such ideas as being foolish and resumed their chatting and idle laughter as someone joked about sheep having conversations with each other. Everybody knew that sheep were stupid and didn't talk. But 'everybody' was wrong on that score. The sheep were busily planning the right approach so that they could creep up to their target without causing any suspicion. All that they now needed was the annoying humans to disappear down the hill then they could begin their attack. Fortunately, many centuries of standing around and doing very little, while guarding a sword, had taught them patience and they knew that the passers-by would soon be gone and they could get on with things.

Eventually the human laughing and chattering faded as they descended down the hill. Only then did the stealthy sheep begin to leave their hiding place. In small groups of twos, threes and fours they allowed the previous clusters of sheep to get in position and start to inconspicuously chew on the fresh grass before the next group proceeded. To any onlooker, or bovine, there was nothing suspicious about a few sheep coming out of the moorland and standing near the cows as they ate. After all that was where the best grass was. The cows looked at the sheep but were more interested in keeping an eye open for any suspicious looking humans, who could be angels really in disguise and, even to demon cows, they knew that angels didn't disguise themselves as sheep. They were just dumb animals and no threat. Eventually the gentle stream of ovine guests, at the cow's eating area, became conspicuous. The sheep were now all in position and outnumbered the cows by more than two to one. The odds would have been higher, but the rest of the forces were busy keeping an eye on the more human shaped demons that were currently making their way across the moor.

To the cows all they heard was the gentle and almost soothing 'Baaing' of sheep, unaware that the noises that were floating around them were whispered final instructions all aimed at their imminent destruction. There was silence as both sides stood either nibbling on the verdant grass or just masticating as they chewed the cud. Then there was a single loud 'Baaaa' and the sheep struck. Twisted and sharp pointed rams' horns penetrating deep into muscle. Some delivering inexact thrusts aiming for the heart, in the region just above the front legs; but the organ was too far inside the body to ever be truly threatened. Moo's of pain, shock and surprise were released to be carried away in the wind. Other sheep sprang upwards, full body weight stabbing into vulnerable necks aiming to puncture the jugular veins close to the surface. Where the target was achieved rich oxygenated blood spurted out, warm and bright red, creating a macabre display like a bloody water fountain; turning the previously green grass to crimson. But despite the element of surprise, and the damage inflicted, all the cows remained standing. Although some of the injuries were severe, they were not immediately fatal. Now, painfully aware of the enemy in their midst, the cows began to issue Moo's as impromptu instructions were quickly given out. They now had enough open ground on which they could move and take up defensive, or offensive, positions. Despite their bulk their bodies were rapidly and agilely moved so that they could make the vulnerable and undefended parts not such easy targets. Heads and horns pointed as best they could to the enemy that outnumbered them. The opposition was definitely the biggest battalion and the best sheep. But these cows were not so easily beaten and destroyed. Their eyes were now red and would have chilled the soul of all but the bravest, or most foolish, human. Snorting they braced themselves for the next wave of woollen warriors.

"Baaaa" ordered the lead sheep and then they struck all at once. Solid and thick heads clashing, with horns locking. Some sheep were unable to get free from the entanglement so the taller and stronger cows simply lifted their heads, with sheep still attached. Heads shaken and the suddenly freed ovines were sent flying into the air crashing down onto the rocks nearby, finding instant death.

These cows would not die as easily as the ones near the cliff and any battle was destined to be harder fought. The sight of the few fallen comrades enraged the sheep. They stepped back slightly so they could catch their breath and assess the enemy. Moos and baas could be heard as each side planned and issued orders in preparation for the next move. Angry red eyes met each other knowing that no mercy would be given or received. Only total victory or annihilation was possible. Then, in unison, the cattle moved first. Unexpected speed and agility as hooves, now able to run on the hard ground, pushed them towards the sheep. The sheer body mass of the heavy cows, hitting the sheep, had the desired effect. Even though they had braced themselves they had no defence against such a force and were pushed backwards, small hooves unable to obtain any grip on the compacted soil or solid rocks. Some lost their balance and fell over only to be gored where they lay, defenceless, on the group; the sound of their agonised Baas running up and down the spines of their compatriots. Other sheep were pushed backwards but managed to extricate themselves from the bovine steam trains. Seeing their opportunity sheep, that were not being directly attacked, seized their moment. Quickly they circled and rammed into exposed flanks and rumps. The pains of the attempted eviscerations making the cows stop their forwards motion and direct attacks. Turning their focus to the sheep at their rear they swung their heads wildly and indiscriminately. Some sheep were not fast enough and were stabbed by the horns. Those that received the impact to heads, or vital organs, instantly fell dead, others managed to retreat with lesser injuries. But, no matter which way they turned, the cattle always left parts of their bodies exposed to the sharp horns of the sheep. Dripping with blood the woollen attackers struck time and time again. Each impact and subsequent wound not enough to bring down a cow but after each attack the number of injuries increased. The bloodletting weakening them, but still they stood their ground and fought. Eventually, one by one, the cattle began to succumb to the continuous waves of sheep and their horns. The losses to the sheep were higher but they had numbers on their side and each cow that fell down, exhausted, dying or dead weakened the combined defensive abilities of the remaining herd.

Sheep began to leap on the back of the remaining cows, balancing precariously they bowed their heads down and used their horns on backs and necks aiming for spinal columns. Then, once the thrust has been delivered, they leapt to safety onto rock outcrops which the cows couldn't climb. Out of reach of thrashing bovine horns and hooves they could stand and wait for the enemy to turn, defend themselves against other sheep and spring forwards again repeating the process. One particularly unfortunate sheep lost its balance and was crushed to death under the hooves of a desperate cow but other than that the sheep were getting the upper hand.

Eventually, surrounded by the bodies of seemingly harmless farm animals, there was just one cow left standing facing seventy seven sheep. Thanks to the thick wool it was impossible to tell where the blood of their injuries ended and the blood, obtained from the enemies, started but still they stood staring at the lone cow, eyes red with the rage and the blood lust of battle. The cow's hide was also encrusted with blood, but his injuries were far more obvious. Open wounds all over its body showing that it had put up a valiant fight, but its time was close to an end. Sensing as much it drew upon almost depleted energy reserves and, aiming at the sheep nearest to him, he charged. Bovine versus ovine - head against head - a clash leaving the rest of his body exposed and vulnerable. The target in front of him succumbing to the impact of the full force of his body but in turn the cow was pounced upon by the other sheep. Like a pride of lions on a wildebeest they brought down their prey. With one last blood curdling Moooooo the demon cow finally surrendered to death. A valiant spirit sent back to Hell to join the rest of the herd.

The victorious sheep, drained of energy, stood glaring at the scene before them. Friend and foe laid out before them in multi shades of red like a nightmare painting by Hieronymus Bosch, if he'd ever decided to add farm animals to his usual depictions of Hell. The leader of the flock gave his remaining troops a vacant stare as red anger drained from their eyes, returning, them to their natural colours.

"Baaa!" he said. A victory cry but lacking any enthusiasm.

"Baaa, baaa. Baaaaa, baa." The instruction given reminding the survivors that there were still demons further away on the moors, currently out of sight but not out of mind, they would have to be dealt with, but all the sheep knew that their high velocity rifles would be harder to deal with than cow horns.

Chapter 37 - A Band of Gypsies

The strange quintet of mismatched angels appeared at their designated location on Earth, empty air suddenly filled with human shapes. The warm and comfortable feelings that the transportation process left them with was a stark contrast to the emetic and feculent effects that the cows encountered. Dedan carried out a brief check to ensure that everybody was there and that they were all alright. He was relieved that Roxy, Bob and Miles had made it but was not so sure about Jimi. But never the less Jimi had also arrived safe and sound so Dedan realised that he would have to live with it, and hopefully not have to die because of his presence.

Looking around he could see, ahead of them, a small wall circling around them. Just beyond that there was a road and after that there was long grass interspersed with heather leading up to a rocky cliff face. Looking to his left he could just make out the squat shape of the Cow and Calf Café with its flags fluttering wildly in the wind. Turning his head, he could see that there was a tall brown brick wall directly behind them with a single window half way up it and a blue door at their backs. Taking in a deep breath the air was cool but not overly cold; it felt refreshing in his lungs. He had always loved being on Earth and after the oppressive heat of the air in Florence this was a pleasant change. Looking up at the sky he saw thin but still leaden grey clouds; except for a small area where they were totally obscuring the sun. The only indication that it was there was the faint orange glow as if a fire was being burnt directly behind the cloud.

"Welcome to bloody England" he muttered disconsolately to himself. "We have been here a minute and it hasn't started raining yet, that must be a record!"

Walking to the edge of the tall wall he carefully looked around the corner. There was a large car park with a couple of cars there and, craning his neck, he was able to view the front of the building. His first sight was of ornate bay windows surrounded by rich green ivy climbing up the wall of the building. Unable to see anything that resembled a demon, or a possible threat, he stepped out to get a better view of the surroundings. Walking out into the middle of the car park, closely followed by the rest of his oddly attired platoon, he stood with his hands on his hips as he took in the view of the impressive old building. At the centre of the façade was a door with small stone columns at either side supporting a stone porch. The rest of the wall was more bay windows and ivy. Above the door, just below the roof awning was a beige sign with bold black lettering announcing that the building was 'The Cow & Calf'.

Jimi Hendrix looked at the sign and smiled. "Hey man, I know this place. This is sooo cool."

The rest of the group looked at him with undisguised disbelief on all their faces. The total and utter remoteness of the building and the actual obscure part of the country seemed to be incongruous and totally at odds to the cosmopolitan wild hippy image of the legendary rocker. He didn't strike any of them as being the type of person to don a backpack and wear dull short trousers as he went hiking into the wilds and communed with nature; although his electric guitar version of 'The Happy

Wanderer' would have been interesting to hear. He might speak the love and peace rhetoric of that generation, but his image was more sex, drugs and rock 'n' roll than that of a tree hugger.

Dedan was feeling certain that if any demons had arrived before them, they were not hiding there in wait for their arrival. Any possible ambushes, or traps, would be better sprung elsewhere. "Alright, shall we go and investigate? We need to be somewhere up there." Pointing up towards the rocky cliff. "Bob, lead the way."

Bob looked embarrassed. "Err, I don't know the way from here. I always approached the hiding place from the opposite end of the Moor when following Ernie."

"It's okay man, I know the way." Volunteered Jimi with a broad smile.

This comment resulted in further looks of disbelief from his brothers, and sister, in arms.

Despite his desire to contain his incredulity Dedan couldn't remain quiet any more "Bull shit!" he said, louder than he had intended.

"No man it is true. I've been here before."

"Okay MAN, before we believe you, and walk another step, I want you to tell us how you manage to know this place so well and happen to know the exact location of the Swastika stone when none of us do. I have no desire to blindly follow you and find myself walking over the edge of a cliff. Don't forget I have worked with you before!" Dedan's voice full of cynical contempt and disdain.

"Hey man, such bad vibes. Let it go man, that was a long time ago and I made one mistake." Jimi's voice frustrated at the implication that he was lying. "Okay I will explain, then perhaps you'll get off my case." Walking to the wall, at the edge of the car park, he sat down and looked at his colleagues, inviting them to sit next to him so that he could tell them a story. As the rest of them sat on the wall, two on either side of him, ignoring Dedan, he smiled at their expectant faces.

"It was 1967 and I was just starting to get big, and by big, I mean massive. I did all the TV shows and was booked to play in Ilkley. The venue was not huge, and they sold out quickly but kept selling tickets so the venue, that was meant to hold about 150 people, was stuffed full of fans. There must have been over 500 there. They were packed like big sardines in a small tin can and the air was electric. I loved it and miss those days." His eyes began to glaze over as he recalled the experience, with his own Experience band.

"Okay, then what? So, you played Ilkley." Dedan, conscious of time, impatiently urged him to carry on.

"I began my set and the noise of the crowd was drowning me out. I could have shouted out my grocery shopping list to them and they wouldn't have known any difference and would have screamed and cheered me like excited monkeys. I kid you not, it was like a sauna in there and the walls were dripping with condensation as if the wallpaper was sweating with the heat. Then some local policeman, that must have had nothing better to do, popped in to see what was going on and saw the death by crushing that was just waiting to happen and decided to step in and stop my gig. I was into my third or fourth song and he somehow managed to fight his way to the front of the crowd, climb onto the stage next to me and pull the plug on the speakers. The crowd went crazy and I thought there was going to be a riot. But somehow, they didn't. They just jeered the copper and, after he'd told them to all go home, they began to leave peacefully."

"Of course, they didn't riot. In Britain, in the 60's, that would have been seen as impolite." Dedan interrupted. He had always found the English and their polite way of dealing with anger and disappointment to be strange. Blitz them in a war, lock up their fathers or push in front of them when they were in a line, after they have been queuing for hours, and they will maintain a stiff upper lip and keep an air of polite manners bordering on diffidence. All done as if showing that being cross would be seen as being rude and impolite. Perhaps a startled 'I say' might be muttered under their breath but, on the whole, they'd rather chew off their own foot than be seen as breaking some cultural taboo and challenge someone else that happened to do something that would have an American reaching for his gun. The only time that they'd even remotely cross the line would be if they saw someone being cruel to a dog or a horse or, sin amongst sins, put up the price of a pint of their beloved warm beer. Then they would be shouting abuse from street corners and foaming at the mouths. So, unplugging a rock concert, decades before it became trendy, wouldn't have been deemed to get them above the status of being *slightly miffed*.

"Yer probably right man." continued Jimi. "Anyway, the band began to pack up the gear but I was feeling down and depressed. I decided to just pick up an acoustic guitar and go for a walk. Escape the mad crowds and get some peace. I ended up walking up that long road behind us and I came to this place. It was dark, and I was cold, so I went in for a drink. English beer is warm but was ideal as I was cold and I ended up sat drinking it next to an open log fire. As the night went on the pints flowed, I did a few songs and then it came to chucking out time. I had to leave so I began to walk aimlessly on the moors. It was beautiful man. The moon was casting amazing shadows and I just walked and walked. Eventually I came across this old flat stone and sat down to rest. Then it got a bit weird. Some sheep started talking to me. It must have been some bad acid, or just too much grass that day, but they actually spoke. They asked me if I was alright and then they led me to safety, back at the road. It was crazy man, like some surreal dream. But they told me that the stone was special and that I must never tell a living soul about my trip. But I am sure that you lot do not count as living souls, so I feel sure that I'm not breaking my promise to them."

His audience stared at him with a mixture of, in the case of Miles and Bob, awe and total and utter disbelief from Roxy and Dedan. There were elements of the tale that made sense and sounded reasonable, however the idea of sheep talking and being some sort of hippy spirit guide just made the whole thing go over the edge of the sensible cliff and go tumbling onto the rocks of insane weirdness far below.

"Righhhhhtttttt," began Dedan, struggling to formulate a sentence that wouldn't sound sarcastic. "So, sheep, little woolly farm animals that go baaa, *talked* to you and guided you back to the road? And you didn't write a song about it? Shame, I am sure it would have been a massive hit. You could have called it something like 'Sheep Lady' or 'Sheep's so fine'." All his attempts at not sounding sarcastic failing.

"How about 'Have Ewe ever been to Electric Ladyland'?" added Roxy laughingly, joining in the fun.

"Scoff it you want, but I am telling you what happened." Jimi's voice calm, refusing to rise to their baiting.

"Well thank you for sharing your story about your very interesting *trip* but I think we need to get on." Dedan suddenly serious as if the joke was no longer funny or important. He wanted to disbelieve the whole thing but there was something nagging away inside him that he didn't like and was wondering if it, in reality, wasn't just some drug induced dream and it was all true. After all God had insisted that Jimi came along and there must have been more of a reason than to just annoy him.

Standing up Dedan strode over the low wall and began to walk along the road leading to the café in the distance. The rest of them, on seeing him get up, followed suit and walked quietly behind him; all deep in their own private thoughts and opinions about 1960's rock concerts, beer, moonlit walks on the moor and talking sheep. Suddenly Dedan stopped and raised his left arm, hand clenched tightly in a fist. At the signal they all stopped and took their weapons from their shoulders and held them in their hands, tense and ready for action. Dedan lowered his arm and pointed towards the café. "Over there" he whispered. "By the side of the café, under the canopy next to it, can you see it? Black and white, it looks like we have some demon cows waiting to greet us."

"What do you want us to do?" Roxy enquired, squinting to see that far ahead. "It looks like there is a path up onto the moors there and it might take too long if we try and find an alternative route just so that we can avoid them."

"Avoid them? Who said anything about avoiding them? The last time I encountered them they were not that well equipped to be any real threat. Horns and dumb confidence are no match for someone with a gun. Hell, they are no are no threat to someone with a long stick and a wooden chair. I suggest we go over there and explain the alternatives that are open to them. I do not speak, or even understand cow, but I am sure they will understand what I am saying to them. Give them a choice of leaving us alone, so that they can remain on Earth and chew on grass in peace or get a bullet in some painful places before they are killed and sent back to Hell. If they can't see the validity of my argument, then we can donate a wide selection of prime cuts of beef to the café. I am sure the owner will find them a nice addition to the menu."

They were about to resume their walk when Bob looked around and spoke, his voice loud and full of alarm. "Look, over there to our left, just by the rocks at the bottom of that cliff. It looks like a lot of cows laid down. It could be an ambush!"

Dedan turned and looked at the pile of cows partially hidden by the undulating grassy ground directly in front of them. "It could be an ambush but if it is then it is rather elaborate and convoluted. Cows, especially demon cows, might attract flies so that is probably normal but the camouflage involving covering themselves with their own blood and scattering their innards around them seems to be a bit melodramatic and over the top. I suspect that something else has happened and they might have somehow been persuaded to come down the cliff quicker than they would have liked."

"But how?" asked Miles, showing disgust at the bloody sight.

"I have no idea, but it will be interesting finding out. Come on, let's go have a little chat with our bovine friends over there."

It is hard to casually remove large deadly assault rifles from shoulders, cock them in preparation of a firefight, and aim them at a small herd of cattle without causing a small amount of concern in the minds of any civilian bystander that just happens to be stood behind a café counter. And any attempts which the five strangely, and disconcertingly unconvincingly, dressed soldiers made to point their weapons inconspicuously and in a casual manner were failing to such an extent that Barry was in grave danger of soiling his trousers. And for someone that was proud of his health and hygiene certificate that was not a good thing to do while he was handling or preparing food. Anyway, the visitors to his café would not have wanted to eat his snacks after that. Looking franticly around he searched for an excuse to desert his post. Perhaps there were some boxes in the back office that needed to be emptied or some stock to be re-ordered? But he was like a deer in the headlights of a truck hurtling in his general direction along the opposite side of the road. Not in immediate danger but still frightened and unable to move and run into the woods; just in case the vehicle swerved and splattered it leaving venison road kill and a dented fender. He had no idea what the cows had done to upset the British military but neither side seemed to be in happy moods. If he didn't know any better, he would have sworn that the cows were harbouring dark and evil thoughts and were planning to attack the soldiers. His social frames of reference were limited so any experiences of life outside of a childhood, spent in a small spa town, and a short period of working in a remote café hadn't prepared him for what was to come next. Mesmerised all he could do was watch. As if hypnotised he saw the officer maintaining the grip on the handle of his rifle, and finger firm on the trigger, with the weapon's butt tight against his shoulder he began to walk slowly towards the cattle. Then to Barry's bemusement the soldier started to engage it what seemed like a two-way conversation with the, now red eyed, cows.

"Look, I don't speak cow, but I hope that at least you understand English. Is that right?" Dedan's voice was firm and confident, knowing that he had the upper hand but accepting that trying to talk to cows, even demon ones, could have high and insurmountable language barriers.

"Mooo." Replied the nearest cow, nodding its head to confirm that the words were understood with big, round and red eyes meeting human ones; both filled with mutual distrust and suspicion

"Good, at least that is a start. Look, I am sure you have been left here to set up some sort of strange ambush and probably make some valiant sacrifice so that your colleagues can carry out their mission. All very noble and, also surprising considering you are demons. Heroics and grand unselfish gestures like that tend not to be your forte. However, there are several things that make such a gesture futile…"

The cows gave him extra nods of agreement and understanding. Showing that they were listening and waiting to see where he went with his conversation.

"Your subtle camouflage, as in black and white with what looks like fleck of brown excrement, might have worked if you were trying to hide in a herd of zebras but look around you" pointing to the green, grey and brown landscape around them "it is hard to maintain the element of surprise here. You stand out like Casanova's dick in a nudist convent." He paused to think about that simile. He wasn't sure that such places existed, but he wished they did and hoped he could visit one someday.

"Moooo" replied the lead cow with a gentle nod, unable to argue with that logic and even if he'd tried to do so Dedan wouldn't have understood what he was saying.

"Exactly, Mooo" added Dedan not realising that his inability to speak any bovine language had made him inadvertently make a comment, in their language, about some grass tasting odd. "So, as you can see, we have the advantage and hold all the cards. And when I say cards, I mean these lovely assault rifles that are held by my friends, stood just over there, and ready to tenderise your flesh in a very messy and painful way. You suffer a torturous death and go back to Hell and we waste bullets and then carry on with our mission as if you had never been there."

Despite the different language the ensuing "Moooooo" was understood by Dedan to be a simple 'and your point is'.

"If you have a little walk over the brow of that hill behind me you'll see a rather large and very dead pile of cows that either all had a massive accident and managed to fall off a cliff thinking that they were a synchronised diving team and there was a warm swimming pool below them or, more likely, they put up a good fight but failed to beat whatever force that attacked them. Soooooo, you can opt to join them. Back, as I said before, to Hell and risk being frightened in Satan's office and spoiling his carpet, or…" pausing to allow the image of answering directly to Satan, for their failure to defeat the heavily armed angels, to sink in. "you can act like you haven't seen us and go for a little walk. Get lost on the moors and spend as long as you like chewing grass and doing all the things happy cows do. I am sure that the absence of half a dozen cows from Hell will not be noticed and even if it were do you honestly think anyone will care? I can't see the 'Big Red and Angry One' sending a force to Earth to retrieve you. Do your best to avoid doing demon things and I am sure God will be happy to ignore your presence on Earth as well. I, for one, certainly have no desire or intention of wasting any time chasing after you once this mission is over."

The knowledge of the experience some of their fellow cows, on their previous mission to Hawaii where they'd encountered an amorous and virile bull, made them wary of the idea of doing what cows do. Jon, the leader of mission, had not been the same since his return to Hell. However, they had to accept that a lot of what they were being offered made perfect sense and sounded attractive. They were treated as the lowest of the low in Hell, and were the butt of much cruelty, so the thought of a peaceful existence on Earth, just minding their own business, had merits. Turning to face each other there ensued a quite conversation as *moo's* were exchanged. The debate weighing up the pros and cons and what could happen to them if Satan decided to look for them. After a round of nods of agreement at the unanimous decision the lead spokescow returned to his position facing Dedan. "Mooo, mooooo, mooo. Mooo!" He then gave the angel a slight bow. Turning he began to walk across the car park to the side of the road, closely followed by his small herd. There was fresh grass waiting for them there and they wanted to start enjoying their new life as soon as humanly, or in their case bovinely, possible.

Dedan turned to face his bemused looking troops, giving them a sly smile, and Roxy a conspiratorial wink for good measure. He clicked on the safety catch of his rifle and slung it, by its strap, over his shoulder. Turning his attention to the café he looked at Barry who was watching him with his gritted teeth and ashen face.

"Hello their young man. How are you this fine day? Can I have five cups of coffee please and some salt and vinegar crisps please?" The expression on Dedan's face was one of blithe indifference as if nothing out of the ordinary had just happened.

"Y-y-y-y-y-yes sir." Barry stuttering because he wasn't sure if he should feel comfortable about all that he'd just witnessed. He felt that, if he was lucky, he would soon wake up and the last few minutes would have been just some strange dream possibly induced by him eating a stale, and long out of date, cheese sandwich.

"I wonder if you could help me? Other than the obvious sight of a grown man having a conversation, with some ordinary cows, have you seen anything else unusual recently?"

Compared to what he'd just witnessed everything that had come before, in his entire life, seemed totally normal and sensible. He couldn't say for certain but even if he had travelled and seen the world then the officer having, what seemed like, a two-way discussion with cows would have probably stayed top of the list of bizarre things that he might witness.

"There were the soldiers just like you, or probably more like soldiers than you lot, and the rest of the cows that went up the hill earlier today. I suppose that could be said to be unusual." But Barry was no longer sure. If such things were to become normal, then he might have to seriously consider a career change.

"Exactly!" Exclaimed Dedan; realising that the enemy was more than just a herd of pragmatic but cowardly cattle. "And can you give me an estimate as to how many soldiers there were? Which way did they go?"

"Oh, I don't have to estimate sir. They ordered 18 cups of tea and they each had a cup. All milk, with just one sugar each." adding that fact, just in case it was relevant. "But I have no idea how many cows there were. But it was funny watching the soldiers pushing them up that there hill."

"I see, thank you. We are part of the same mission and it is important that I catch up with them as quickly as possible. A point of regimental honour, I am sure you understand."

"Of course." Barry's response was a lie and Dedan knew it but didn't care. He paid for the refreshments and carefully carried them to the waiting troops.

"There you go, sup up quickly as there are 18 demons up there and they could be waiting for us and I am sure that they will be more of a threat to us than those cows" He paused then looked across the car park at Barry. "Oh, crap." Muttered Dedan. "I'll be right back, I forgot something."

"Cake?" enquired Bob hopefully; the comment getting a two fingered response from Dedan, arm raised in the air but not turning away from the café.

"Sorry to bother you again, but we are looking for the Swastika stone. Can you tell us how to find it?"

"Of course," Barry's face full of forced jollity, hiding the wish that all soldiers and cows would just go away forever and leave him to stare blankly at the scenery. "That's easy. Just go up the hill there" pointing to the narrow path that the demons had climbed "follow it for about 2 miles, then you'll get to a ridge. Turn left and follow it for about 3 miles and it is just by the side of the path. You can't miss it." Then he paused and bit his lip pensively with a look of panic filling his eyes. "I think I have just given you, and them, the wrong directions!"

"Really? Why?" Dedan asked trying to avoid sounding overly excited in case he frightened the already scared café worker.

"It is more like 3 miles and it is the furthest ridge. The soldiers, up there, will never be able to find it from what I told them. I am SO sorry."

Allowing his genuine sardonic smile to appear at the extra piece of information Dedan gave Barry a shrug of his shoulders. "Don't worry these things happen. When we catch up with them, we'll make sure that they know that they've taken the wrong path and will send them where they belong."

Returning to his own waiting troops he gave them the news. "Right, I think we have a chance. They have been given incorrect directions, so we should be able to beat them to The Sword. But let's keep our eyes open. I am sure that they'll shoot first and not ask questions later."

Having adopted human forms on Earth, just like the demons that had arrived before them, the angels became susceptible to the same faults and limitations that normal humans had to deal with. The need to perform basic body functions would perhaps become an issue but for now were not a problem. The need for sustenance, to maintain energy levels, had been met thanks to Barry and his cafe. However, just because they were dressed in a lame attempt to look like fit and well-trained soldiers, the choice of body shapes was not exactly fit for the purpose intended. Roxy was naturally fit, strong and healthy although, if she'd got hold of any cigarettes, she'd have soon changed her health status to gasping and wheezing. Dedan might have been shaped like a badly sewn bag of potatoes but he had done enough missions, on all the continents, so was fitter than he looked. But for Bob, Miles and Jimi they had to cope with bodies that had gone past their sell by dates and would have not been bought if reduced in price and sold in a Black Friday sale. Lives of excessive ease and occasional recreational drugs had taken their toll, with inappropriate footwear, in Miles Davis's case, not helping the situation. Having to carry their heavy equipment, while ascending the first hill, had already revealed their limitations. Although it was not a great distance reaching the brow had left them exhausted and gasping for breath. Shoulders were aching, lungs gasping for air and blood pounding in their heads, making their faces flushed. Finally, at their first objective, they took the unoffered opportunity to sit and rest. Miles removed one of the sticks of celery from his helmet and began to chew on it. Responding to Dedan's bemused look he just replied, "I told you I like celery!"

Ignoring the comment Dedan saw them on the ground and wanted to chastise them but knew that shouting wouldn't give them the energy or motivation to carry on. St. Michael might resort to such methods but thankfully he wasn't here. And, besides, Dedan knew St. Michael was a pompous arsehole. "It's alright, just rest a couple of minutes and … catch your breath." The last words trailing off as he saw a trail of bloodied black and white leather and woollen carcasses leading around the corner of a rocky outcrop. Unshouldering his rifle, he clicked off the safety catch. "Just wait here, I'll be right back." Despite their exhaustion they recognised his action and copied it. Weapons ready, just in case. Watching intently as Dedan walked around the corner and out of sight.

What he saw left him astonished, the blood strewn scene would have been worthy of any human battlefield, only the bodies had four legs and horns. Scanning the area, he saw no sign of any dead human formed demons or survivors so turned and returned to his allies.

"And...?" Roxy asked, her voice full of undisguised concern and anxiety.

"Well, perhaps Jimi, I think I just might owe you an apology. I get a feeling that there is more to your sheep story than a few bad drops of LSD and some warm English beer." Shouldering his weapon once more, "come on, I think we have some unexpected allies that might just need our help."

Forcing themselves up the trio joined Roxy and Dedan and they continued their trek along the moors. Walking along the muddy path was not easy as it was uneven and overgrown in places, but they managed to keep upright and, despite some of them being tired, they maintained a steady pace. As they walked Dedan was able to look at the views. Despite originally expecting it to be cold, bleak and depressing it was mild, and the views were magnificent. Other than the noise of breathing and feet hitting the ground there were few other sounds to break the spell of the place. The wind whistled past his ears and, in the distance, he saw some Red Kites gently hovering in the breeze as they hunted for small prey. Other than them he could see nothing but undulating moorland. Then, as they reached the brow of another slight incline, they were able to see into the distance and what looked like a long line of people all carrying large backpacks. It was hard to make out but there were thin objects protruding above the heads of the hikers and they could easily have been the barrels of shouldered assault rifles. "It could be just a party of hikers in fatigues and carrying a lot of military equipment but I think that it looks like the demons could be over there. Sneaking up on them might not be easy but I think we need to pick up our pace and try and get closer. Maybe we will get lucky and surprise them."

Assorted weapons were carried in arms, ready for any surprise attacks. Just because Barry had counted 18 people and there were 18 in the distance didn't mean that there weren't forces that had made their own separate way to the Moor. Suddenly they stopped, their path blocked by a small flock of sheep staring at them through dark and intent eyes. Instinctively Dedan raised his rifle at them and the others quickly followed suit. Lowering his rifle in one hand Bob gestured to them to do the same with his other. "It's alright; I think they are on our side."

"Hey man, look, I recognise my old buddies. It's them. It's the sheep I told you about." Jimi was holding Roxy by the shoulder shaking her in excitement.

"Calm down Jimi." Replied Roxy shaking her shoulder to free it from the over enthusiastic grip of the musician. "I am not sure if it is a sin, but I am sure it isn't right that a grown man should get THAT excited at the sight of sheep. Lonely farmers in remote cottages maybe, but you have the ongoing en suite orgy in Heaven, so you should just calm down a little." Giving the sheep a quizzical look, she then added "Besides, if you've seen one sheep you've seen them all so they might not be the same sheep!"

Realising that he had got carried away in the moment he relinquished his hold on Roxy's uniform. "Sorry Rox, it's just that I thought I'd never see these guys again."

The lead sheep raised his head "Baaa, baa, baa."

Dedan looked at his colleagues. "Well, I can add sheep to the long list of languages that I don't speak."

"It's okay, I've got this." replied Jimi, regaining his composure and acting less like a pervert that had been turned on by farm animals. "I know what they are saying. Hi, you guys, I'm Jimi Hendrix and we are on a mission from God to retrieve The Sword."

"Baaa. Baaa, bahaha, baaa."

"Hey Dedan, they say that they know who I am, and they love my music."

Dedan looked quizzically around him. From what he could see of the moors any form of audio equipment was conspicuous by its absence. There wasn't a stereo to be seen anywhere and, even if there was, he wasn't sure how the sheep would be able to operate it. "What the..., how the..." He was struggling to formulate the best way of demanding clarification on the claim but decided that such things could wait. "Never mind, can they understand what I am saying?"

There was a chorus of Baas in response.

"They say of course, they aren't stupid." translated Jimi helpfully.

"Good, tell them…, scratch that." turning his attention from Jimi to the sheep. "Look, over there, there are some demons disguised as soldiers and they are after The Sword. We need to stop them. Can you help us?"

"Baaa, Baaaaa, baaa. Baaa!"

"They say that they know and were following them and waiting for the right moment to attack. But, now that we are here, they are happy for us to help them."

"Sure, whatever." unsure whether it might be the sheep that needed the angel's help and not the other way around. "What are your plans?"

"*Baaaa.*"

"He says that he wants us to try and get as close to them as we can and then, once we get spotted, we draw their fire and they will strike. The demons do not suspect the sheep of being anything other than neutral, so that works to our advantage."

Dedan looked at Jimi in astonishment. "One baaa said all that? I really do need to learn their language." facing the sheep again. "Alright, I am sure we can do that. Maybe our weapons can be almost as much use as your horns!"

"Baaa." replied the lead sheep, tilting its head in a disgruntled manner. It was hard for sheep to look cross or offended but he managed to pull it off perfectly.

"Yes, he is. A complete asshole but he is alright once you get to know him" Jimi could tell that Dedan was holding back the abuse but he couldn't resist the opportunity to wind up his commander.

"Alright, I apologise, it is just that I am not used to going into battle side by side with sheep. Let's work together. We will get as close to them as we can and then once the firing starts will try and make sure that we don't hit any sheep in the cross fire."

With that the sheep disappeared back into the short, but dense, foliage. With only the occasional tufts of heather being disturbed, as they moved, revealing any evidence that they were there and heading towards the small demon army. Dedan and his troops took the less direct route along the path. When they got to the part of the moors, where they needed to go left, he paused. Ideally, he'd have loved to be able to send Bob and Miles the correct way to the Swastika stone and dig up The Sword but his resources were limited and he couldn't risk splitting his forces. They were outnumbered almost 4 to 1, as it was, and he didn't want to make it 6 to 1. Stooping low they set off along the path towards the demons. Despite tired limbs and aching backs, from the enforced posture, they were able to progress rapidly; the plants ahead of them ensuring that they remained invisible to the demons. At each patch of greenery, which lay in their path, Dedan paused and poked his head over it to ensure that the demons were not within sight. Once he was certain that the coast was clear he would walk around the obstacle and carry on the stealthy march. Bent over like strange hunchbacked primates.

Finally, after too much crouched running for comfort, they got to another grassy outcrop and saw a solitary sheep stood just on the path running around it. "Baaa." It said. Its voice was low and gentle but all five of the soldiers knew that the message was more than just a casual hello.

"He says that the demons are just ahead of us, but they haven't seen you and are just marching along the path." Jimi's quiet translation once again surprised Dedan with the complexity of the sheep language, one seemingly simple *word* conveying so much.

Checking that all had their assorted weapons were at the ready Dedan was pleased that Bob had opted for the heavier fire power than the standard British army issue SA80 assault rifles. Even the angelic musical section's choices of the M16 would be useful. But before he could whisper the instruction to attack Jimi put his hand up in front of his face. Forefinger sternly raised to indicate that he needed to speak. "One minute" he whispered. "My axe!"

"For God's sake Jimi leave the guitar, and the case here. I don't think the demons are going to drop dead just because you play them a verse of 'Crosstown Traffic' and set fire to your guitar!" Dedan's voice was muted but still managed to carry the full force of his frustration and anger.

"Relax Dedan man" responded Jimi in an equally quiet voice. "Who said anything about a guitar? I said axe." With a conspiratorial wink and sly grin, he opened the rigid case and pulled out a big and heavy shiny double headed metal Labrys battle axe on a thick wooden handle. "A fan from Greece gave me this as a present and I've always wanted to have a go with it." Carefully placing the now empty guitar case in the heather he held his assault rifle in one hand and the axe in the other. "Ready when you are Dedan." Giving him a further nod and a wink, the combined actions making him look more like someone on the pull in a night club rather than a warrior prepared for a battle.

"Right, come on then. Oh, and Bob, no bloody battle cries. I want to surprise them."

"As if Dedan." Bob's expression betraying the fact that he had been planning to allow the Alabama part of his soul to escape and let out a Confederate 'Yee ha' war cry.

Waving his small band of soldiers to proceed Dedan stood upright, rifle tucked into his shoulder, eye close to the body of the gun looking down the sight. He was ready to provide covering fire when it was required. Carefully the four soldiers walked forwards, careful not to disturb any stones underfoot and alert the unsuspecting demons. However, a pebble was knocked by Bob's boots and fell off the path disturbing others on its journey. The noise, they made on their short journey, was not loud, but it was enough to get the attention of the demon at the rear of the procession. Turning he was met by the sight of Dedan's mini armed force in mid crouch and aiming their combined fire power directly at him. He attempted to raise his weapon but Dedan released a burst of three rounds at the member of the Marching Horde, each bullet hitting their target; leaving the front of his face with three neat round red holes and removing the back of his head in the process. Even before his dead body had time to hit the ground the rest of the demons had their weapons ready and were turning to engage their eternal enemy. At that moment the sheep, that had been shadowing the demons from the undergrowth, struck. Leaping into the air their horns impacted with hard helmets, thick padded uniforms or just back packs. Minimal injuries were inflicted but the demons were able to fire off a volley at the sheep as they clambered back into the ferns, so that they could regroup for the next attack. Several sheep were not fast enough and were killed instantly. Seeing that the opportunity for some close quarter, hand to horn, combat the Chaldean demon shouldered his rifle and pulled the cord to start his chainsaw. The noise of gunfire between angel and demon was drowned out by the deafening roar as the blades span and the unconventional weapon was twirled in the air like an evil cheerleader getting ready to put on a show.

As bullets whizzed past their heads the angels took the opportunity to dive wildly into the heather that lined both sides of the path. Dedan fired some more rounds before he, in turn, ducked down and found cover. The demons followed suit leaving just the Chaldean demon stood swinging his chainsaw. His mind now full of his own private rage he was oblivious to the bullets that were flying past him. He was challenging any, and all, to come and meet him in a private battle to the death. Several sheep, hiding in the undergrowth, watched him and waited. Seeing him sweep the yellow machine in front of him they saw their opportunity to jump at his exposed face and chest, but the demon was too quick for them. With reflexes, that would be impossible for any human, he saw them and was able to swing the chainsaw back again so that it decapitated all the sheep in one single blow while they were still in mid-air. Some blood spurted skyward forming a fine mist before it fell to the ground as more was thrown, by the blade, across his chest and his maniacally grinning face. He wiped it from his eyes with his free arm then, with the other, he lifted the chainsaw above his head in triumph. "Is that all you've got?" he roared, demonstrating that he was no coward when it came to battling sheep. Seeing another possible chance to attack a couple more sheep, who were in hiding behind him, thought they'd have more success than their now dissected friends. Silently they pounced but once again the demon was too fast. The chainsaw was thrust into the belly of one of the woolly jumpers and before it had been able to cut through all of the body, he swung the blade, with sheep still attached, and struck the other attacker so that the part of the unexposed blade was able to remove one of its front legs. As it fell injured to the ground the demon extricated his weapon from the now disembowelled sheep and brought it to bear on the surviving animal laid at his feet. With an evil grin on his face, that befitted a demon, he utilised his weapon with accuracy and skill that would have made a lumberjack, or butcher, look at him in awe and ask him for advice. Sadistically he sawed off the remaining limbs and then cut along the exposed stomach, allowing vital organs to slip out. It wasn't until he had issued the final coup de grâce that the haunting and agonised screams turned into the silence of the lamb. Even with the din of his saw and the noise of the bullets the deathly cries had carried in the air and made the angels shudder. Enraged sheep began to blindly break cover and jump at the demons that were nearest to them. Many were hit in mid-air, like targets at a fairground shooting range. Others managed to impact with their foes but they were unable to inflict any serious injuries and were shot as well. Seeking vengeance more sheep focused their attention on the Chaldean demon, but they met the same fate as all the others. Flesh ripped open by spinning blades and body parts sent up into the air, escorted by fountains of blood.

Seeing the carnage, that the sheep were suffering, Jimi decided that he had seen enough and had to act. "Cover me!" He screamed as he stood upright and dropped his M16 rifle. Around him his colleagues let loose a barrage of hot metal trying to avoid hitting him while they kept the demon's heads down. Indifferent to the demons crouched down at the side of the path he ran past them screaming with rage and waving his axe. Seeing that he was not intending to use the axe on them the demons instinctively refrained from opening fire on such an easy, and obvious, target. They easily knew who the object of his anger was, and they hated to miss out on the opportunity to witness what could be a spectacular battle. Some recognised the angel for who he was and if they couldn't see him play guitar then they could, at the very least, watch him be brutally killed.

Seeing the oncoming axe wielding Hendrix, the Chaldean demon lowered his chainsaw and pointed it at him. "Come on then pretty boy!" He shouted and gestured with his free hand giving Jimi the invitation to come and engage with him in some deadly contact sport. Whether he'd been given the invite or not he was sending an RSVP in the shape of a double headed axe aimed directly at the waiting demon's head. Had it made contact then the battle would have ended before it had truly begun, leaving the demon with a splitting headache that no tablet would have cured. But the blow was blocked by the edge of the chainsaw blade. Attempting a counter swipe the demon swung the saw, aiming for Jimi's unprotected stomach. With surprisingly fast reflexes Jimi saw the blade and jumped back so that the blade missed him by mere inches. Jimi took his turn, making a sideward sweep he aimed at the demon's ribs only to find his weapon releasing a plume of brilliant sparks as the metal blade made contact with revolving hungry chainsaw blade teeth. Using both hands to keep the saw in position, and avoiding being injured, muscles strained as weapons locked in mid-air. Seeing an opportunity Jimi freed one hand from the axe handle and punched the Chaldean demon as hard as he could in the face. The sudden, unexpected, impact was enough to stun the demon and make his step backwards. Weapons became free, but the demon lost his footing on the uneven path and fell heavily to the ground. The momentum of the fall sending the chainsaw flying over his head and making it hit a large grey rock. The impact of the stone on the spinning blade was hard enough to shatter the chain and send teeth flying off at a velocity so fast that if it wasn't for them glowing red-hot, they would not have been visible. Most flew harmlessly along the path or into the heather, but one single tooth shot deeply through the demon's uniform and into its shoulder making him release a cry of pain. Seeing an opportunity Jimi took it. Swinging his axe high he brought it down onto the chest of the prostrated demon. It sank deep into the sternum, breaking the ribcage and destroying its heart. Jimi had given vengeance on behalf of his old friends, the sheep, and the debt of honour for them saving his life all those years ago was repaid.

On seeing that the side battle was over, and their champion had been defeated, the demons decided that Jimi was no longer the subject of the vague and unspoken truce and aimed their weapons at him, intent on seeing that the Chaldean demon wouldn't be the only body laid on that stretch of the path.

As the rage abated, and he began to take stock of the situation, Jimi began to see that he was now becoming the focus of some unwanted attention. "Oh shitttt!" he cried as he dived into a patch of thick heather, escorted by a fusillade of bullets narrowly missing him. There was soft padded thud as he landed on top of a sheep that had been watching the fight from a safe vantage point. The shocked sheep released a startled Baaaa which was roughly the same expression that Jimi had only just made.

As their target had now disappeared the demons turned their attention back to the angels that were entrenched in the heather to their rear. A demon lifted his head a little too high and received a single fatal bullet from Roxy. Having hit her target, she managed to duck back down again before several rounds, sent by the demons, flew over her head.

"Sod this for a game of soldiers!" Muttered Bob in frustration. Reaching into one of his many bulging pockets he removed an orange stick of dynamite with a short black fuse sticking out of the end. Placing it on the ground, in front of him, he pulled out a lighter from another pocket and lit it. Bright sparks were released as the flame made its way towards the explosive. Kneeling up he fired his weapon, the ammunition belt flying through the machine gun, and, with his spare hand, he threw the dynamite. "Fire in the hold!" he shouted before jumping back down into his cover. Fast, but not fast enough, he winced at the pain from a round that had found its mark in his right shoulder; painful but not fatal. "I've always wanted to say that." He shouted gleefully to the world in general.

On seeing the explosive, the demon, nearest to it, attempted to pick it up and throw it back in the direction it had come. But, just like Bob when it was first thrown, he was not fast enough. The explosion ripping him apart; with the blast also catching two other demons in the discharge, killing them as well.

Seeing what Bob had done, with his dynamite, Dedan began to fire in the direction of the demons in the hope that they would fire at him and not decide to look for the easy target of Jimi. "Dynamite?" He shouted to Bob. "What is this, a bloody cartoon? Have you never heard of hand grenades?"

Bob gave Dedan a wide and toothy smile "No worries Brah", slipping into Hawaiian slang, "it worked didn't it? Anyway, TNT is more fun."

Bob's choice of archaic weapon was basic, crude and messy but Dedan had to admit that it was effective. Usually, when in a battle, allowing the enemy the opportunity of spreading out could give them a tactical advantage, but the three demons that took the brunt of the blast had their bodies spread out in such a way as to ensure that they were definitely disadvantaged. The action of picking up the dynamite, in an uncharacteristically valiant attempt to throw it back in the direction of the angels, had proven that that particular demon had guts. Evidence of which could now be seen decorating the nearby plant life. "Good point well made. Got any more of those wonderful little candles?"

"Sure, you didn't think that the bulge in my uniform was because I was pleased to see you?" Bob removed a couple of sticks of dynamite and tossed them to Dedan.

"Any for me?" added Roxy as she stuck her head above the grass to fire a volley at the demons. "I think I can get a few demons with one."

"For you Roxy, my dear, anything. Happy to oblige." He threw a couple more sticks in her direction before ducking down again to avoid several rounds that flew over his head. "Miles, you want a few fireworks?"

"Yeah Bob, send 'em over. Let's have a party!"

From the demon's vantage points most of what they could see was numerous sticks of, as yet, unlit dynamite being tossed from one clump of heather to another. They expected them to be ignited soon and sent in their general direction but thanks to the bullets, being sent flying over their heads, there was little that they could do to prevent the impending cascade of TNT. In desperation one of the Marching Horde sat up, so he could see properly, to spray his gun in the direction of the enemy. In one respect his timing was right as it hit Miles in the chest just as he was lifting himself up to throw his lit stick of dynamite. He fell down, his back on top of a clump of heather, the explosive still in his hand. The blast left little trace of the jazz musician, or the plant he had landed on. What was left of his equipment was sent flying up into the air and a bent and mangled trumpet, that he'd managed to conceal from Dedan, landed next to the demon that had dispatched Miles back to heaven. Instinctively he saw it land by his side and, without processing the sight fully, assumed it was some form of explosive device. In an attempt to put some distance between the object and his body he leapt to the side. This new target was spotted by Roxy and she was able to fill his uniform, and the body underneath, with a series of additional holes. The demon was dead before he'd even touched the ground; proof that in war a fear of jazz can be fatal.

Even though Finley had no idea of the number of the angel's in Dedan's team he knew that he had already lost a third of his force and was sure that once the dynamite started flying his numbers would decrease even more. Tactically, as he saw it, staying put would only lead to them being blown to pieces so there was either fight or flight as tactical options. Neither choice seemed attractive to him as the risks of being shot were almost as great as the odds of being blown to smithereens. Although, to serving troops, it was usually said in a sarcastic and ironic way but to Finley, who was a great believer in a common military philosophy, *there is no greater love that a man lays down his life for his commanding officer*. To him his minions were expendable, whereas he had a mission to complete, so was willing to make a few sacrifices to ensure *his* success.

In close quarter battles, with the noise of bullets flying around people's heads, it is difficult to speak at the appropriate level so that the right people, close by, can hear you and the enemy is left ignorant of any new orders. Whispering is pointless, but shouting tended to reveal plans to anyone that cared to listen. "Men" he began; his voice carrying to the demons nearest to him. "On my command we attack, pass it on."

The instruction was passed on from demon to neighbouring demon until all were ready and waiting for his word. In such situations seconds can feel like hours and the sporadic gunfire, that was keeping them pinned down, was random and scattered enough to avoid giving them a clear point at which to mount their offensive. War might be hell but to the demons, who had already technically died, liked being alive and had no desire to be killed once again and sent back to the real place. So, to them, war was more akin to a form of heaven and they were happy to wait seconds, hours, or even weeks, before facing anything that might see them dead. Attacking seemed to be a way of ensuring that their brief tenure back on Earth was cut shorter than they would have liked. There was a short lull in the shooting in their direction, so Finley took that moment to press forwards "Charge!" the instruction shouted at full volume. With that word the remaining demons stood up and began to return the fire. The timing was such that a rogue round was able to hit Roxy in the abdomen. She had stood up to allow for her lit stick of dynamite to be thrown. Luckily, she had more success at throwing it than Miles and it flew forward landing in a patch of heather by the path. With the burning projectile dispatched she collapsed back into her protective covering. As the demons ran forward the burning fuse reached the dynamite and exploded sending heather, mud and demon body parts flying across the moor. Three of the Marching Horde were caught directly in the blast and returned to Hell with a further four sent flying backwards towards Finley and making the other troops fall heavily onto the now blood strewn path. Seeing that the demons were disorientated Dedan took the opportunity to stand up and fire. Years of experience of demon killing ensured that his bullets hit four of the enemy that were still left standing. Each single round, on its own, would have been fatal but the full magazine that was emptied ensured that there was no risk of them getting up again. Seeing the last of his upright troops killed Finley decided to dive out of sight and return to the relative safety provided by the greenery. In his hiding place he was unable to witness Bob get up, despite the pain from his injury, and help to shoot the four demons that had been knocked off their feet by the blast. His belt fed machine gun ensured that they wouldn't be getting up either.

"There looks like there is just one left. Leave him to me." Bob's words making it clear that he wasn't leaving it open for discussion. "Dedan, you look after Roxy, she looks like she's been badly injured".

As the metal ammunition belt sped through his machine gun bullets began to force their way through the undergrowth surrounding Finley, forcing him to lie down behind a small earth mound, face into mud, to avoid getting hit. He still had his SA80's handle tightly in his grip but didn't have the opportunity to lift himself up and return fire.

Sensing that the battle was nearing its conclusion, and the risk of being shot by a demon was minimal, although Bob's wild firing was a different matter, Jimi decided to get up. Released from its enforced place, underneath the 1960's rocker, the formerly trapped sheep ran to find a place where falling soldiers were less of a risk.

From his vantage point Jimi could see Finley hiding in his cover and decided that now was an ideal time to re-join the fight. Having left his rifle behind, in the heather, he looked around for a weapon and spotted his treasured axe, still protruding from the chest of the Chaldean demon. Grasping it with both hands he yanked it free, swung it around his head twice and then launched it at Finley. Turning Finley saw Jimi and then he spotted the flying axe. As if in slow motion he watched helplessly as the anachronistic weapon spun gracefully through the air before one of the two blades buried itself deep into the demon's face, just to the left of the nose running from his eye down to his mouth.

Sensing that the last of the demons had gone Bob took his finger from the trigger and collapsed to his knees, his injury and general exhaustion preventing him from remaining standing.

Free from any risk of injury Dedan rushed to kneel on the soft heather by Roxy, one hand placed over the wound to prevent further blood loss while the other removed bandages from his pack.

"It's alright Roxy, it's just a scratch and you'll be okay!"

"I have said it before, and I'll say it again, you are full of shit Dedan."

"Yes, I certainly am but you love me for it!" giving her a reassuring smile and an un-reassuring wink. "Okay, it isn't great, but I have no intention of letting you go back to Heaven just yet. We still have to retrieve The Sword and you don't get out of doing your share of digging so easily!"

"Thanks, Dedan" coughing and wincing at the additional pain it caused "You are all heart."

Having retrieved his, now blood encrusted, axe Jimi stepped over the bodies of demons strewn along the path and joined his colleagues. Helping Bob to bandage his own wound he looked at Dedan. "Hey man. Not bad for a stoned and useless hippy was it?"

Dedan returned Jimi's gazed and gave him a slight nod. "Yes Jim, you did alright. Well done…. And thank you."

Recognising the words as finally being a sign of respect and forgiveness Jimi returned the nod. "I wish I'd brought my guitar now."

"Don't push it Jimi." Dedan responded, his voice full of laughter.

Chapter 38 - Digging To Be Done

Despite her injuries Roxy had refused the opportunity to take a portal back to Heaven and be free of her injuries. Her display of Italian temperament and strong will had made it perfectly clear to the three other survivors that she had no intention leaving the mission while she still had breath in her body. She might not have been able to walk, turn or even blink her eyes without feeling the pain that the wound, inflicted on her stomach, was sending through every nerve in her body and making her tighten up in agony. A pride in her mission but also her reasoning was that there could be other demons about and as long as she could carry a gun, and pull the trigger, she had to be there. With that simple argument Roxy adamantly maintained that she was still a valued part of the team. Dedan, Jimi and Bob all wanted to disagree with her, and insist that she go, but none of them had the strength or courage to contradict her. They had happily just faced the fury of Hell, but they had no desire to face the fury of Roxy's scorn.

The tired quartet gathered their weapons, and as much equipment as they could carry, and began the last part of their journey. They made a strange sight, Bob carrying his machine gun over his shoulder, the bullet belt wrapped around his neck like a deadly cravat. If he'd have accidentally pulled the trigger the tightening of the belt would probably have decapitated him. Jimi gave him support, ensuring that he didn't slip or fall. Dedan walked with his assault rifle draped across his back and Roxy held firmly in his arms. Her arms were wrapped around his neck with her weapon still in her hands. Body badly damaged and wracked with pain but mind still alert for any possible dangers. The pace was slow, but they felt confident that they didn't need to go any faster. They traipsed back the way they had come and re-joined the path heading the correct way, towards the brow of the next hill in the distance. The sheer number of miles disheartened them, but they knew they had to get there. In their condition the uneven surface was unforgiving and punished any careless step. Despite all his caution there were several occasions when Dedan slipped on some mud, or a wet and mossy stone, and had to struggle to maintain his balance. He could see the pain that each jolt was inflicting on Roxy but there was nothing he could do about it. She did her best to hide the agony, but he could see it in her eyes and feel it as her body winced. Following the proper instructions, that Barry had given them, they finally reached the Swastika stone; tired bodies welcoming the opportunity to stop and rest. Thanks to Dedan having lived in the early Biblical times he had seen and experienced many things so wasn't surprised by its appearance. However, the others, having lived in the second half of the 20th and early 21st Century, had been expecting something more recognisable and identifiable as a Swastika. Instead of the bent cross with right angle corners that had been stolen by the Nazi's, and turned into the symbol of hatred and death, they saw something that, to them, didn't seem to fit the bill. It still had four arms sticking out, and meeting in the middle, but they were far more rounded and haphazard in their design, looking more like a child's toy boomerang than an ancient symbol of fertility and peace. Despite being weathered and covered with small patches of cream and green coloured lichen the engraving could still be clearly seen in the grey rock.

Roxy was carefully placed down on a nearby patch of soft heather, overlooking the stone, giving her a vantage point from which to spot any possible demons. From there she was she could see across the wide valley that had been carved during the last ice age and anybody that approached could be seen before they got within a mile of them. Once Dedan was sure that she was as comfortable as possible he moved to the stone and gently rubbed it with his hand. "Alright Bob, I hope you have a shovel in that big bag of tricks stuck on your back."

"Have no fear chief, like a good boy scout I have come prepared. Although I don't know of many scouts that carry machine guns and sticks of dynamite. I know it was shunned in my pack when I was a lot younger." Removing his back-pack he opened it up and removed a black NATO style folding-head entrenching tool. Opening it out fully he then passed it to Jimi. Thanks to his injury he wasn't able to use the shovel and dig, but he knew how to delegate.

"I suppose the Swastika 'X' marks the spot. Where shall I start?" asked Jimi, pointing to some soil below the centre of the stone as he spoke. "Just here?"

"Yes, I suppose so. It looks as good a place as any to start the dig."

There followed several hours where Dedan and Jimi took it in turns to dig and remove the excavated soil out of the way. The wind was still strong, but it was blowing the clouds so that the sun kept making a brief appearance before being hidden again.

As they dug the exertion from the work, and the warmth of the periodic sunlight, forcing them to strip down to their waists. Jimi's dark, lean and taut stomach a stark contrast to Dedan's flabby gut but, despite the differences in appearance, Dedan was able to work at a faster and more energetic pace than the guitarist. Eventually the hole was so deep that the only way to access it was for the designated digger to climb inside, via a small entrance hole, and pass the freed earth out so that it could to be put elsewhere, out of the way. Finally, exhausted and frustrated, Dedan threw the shovel out of the hole and clambered out after it. Wiping the muddy sweat from his forehead with his uniform jacket, that had been laid on the ancient stone; he sat on the large rock, leaning forward with his arms resting on legs. "This is pointless. Either it is buried so deep that we'd need an excavator to retrieve it or it simply isn't there." his tired voice full of despair and failure. "Maybe Ernest lied to us or maybe he genuinely believed that it was here but either way I think we have just been on a wild goose chase!"

"Do you think that the demons got it before us?" the pain audible in Roxy's voice as she spoke; an equal mix of physical and emotional suffering.

"No." Replied Dedan his words sounding casual as if he were deep in his own private thoughts. "The ground here is too compacted and if it had ever been dug up it certainly wasn't recently. If Satan did have The Sword I can't imagine that the demons would have gone to the trouble of filling in the hole so carefully and besides why would he bother to create such subterfuge with the demon soldiers and cows? If Satan had it, he'd more than likely have made his move and probably have been sat on the throne of Heaven long ago. I just don't know. Maybe each one of the many Guardians, that are spread all over true planet, truly believing that they are the keepers of the true Sword's final resting place and they wouldn't know any better. Ask them and they'd all say that they were the one and only true Guardian. All wrong but as far as they know it is the truth. Maybe we'll never know where The Sword is. But one thing I do know - it isn't here."

Putting his jacket back on Dedan despondently summoned the portal to open so that they could return to Heaven, and all the safety and comforts that were to be found there. Tenderly picking up Roxy, in his muddy arm, he gave Bob and Jimi a resigned look. "Come on, let's go give God the bad news and Jimi, you can give Miles the bad news about his trumpet."

"But what about the mess we've made?" Bob enquired. "Surely, we can't just leave a pile of dead bodies, of various shapes and sizes, just littering the place. Somebody's bound to notice. If nothing else the smell would attract the attention of some confused authorities."

"Don't worry Bob, God will send down a team to tidy up the mess and a special public relations team to spread bullshit to explain the cows and the carnage." Dedan spoke without turning to face Bob. Before he could be asked any further questions both he, and Roxy, were gone. They were closely followed by Bob and just as he was about to walk through the barely visible portal Jimi turned to give the moor one last look. "Baaaa" he shouted to be met with a chorus of grateful Baaa's in the distance. Smiling he turned, took a step forward and also disappeared like a 1960's ghost blown in the wind and caught in the daylight.

Chapter 39 – Return To Better Thinking

He usually liked being on Earth and could cope with suffering some of the discomforts that entailed but, on this occasion, being free of the constraints of his former human body was a relief to Dedan. He might always keep the same appearance and shape but the ability to rid himself of the stupor that had engulfed him, by the end of the mission, was like taking an invisible Swastika stone from his back. Physically he had renewed vigour, energy and no longer felt any of the aches and pains that he'd received during his brief trip to the moors. Even the most battle-hardened trooper's body had its limitations and Dedan's was no exception. Although emotionally he still felt the pains of disappointment.

Leaving the rest of his small strike force, to make their own way back to their respective homes so that they could rest, he set off to God's office. The journey was like a blur, angels saw him and greeted him cheerfully hoping that he would stop and engage in conversation with them. Perhaps even telling them all about his exploits or, at least, telling them the basics, with good news somewhere in the story, but he hardly noticed them. A few got a distracted and distant sounding 'hello' while the rest were totally ignored. Not due to bad manners but more to the fact that his mind was in its own private hell trying to work things out and find answers that weren't there. Each possible solution sending out more complex questions, muddying his mind like feet walking through a silt filled stream lifting the dirt and clouding the water. The Swords mere existence on Earth posed a direct threat. If Satan found out that Dedan hadn't retrieved it then he'd redouble his efforts to get his hands on it. The unearthly arms race continuing as they all tried to find a single small sword hidden somewhere on a big planet.

He felt that it was his duty to break the bad news personally to God and any disappointment would be borne just by him. His friends had done their best and it wasn't any of their faults that The Sword wasn't where it was supposed to be. Their returning to their homes was scant reward for all they had done but, for now at least, it was all he could offer them.

Walking into Angelica's office he saw her sat at her desk busily typing away. On seeing him enter she immediately stopped her work and gave him a wide smile and stood to greet him. "Hello Dedan, welcome back."

He always enjoyed seeing God's private secretary and under different circumstances he would have found time to engage in some banter filled with gentle smut, innuendo and double entendres but at the moment he felt despondent and just wanted to deliver the message, get the meeting over and done with, and go home so that he could sleep. As days went, he could honestly say that he'd had better. "Hello Angel" His words lacking their usual energy and enthusiasm. "Is the Boss busy?"

"No Dedan, go straight in." She could see his undisguised troubled expression and her voice was full of concern for her friend and verbal sparring partner. "He's been expecting you."

Giving the door, into God's office, a firm knock he heard God invite him in. Silently opening it he walked into the large office and closed the door behind him; leaving Angelica worried. She was glad that Dedan had returned safely but was also wondering if he was the bearer of bad news that could mean that Satan had The Sword and was on his way.

"Ah, Dedan. Come in and sit down." pointing at a large brown leather-bound sofa chair that had been placed in front of his desk in anticipation of Dedan's return. God was, as always, happy to see His trusted emissary and seeing the defeated look on Dedan's face He lost His usual happy demeanour and replaced it with a concerned look. "How did it go? Tell me all about it."

"Well…" taking a deep breath "long story short, those Lambs of yours managed to see off most of the cows before we even got there. I persuaded the last of them to go and do what cows do. So, as long as they are behaving themselves, I think we can leave them on Earth. Any human that is tempted by a demon cow will probably end up in Hell anyway, whether those cows help out in the process or not."

"Agreed, not a problem." Nodding sagely God gestured for him to continue.

"Good. Anyway, we caught up with the main demon force. There were only 18 of them but they knew how to fight. Miles, and his trumpet, got blown to bits and Bob and Roxy were injured but we managed to send all the demon soldiers back to Hell. There is quite a mess down there, so we'll need to send a containment team down there to scrape up the pieces and placate any curious journalists or police officers."

"Consider it done." God was casually stroking the neatly trimmed white beard on His chin as He listened to Dedan's report.

"We then found the Swastika Stone and began to dig. And dig, and dig, and dig. We must have dug down about 9' and looked like large rabbits, making a burrow, but The Sword of Uncreation wasn't there."

"I see." God's voice calm and His face inexpressive. "You don't think you could have missed it or that the demons had somehow got there first?"

"There was no indication that the ground had been disturbed before we got there and when we dug there was nothing. I think we could have dug down to Australia and not found anything."

With a cold and unemotional voice God spoke "Oh well. You didn't find it but at least Satan doesn't have it either. He'll have to keep looking and I am sure that, every time he sends out a search party, we will stop him and make sure that any digging he does will leave him empty handed."

"Yes, I suppose so." Replied Dedan, not reassured by the words of God. "But I wish it were safe here in Heaven."

"Did I ever tell you that the discovery of Tutankhamen's tomb was due to a race between some of my angels and a few demons? Satan thought The Sword was buried in the desert but all that they found was a lot of sand, an old coffin, with a mummified body in it, surrounded by a few glittering baubles. Poor old Satan was

385

furious." Chuckling to Himself. "You see in his eagerness to wreak havoc and destruction he virtually single-handedly created a global tourist attraction which saved a whole country from poverty and starvation. The devil doing some good, whether he likes it or not! If only he'd knocked through a wall, he'd have found even more treasures as well."

"But you're playing a dangerous game. What if someday he becomes lord of the dance and gets one step ahead of you? It could happen." Dedan gave God a concerned expression.

"I very much doubt that Dedan. I can assure you he will never get his hands on it." The reassuring voice backed up by an appeasing shrug of his shoulders.

"But what if..." Dedan paused, his expression changing from concern to surprise then to realisation. "Hang on, hang on, hang on, HANG ON! You devious and tricky little bastard!"

It was God's turn to change his expression, this time from smugness to one of being offended. "I beg your pardon? Don't forget who you are talking to!"

"My humblest apologies my mighty Lord! You devious, tricky and mighty giant bastard. I might not know where exactly The Sword is, but I do know where it isn't. It isn't buried down some dirty hole on Earth, is it?"

Despite the profanity, aimed at Him, God gave Dedan the sort of innocuous and innocent look a school boy adopts when trying to tell a big lie in order to hide an obvious misdeed. Putting His hands up as if to surrender

He cleared His throat and finally spoke. "I was wondering how long it would take you to work it out. The Sword is indeed safe and unless Satan finds his way into my inner sanctum then I assure you there is nothing to fear."

"But why all the drama, why all the lies and all the pretence? Why not just stop all the silly games? Maybe even put it to some good use now and again?" Dedan was doing his best to keep calm and not shout at God. Not the best thing to do, especially in His own office and when He was sat right in front of the angel. He'd got away with swearing but there were always lines that could be crossed but shouldn't be. "We went through a lot of pain down there for no reason."

"Yes Dedan, I understand but when you play the devil at his own game you need to understand the rules; which, in the case of Satan, means that there are none! Smoke and mirrors if you like but the trick is to make him look one way while you use sleight of hand. Of course, I know he deals from the bottom of the deck and has 12 other aces stuck up his sleeve but while he thinks he is being smart, and fooling Me, then I have the true advantage. It is only when he realises that game has changed does, he become truly dangerous." Sensing the fountain of questions that Dedan wanted to release God raised His hand to silence Dedan and allow His explanation to continue. "And you want to know why I didn't let you in on the secret?"

"Well, yes, that is one of my questions."

"It is simple really. Knowing the truth might have changed how the game was played. You might not have been so desperate to stop the demons. Not been so willing to see Roxy get so badly injured and suffer the pain. Forgive me changing metaphors but if you'd have taken your foot off the accelerator then the demons might have noticed and got suspicious. Then if they'd got to the stone first, done the digging and found nothing Satan might have started using his brain and put two and two together to make four. Plus, if you'd been captured, and inadvertently let on that The Sword was really in Heaven then the whole show would have come to an abrupt end. Take a bow as the curtain closes!"

"But why the charade?" Dedan felt that the answers should be obvious, but he couldn't see them in the fog that was his current state of tired mind.

"Because my dear Dedan the more demons he sends to Earth in a futile attempt to look for a sword, that isn't there, the fewer demons he sends out to trick and deceive humans into giving him their souls. Thanks to free will Humans can be good or evil on their own so why have Satan adding to the difficulties of staying Heaven bound?"

"So, what now?"

"Now?" God appeared to be momentarily deep in thought before looking into Dedan's eyes and giving him a serious stare, His eyebrows furrowed. "Now the game goes on. The same dramatic moves but at a different location. I will ensure that a few innocent and uninformed angels are sent down to Earth to try and continue the search for The Sword. The Demons will soon find out and he will divert a lot of resources to ensure that he pulls one over on me and gets the weapon. I am sorry Dedan, I know that I used you, with Roxy, Bob and Miles briefly receiving some pain, but, if it is any consolation, I promise you that I will not use any of you for any similar missions in future. After all you know the secret now so are compromised. But of course, you must also understand that what I have just told you has to stay between you and Me. None of your brothers, and sister, in arms can ever know the truth."

Dedan thought, for a few seconds, about all that he had just been told. He realised that he had been a simple pawn in a bigger chess game but that was life, be it on Earth or in Heaven. Not everybody could be the grand master and control every piece. In a way he was relieved that The Sword wasn't really on Earth. Instead of failing he had inadvertently played his role to perfection; a warrior desperately defending something precious. The fact that The Sword wasn't really there was academic, Satan thinking it was on Earth was the truly critical thing. "Okay God. One last thing, where is it?"

God laughed gently. "It's in here and has been for centuries. Can't you see it? It's there if you look!"

Dedan stood up and began to look around the room. Starting his search, he looked at God and His large ornate desk, nothing but the usual attributes of a high-powered executive. An antique leather-bound desk pad blotter and a pen holder, with two fountain pens protruding out of it, all where they should be. And, of course, His seemingly ever-present novelty mug full of strong black coffee. Across the room he saw nothing out of the ordinary and certainly nothing that he hadn't seen hundreds of times before. All was the same and seemed in keeping with the office of God. Plush and comfortable chairs were placed around the room with coffee tables nearby, ready to support any drinks placed on them. The drinks cabinet looked too small to hold all the exquisite and rare spirits along with The Sword. The oak umbrella stand, just next to the door leading to Angelica's office, was tall but just had several umbrellas' protruding out of it, handles of various colours, shapes and sizes. Then there was the large fish-tank at the other side of the door. That had always seemed odd and incongruous to Dedan with the anachronistic fish, from prehistory, happily swimming with modern and brightly coloured tropical fish. But, yet again, The Sword didn't seem to be there.

Moving his attention from the furniture he began to look at the walls. There was the cavernous fireplace with its roaring log fire, always burning and never needing replacement fuel. The eternal flames a perk of being God. There was a brass fireplace poker set next to the right-hand column of the fireplace but none of the five little tools, hanging from the metal branches, were big enough to be The Sword. Half expecting to see the sword in a wooden frame, clearly visible, yet ignored by all visitors, he moved along the walls. Works of art created by the masters were on display. Some depicted Saints wielding swords but there was no physical sword he could touch. His eyes passed over doors in the far and side walls, that he hadn't noticed before, but had always been there. He had no idea where they went to and had never seen anyone use them. He finished his visual inspection of the office and turned his attention to God. His Master was sat with a grin on His face as if He was suffering from terminal smugness. Not a deadly sin but still annoying, especially coming from God. He was enjoying His little game far too much for Dedan's liking. He half expected God to start saying 'You're getting warmer, Oh, you're cold, cold, freezing' as if he were a little child. Suddenly it was Dedan's turn to smile. Something in his mind had just created a mental jigsaw puzzle picture and put the last piece in place. The scene was one of the sun on the horizon and it was called 'The Dawning!' "You sly old Sod!" The gentle insult making God chuckle rather than chastise. "Of course, it is obvious when you think about it. When does it ever rain in Heaven? Okay, there might be some that find rain their idea of paradise but when did it last rain on you?" Dedan walked to the umbrella stand and began to empty it, removing the contents one by one. Gripping each handle carefully, inspecting each umbrella on removal before placing it on the floor. Until finally he saw one that didn't look like any umbrella handle he'd ever seen before; black leather in the shape of a cross. Pulling it out slowly he looked at the furled up black canopy held tightly shut by the long and thin metal ribs. Inspecting it closely he saw a small button on the shaft, just below the handle. Before he could push it, God spoke, casually, to him. "Be careful Dedan, some say that opening an umbrella indoors is bad luck."

"It's alright Sire, I promise to watch what I am doing. And besides I think I have suddenly become lucky."

Pressing the button, instead of it releasing the runners and opening it in anticipation of rain, the cloth and metal separated from the handle and slid to the floor revealing the bright blade and jewelled handle of The Sword of Uncreation. For once Dedan could have made a rude joke about holding a mighty weapon in his hands and he'd have been telling the truth.

"Bravo." God clapped enthusiastically. "I wondered how long it would take someone to ask if they could borrow an umbrella. Admittedly a rather showy affectation but it was effective. Ready for me to use just in case Satan and his armies of darkness should ever breach Heaven's defences and end up being my uninvited guest. A last resort but always there if needed."

"Now what?" asked Dedan, looking uncertainly at The Sword that he was carefully wielding in his hand. He felt like a dog with a large stick in its mouth. He had it but didn't know what to do with it.

"Now what?" God repeated the words as if He was encountering an alien concept. "We put it back in its cleverly disguised scabbard. Very carefully back in its scabbard I must add. Then it goes back where it came from. Finally, you say nothing about its location to anyone; ever!"

"Understood!" said as he picked up the cleverly disguised sheath and returned The Sword so that the blade, and ornate handle, was not to be seen and all anyone would see was a large umbrella. Placing it back in the stand he then picked its umbrella brethren so that they could re-join it.

"Well, if you'll excuse me Sire, with your permission I would like to retire. Go home, have a long soak in the bath and then sleep. It has been a very long and busy day and I could do with relaxing."

"Of course, Dedan. I know it might have seemed like you have been used but please believe me when I say that it was for a greater good. Sleep well my friend."

Dedan bowed slightly then left the room, leaving God to sip His coffee and stare absent-mindedly into His fire.

Chapter 40 – Experiencing Jimi Hendrix

Angelica was facing God's door, leaning against the edge of her desk, legs outstretched and feet flat on the floor, crossed at the ankles; the tight black pencil skirt revealing her legs from just above the knee. They were tanned and slender and would have made a weak man collapse onto his knees and worship them, perhaps a new religion starting up in God's secretarial office? Her equally snug fitting white blouse just completed the package of perfect sex appeal, and many male angels wished they could donate generously to that cause! A deliberate beauty which was carefully planned, by her, but still looking natural and unforced.

Although she was there waiting specifically to talk to Dedan she was trying to maintain a casual and nonchalant appearance. Even though she had a folder in her hands, and wasn't looking at its contents, if you'd asked her what the pages said, or the document was about, she wouldn't have been able to answer. The paperwork could have been upside down for all she knew. Curiosity had been burning her up inside, the more walls she encountered, while looking for answers, the more determined she became to find the definitive answer. Although it pained her to admit it the only person that might be willing to fully answer all her questions would be Dedan. If he found out the lengths, she'd gone to in attempts to find answers she knew she'd never hear the end of it. God had given her a little information but the gaps made the story even more painfully tantalising.

As he appeared, exiting God's office, she maintained her casual demeanour and lowered her documents, and placed them on her desk, making it look like his appearance was just part of the routine and she just happened to be stood there as she studied a critical piece of data.

"Oh, hello Dedan. How are you? You didn't seem too happy when you went in to see the Boss. I take it that The Sword is safe, and I don't have to start barricading my door in preparation of Satan rampaging through Heaven?"

Dedan was deep in thought, going over all that had happened over the whole day so her cheerful words, and seductive voice, snapped him out of his own private world. He might not have liked the way that he'd been used but understood the rationale behind it. When it came to the machinery of war there were wheels within wheels and it was sometimes best not to try and dismantle it or, even worse, stick your arm in-between the moving cogs. After all Satan and all his demons would be kept busy trying to find The Sword and while they were doing that Earth would be a safer place. Humans could be idiots without having a devil whispering in their ears and giving them suggestions. "Hello Angelica, my beautiful angel. You are looking stunningly beautiful today. But then again you always do." The excuse to light heartedly chat with someone was just the diversion he needed; the fact that it was Angelica was even better. "You can rest easy, Satan hasn't got his hands on The Sword, so you can leave your bedroom door unlocked, especially for me, you provide the body and I'll bring the chocolate sauce, whipped cream and wine."

"You really should get hold of a modern dictionary and look up the word *inappropriate*." Feigning mock shock and disapproval as she spoke. "Nought out of ten for subtly but ten out of ten for consistency and effort."

"Well you can't blame a man for trying." the impish look in his eyes showing that his focus was no longer on the negatives of the day.

"Well you can be very trying." giving him a coy smile. "Dedan," her tone suddenly serious. "I know that there is some bad blood between you and Jimi Hendrix. What is the story behind it?"

"Oh, that is all sorted now. He and I are good. But it is a long story."

"It's alright Dedan, I like long stories and don't mind." She was determined not to let him leave her office until she knew the full story. After all, to her, Jimi was a legend and seemed like a great guy so how could anyone, especially an angel, not like him? "God gave me the brief details but that left more questions than answers."

Adopting the same position as Angelica, Dedan rested his buttocks against the edge of the desk next to her. His motivation a mixture of wanting to be comfortable, be close to the target of his flirtations and also to enable him to have a better view of her legs and cleavage as he recounted his story. If nothing else Dedan was an opportunist that admired beauty.

"Well, it all began at the end of 1970. Jimi had drowned in his own vomit, in his London flat, died and, when he had arrived in Heaven had quickly got bored. He heard of me, and my missions, and started to pester me, asking if he could join me on one of my trips to Earth. I wanted nothing to do with him, after all who needs a dead-weight stoned hippy with them when you are up against demons? I liked his music but that wasn't enough to convince me that he'd be any use in a battle. Whenever I returned to Heaven, he'd be there asking me, pestering me like a spoilt child. He got to be a real pain in the arse so I eventually told him to go away - although I might have used stronger words than that. But not being one to take no, or even feck off, for an answer he went over my head and spoke directly to God, which he did. Unfortunately, for me, He didn't share my concerns and promised Jimi that he could escort me on an operation at some point. I tried to avoid seeing him for a while but eventually he caught up with me and I had to fulfil God's promise. By then it was February 1972 and I had to track down a pack of particularly vicious Crandial Demons. They are beasts that are cunning gamblers and adapt at obtaining the souls of those that like to wager more than their ready cash. You could bet everything you own on a dead certainty and end up losing more than your shirt. At first all went well, we tracked them across America but thanks to Jimi running off for a few days, so that he could see the Grateful Dead in concert, we lost them at San Francisco. But we soon picked up the trail again and found them in Hong Kong. I managed to pick off a few in a very friendly brothel and gambling den but the rest escaped. We followed them and as we got to the harbour, we saw them steal a boat and take it to the Queen Elizabeth cruise ship that was anchored not far away. It was night and we chased them all over the big boat. I told Jimi that, no matter what, we mustn't let them escape so he took my instructions far too literally and decided to ensure their demise and immediate return to Hell. The problem was that his way of following instructions was far too literal and extreme. We closed bulkheads and managed to contain them below decks. I was planning to carry out a room by room sweep and just deal with them as we encountered them. Slow but we would have got them eventually and a containment team would have been able to clear up the mess before the workers came on board. But, oh no, not Jimi 'The End Justifies the Means' Hendrix, that was far too convoluted a plan. He decided to light a few fires and smoke them out of their hiding holes. Unfortunately, the ship was in the middle of a refurbishment and there was welding gear about - A LOT of welding gear about. And the thing about Oxyacetylene cylinders is that they do not particularly like the gentle caress of bloody great flames warming them up. They tend to get temperamental and explode in a rather spectacular fashion. If you have never seen it happen close up then you are lucky because, if you have, then it would be more than likely the last thing you'd see as a human. If you are thinking subtle pyrotechnics like a 4th July firework display then you are being a bit too romantic. In the confines of a ship it is like being inside a volcano or, I would imagine, it is not dissimilar to one of Satan's fun chambers. The remains of the canisters, mixed with the red and golden flames, shot through the corridors like someone going mad with a flamethrower. A brief but painful way to die, you can take my word for it. Jimi suffered from over exuberance and a bad case of demon overkill but, credit where credit is due, he did destroy all the demons. However, he also managed to kill me and send me back to Heaven and sink the ship in the process. A spectacular sight from what I have been told, alas my body had just been cremated so I missed that show. Somehow, and to this day I have no idea how, he managed to escape his own firestorm and make it back to shore. He was unscathed, and God had to send the an eager Archangel to retrieve him. He found Jimi in a casino getting drunk with Bruce Lee. Suffice to say that, up until today, I had avoided Jimi and he hadn't been allowed on any more missions. But he acquitted himself well on Ilkley Moor, so perhaps he'll be allowed back on Earth again, maybe even with me."

Throughout the recounting of the story Angelica had sat open mouthed listening intently to Dedan and visualising it all; a once glorious cruise ship burning on the inside and giving several demons, and an angel, an extravagant Viking funeral in Asian waters. As a child she had seen the black and white news broadcasts on a small television screen and witnessed the demise of the famous liner. The cause of the fire had always been a mystery and no human, no matter how much they loved conspiracy theories, had ever put forward a hypothesis that even came close to the truth. "Wow" she muttered. "But why all the secrecy? I tried to find out why you disliked him so much but it was locked away tighter than St. Margaret of Antioch's chastity belt. No-one was getting into those files."

"You must have been extremely nosey to have dug so deep and found all the barriers." giving Angelica a sly sideward glance as if to tease her. "You could have searched for all eternity and found nothing as I deleted the folders and all official records of the incident. But I am flattered that you looked."

"But why?" she reiterated the original question.

"Why? That is simple. I was embarrassed. I was in charge of the operation, so the buck stopped with me. I have had missions go wrong before and, sometimes shit just happens, so I have failed occasionally but to be seen as the one that destroyed such a beautiful ship just to kill a few relatively harmless demons, armed mainly with sleeves full of aces and pockets full of weighted dice? No, better that tale be put down to experience and just forgotten about." He stared at his feet as he paused to contemplate all that he had just revealed to the target of his affections, or at least lust. "Guitarists! I suppose Satan has the same problems and that is probably why he's never sent Robert Johnson back to earth."

Although she had no idea who the musician was, that he'd just name checked, Angelica smiled. Records by 1930's guitarists, who had sold their souls to Satan, were never part of her record collection when she'd been alive on Earth.

The fatigue of the day was finally making itself known to Dedan. Even the invigoration received from returning to Heaven, and resuming his Angel form, had still not managed to make him feel totally awake and free from aches, stiff limbs and sore feet. "Well my beautiful angel, if you will excuse me, I think I need to go home and have a soak in a nice hot bath and go to bed. Care to join me in one, or both, of those?" Exhaustion had done nothing to diminish his ardour and sense of delusional optimism.

"Why thank you Dedan for such a tempting offer but I think I will give it a miss. I'll let you soak and then sleep alone."

"Alright but it is your loss. You don't know what you are missing." Dedan stood up and gave her a lascivious smile that wouldn't have been out of place on an Incubus Demon's sly face.

"Well from what other female angels have told me I have a pretty good idea of what I am passing up and I am sure I will survive." She gently put her hands on his cheeks and tenderly kissed him on the forehead. "Now go home my friend, you look tired. Good night!"

Standing he gave her one final smile, this time one that was full of genuine caring and attachment. Friendship meant a lot to him, and if he couldn't have more, than he was happy to have that and cherish it. It had been a long day and he no longer felt like putting on the act that people had come to expect from him. Sleep and rest were what he needed.

Chapter 41 - Hell Hath No Fury...

If there were ever any demons, in Hell, that had any doubts about the level of rage that Satan could reach then they should have had a look around his private office. He tended not to take bad news well and it was fair to say that when Finley, Collins and the rest of the demon army finally reappeared in Hell, found their way to Satan's room and delivered the fine details relating to the battle and subsequent failure to obtain The Sword, he was extremely unhappy. Their dark master's reaction was far from favourable, and it showed. A fact that could be evidenced by the redecoration that he had personally done to the surrounding walls, floor and ceiling. Thanks to his quick and vicious temper the inner sanctum frequently took on the same hue as blood. However today the 'paint' was particularly thick and was not a non-drip emulsion. Blood was indiscriminately splattered into every imaginable, and some unimaginable, nook and cranny of the place. In addition to the various shades of crimson there were the added hints of grey brain matter, some browns that had escaped from internal organs and some light green substance that an anatomist would have easily recognised but most people wouldn't want to know what it was. The wet and fluid artwork was given a three-dimensional texture with the addition of various sized pieces of shattered and dislodged bone. The whole motif was akin to Jackson Pollock having been force fed explosives before it detonated, leaving the result on one of his own canvasses. All that was missing was a signature at the bottom to prove its authenticity.

Panting heavily, like a bull that had just been on the rampage and had briefly stopped to catch its breath, Satan stared intently at his hands, covered in blood with chunks of flesh still stuck in his claws. The rage inside him had still not been fully sated but his tornado of anger had been forced to come to a premature end as he'd run out of demons to rip to shreds. On the floor, at his feet, lay the small demon army. Or, more accurately, it was the remains of them. It would have been difficult to recognise individuals or, in the case of one particular pile, decide where one demon ended and another began. The remnants looked like they were in the process of being made ready to be processed and turned into burgers. All that was missing was salt and some spices. He would need his carpet to be replaced, yet again but, fortunately for him there were plenty of carpet makers in Hell and they were spared the charms of punishment chambers thanks to them being kept busy with making replacement flooring for Satan's office. They could easily make a product that would allow the blood to be washed out, but they knew a good thing when they had it and preferred working on their trade rather than being sent into some chamber where their comfort was not part of the room service.

The usually ever present Stuart was now nowhere to be seen. He had witnessed Satan's temper tantrums before and had learnt to recognise a storm well before it happened. On seeing Finley eventually appear, without The Sword proudly held up high in hand and accompanied by a triumphant smile, he knew what was coming and had decided to make himself scarce. He was sure that it was an ideal time for him to do his rounds at some of the outer rings of Hell and, as a coincidence, he thought that it would take just enough time so that his return to his office coincided with Satan calming down to an extent where Stuart would manage to keep vital organs inside his body rather than seeing them redistributed across the floor. When he was out and about, he used his chameleonic skills to remain hidden, so that any conversations were carried out by other demons and he could maintain his obscurity, hidden and unobserved. He didn't need to tell anyone else the details as the news of the empty-handed return had spread throughout Hell like the after effects of a strong curry across a toilet bowl and it was just as unappetising. Creatures that would normally have avoided each other were deep in furtive conversation discussing all the details that were available and speculating on the repercussions of their leader's rage, once it spread out to their personal corners of Hell. They all felt sure that, irrespective of them not having had any involvement in the operation, they would all suffer in one way or another. Losing their heads was one thing but having it cut off, and used as a suppository, might mean that they kept their heads but it was something that made them wish that they didn't have eyes or such long horns!

As Stuart progressed, he encountered the same level of fear and panic wherever he went. After the earlier revolt, by the damned souls, the demons had been spared any punitive injuries as Satan had wanted to ensure he'd have enough troops for the impending storming of Heaven. Now that that requirement had gone there was little to prevent them from experiencing a level of pain beyond the comprehension of any human. Even Stuart didn't feel immune to any random acts of extreme violence that would soon be making Hell an even worse place to experience. Deciding that he had seen enough he decided that he had better return to his office. There were risks but, in balance, being absent while Satan called for him would be far worse than being there and answering any call. He had other news to deliver to him, relating to the few damned souls that remained on the loose and managed to escape to Earth, but that could wait for a quieter moment. Waiting for the particular area around his hiding place to be free from other demons he moved away from his section of wall and returned to his human colour scheme. Opening a door that had, up until a second earlier, not existed he stepped through it and as soon as he had disappeared so did the door leaving only the patch of rocky wall that had previously been there.

Back in his office he paused and listened attentively. Moving closer he pressed his ear to the wall, being a sneaky spy, he recognised that often the old ways were the most efficient. He couldn't hear any noises emanating from his master's office, no shouting, no screams and no sounds of body parts being displaced and redistributed across the room. Even the public address system had respectfully gone quiet so Barry Manilow's voice was not serenading Satan with lyrics describing tropical bars or his inability to smile in his absence. However, that lack of things to hear wasn't as comforting as it should have been, Satan being silent and alone with his own burning angry thoughts was a dangerous place to be close to. There was an evil blast zone, on the other side of the wall, which could be unpredictable and inescapable. Satan was liable to plan more arbitrary ways to vent his rage on any unfortunate demon that happened to walk into his line of sight. Stuart shuddered as he remembered what happened to a couple of Winderrigheid Demons that had been tasked with cleaning up his office last time he'd flown into one of his wild and uncontrollable rages. Ever since then he'd never been able to look at mops and buckets in the same way and volunteers for janitorial duties became impossible to find.

There would come a point when either Satan came out of his office, or more likely, Stuart would be summoned to leave the relative safety of his own quarters and enter the danger zone that was Satan's room. Hell was large and almost infinite, and he knew the place like the back of his hand, so running and hiding was always an option, but he liked his position of power and had no desire to act like a Chameleon lizard for the rest of eternity. Scurrying along walls and trying to remain invisible was not his idea of fun. Plus, if he tried it, and failed, then the punishments would not bear thinking about. His cunning machinations had allowed him to rise at the expense of others, he had seen what had happened to them and he was happy to avoid such fates. Sitting at his desk he busied himself with clerical duties. There were reports to be made and ledgers, listing all the new arrivals to Hell, which had to be compiled. Even though he seldom read them the large skin bound volumes were carefully placed on Satan's desk on a daily basis. They were invariably ignored and Stuart would duly collect them later and then file them away in a vast archive room that could be accessed through a door at the far end of his office; an ancient tradition that Stuart wished that he could skip for just one or two days. Noticing the clock on his wall he saw that the time had come for him to perform his duty. Some bullets had to be bitten, but he was more concerned that the metaphor could be more of a reality and he'd end up with his head being blown apart. Picking up the latest book he held it carefully in both hands, it was heavy and occasionally, due to its listing so many evil people, and their deeds, the document itself came alive and performed evil deeds. Several times he'd found himself being attacked with the paper giving him more than minor cuts. Violent journals were not something he'd encountered on Earth when he had been an accountant. The height of excitement, in that profession, usually involved adding an extra sugar to a cup of drinking chocolate at Christmas time.

Manoeuvring his hands, so that he could hold the book safely in one hand, he knocked on Satan's door. He could hear the resultant sound echoing coldly throughout Satan's office.

"Enter!" Satan's voice was booming and tinged with barely suppressed wrath. If words alone could cause real physical damage then that small sentence would have had the power to crush the skull of the toughest demon.

Utilising his shoulder, he used all his weight to push the belligerent and uncooperative door open, reluctantly it finally allowed access but gave Stuart a deep groan just so that he knew that it was complying under duress. Upon entering the room, the first thing that he saw was the unavoidable carnage that would have kept a human forensic team busy for a month. The next thing that he noticed was the smell. In his enthusiasm for the punishment process Satan must have ripped open a demon's spleen, bladder and bowels so its contents were releasing a far from delicate bouquet of excrement in various stages of ingestion. Then, at last, he saw Satan. He wasn't sat at his usual place, behind his giant desk, but was currently stood in front of the vast fireplace staring intently into the flames, there being the only place where the warmth from the fire was cooling when compared to the normal ambient temperature. Unsure if the latent avalanche of rage syndrome had dissipated Stuart silently proceeded to the desk. With the sound of squelching body parts and blood-soaked carpet accompanying his every footstep he walked across the room. Reaching the desk, he dutifully placed the book on it and stood waiting for any further questions or instructions. He felt unconvinced that getting his satanic majesties attention was the best career move but he knew that trying to leave the room unnoticed was unlikely. Standing, waiting, he could feel his feet sinking slightly in the now marsh like handmade flooring. He always hated cleaning his shoes after days like this; the black leather became stained and made them look a ruddy colour.

Slowly Satan dragged his gaze away from the dancing flames and turned to face his underling. Stuart tried to read the expression on Satan's face but, thanks to the red shadows cast by the flames behind him, he was unable to. As he drew closer Stuart stood stock still, maintaining his polite posture. Normally he would add a hint of arrogance and surliness to the way he stood but for now he would avoid any gesture that would result in him suffering the same fate as the Marching Horde that had recently redecorated Satan's walls. Although Satan was walking no slower than he normally did, to his menial the progress seemed to be agonisingly slow, step after step he moved closer until he was stood in front of Stuart. Daring to move his head he turned his face to look into his master's eyes but instead of a face he saw Lucifer's chest covered by a suite that had previously been a charcoal grey pinstripe but was now a crimson colour. Raising his chin higher he was able to see Satan's face, far higher than it used to be. Then he made a quick glance downwards at his feet and realised why Satan had grown even taller; he was stood on a pile of demon remains. Unmindful of the fact that he was stood on a pile of minced flesh Satan looked down and gave Stuart a severe scowl full of contempt and abhorrence for his weak and pathetic assistant. The wrath was still coursing through his veins and making his brain feel like it was going to squirt out of his nose but, despite that, he couldn't be bothered to vent any of his aggression on Stuart. If he was to destroy anything then it had to be worth the exertion, not some snivelling sycophant.

"Stuart, in the past I think that that I might have likened you to a worthless maggot, insignificant and only worthy of being squashed underfoot. But on reflection I think that I have been grossly unfair and cruel to maggots. At least they serve a purpose and can help to make dead bodies disappear and in their own way have a mesmerising beauty. You, on the other hand, lack all the attributes of those creatures. You are pathetic and other than filling out paperwork and spying on people you serve no real purpose. In the hierarchy of demons, you are the bottom of the dung heap that the demons, with spines, use to shit on. Isn't that right?"

Inside Stuart was seething; the character assassination was totally unfair. At least it was in his mind, if not the minds of every other demon that had ever met him. Especially as one of the things that had sent him to Hell in the first place was his ability to make bodies disappear. No matter how much he wanted to disagree with Satan he knew better than that. "Totally right sir, as always." He wished that he could add 'just like your idea to send the cows on the last mission was well thought out'. But self-preservation was winning today's battle with his sarcastic nature.

"Well, I think I will give you something to make you feel worthwhile. I am going to send you on a mission to Earth. But first send for Grank."

Chapter 42 – The Great Gig in the Sky.

Despite his sudden, spectacular and messy exit, from Earth, Miles Davis had materialised back in Heaven and was back to his normal self with no untoward side effects. He did feel blue about having lost his favourite trumpet but there were plenty of horns in Heaven that he could use so he soon managed to purloin a silver one from Moses and was busy playing a jazzed-up version of Pink Floyd's Money. After adding a few embellishments, to the classic tune, he was currently on his 57th minute of his solo and showing no sign of nearing the end. Despite this Bob and Jimi were sat in awe filled silence as they watched and listened to him play. Jimi was ready with his guitar and waiting for a nod indicating that he should join in, but from the looks of it he could have left his private recording studio, enjoyed himself with his large army of naked, but hot, female fans in the room next door, and on his return, Miles might *just* be ready for him to make it a duet.

Bob took a deep drag of a joint that looked like it had been in a competition with a walking stick to see which could be the biggest and won. Then he passed it to Jimi for him to enjoy.

"Jimi, where's Dedan and Roxy? I thought you invited them to come 'round and chill out after they had got some sleep."

"Yeah man, I did. But Dedan said that he had to go see Sinatra and the Rat Pack. There's some sort of party going on at Deano's place."

"Hey, why don't we go and crash the party? It sounds cool." Bob was making a move to stand up when

411

Jimi gently held him by the shoulder and gave him a slight head gesture, indicating that he should remain seated.

"Man, are you joking? Last time I went to one of Frank's shindigs Bogart smoked all the grass, but it was great jamming with Sammy Davis Jr. though. But no, I am happy here."

"Okay Jimi. I am happy here too. And what about Roxy? Did she finally succumb to Dedan's lascivious charms?"

A loud and discordant note was released from Miles's horn indicating that, when he was playing, they should be listening and not talking.

Jimi gave Bob a quizzical look then whispered "Are you kidding? She likes him but isn't insane. No, she's gone back to Florence and taken Limbo up on his invitation to join him for an 'English tea'. Apparently, she finds him charming and enjoys the delicate sophistication of his room. I suppose he doesn't get many visitors, is short of real angelic company, and likes her as well."

"Oh well, each one to their own." Bob nodded his head before, once more, taking the spliff from Jimi and savouring another long and satisfying drag. He'd enjoyed his brief sojourn down to Earth but he had to admit that life, or the afterlife, just didn't get much better than this.

God was sat in one of His comfortable leather chairs close to the fireplace, positioned so that He could relax and stare into the flames as He enjoyed a strong black coffee drunk from his favourite mug. Yet another mission had been a success and Satan was still none the wiser and would continue wildly chasing metaphorical geese, as he had always done in the past. Then His thoughts were interrupted by a gentle knock on the door followed by Angelica, and a small and sallow looking man, entering his room.

"Apologies for disturbing you Sire but I have someone here that needs to speak with you."

Standing up He gave His guests a smile and proceeded to go to the chair at the far side of His desk and sat down again. "Not a problem Angelica. So young man, what brings you to my office on such a lovely day?"

The man stepped forward awkwardly. He wasn't sure how he should stand or talk when in front of God. "Sir, Sire, my Lord" He stammered "I, I, I"

"Please, relax, I am God not some ogre waiting to smite you. Please take a seat and consider Me a friend. That should help you to avoid repeating things three times."

The man thankfully sat down. Despite his faith and belief that God was a loving and kind deity he was still frightened enough to soil his trousers. When it came to meeting his maker, he was not prepared or even certain of what to expect. "Sire, my name is Brian and I have just been judged by Limbo and found to tip the scales on the side of good. I am not proud of my life but I am pleased that I wasn't found to be all evil."

"I am glad to hear it Brian and welcome to Heaven." God took another sip of coffee as he listened.

"Well Sire, before I came here Limbo asked me to personally give you a message. It is 'Ernest is good but wants to stay here for a while and be my assistant'. I hope that makes sense Sire." Brian finally relaxed, relieved that he'd been able to deliver his message without making any mistakes.

"Thank you Brian I appreciate being told."

Once a few pleasantries had been exchanged Brian made his excuses and left, closely followed by Angelica. He was relieved to be out of the overwhelming office and be allowed in the parts of Heaven where he could enjoy all that the place famously had to offer.

Alone in His office God smiled to nobody but Himself. He was not as vindictive and vengeful as many Christians wanted to believe that He was and bore no malice towards His wayward Sword Guardian. He was glad that Ernest had proven to be good and finally found a place where he could find happiness. Heaven wasn't the only place for that, but He hoped that someday Ernest would learn to forgive himself and pass through the Pearly Gates. He'd be made welcome when he did.

Chapter 43 – The Odd Couple

Thanks to their previous mission together, where they had continually tried to outsmart the other, on a scale of one to one hundred on a 'love-o-meter', if such a thing existed, the harmonious feelings that Grank and Stuart shared for each other would have scored somewhere in the high minus numbers. Mutual hatred and loathing wouldn't even have come close to describing what they felt for each other. It was worse than a couple that had been married for 30 years. Reluctantly they stood, side by side, before Satan. Both recognising that a mission was about to be issued and hoping that they would be given the role of leader. Both felt that they deserved it and they felt naturally superior to the other.

Satan was leaning on the edge of his desk and was ignoring the noise and bustle being made by a team of frightened Masturbasi Demons as they hurriedly cleaned up body parts from the floor and attempted to remove all traces of blood from the room. Not an easy task, especially with the fear of making too much of a noise, attracting Satan's attention and ending up in a similar state to the demons they were currently shovelling into large wheelbarrows. Their gigantic hands made light work of handling the shovels but the fine skills, required for cleaning the bloody demonic works of art hung on the wall, was not something they were good at. They were happier making messes rather than cleaning them up.

"Right you two, I have a lovely job for you which I am sure you will enjoy immensely. I want you to select 100 demons and go and find the mythical city in the desert and persuade them to make me my own personal Sword of Uncreation."

"But Your most evil one, nobody knows where the fabled city is." Stuart's voice was back to its usual mix of obsequiousness and thinly veiled contempt.

"Well, you moron, that is why I used the word 'FIND'!" Satan lubricated the final word with droplets of white foamy spittle. "You'll just have to look for it won't you!" He paused allowing his words to sink in before he continued. "I don't care how long it takes but I want that sword, and unless you want to suffer a similar fate to the Marching Horde, that you are currently stood on, and then once you re-grow any missing bits, spend the rest of eternity in the worst punishment chamber in Hell then I suggest that you are quick in taking your time and return with the sword!"

Both of them knew exactly how serious Satan was with his threats and that failure would result in loss of all privileges that they currently enjoyed. Grank nodded solemnly, he understood what was required and could guess what his enforced travelling companion was going to ask next. He didn't have long to wait and wasn't disappointed.

"Master, which one of us will be the leader?" Stuart's sly voice had enough oil in it to make a Texan rich.

"I don't care, sort it out between yourselves. Just get me a sword. Now get out!"

They both headed for the door reaching it at the same time and squashing through it, shoulder pushing tight against shoulder as both claimed the right to go through first.

Satan rubbed his brow as his mind allowed him to, yet again, dream of battling God and being able to use a sword to claim final victory. Legend said that the original weapon had taken a decade to make and the city was hidden deep in the shifting sands of Arabia, but he didn't mind. After millennia of waiting he could be patient if he needed to be. Then he allowed himself one last thought:

'The Time will come and that time will be mine....'

If you would like to know about future novels, my strange writing, book events or any other random stuff then please feel free to pop in on my website:

http://darrenwalkerauthor.com/

Or why not follow me on Twitter?

https://twitter.com/DarrenWAuthor

www.blossomspringpublishing.com

38289209R00251

Printed in Poland
by Amazon Fulfillment
Poland Sp. z o.o., Wrocław